Following her graduation from the police academy Kelly McKenna joins the ranks of Red Oak police department as an officer. At the same time her long-time friend and roommate Susan Hammond has accepted a job in Los Angeles leaving Kelly with the choice of going it alone or finding another roommate. Kelly soon finds what starts out to be a near perfect roommate named Natalie. In the midst of settling Natalie into her house Kelly also finds herself contending with a competitive and conniving badge bunny in dispatch, one who makes no effort to hide her disdain for Kelly and her new roommate. Natalie, it seems, has her share of issues, not the least of which is being manipulative and something of a drama queen. While Kelly shrugs off most of Natalie's drama, there is someone out there who doesn't find her at all tolerable.

Meanwhile Kelly's long-time love, AFT Agent Ryan Michaels, is about to arrest the key member of a major criminal gang. Its members are determined to protect their leader and will stop at nothing to protect him or her.

Is Natalie the real target, or is someone out to get Kelly?

The Roommate
Copyright © 2020 Regan Taylor
ISBN: 978-1-4874-2640-8
Cover art by Martine Jardin

Published by eXtasy Books Inc or
Devine Destinies, an imprint of eXtasy Books Inc

Look for us online at:
www.eXtasybooks.com or www.devinedestinies.com

THE ROOMMATE
McKenna Crime Book 3

By

Regan Taylor

DEDICATION

To Everyone who has had that *Roommate.*

CHAPTER ONE

"All units standby for emergency traffic!"

Three tones came through the unmarked car's onboard radio in rapid succession. Despite being fifteen miles from her city, the dispatcher's calm and collected voice sounded as if she was in the car beside Officer Kelly McKenna as she drove her patrol car back to her station after an evidence transport to San Francisco, items collected in a joint task force case. The newly minted officer didn't want to miss a beat. Whatever the emergency was being called would mostly likely be code four'd before she hit the Red Oak city limits. Still, one never knew what one could learn just by listening to radio traffic.

The tones sounded again a moment before the dispatcher continued, "All county Code 777 in place for blue Dodge Charger license 4 x-ray, Robert, Henry 441. All units to channel one for further on blue Dodger Charger license 4XRH441."

Heart starting to race in anticipation of what was to come, Kelly quickly switched the car radio over to channel one, the secure police channel, and brought the call up on her CAD-computer aided dispatch monitor. The 777 code indicated multiple agencies could be involved, even other counties. The onboard GPS began to track where each of the other agencies, as well as her own department's units, were moving.

One by one units from all over the county began to call out their move to channel one along with their physical locations and which staging point they were headed to. Kelly clearly visualized where her fellow Red Oak officers were headed to their staging points along the freeway. The 777s didn't

1

happen all that often, but when they did, there were always a few moments of pure adrenaline rush. More often than not, another agency picked up the vehicle before it hit Red Oak.

Radio traffic continued, "Suspect vehicle, blue Dodge Charger license 4XRH441 associated with 211 just occurred on Presidio grounds. RP-victim advises two suspects, both wearing ski masks armed with semi-automatic handguns. Vehicle last seen headed northbound over the Golden Gate Bridge at high rate of speed. Approach with caution."

Kelly made note of just what was going on—an armed robbery happened over in San Francisco and the reporting party saw two armed suspects.

A car blew by Kelly, and despite the weight of her patrol car, the speed of the other vehicle caused hers to rock ever so slightly.

"Asshole," she muttered just before a sliver of moonlight hit the speeding vehicle to reveal a dark blue Dodge Charger. Adrenaline surged through her as Kelly fumbled a moment reaching for the car's radio and cut off the dispatcher's most recent transmission. "Dispatch, D-18 out of Red Oak, confirm license 4 x-ray, Robert, Henry 441?"

"Affirm, D-18," the dispatcher answered using her call sign, D for graveyard shift and 18 for her officer number.

"Dispatch, I am in an unmarked Red Oak unit traveling northbound on 101 and behind a Dodge Charger, license 4 x-ray, Robert, Henry 441. We are traveling in the number 1, passing Spencer at this time at . . . 80 miles per hour. Advise."

"D-18, confirm, you are behind the suspect vehicle, northbound 101?"

A knowing calm took over and Kelly replied, "Affirm." And then added, just in case they missed it the first time, "I'm in an unmarked."

"Copy that 18. All units copy?"

A series of clicks came over the airway while a second

dispatcher called over the air, "Any unit in position?"

"S-1 out of Sausalito copies and en route," the lead Sausalito sergeant responded.

"34-20, en route," a Highway patrol unit called in. "Color of the unmarked?"

"Black," Kelly responded before continuing, "Approaching Richardson bridge in number two at 80."

"S-1 to 18, does he know you're behind him?"

Kelly peered into the night. "I, I don't think so. I'm keeping fairly far behind . . . just enough to keep him in sight, but not so he'd make me . . . at least I don't think so."

"34-20 passing Highway 1, coming up behind you. Dispatch, advise all units, traffic is light, moving at speed."

"All units copy?" dispatch asked.

The question was followed by a number of units calling in they copied. Kelly could hear the building excitement in their voices.

"D-18, advise location."

"Approaching Lucky Drive, back in number 1." Out of the corner of her eye, she saw what she was certain was a Corte Madera unit pull on to the freeway. A flash of light shot out of the Charger's window.

"Corte Madera unit to dispatch, shots fired."

"Copy, shots fired. D-18, your location?"

"Passing Lucky." Given that she was in an unmarked and barely out of training, Kelly figured it might be time to ask if they wanted her to pull out, but so far, no one was questioning her presence or what she was doing there.

"S-1 to 18, coming up on your right."

"Copy that." She glanced over to the right and saw the sergeant's SUV pulling up alongside her. Without being told, she knew it was time for her to drop back. "Dropping back."

"Copy, 18 is dropping back," dispatch advised over the air. "All units, be advised CHP has completed round robin stopping all northbound traffic just south of central San Rafael and is laying the strip just north of 580 on."

"Spike strip down," a unit responded, alerting Kelly to the fact that either CHP or one of the other patrol cars had laid down a spike strip to stop the suspect vehicle. While the suspect vehicle may have taken a shot at the Corte Madera unit, they weren't aware, from what she could see, of the CHP and Sausalito units closing in on him.

"S-1 and 34-20 behind suspect vehicle, ready to light him up?"

"Dispatch copies, light him up."

At the same moment, both units hit their lights and sirens along with eight other units that had come up behind Kelly. "Oh yeah!" Kelly yelled, unable to keep her excitement contained. There was nothing like the feeling of a pursuit coming together.

The suspect vehicle momentary lurched from side to side before hitting the gas and trying to pick up speed. A moment later, they hit the spike strip and spun out of control. Twelve patrol cars converged on the area and formed a barrier around the now disabled car. Still, the suspects tried to limp along the road . . . a door burst open and one of the suspects ran out onto the freeway, firing blindly into the roadway. Shots reverberated as several officers opened fire, and a moment later, the first suspect stumbled down on to the pavement.

Not wanting to miss the takedown or get in the way of the officers surrounding the vehicle Kelly pulled over to the side, her badge held high over her head to alert them to her presence. A moment later, the rotors of a helicopter sounded above and a broad beam of light illuminated the freeway.

"Down on the ground! Down on the ground!" one of the officers yelled at the suspect who'd already gotten out of the car and had fallen. Long rifles out, several other officers approached the suspect vehicle from the other side, yelling for the second suspect to stay inside the car.

"S-1 dispatch, roll medical."

"Copy, rolling medical. Advise best for staging."

As Kelly headed over to what was looking like the incident command center, she listened to the radio traffic back and forth, directing medical and requesting a warrant check on the injured suspect. Even though he'd been hit, no one was taking any chances that he had a back-up weapon before he was searched and transported to the hospital. Several other officers had surrounded the suspect vehicle, long rifles pointing at him, everyone ready to shoot at the slightest provocation. She glanced over to see that traffic on the other side of the freeway had apparently been stopped or detoured, as had the side they were on, in the event stray shots were fired.

"D-18?" An officer in a tan CHP uniform approached her.

"Yes, 34-20?"

"That would be me. Nice driving up there at the bridge and good call."

Kelly shrugged. "Just my luck. Seems to be the way my life goes."

"Well, score one for our side."

Together they stood and watched as first the injured suspect was put in a waiting ambulance and then as one of the sergeants began to order the other one out of the car.

Using a bullhorn, he directed the suspect to lower the car's window and open the door from the outside. The whole process of removing a suspect from a stolen car was one of the subject matter areas that Kelly found the most useful from her eight weeks of POST or Peace Officer Standards Training. The whole course was exceptional and she felt it more than readied her for the on-the-job training at her department. That part, though, and all the things that could go wrong really stuck with her. Suspects were taken out one-by-one in a slow and steady manner to ensure they couldn't get to a weapon and no one would be hurt. Seeing it up close and personal for the first time, she found herself checking the elements she'd learned in class.

Slowly the suspect backed out of the car and arms raised and starting to turn to the officers. One quickly yelled at him to get down on his knees.

"I got bad knees," the guy whined.

The officer ignored the pitiful whine and calmly yelled once again to get down on his knees.

"Aw, man, come on. We didn't mean anything by . . ."

"*On your knees, now!*" a second officer demanded of the suspect.

With two of them now in relatively close quarters to the driver, he dropped to his knees.

"Now," the first officer told him, "walk backwards on your knees."

"You're kidding, right?" The driver balked.

"Serious. Start moving."

Slowly the suspect began the backward crawl on his knees to where two officers stood by. One kept his gun trained on the suspect while the other patted him down and cuffed him. Two other officers approached and duck-walked the suspect to a waiting patrol car, placed him in the backseat, and took off for the jail.

One of the lead officers called out to anyone still in the car. When no one responded after several attempts, several of the officers, guns raised, approached the car. Assured no one was inside, they popped the trunk to find a young woman curled on her side and crying inside the trunk. As one helped her out another radioed for confirmation that the woman had been a hostage and not part of the group that had robbed the bank. Satisfied she was a victim, one of the female officers approached to take down her information.

By this time, one of the Red Oak units had made its way down to the stop and headed over toward Kelly. "Nice call, McKenna. Lieutenant Napolitano was mighty pleased to hear it was one of ours who spotted the car."

"I'll tell you, Doug, the last thing I expected coming back north tonight was to get into a car chase but then . . ."

A frisson of awareness coursed through her. Not the cold kind of shudder that accompanied bad news but one she'd come to recognize over the past year . . . one as familiar to her as her name . . . one she'd known since her own time began.

A black Ford Mustang cruised into the command area. A moment later, a tall, blond-haired man emerged and raised his arms showing his badge. He quickly took in the scene before focusing his gaze on Kelly. In purposeful strides, the man started toward her. Instinctively Kelly's hand moved not to the gun on her hip, but to her chest, across her heart. Without even seeing the deep green of the blond's eyes, she knew he was focused entirely on her. Any other woman would have been taking in the pristine white button-down shirt tucked into form-fitting jeans. Any other woman might well have been turned on by the shoulder holster fitted snugly to his shoulder. It was the powerful aura of the man himself that drew Kelly's attention so completely she barely heard Doug laugh while he told her, "Yeah, well, that's part of what makes the job fun. Serious, but fun. So now, anyone talk to you about the paper you're going to have to do?"

She'd caught one word, and sounding dazed, she repeated it. "Paper?"

"Yeah." The blond had come to stand before her, making her mouth dry and a pleasant awareness of what he could and would do with her tingled between her legs. "Someone has to write the report and technically, as first on scene, that would be you."

CHAPTER TWO

"I can't believe I missed the car chase of the decade!" Chris Tanner screeched in her usual nails on a blackboard voice. "I go on code for my dinner and *this* happens."

"Say what?" Dispatcher Maria Ramirez turned to look at the skinny blonde that one of the other dispatchers had once described as being so thin that if she turned sideways and stuck out her tongue, she'd look like a zipper.

None of the women cared much for Chris—it was the parade of male officers, including the chief, through her bed that liked having her around. There'd been more than one occasion when an officer's life had ended up on the line because of her antics and yet not once had discipline been meted out because every time she'd been caught, it was a male internal affairs officer who oversaw the process. Each time the review board found Chris had been doing her job. Indeed, it *was* the job no one else wanted to do with some of the out of shape officers, but still . . .

She was also quite the adrenaline junky and had been known to stir up trouble on an otherwise quiet night just so she could get her fix.

"The car chase. I can't believe I missed it. Tonight's my night as primary on the radio." Hand on hip in a parody of a sexy Hollywood siren, she continued, "Well, I'll have to give the officer who caught the guy a special treat."

The other dispatchers looked at each other with sly smiles on their faces. Even as self-absorbed as she was, Chris caught their looks. "What?"

"It was D-18, McKenna, that caught them. She probably won't be interested in any special favors."

"McKenna? The newbie? The one who got the job cause her boyfriend is an ATF agent? No way."

"Way," Maria answered her. "And I believe she got the job because she's good at what she does and in case you missed the memo, she was number one in her class at the academy . . . all the way through."

Chris sat down heavily . . . well, as heavily as she could . . . in the second chair. "How the hell did that dumb bitch end up getting a stolen? I bet she planned it so she'd find it when I was on code just to deprive me of the call."

Maria shook her head more to herself than anyone else in the dispatch center. This was typical Chris at her best—everything was always all about her.

"McKenna's been nothing but trouble since the day she started," the skinny blonde groused. "Just because she's got that federal agent boyfriend everyone thinks she's so special. Well, she puts her bra on just the same as the rest of us."

At that, Maria glanced over at Jess Clarkson, one of the other dispatchers, and the two shared a smile—it was well known that unlike the other more endowed women in the department, Chris didn't really need to wear a bra.

Jess mouthed to Maria, "Zipper." That, unfortunately, caused both women to giggle, catching Chris's attention.

"What's so funny?"

"Nothing," Jess mumbled before turning back to the console to answer an officer leaving the scene, but not before Maria caught her eye right back and gave her a thumbs up.

"So, fill me in. How did she manage it? Show her tits to the suspect and he couldn't believe they were so ugly he just stopped?"

Neither woman responded. Despite the fact that the highway patrol, as well as probably every other department on scene, had run the two suspects, Jess ran them one more time ostensibly to have copies for the report she was sure Kelly would at least have to contribute to if not write.

"Well? Is anyone going to tell me?" Chris demanded.

"Um, not quite," Maria finally answered her. Despite Chris's glare in her direction, Maria looked past her to see Jess's shoulders shaking with laughter.

"So how?" Chris squealed.

"Well, remember how we had that evidence transport over to the city?"

"Uh-huh."

"The one that one of the community service officers could have . . . probably should have . . . taken?"

Chris took that moment to look at her nails. "Yeah. So."

"The one you sent D-18 on?"

"It's my job to decide who best to send on different calls." It wasn't hard to miss the growing defensiveness in the blonde's voice.

"Yeah, well, she went and the call on a 211 in a 10851 went out just as she was crossing the bridge back into Marin and from what the radio traffic sounded like she happened to look up just as the suspect vehicle cruised by her, she caught the plate, confirmed it and the chase was on."

"She was in an unmarked . . . by herself," Chris muttered almost to herself before turning an evil grin in Maria's direction. "She's still on FTO—field training—and was on that transport by herself. I didn't have another woman to send with her."

"So?" Jess looked up from her CAD.

"So she's in training. She can't just up and play police officer."

"She didn't . . ." Maria started.

Chris's grin turned to pure malice. It was a grin Maria had seen on Chris enough times to know nothing good was going to come of this.

"Guess there goes her badge. Poof, no more AFT agent's girlfriend."

CHAPTER THREE

K elly watched as blond-haired, green-eyed Ryan Michaels took in the scene at a glance before zeroing in on the love of his life. At six-foot-four inches, he towered over a number of the men assembled. Kelly knew beneath the stark white button-down and form-fitting jeans the man was all muscle. Assured all was under control, he moved next to Kelly before showing his credentials to the CHP on-scene commander. "Ryan Michaels, ATF."

Brow raised in question the on-scene answered, "Lt. Frank Dickerson. What brings ATF on scene? You guys know something we don't yet?" He clearly wasn't pleased ATF was there.

"No." Ryan glanced down at Kelly with a smile. "I was listening to the radio and heard Kelly . . . Officer McKenna's voice and followed the call. When I heard the takedown happening I wanted to be among the first to congratulate her."

Dickerson nodded and stroked his jaw. "I take it there's more than just professional interest here?"

Ryan smiled. "You could say that."

One of the other officers ran over and exchanged a few words with the lieutenant. A moment later, a flatbed tow truck pulled up and began to load up the car.

"Word of advice," Dickerson said to Kelly.

"Anything, sir."

"Even though we'll take lead . . . and that paper someone mentioned to you . . . you may want the honors of having your dispatch contact the vehicle's owners and let them know where the car will be and when they can pick it up."

Ryan watched as Kelly nodded and turned to speak into her shoulder mic. "Red Oak, D-18."

"Go to 18," Jess answered.

"Vehicle secured. CHP will be entering it into the system. Could you notify the owners where and when they can pick up?"

"Affi—" Jess started.

"1023 just one." Chris came out over the air directing with the code to wait a minute. "It happened on the freeway. That's CHP's call. Have them make it."

Kelly looked up at Ryan and smiled.

"Chris?" he whispered.

"Who else?"

"Tanner?" Dickerson asked the couple.

"Yeah. You know her?"

Dickerson nodded. "Her reputation precedes her."

Kelly shrugged.

Ryan, however, commented, "Hops around, huh?"

Dickerson smiled. "Like a true badge bunny. Word is she cut quite the swath through the fire department before going off to be a police dispatcher. Manager over at county said she'd never make it at county so Tanner basically had to go to the local PD—not that there's anything wrong with local PD's. You guys work damn hard and your dispatchers are top of the line . . . at least most of them. From what I understand when some of the fire guys heard she was testing for county dispatch they passed on their concerns to the manager. She didn't pass background—but got on with Red Oak. I'm not telling you this out of gossip, mind you. Just want to give you a heads up that she's not the most reliable when dealing with female officers."

Kelly glanced up at her guy.

Ryan nodded and stuck out his hand. "Thanks for the 411. I'll leave you guys to finish clearing the scene."

13

Dickerson nodded and strode off to the units processing the scene.

Kelly turned briefly to Ryan. "See you at home later?"

"You betcha." Ryan smiled and turned to walk back to his car. "Oh, one thing."

"What would that be, Agent Michaels?"

"I'll be planting a big wet one on you as soon as I get you alone."

"I hope it's more than just a wet one, Michaels."

CHAPTER FOUR

Chatter in the dispatch office came to an abrupt halt as the three women became aware of their on-duty sergeant, Mack White, standing in the doorway.

"Sergeant." Maria greeted him.

"Ladies." White cleared his throat and cast a glance over to the blonde dispatcher. "Not that that would upset many of the officers, at least the males here. Tanner, you got a minute?"

The blonde's gaze took in the room before she smugly smiled. "Of course." She rose and followed White out of dispatch and into his office.

"Have a seat, Tanner," he told her.

A bemused look across her face, Chris sat in the chair across from the sergeant.

"Did I hear that right that you sent McKenna on that transport?"

Chris slid around in a parody of sexy slink before answering, "I did."

"And why was that?"

"She's on FTO. Her training officer is off today and I had to do *something* with her. I decided sending her into the city would cause the least amount of trouble."

White tapped his pen on the desk a beat while gazing at the dispatcher. Finally, he spoke. "That wasn't your call to make."

Chris sat up straighter. "It certainly is."

White shook his head. "No. You do not assign beats or duty assignments. You relay traffic to and between the officers. If

15

McKenna's FTO is out you notify your command and we decide if she should remain in station to study our policies and procedures, if she should ride with another training unit, or make a transport. Understood?"

The blonde shrugged. "If that's what you want. Other sergeants let me make the assignments."

"I'm not the other sergeants and I'm sure if I asked I would hear something a little different."

"Is this because I haven't put out for you?"

"Excuse me?"

Instead of answering, she slid a hand up to her collar and traced a finger around the edge. Before she could move further, White cut her off.

"Tanner, just because half the men around here like an hour or so with a badge bunny doesn't mean everyone does. It would behoove you to be a little more aware of your audience. And to return to the subject at hand, McKenna did a fantastic job tonight. She was cool, calm and collected. Every move she made was textbook. And for the record I'm glad Jess and Maria were on the radio because I hate to think how your petty indifference for female officers could have cost McKenna not only that collar, but could have endangered her and every other unit out there."

Appearing totally unconcerned by what she was hearing, Chris looked at her nails and shrugged.

"Tanner?"

Finally, she glanced up. "I understand. Can I get back to my radio?"

White studied her a moment before nodding. As he watched her sashay out, he knew without a doubt Tanner wasn't going to let either the fact that McKenna brought in a good bust or that he called the dispatcher on her attitude and behavior go.

CHAPTER FIVE

With the scene processed, Kelly took her leave and started north to her station. The hum of adrenaline still pumped through her as she relived each moment of the pursuit. The whole action, at least her part of it in spotting the car, calling it in and watching as the spike strip did its job, took maybe twenty minutes. It was a good bust . . . no one was hurt and they got the bad guys. *She* got the bad guys.

Okay, someone would eventually have caught them and probably not long after she spotted them, but it still felt pretty darn good. And all because her FTO had called in sick and one of the dispatchers sent her off on a minor transport. Damn, she felt good.

Driving past a few late-night businesses that were still open, Kelly reflected on how while she'd turned in some breath-holding stories as a reporter, nothing came close to what she felt as a police officer, even a newbie. She'd always enjoyed watching Ryan when he discussed his cases, at least the parts he could. The way his eyes lit up and his arm and shoulder muscles bunched as he described his movements on an arrest. With tonight's arrest, she got it in ways she never did before about why he loved his job.

When she walked into the station, Kelly was met with a round of applause from the officers on duty that were currently in station along with the dispatchers and the incoming graveyard shift. Well, all but Chris. Kelly caught the dispatcher's sour expression. But it went beyond sour. It was a look she'd seen before and not just from Chris here at the station. Oh no, it was a look she'd seen in other lifetimes from other women and an occasional man.

No, that wasn't right. There was only one man who ever looked at her with such hatred and malice, and right now, he was in prison. Adrian James would be up for parole in a year or so in large part due to Kelly's speaking up for him. Odd as Kelly speaking up for the man who tried to kill her may have sounded there was a part of her that knew her role in his actions. Yes, Adrian had free will and could make his own choices, but the tie between Kelly, Ryan, and Adrian went back lifetimes, beyond even Rome and Egypt. What bound them together began with a spell Kelly cast, in the embodiment of a woman named Khorla in long ago Atlantis. It was only about two years ago, just before Adrian almost killed her, Kelly remembered not only the lifetimes the threesome had been together, but for the first time, what brought that final attack about.

Justice demanded Adrian be punished for what he did in this lifetime, however when Kelly uttered the words unbinding that original spell, they were all free of that long-ago curse. Or at least they were supposed to have been. Then there was the matter of Clarissa Siegal from Hamilton & Myers and her cadre of adoring sycophants. Kelly had no doubt that the woman's actions against her a few months ago were part of that badly done spell. Now though, in this lifetime, Adrian agreed to pay his dues as it were and a time would come for him to move on with his life.

Now though, it was Chris casting a menacing look her way before the blonde turned and sashayed out of the room. With a brief chill, Kelly made a note to watch her back around the other woman. Was she, too, part of Kelly's past-life *faux pas,* or was she just a mean-spirited little bitch who was out to get all women in general?

"Great catch tonight, McKenna!" Officer Bruce Sterling

called to her as she entered the building.

"Definitely way to go," one of the day shift officers told her.

"Awesome on the radio traffic," came from Jess.

Maria reached over to hug her and whispered, "You sure show'd em, lady."

On and on as Kelly made her way to report writing, the officers in house congratulated her. In moments she forgot the look Chris had sent her way.

Mack White followed her into report writing. "Congrats, McKenna."

"Thank you, sir."

"You did us proud out there."

Kelly nodded at him. "I tried."

"And I heard you agreed to take the paper on this one."

Despite her frown, Kelly's eyes twinkled. "I did. Good practice for when it's really my call, right? And makes for good relations with the other departments."

White agreed. "It does. Dispatch will have the vehicle and suspect printouts for you."

"Got it." She put down her go-bag, booted up a computer, and headed down the hall. Along the way, a few other officers ambled in, and as word spread through graveyard shift, each one gave her a fist bump or *good show* comment.

Jess grinned as she handed the printouts to her. "You were great on the radio tonight. I've heard seasoned officers who weren't as calm as you were out there."

"Th—"

"Oh please." Chris cut her off. "How stressed could she be when all she's doing is playing at being a cop and had all those other officers, real police officers, out there doing the real work."

"Don't mind her, Kelly," Maria put in, "she's just jealous there were what? Fifteen or twenty male officers out there with you?"

Kelly shook her head. "Thanks for the printouts, Jess. You and Maria were awesome tonight. I couldn't have done it without you."

"She got that right," Chris muttered from her console.

Shrugging Kelly made her way back down the hall to report writing and her computer. She looked at the printouts a moment before picking up her phone and dialing Ryan's number.

"Hey, beautiful!" He greeted her when he answered the phone.

"Hey, yourself."

"Coming off your arrest?"

"I am. Um . . . you know I agreed to take the paper on this one?"

"Uh-huh."

"Well, I'm back at the station and starting my report, but I'm thinking it's going to run a little late."

"That's to be expected. All part of the job."

"I know. I just wanted to let you know I probably won't be over till way later tonight or rather this morning."

"I figured." Ryan's voice was like a caress through the phone. "I'll be here when you get off."

"Keep the sheets warm for me."

"Not as warm as when I get you in there beside me. Love you."

"Me too," Kelly told him before hanging up.

*

It was almost 4:00 a.m. when Kelly finally stood and stretched. As she bent side to side, her spine offered up quite the symphony of creaks and cracks. At that moment, she felt a bit older than her twenty-eight years. A jaw cracking yawn completed the moment, along with the last page of her report popping out of the printer.

In the dimmed overnight hallway lighting, she made her way to the records area and sat down at the main desk to leave a note for the morning crew about the report. When the non-sworn staff came in, they'd log in her report and forward it down to the CHP office to include with their report when it went to the district attorney. Given the level of felony and the suspects' pending arraignment, the report would go through relatively quickly.

She started for the door to leave and then stopped a moment to listen to a piece of radio traffic going on. Hearing Naomi, one of the day shift dispatchers who'd apparently come in early, confirming plate information on a stop, Kelly headed into dispatch. It was probably bad form and manners to have planned to avoid dispatch if Chris was in the room, but the last thing she wanted was to deal with the bitchy blonde. One never knew what kind of stunt Chris would pull the next time she sat on the radio when an officer who didn't adore her needed back-up or even some cite info.

"Hey!" Naomi greeted her. "Nice call on the stolen earlier."

Seeing Chris was nowhere in sight, Kelly sat in one of the empty chairs. As much as she wanted to head home and into her bed, she enjoyed her all too infrequent chats with this particular dispatcher. Their shifts seldom intersected, so when the opportunity to chat came up, she went with it. "Thanks. I'll tell you though, that if I hadn't heard the call moments before I saw the car it wouldn't have happened. And then once I saw it, Sausalito and CHP did all the work."

Naomi shook her head in disagreement. "That was good police work and don't let anyone tell you otherwise."

"Well, thanks. My portion of the report is up front if you want to look at it—pretty dull reading, but it's there."

"I might. Fortunately for graves tonight the shift has been pretty mellow. I've read the CAD log and it looks like it was a pretty exciting call."

"For my first stolen I have to admit it was."

Naomi looked around the room. Small as it was, it never hurt to be aware of your audience. "Lucky for you Tanner wasn't on the air when it happened."

"That's what I hear," Kelly answered with a wry smile. "Has she always been like that?"

"Since I've been here. Badge bunnies are born, not made . . . I'd be willing to bet she was born boy-crazy and it went downhill from there. Thing with Tanner is she's nastier than most. Not that all bunnies are mean . . . a lot of them stick together to do their hunting. Tanner sees pretty much every female, be it human or animal, as a threat to her quest for the attention of every male on the planet."

"I see. Well, I have to tell you, as much as I wish we could chat for the next hour or so, I'm beat. My bed is calling me, but I didn't want to leave without taking a moment to say hi— one of these days we've gotta get on the same shift."

Naomi paused a moment to respond to an officer calling in his status before answering Kelly, "I hope so too. Have a good one and see you around."

With another timely jaw cracking yawn Kelly rose and headed out the door. With no moon and only a few buildings near the station, the night sky looked like a deep rich velvet littered with diamonds. A slight chill in the air reminded her fall was on its way . . . and that Ryan was waiting between her sheets for her to join him.

Turning the key to the ignition, Kelly shook her head. Ryan arriving at the scene of the arrest was so typical of him. One of these days, he was going to have to stop thinking of her as a fragile flower and accept that she was a modern 21st-century woman. They'd had their problems over his protective streak—and had come close to breaking up while she was working at Hamilton & Myers when she and a few of the other women decided to investigate Clarissa Siegel. He'd had his reasons for not wanting her involved . . . reasons he could have . . . should have told her. Some of it may have breached a confidential investigation, but somehow, someway, he could have let her know why he needed her to back off. Like maybe he could have said, "Hey, I'll look into it." Or "I can't tell you much, just believe me, Siegel is on our radar."

Well, that was over and done. They'd talked and he supported her decision to become a police officer. Maybe he thought it was just another career switch for her. After all, since they'd met two years ago, she'd been a journalist, then a secretary at Hamilton & Myers and was now a cop. Kelly frowned . . . no, she hadn't been career hoping. She'd been a journalist for a number of years and the job at H&M? She'd taken it, with her newspaper boss's agreement to do a story on Clarissa. It was while investigating the woman along with what she'd learned about Ryan's job with ATF that led her to consider a job in law enforcement. Being a cop tied together all the aspects of her earlier jobs along with her college degree in psychology and journalism into one neat package. She and Ryan had talked about that and he agreed with her — it was a make-sense career move.

And as to Ryan's protective streak? He'd get over it. Not too soon though. At least she hoped not — there were times that his pure alpha male mentality was a major turn on. At least tonight, he backed off and headed out from the scene after a quick chat . . . and seeing that she was just fine. How many other female officers had their boyfriend show up at crime scenes ready to go all protective of them?

Kelly chuckled to herself . . . probably more than the number of male officers that had their girlfriends showing up worried about them. Well, maybe not showing up, but waiting for them to come home at night.

From behind the curtains, a dim bluish light illuminated the living. Either her roommate Susan, or Ryan, left the light on for her or, instead of sleeping himself, Ryan was waiting up for her. Kelly's money was on Ryan waiting up . . . waiting up as he had, so many times in so many lifetimes . . . lifetimes such as one in ancient Egypt where as Khorla, while married to Ryan, who was then known as Royok, she sought love outside that of her husband. Or as Richard in early America. Or any number of other lifetimes when Ryan loved her more than life itself yet time and time again Kelly sought out another . . . or another came between her and the man now known as Ryan. And all because of a spell she had cast in ancient Atlantis.

In that long-ago time, she was betrothed to Ryan but desired another. Willful and defying higher powers, Kelly cast a spell to win the heart of the man now known as Adrian. And in lifetime after lifetime, Adrian sought out and pursued Kelly . . . until this one when she realized what she had done and wove another spell to undo the one that almost ruined their lives once again.

As quietly as possible, Kelly let herself in the front door and relocked it. Yes indeed, Ryan was sprawled out, sound asleep, in front of the television, which was caught in a cycle of ridiculous home shopping products. Exhausted as she was from the long shift and post-adrenaline let down, the idea of getting up close and personal with her guy was still pretty darn appealing. Instead, after a quick glance down the hall, she toed off her shoes and settled into the overstuffed chair across from the couch where Ryan lay. The slight morning chill had her tugging the colorful afghan that lay on the back of the chair around her. It wasn't often she could simply sit and watch Ryan. Handsome, smart, and loyal, even sitting still, he gave off an aura of movement. His gaze never seemed to still when he entered a room, always looking out for the next suspect, the next crime, the next time he'd need to protect her. Not that Kelly needed protecting. At least not in this lifetime. Not anymore. She'd just snuggled under the blanket and the soft padding of her big gray cat, Ginny, sounded coming down the hall. The cat stood a moment at the threshold and glanced around the room. With a barely audible meow, she walked into the room and jumped up on Kelly's lap. Together they turned their gazes on Ryan.

It wasn't long before he stirred more from that sixth sense Marines and cops seem to have than the jaunty tune on the latest product being hawked on the TV. For a moment, he stared ahead, blinked his eyes, and turned to look directly into Kelly's.

His voice gravelly with sleep, he whispered, "Hey, gorgeous. What are you doing over there instead of snuggling up with me over here?"

Kelly stroked Ginny's soft fur and smiled. "I might ask you what are *you* doing watching trash TV instead of keeping my bed warm for us?"

"Trash? I'll have you know the perfect workout outfit goes for a mere $19.95 and is entirely washable after you've made your own homemade pasta and sauce in one simple machine with only the touch of a button."

"All that?"

"And more." With one smooth move, he was up and at her side.

Hand on his crotch, she asked, "Care to show me that more?"

Ryan glanced down the hall.

"Ah, Susan's home?" Kelly asked, referring to her best friend and roommate. Susan, a total techy and computer guru, had moved to the San Francisco Bay Area with Kelly a few years before. Actually, she was more than a best friend — they'd met in high school, and rather than run and hide when she became aware of the stalker threatening Kelly's life, Susan became an even better friend. She was the sister Kelly would have wanted. At times Kelly thought she would have lost her mind from the things that happened if Susan hadn't been there for her.

"That she is."

"I thought she'd be at that job she was contracting for another week."

Ryan shrugged. "She was home when I got here, said hi and that she was bone tired and headed off to her room."

"Guess we'll catch up with her later."

Casting another look down the hall, Ryan nodded.

Kelly leaned into him. "That doesn't mean I can't have my wicked way with you in my room now, does it?"

"And just how wicked would that be?" He cast her a smile that had her tingling down to her toes.

Kelly toyed with one of the buttons on his shirt. "Very, very wicked. I've got my cuffs all ready to take you prisoner."

Ryan leaned down and whispered against her ear, "Not if I capture you first." With that, he slid his hand down her back to her knees, bent enough to pick her up, and carried her down the hall. Over Ryan's shoulder, she watched her cat glance her way, and she, with a decidedly feline shrug, headed over to the chair Kelly vacated.

In her room, Ryan gently laid Kelly on her bed before turning to shut the door. As soon as her butt hit the mattress, Kelly began to work the button and zipper down her jeans. Ryan turned to her with a look of pure longing and his hands on his own fly. Kelly scooted over on the bed at the same time she tugged her jeans off, "I want you, Michaels. Right here, right now."

"You got me, babe."

"I want all of you, always."

"You've got me."

He tugged off his t-shirt giving her access to his smooth chest. Kelly stroked his pecs, up and over, down his rib cage and over on to his back. Clearly frustrated with her impeding his need to remove her blouse, he grabbed her hands. "You aren't going to get me . . . all of me, if you don't let me get this top off you."

"What? You can't take me, hard and hot, with a blouse on?"

"Oh I can take you and take you again, but I want to feel all your skin against me. I want to feel your nipples all hot and hard grating against my chest."

Kelly pouted. "So you don't like the feel of my hands . . ." She raked his chest with her nails causing him to groan ever so low. "On your chest?"

"I like. Oh yeah, I like . . . but I like more skin than your hands." With that, he quickly pulled her up by her shoulders and, in a flash, removed her blouse. With deft fingers, he pulled the clasps to her bra apart, sending it the way of her blouse. She watched as he stopped a moment, hovering above her, taking in the woman he loved beyond reason.

Beneath him, Kelly watched her man's every move. The tautness he held himself with sent a shiver through her down to her girl parts. His want showed strongly on his features and, at the same time, a vulnerability that never seemed to leave him when he was with her. Lifetimes of wanting, finding, and losing her were forever etched on his psyche. Sensing he wouldn't move until he was sure her need matched his, Kelly slid her legs up over his thighs, locking him to her in an embrace. "Take me, Michaels. Take me hard."

Chapter Six

The sunlight spilling across the pillow where Kelly rested on Ryan's shoulder woke her mid-morning. She chastised herself for not pulling the blackout shades tight before she and Ryan fell asleep. Then again, she'd been pleasantly distracted for some time after they slid between the sheets. A moment later, he stirred beside her. She shifted her head ever so slightly so she could look into his eyes. Without looking, she unerringly traced her finger around his nipple, causing him to intake a quick breath. She smiled up at him, reveling in the knowledge that her mere touch could make him want her.

"Hey, beautiful." His voice was slightly rasped with sleep.

"Hey, yourself." She leaned up enough to give him a light kiss on the cheek.

"We good?"

She stilled her finger and looked directly into his eyes, drinking in their moss green depths. "Why wouldn't we be?"

"Why?"

"Yes. What would make you think we weren't . . . especially after I did that . . . thing to you . . . twice last night."

"Not to argue, but I think it was early this morning. Not that I'm complaining. It was nice. Very nice."

"So why wonder if we're good?" She scooched closer to him, pressing her groin against his hip, letting him know she was just about ready to couple with him again.

Ryan reached over and ran his hand along her hip, down her thigh, debating if he should ruin the mood by telling her why he wanted . . . needed to know if they were good.

"Ry?"

"Last night . . ."

"Yes?" She probed when he didn't continue for a few moments.

"Your crime scene . . ."

"The stolen and arrest?"

"That would be the one."

"What about it?"

"I came . . ."

"Yes . . . twice last night and if you play your hands . . . I mean your cards right, you will again in not too long a time."

He smiled. "I mean about showing up . . . unannounced. It was your scene and I . . . I . . ."

"Crashed it?" She bit her lip to keep from chuckling at his discomfort even though she knew he was thinking of their history, and not just their history in this lifetime. That, and Adrian's attempts on her life when he tried to run her down with a car, when he attached a bomb to her car, and at the last, when he kidnapped her and was going to kill her in a ritualistic ceremony. At times it seemed that even a crack in a sidewalk had Ryan in protective mode. When she first saw him emerge from his car last night, a part of her wanted to scream—and just because she was chuckling about it now didn't mean she wanted to put up with him showing up at every call she went on. Her credibility with her department aside, he needed to realize she was a strong and independent woman who could hold her own. "Well . . . you know, showing up . . ."

He was clearly struggling there, feeling guilty for showing up, wanting to be part of her life, his own protective instincts coming to the fore. Knowing Ryan, he wasn't going to let the subject drop, no matter how playfully she treated it. And, now was a good a time as any to lay down the ground rules on her job.

Kelly shifted a bit away from him but, at the same time, kept her hand on his chest. Ryan Michaels may be a former Marine and ATF agent, but he had a tender side, especially when it came to Kelly McKenna. Moving away from him to have this conversation would send him deep into that very protective mode, coupled with his concerns about their relationship.

"Yeah . . . you did show up."

"And? How did it make you feel? About me?"

Kelly looked down a moment to gather her thoughts. "Ry, I love you. I love you more than life itself."

"But?"

"No, but. Just . . . I didn't expect to find you there. It surprised me, and well . . ."

"You think it made it look like you couldn't control the situation. That you needed my help or that I didn't trust you or . . ."

"That I couldn't handle it?"

He blushed, something Ryan did not do . . . he blushed.

"So, I'm thinking," she continued. "Maybe laying some ground rules might be a good thing."

Ryan sighed. "I suppose rule number one will be to stay away from your crime scenes."

Kelly chuckled. "That would be a start. Unless, of course, we're working a case together."

"Kelly."

"Ry, I know you worry about me. I know you want to keep me safe. But sometimes you can't do what you want just because you want to. Sometimes you need to accept that I can handle things, like an arrest. And last night I wasn't out there by myself. Heck, I wasn't even the lead officer. All I did was call in the stolen and the 20s as we went by them."

"Twenties?"

"Cop talk," she answered with a smile. "1020s are

locations, where you are. We refer to them as 20s."

"Okay."

"Ryan, don't."

"Don't what?"

"Don't feel like I'm closing you out when I say something like 20s or other basic PD slang or abbreviations. It's just part of me learning to talk to my peers, to be a responsible officer. Like I was saying though, I wasn't even the lead. As soon as they had the stolen in sight, CHP took the call. They're the ones who threw the spike strip, the ones who pulled the suspects from the car and the only reason I took the paper was as a learning opportunity."

"Kelly, next time you could be the lead officer. You could be out there with a stolen and an armed suspect on your own . . ."

"And I'll deal with it. You know the training I went through. You know what POST demands. I'm still in training with my department. Most important, I don't have a death wish. Like you with your ATF work and when, when you were a Marine—you train, train and train some more. Then you go out and do the job and let the training take you where you need to go. I'll be fine."

"And if you're not? If some guy with a gun gets trigger happy?"

Kelly sighed. "Ryan, could we please not borrow trouble? Let's take it one step at a time. I'll stay out of your crime scenes and you stay out of mine. We'll talk about them after, but we won't second guess each other. Okay?"

They entered the kitchen a short time later to the smell of fresh ground coffee brewing and pancakes on the griddle. "Mmm, Suz, I do like it when you are home and in a cooking mood." Kelly greeted her lifelong friend and roommate, Susan Hammond.

"Well, how often do you get to celebrate a major felony arrest?" The petite blonde smiled at the couple just before swatting Ryan's hand for snagging a slice of bacon.

"Sure you got enough for all of us?" Kelly asked, ignoring the arrest part, at least for the moment.

"Definitely. Like I said, how often do you get to celebrate a major do like you had last night?"

"So Ryan filled you in?"

"In glorious after-the-fact detail. What I want to hear is how it all came down before Ryan arrived . . . or . . ." She glanced from one to the other clearly aware of Ryan's past protective history and Kelly's craving for independence.

Kelly finished pouring coffee for the threesome, and Susan put the platters of pancakes and bacon on the table.

When all three were seated, Susan gestured with her fork. "So?"

"Well," Kelly began. "It was kinda cool. Chris, you know the perky blonde at the police department."

"Perky? Isn't she the one you call the badge bunny?"

"Yup. That one. Anyway, we had a minor evidence transport and she decided that instead of me doing some in-house training—training my sergeant would have given me to do, that it was up to me to hustle it into the city. So off I went into the city, made the delivery and was headed back across the bridge which, by the way, the bay looked amazing last night. I'm cruising along, listening to the county-wide radio band and I hear a call for a stolen that was just taken in the city. I take note of the plate and description and lo and behold, I look over to my right just as a car blows by me going at least eighty. I radioed in to dispatch and asked them to confirm the plate and it comes back to the stolen. Dispatch took it from there—calling in back up, getting info from me. CHP brought in the spike strip and downed the car. It was over in less than ten minutes from when it started, at least the pursuit was."

"That's it? Ten minutes?" Susan jabbed at a bite of pancake and sluiced it through a puddle of syrup.

"Yup. They don't last long."

"But what about the ones we hear about on the news — the ones that go from county to county?"

Kelly looked over to Ryan, silently giving him the okay to respond. "Some can, but they depend on a number of factors. I've never been involved in one but from what I've heard is it depends on traffic — how many other cars are out there, number of units in pursuit, how safe citizens will be depending on which actions the officers take."

"My pursuit last night was pretty straight forward . . ." Kelly began.

"Not that she didn't do an awesome job." Ryan smiled at her.

"Later at night, not a lot of traffic, plenty of units in the area. It was textbook. And it was fortunate the suspects stopped after they hit the spike strip."

"They don't?" Susan's voice cracked with her surprise.

"Some don't. They're just so intent on getting away from the officers they disregard even their own safety and some keep riding on rims. That leads to a whole other series of problems for them because the rims hitting the pavement can spark and cause a fire. Anyway, the strip stopped them and CHP took over the arrest."

"Then how come you got home so late?"

"It takes a while to get them out of the car — gotta watch for officer and citizen safety. These guys are driving a three to four-thousand-pound potential weapon — and that's just your average, every day car, some of them are armed and aren't the sharpest tools in the shed. They don't want to get caught and think by firing a gun at someone they're going to get away. The longest part though is doing the paper. Making sure you've got all your details lined up and everything is factually accurate."

"Got ya. So, anything else going on with you two?" Susan popped in her last bite of bacon and picked up her coffee while she waited for their response.

"No. Not really, at least not for me," Ryan told her.

Kelly took a sip of coffee before shaking her head no. "Just training, training and more training. You have a little break before your next contract?"

"Well, no, not really," Susan told them.

"Wow, so no break between jobs this time?" Kelly asked, clearly surprised. For years Susan'd made a good living doing contract computer work mainly because she liked calling her own shots on her time. Generally, she took two to three weeks if not a month or so off after each job.

"No. No break because . . . well . . ." Susan sighed. "This last job was pretty lucrative but more than that . . . I really enjoyed the people I was working with."

"So you're going to take a longer break? Retire?"

"Not quite." The petite blonde rose and refilled her coffee cup, stirred in her milk, and took a swallow before continuing.

"Suz, is everything okay?" Kelly reached out a hand to her friend.

"Better than okay except for one thing."

"Susan, you're scaring me."

"Sorry, I don't mean to. I'm just trying to figure out how to tell you."

"Tell us what?"

She drew in a breath and slowly released it. "I took a permanent, full-time-comes-with-a-pension and profit-sharing job."

"Suz! That's great! That's fantastic! Why would you be nervous about . . . well, I can understand nervous because you've freelanced for so long, but if this is the real deal, if it's what you want, that's awesome. What kind of position did you take? When do you start?"

"I'll be managing a group of fifty techs to start . . . in Los Angeles."

"Los Angeles? So you'll be telecommuting?"

"No. Not telecommuting."

"It's easy. We'll just turn one of the spare bedrooms into an office and . . ."

"No, I need to be onsite. In L.A."

"So you'll be commuting? Like flying up here weekends?"

Susan shook her head. "No. I need to be onsite, onsite for at least the first year. But they're looking to expand into Missouri, Ohio, and Virginia. They're looking to provide support during convenient hours for pretty much everyone in the U.S."

"Call me clueless, but I think you're telling me you're moving."

Susan sighed again, picked up the salt shaker sitting on the table, and finally answered, "Yeah . . . that's what makes it so hard. I hate to . . . well, bail on you, I guess."

Kelly leaned over to hug her friend. "No, oh, Suz, no, you aren't bailing on me. Seriously. If this job is what you want you totally deserve it. For so many, too many, years you've stood by me and while you'll deny it, you've put parts of your life on hold because mine was so screwed up. This is awesome for you and I'm one hundred percent behind you. What do you need from me?"

"From us," Ryan put in.

Susan thought for a minute. "Nothing right now. I just need to get packing."

"Do you have a place down there?"

"No. The company said they'd put me up in a hotel and pay for shipping my stuff and all."

"When are you expected down there?" Ryan asked.

"They're hoping by the end of the month. But I can commute the first few weeks."

"So a month? Well, let us know what you need from us and . . . wow. I gotta admit this is sudden, but Susan, I'm so happy for you. Really happy for you."

Ryan sat on the edge of Kelly's bed while she dressed for her upcoming shift. "You're okay with Susan moving?"

Kelly checked her utility belt before putting it on. "I'm happy for her."

Ryan reached for her and pulled her onto his lap. "I know you are. But how are *you*?"

Kelly let out a breath. "I'm okay. It's like a family member moving out, you know? Susan hasn't been just my best friend for pretty much my entire life. She went through — stood by me — through all those horrible years when Adrian was stalking me. There were a few times her life was on the line because of things he did. When his jealousy would overcome him, when he'd get into that violent place he'd sometimes get into, she could have bailed at any time. She didn't. She just stuck with me . . . when I moved here she came with me. She's the sister I would have wanted. Now it's time for me to be supportive of her. I'm just . . . well, it's going to be weird."

"I can see that. You know you have me?"

Kelly quickly kissed him. "I know and I'm glad I've got you. Especially when those chilly nights come around. It's just going to be different not having her down the hall to talk with . . . it's like when you move out of your family home and suddenly you're on your own."

"It's early yet, but do you know what you're going to do?"

"Get a roommate I guess. My mortgage is fairly reasonable, but I feel better if I have a bit of a financial cushion, you know?"

"Totally get it."

Kelly ran her hand along his cheek. "I'm going to give it a few days, see if Susan is really going to take this job and plan from there. It shouldn't be too hard to find someone decent and since it looks like I'll be working nights and weekends chances are whoever moves in and I won't be crossing paths all that much."

Ryan nodded.

"And right now? I need to get going to work. You be here when I get home?"

"If you like."

She gave him a quick kiss. "I like."

A few more kudos were sent her way when Kelly entered the station that afternoon. Several of the officers from swings were still on site and took the time to congratulate her on recovering the stolen vehicle. At briefing though, if looks could kill, the daggers Chris sent her way would have been among the most deadly. A few of the officers noticed and merely shrugged — it was, typical Chris.

Briefing over, Jen Donnally and Kara Serling ambled over to Kelly and complimenting her on the arrest.

"Don't be surprised," Jen, the on-duty sergeant for the night shift, told her, "if Chris manages not to hear your traffic tonight. She's on a real snit about not being on the radio when the pursuit went down."

"Seriously?" Kelly asked.

"She's sure you planned it to get back at her for the evidence run," Kara told her.

"Huh? How on earth can you plan when you're gonna . . . gotcha . . . she needs someone to be pissed at."

"Yup," Jen answered her. "Chris has a pretty warped idea of how calls are supposed to go, but the main idea is she must always, no matter what, be the queen bee."

"So great, are you telling me if I have emergency traffic she might pretend not to hear it?"

"With Chris you never know. Don't worry, we have your back."

"I appreciate that, but tell me this, if you know she does this or is capable of it, why is she still working here?"

Kara answered for the duo, "She . . . dispatches . . . important services for someone higher up on the food chain who manages to overlook things most of us wouldn't take too kindly to."

"And no one does anything about either of them?"

Kara looked around where they stood, and after making sure they were alone whispered, "More than one, and no, if we want to keep our jobs and make sure we've got the right back up, no, we can't do anything about it."

"Sounds like a third world dictator."

Jen snorted. "Something like that. Anyway, you'll be riding with Jack Coburn tonight and since she . . . likes him there shouldn't be any issues.

"Yeah," Kara chuckled. "As long as you make it sound like you aren't much interested in him because she wants him all for herself."

Kelly shook her head as she headed out to the car.

"Nice call last night, McKenna," Jack told her while they checked out their patrol car, making sure the shotgun was cleared and in place, that the cage of the backseat was in working order and their EMT supplies stocked in the trunk.

"Thanks."

"Are you getting tired of hearing about it?"

"No. The recognition is kinda nice, you know?"

Jack nodded. "And talking about it?"

"Well, there's not much to tell."

Her partner gestured for Kelly to take the wheel. Buckled up, she picked up the radio and called out, "D-18 with D-22,

10-7."

"Copy 18 and 22 on duty," Jess responded from the dispatch radio and then continued, "18 and 22, 1182 at Redwood and Grant. RP advises black Toyota Tercel and red BMW on right-hand shoulder requesting a unit."

"18 copies, en route," Kelly responded, letting dispatch know she and Jack were on their way to a non-injury accident on Redwood and Grant. From the way Jess put out the call, it didn't sound like they needed back up, and they were a two-person unit. Still, Kelly and Jack scanned the sidewalk for the parties to make sure no one was having a temper issue.

A few minutes later, as they rolled onto the scene, Kelly announced, "18 and 22, 1097," letting dispatch know they had arrived.

Kelly and Jack each took a driver aside and took down their relevant facts. The BMW driver took responsibility for the crash, advising that he was new in town and realized he almost missed his turn and then cut it short, hitting the Toyota. Since the Beemer driver was new in town, the Toyota owner wanted the police report.

The report taken and assurances that no one was injured, Kelly announced, "18 and 22, report taken, units 1098," letting dispatch know they were done with their call.

The rest of the shift moved along pretty mellow with some decent breaks between each call. During one break, while driving patrol along the streets, Kelly mentioned Susan's plans to move for her new job.

"You live in Red Oak, right?" Jack asked her.

"Yeah, actually a couple of blocks from the station."

"Given any thought to what you might do?"

"Right now, nothing specific. I'm pretty sure I'll be getting a new roommate. You know anyone?"

Jack thought about it for a minute. "No, not off the top of my head, but if something comes to mind I'll let you know."

"Thanks, I appreciate it."

"Sure. You know, you can post a notice on the bulletin board."

"That's true . . . with my luck Chris would apply."

Jack laughed. "Nah, she'd try to rent the room by the hour."

"I am beat. Exhilarated, but beat," Kelly announced to Ryan as she walked into the house at the end of her shift.

"No hot pursuits tonight?"

"Nope. And that's fine with me. One of those a week suits me just fine. Only hot pursuit I want is a certain blond ATF agent in my bed."

"You know there's some who'd say if you're not going to be an adrenaline junky, maybe you don't want to be a cop."

She toed off her shoes and asked, "What about you? Do you need an adrenaline rush every time you go to work?"

"Nope. But keep in mind, seventy-five percent of my job is spent doing analysis behind a desk. We gather intel and follow leads."

"Mmm, I think I'd like one high profile case every other week."

"Every other week?"

Kelly snuggled up to him and slid her arms around his neck. She threaded her fingers through his hair, cresting just below the collar of his pale blue button-down shirt. "Yeah, so I don't have to take so much paper. Besides I have a much better way to get my heart racing."

"Do you?" Ryan lowered his head toward Kelly's.

"Mmm hmm. Consider the comment about the hot guy in my bed." She leaned into him and rubbed her hips against his groin. Heat raced to the juncture between her legs when she felt his hardened cock through his jeans. "You know," she whispered in his ear, "just being near you makes my heart race . . . and my panties wet. Very, very . . . wet."

"That so?" He sounded ever so slightly out of breath, like he'd just come in from a quick run, as he pulled her closer to him.

"Very wetly so. And you know what, Michaels?"

"What?"

She loved how his voice sounded ever so strained with need. "I get all hot, bothered and wet just thinking about you. Sometimes I sit in that patrol car and want to pull to the side of the road, call you over and have my very naughty way with you."

"Do you have a naughty way about you, Ms. McKenna?"

"Only with you and you know what, Agent Michaels?"

"What?" His whisper was full of need.

"If I don't get you up close and buck naked personal right now . . ."

Not letting her finish the thought, he brought his lips down on hers. Kelly practically purred as he picked her up and carried her to the bedroom. While he strode down the hall with the determination of a predator, she worked the buttons of his shirt, peeling them open one by one.

In the bedroom, she reached for his fly and made quick work of dragging his pants down over his hips while he returned the favor tugging down hers. A shot of liquid heat coursed through her body as she rubbed her breasts against his chest. "Ryan, Ryan."

She wrapped her legs around his hips as he carried her to the bed and placed her on the edge. Kelly held on tight to him and pulled him up and into her. "Ryan."

"I'm gonna come, babe, I'm gonna . . . ahhh."

CHAPTER SEVEN

A month later, Kelly stood on the front step of her house fighting tears. Despite being happy for her friend and the fact that she was going to be only a short flight away, there was a certain sadness in saying goodbye. In the background, she could hear Susan giving some last-minute instructions to the movers along with her plans when she arrived in L.A. When the sound of her instructions faded, Kelly presumed, Susan had walked further into the Victorian, probably for one last walkthrough.

"You okay?" Ryan quietly asked her.

Wrapping her arms around her waist as if fending off a chill, Kelly nodded. "I'm happy for her — not so much for me. It's not like she's leaving my life forever. She's only moving to L.A. and will just be a phone call, Skype or plane ride away. Right?"

"True."

"It's just . . . just . . . well, shit, moving away from home, from my parents' home wasn't half as difficult. Susan's been there for pretty much all the major events of my life."

"And she'll continue to be."

"I know." Kelly hated how her voice cracked. She and Susan weren't lovers going through a romantic break-up. They were friends, best friends, so why did she feel like a part of her life was ending?

Well, in reality, it was. For the first time in her life, she was going to be on her own. She had Ryan, yes. He knew a lot about her past, especially that with Adrian. But Susan had been there, by her side, when almost all of it happened. Sure, Kelly was alone when on a business trip. That wasn't a permanent situation. They were relatively short trips, a few weeks, and she had a home to come back to. And really, she wasn't losing her home. She owned the quaint Red Oak Victorian.

It was her roommate who was moving out. That was all.

And she'd be getting a new roommate.

Taking Jack's suggestion, she'd posted a notice at work . . . which quickly disappeared . . . all four times she posted one. No one knew for sure, but most everyone thought it was probably Chris just starting to stir up trouble. The chief finally said something about it during one of his rare visits to briefing and the next notice didn't disappear.

Ryan had also posted a note at his office — with the warning that none of the guys he worked with need apply.

The local paper and the online list also had a *roommate wanted* section, and in the past few days, some prospective candidates had called.

"So when do the interviews begin?" Ryan asked while they waited for Susan to return.

"Tomorrow morning. I figured I needed tonight to just be by myself, be me, before opening the door to strangers."

"Got ya."

Kelly turned and smiled up at him. "I didn't mean you, you know. And Susan might not stay here tonight."

"No?"

"No. Just think about it, if she stays with Craig or whoever her latest is . . . tonight we can run around the house naked and not have to worry Susan might walk in on us."

"Ah. I see."

"See what?" Susan asked as she followed the last of the movers out the door.

"The roommate interviews tomorrow . . . unless you've

43

had an attack of second thoughts . . ."

"No . . . I wish the job were here or that it didn't involve a move, but I have to . . ."

Kelly reached over and hugged her friend. "It's time you put you first."

"I do. I have. Trust me, if my own goals and dreams didn't fit with yours I wouldn't have put them aside. And lest you think I never had apron strings going back the other way, you're wrong. Our plans just fit together for a long time and now my life is going in a different direction. And consider this, maybe when you did that spell releasing Adrian it also freed us up to our own things without each other. Maybe we were bonded together through that spell too."

Kelly considered Susan's words. "Maybe. Anyway . . . roommate interviews are tomorrow."

"So make copious notes and we'll gossip about them tomorrow night."

"Sounds like a plan."

The sound of the moving van's engine drew their attention. "Give me a sec," Susan told her and hurried over to the truck. She looked like a little kid looking up into the cab and, with a few hand gestures, seemed to conclude her business with them. She watched for a minute as the truck started to roll down the street and turned the corner. Once it was out of sight, she came back to Ryan and Kelly. "Now where was I?"

"Me taking copious notes about the potential roommates."

"Right. You create a huge number of notes and we'll laugh about the ones who aren't moving in."

"Sounds like a plan. A mean one, but a plan."

"You know we really don't mean that. I just want to find someone reliable."

"How many are coming?" Susan asked her.

"Six. Four women and . . ." Kelly started to tell her, but her cell phone ringing on the entryway table interrupted her. The threesome entered the house and Kelly answered the phone.

"Hi, Kelly?"

"Yes." Kelly's brow furrowed, trying to place the voice.

"It's me. Natalie."

"Oh, hi, Natalie." To Ryan and Susan, she mouthed, "Natalie."

Ryan whispered, "Who?"

"One of the possibles," Kelly whispered back.

"Hello? Possible what?" Natalie asked her.

"Uh, oh, you're coming to see the house and talk about rooming together tomorrow, right?"

"Yes, I want to move in," Natalie told her. "My friend and I drove by this morning and liked what I saw."

A slight chill, not unlike the ones she would feel when Adrian was stalking her, raced up here back.

"Uh. Right. Well, the outside is pretty nice so we'll see what you think when you see the inside."

"I'm sure I'll like it. Listen, I was wondering if Martha, my friend, and I could come by this afternoon."

Kelly looked from Ryan to Susan. "This afternoon? Well, I'm kind of busy and . . ."

"That's okay. I only need a few minutes and I'll bring a deposit check."

"Um, listen, Natalie, I'm not ready today to interview anyone. Let's leave it for tomorrow and . . ." While Susan closed the front door and followed Ryan and Kelly into the den.

"I have a ride today."

"A ride?"

"Martha, the friend who wants to see the house with me . . . today. Tomorrow won't work."

Kelly reached her desk and flipped through a few papers sitting there until she found her roommate notes. She pulled out Natalie's and quickly scanned the page. The woman was employed by a car dealership here in town, worked four 10 hour days and said she was quiet and kept to herself. Given they would be working different hours and days, the quiet part was a pretty key requirement.

"Well . . ." She glanced at the clock and then over to Ryan and Susan standing in the doorway. "I guess I could arrange to be here about three . . ."

"One," Susan stage whispered to her.

"Who's there?" Natalie asked her.

"My roommate. Can you come at one?"

Natalie sounded awfully petulant when she told Kelly, "I thought I was your . . . coming to see about being your room-mate."

"Uh, Susan's the one who is moving out. Can you come by about one?"

"Three would work better for me."

"But I will be here at one."

Kelly heard some discussion in the background before Natalie told her, "Okay, we'll be there at one."

Kelly stared at the phone a moment after hanging up. Finally, she looked up at Ryan. "That was odd."

"Sounded like she really wants that room," Ryan told her.

"Yeah. Can't wait to meet her." Susan chuckled.

"Can you hang out to see what's up with her?" Kelly asked.

"I sure can. I can hit the road anytime and technically don't have to be in L.A. for three days so this should be good."

Kelly glanced down at the phone again. She'd had everything straight in her mind to meet her potential roommates the next day. She'd set the interviews up to be an hour apart, figuring each one needed maybe twenty to forty-five minutes to look over the place, ask their questions and take one of the applications she'd put together. Maybe she and Natalie would hit it off and she wouldn't need to meet the others.

Maybe.

CHAPTER EIGHT

At precisely 1:00 p.m., not 12:59 or 1:01 but 1:00 p.m., the doorbell rang.

"Well, she's punctual if nothing else," Kelly wryly told Ryan and Susan.

A moment later, she opened the door to a neatly dressed woman, tastefully made up with copper-colored hair and hazel eyes. The woman smiled a genuine and warm smile. "Hi, I'm Natalie and this is Martha. I'm here about the share rental."

"Hi, I'm Kelly. Come on in."

Natalie and Martha followed behind Kelly into the living room, stopping every few steps to look over the floor, the entryway table, the coatrack, ending with a *tsk* as they walked by the shoes lined up near the hall closet.

"Oh, um, we're usually running out the door at the last minute so it's easier to . . ."

"I think barring shoes in the house is a good thing," Natalie told her with a smile.

"Hm, well, that's a good point. So this is the living room and that's my roommate . . . or rather my soon to be former roommate, Susan, and my boyfriend, Ryan. Suz, Ry, this is Natalie."

"Hello." She beamed up at Ryan. Clearly, Kelly's blond-haired, green-eyed boyfriend had made yet another conquest the moment he turned that lethal smile of his on Natalie.

"Natalie? Good to meet you." Ryan extended his hand.

"Me too," Susan told her.

"I'm glad to meet you." Natalie turned to Susan. "You can give me the 411 on living with Kelly."

Susan glanced at Kelly. They'd known each other long enough to know that the other was thinking Natalie was perhaps a tad pushy. Then again, she could be just as nervous as Kelly was looking at a living situation with a total stranger.

"Could be," Susan told her.

"Well, let me show you the house," Kelly offered. "As I said, this is the living room—we share a few spaces in the house like the kitchen, living room and dining room. I have my bedroom and an office and you'd have your own room plus an extra to use as either an office or guest room if you . . ."

"Oh, I don't have people stay over."

"Well, it's basically there for you to use."

Kelly's cat, Ginny, meandered in at that moment.

"You have a cat?" wide-eyed Natalie asked her.

"Y-yes. It was in the ad. She's well behaved."

"Of course she goes outside to do her business." Natalie made it a statement, not a question.

"No, Ginny's an indoor cat, but I change her box every morning and like I said, she's well behaved."

"I hope so." But her tone indicated she doubted it would be that simple.

"Um, if Ginny's going to be a problem—"

"Oh, you don't have to get rid of her. I'll just keep my door shut and things out of her reach. Shouldn't be a problem. If it becomes one I'll let you know."

Kelly nodded—she hadn't had a chance to tell Natalie that if Ginny was going to be a problem, then Natalie could forget about considering the room. "Okay, well then, we have our own bathrooms and there's a guest bathroom here."

Susan reached over to open the half-bath guest bathroom set slightly down the hall from the living room.

"The kitchen is this way." Kelly led the small party, Ginny padding behind the five humans, into the kitchen. Kelly gave her head a slight shake when she saw Ginny about ready to jump on the table. Despite telling the cat over and over again the table was off-limits, Ginny had some definite ideas about where she could and should be allowed. Apparently, this afternoon, she was on good behavior because all she did was walk in and out around Ryan's legs.

Natalie inspected the kitchen, opened the refrigerator and dishwasher. She finally announced, "I don't leave my dishes in the sink."

Ryan, Susan, and Kelly all nodded.

"So, the bedroom is back this way." Kelly led the party down the hall, noting that as they left the kitchen, Ginny jumped up on the table and settled down on one of the placemats for a nap. Fortunately . . . or unfortunately . . . Natalie didn't see the cat's defiant act.

"Do you hear much street noise?"

Kelly shrugged. "No, not really. If a car is out there laying on its horn, sure you'll hear it. But otherwise it's pretty quiet. We have nice neighbors, no one gets in anyone's face." Kelly crossed her fingers behind her back. While the neighbors were generally pretty friendly and kept to themselves, there were times in the not too distant past when they'd regularly come out and stand in the street to watch the goings-on caused by Adrian's antics. Then, when Kelly's life had been threatened, there was a protective detail parked out front for several days.

All that drama was long over, so there was really no reason to bring that up to Natalie.

"Does it get very dusty?"

"Dusty?"

"Yes, I have allergies and dust is very rough on me. I use a dust cloth on my furniture every day, but it helps if the area I live in isn't very dirty."

"I see. No. It's actually pretty clear in this part of town."

"Good. So maybe we should talk a little about our schedules and likes and such?" Despite the inflection of a question, the woman was clearly demanding they sit down and scope things out.

"Sure. Kitchen?" Without waiting for a response, Kelly turned and led the way back down the hall, but not before catching a rather amused grin on Susan's face. Ryan, on the other hand, looked less than happy. Not that he looked unhappy — more like he wasn't quite sure he was really hearing and seeing what they were hearing and seeing.

With a quick glance about the room, Natalie chose a chair and sat down . . . interestingly it was the one Kelly usually chose for herself. If that meant something, it was beyond considering right then and there. At least Ginny had moved on to another location that wasn't directly in line of sight in the kitchen.

"So?" Natalie looked from one to the other.

"Oh, well, I guess I can go first," Kelly told her. "Right now I work nights and weekends."

"I see. That works because I work Monday through Thursday during the day. We'll have lots of private time, right?"

"That was my thought."

"And you" — she looked at Ryan — "You don't stay here much, do you?"

Ryan quirked a brow at how she'd phrased the question. "Depends on Kelly's schedule and mine. That a problem for you?"

After looking at her nails for a moment, Natalie responded, "I guess not as long as we're not running into each other all the time. And Susan, do you plan to visit often?"

"Me? No. I'm moving out of the area and the most you'll see if me is if you walk in on Kelly Skyping with me."

"That should work."

"So, Natalie, what is it you do?"

"I'm the receptionist at the Jaguar dealer here in town. One of the courtesy car drivers picks me up in the morning. He also brings me home at night."

"That's nice. Saves on gas," Kelly commented.

"Sure does and I don't have to deal with a car."

"How do you do your grocery shopping?" Ryan asked her.

"I pretty much walk everywhere. That's why I need to live near downtown and the stores so this location would be pretty ideal for me."

"How's business at the car dealership?" Again it was Ryan who posed the question.

"Fine. Jag's, you know, they're expensive cars and in this county there are lots of people with that kind of money. I keep waiting for a single rich guy to come in and fall head over heels for me."

Kelly noticed that Natalie didn't seem to be joking about it, but rather seemed pretty certain it would happen. "How long have you worked there?"

"Seven years. So what do you do?"

"Me? I'm a police officer."

"That's good. We'll be safe, right?"

"Right."

A short time later, Kelly told her prospective roommate, "Thanks for coming, Natalie. I'll let you know about the room and all later in the week." Kelly reached out a hand to shake the copper-haired woman's.

"Sure. Look, my mind is made up so I hope you decide in my favor. I'm ready to move in any time."

"Great. Well . . . I'll let you know."

Kelly closed the door. With Ryan peering out the side window of one side of the door and Susan on the other, Kelly opted to look out the peephole to watch as Natalie and her friend ambled up the walkway.

Once she was out of sight, Kelly looked from her boyfriend to her best friend. "Well?"

Ryan cleared his throat. "Her friend is nice."

"Quiet . . . the friend," Susan told them.

"Yes. I don't think she said a word after hello," Ryan answered. "And Natalie certainly seems to know her mind."

"All those questions about cleaning and dusting." Susan shook her head. "I'm all for clean, but . . ."

"Kinda overkill?"

"Right," both nodded as they said it.

"Maybe she just emphasized that so she'd let me know that she wouldn't be a slob."

"Could be," Ryan told her.

"You know," Susan began, "I'm thinking instead of leaving tonight maybe I'll start out tomorrow after you interview your last candidate."

"Not that I wouldn't mind you being here for as long as possible, but what? You don't think I can pick a good roommate?"

"Not at all. You picked me. I figure if the others are half as entertaining as Natalie it would be worth my while. Besides, Ryan will be here, right?"

"You bet."

Kelly sighed. "You two. If you're staying let's order in some Chinese, huh?"

"You're on," Susan called over her shoulder as she headed into the kitchen to call in their order.

"Uh, Suz . . ."

"Don't worry, she knows what you like."

The parade of roommates started by ten the next morning with Betty, a former school teacher.

After showing her around the house, Kelly showed her into the living room. "So, Betty, what do you think?"

"It's a charming little house—I can't resist a Victorian—and your friends are very nice, but I'm not sure I'm really ready to live with someone else, especially someone significantly younger than me. Not that I think you'll have wild parties and such . . . although I'm sure you police officers have your share of good times. I just . . . well, I've lived alone for almost twenty years since my husband died and I'm not sure I'm ready to give up my independence."

"I understand. I can promise you with my hours I wouldn't be in your way—not working the shift I currently have and given I'm low person on the totem pole I'll be on nights and weekends for the foreseeable future."

"Can I let you know in a few days?"

"Of course."

Once again, the threesome watched Kelly's potential roommate walk down the walkway. "She was nice." Kelly sighed.

"I liked her," Susan put in.

"She did seem stable," Ryan told them. "You two would be a good match I think."

"I think so too, but I don't think she's going to go for it."

After waiting around for almost three hours for her second candidate, Kelly figured the guy, this one a postal worker, wasn't going to show.

About two, the third candidate arrived, stumbling up the walk. He rapped smartly on the front door and kept his hand raised to keep knocking when Kelly opened the door.

"Oh, hey. Callie?" Alcohol fumes wafted off the man who looked like he hadn't shaved in a few days.

"Um no, Kelly. Dave?"

"Thachs me." The guy stumbled into the house and wove his way into a wall before finding the living room entry.

"Ryan?" she whispered . . . not that Dave was in any

condition to hear her.

Ryan was already dialing. "Yeah, we have an unconscious male, but breathing, male at 445 Grand."

Ryan stayed on the line and answered a few more questions while waiting for the ambulance to arrive.

"Dave." The one paramedic shook his head.

"You know this guy?" Ryan asked him

"Yeah. We pick him up three or four times a month."

"What will you do with him?" Kelly asked.

"Take him over to detox . . . again. He'll promise to stay sober, get into a treatment plan and that all will be well. How'd you end up with him?"

"That would be me . . . I'm looking for a new roommate and he answered the ad. I thought since he was a bus driver for regional transit he'd be pretty stable."

"Not this guy."

"Well now, that's scary thinking about him getting behind the wheel of a bus."

"Yup. And as long as he tells his supervisor and HR department he's in recovery or doing a treatment plan they'll keep him on and he'll keep on drinking until he kills someone."

While Kelly and Ryan watched the paramedics wheel the now waking Dave down the walkway, Susan came up behind them. "You guys, I'm gonna hit the road."

Kelly glanced outside. "It's getting late . . . you sure? Don't want to stay and post mortem the candidates?"

"Yeah."

"Dinner?"

"I'll grab something out on I-5 and yes, I'll call you when I get in."

Kelly noticed Ryan quietly slip down the hall, giving her lifelong friend and herself a few private moments to say goodbye. "It's gonna suck without you around."

"I'll only be a phone call away."

"Promise?"

"Promise. You gonna repost your ad or . . ."

"I'm going to call Betty tomorrow and see if she's interested. If she is, she's my first choice. I think we'd get along
really well. If not . . ." Kelly sighed. "I don't think Natalie
would be that bad, especially since we probably won't see
each other all that much."

Susan nodded and then reached over to hug her friend. "I'll
talk to you in a few hours when I get into L.A."

"Okay, drive safe."

Kelly watched Susan pull out of the garage and head down
the street before heading to her room and Ryan.

"Hey."

His smile was warm and gentle as he opened his arms to
her. "She's only a plane ride or phone call away."

Kelly curled up in his arms. "I love you."

Ryan kissed the top of her head. "And I'm not going to
leave you."

"I know. You never have—not in this life, not in any of the
others."

"I never will and not because of any spell but because I love
you."

"I know. And you know what?"

"What?"

"I'm the luckiest woman alive. I not only have an incredibly good looking, totally hot, boyfriend, I have some pretty
awesome friends."

"That you do. That you do."

CHAPTER NINE

"Okay, Betty, thanks. If you change your mind in the next few days, let me know."

"She said no?" Ryan asked Kelly as she hung up the phone and he poured their coffee the next morning.

"Yeah. Bummer. I was really hoping she'd be interested."

"So?"

"While you were in the shower I thought about trying to go it alone."

"And?"

"I'm not quite ready to do that. Not because I'm afraid to be alone, but financially it would be tight."

"You thinking of a second interview with Nervous Natalie?"

"No . . . at least not yet. I'm going to repost the ad and see if anyone more . . . more . . ."

"Normal?"

"Well, that too. I was thinking someone more like me might apply." Kelly sipped her coffee and had to put her cup down when she started to laugh.

"Am I missing something?" Ryan asked her.

"Maybe. Can you imagine two like me out there? Or in here?"

Ryan shook his head. "I can see your point . . . two psychics who remember their past lives under the same roof. Well, it might work if you knew each other in those lives and got along. The issue would be if she was one of your old lovers and remembered being a guy in one of your lives."

"Or he? If I remember those flashbacks to other lives, Adrian was the only former lover."

"Yeah, about that."

"You don't trust me with a guy roommate?"

"I trust you. I just like being the only guy in your life."

"And you are. I promise. For keeps this time."

"Me too."

"So I'm going to re-place the ad and see what comes up this week." Kelly glanced at the old fashioned cat clock — the kind where the cat's eyes and tail's flicked back and forth counting the seconds.

Ryan swallowed his coffee. "Yeah, it's about that time. You up for company tonight?"

Kelly rose and put her arms around him. "I'm up for company from you any and every night."

"Hey, McKenna." Maria greeted her as she walked into the station. "How goes it?"

"Slow and easy."

"And the roommate hunt?"

"You heard about that?"

"Saw the sign in the break room. Any nibbles?"

Kelly shrugged. "Not really. I interviewed four people last weekend. That would be four that sounded like good possibles out of the first ten that contacted me. There were three who mentioned in their queries that they were on medical marijuana and while I get it that it helps with certain conditions it *is* a federal offense and dating a federal agent . . ."

"Yeah, that would so not work."

"Neither would it with my job. Then there was the one who was getting out of jail for several B&Es — again, not a good match."

"Any chance on the . . . four . . . you met?"

"One was a no-show, one was drunk and we had to call for

an ambulance because he passed out in my hallway. I really thought one would be a good match—a retired school teacher but she's not sure she's ready to live with someone else just yet. I get that—I suspect that if she moved in with someone it would be a compromise to her independence. Even though we'd probably never see each other she'd still be living with someone younger and her family might think . . ."

"The last one work out?"

"Natalie. That's her name. She was interested. *Very* interested. She came by with a friend and the two of them seemed pretty solid."

"I'm hearing a but there."

"She . . . I'm not sure how to put it. It could be she was nervous and worried about making a good impression so it made her seem wound a little tight. I'm thinking of seeing if she wants to go for a coffee and talk a little more."

"Sounds like a plan."

"And then . . . if no one else steps up well, I'll have to see how the re-interview goes."

"Can't say I envy you. Too bad no one from the department is looking."

"Yeah. When I was a journalist it would have been a lot easier. Now, well, even from when I started dating Ryan, I've been a lot more cautious about things like this. I'm going to call Natalie on break, see when she can get together and then see how she feels about me checking her references."

"And if she wants to talk to yours?"

"No problem. Can I use you?"

Maria laughed.

It didn't sound like she thought it was a funny situation.

"Wait. Before you do that . . ."

"Jess, didn't see you walk up," Kelly told the dispatcher.

"Practicing my stealth skills. Anyway, I could move in with you."

"What?" Maria's voice rose in question.

"I could move in with Kelly. I'd be a great roommate and since we work the same shifts we could come to work together and we'd be sleeping and all at the same time."

"Uh, I thought you and, um, Drew were looking at moving in together," Maria put in.

"Don. Well, we are. Or will be, but, well, Kelly, we could both move in with you, huh?"

"Oh . . . I don't know, Jess. You guys are just starting off your relationship, and well, he works days, right?"

Jess shrugged. "Yeah, but so would all the other people you're talking to. And doesn't Ryan stay with you a lot?"

"Yeah . . . but we've been together for . . . a few years. I . . . I'm not sure I'm ready to live with two other people and a couple just getting together."

"We'd be fine," Jess assured her.

"Um, well, let me think about it. It's . . . quite a change from rooming with Susan after so many years, you know?"

"Oh. Yeah. Sure." With that, Jess turned and walked away.

When she was out of earshot, Maria leaned over. "Your call, of course, but I wouldn't."

Kelly nodded. "I wouldn't either. I don't know why, but I wouldn't either."

CHAPTER TEN

"Why don't we meet at your place?" Natalie asked Kelly a few hours later.

"Um, well, I'm thinking if we meet some place neutral, just the two of us, we'll have more of a chance to see what each other's like. See if we're compatible as roommates without other people around."

"There will be other people in the coffee shop."

"That's true. But if we leave our friends home . . . just us . . . you know, like not being on my turf or anything . . ."

"If I move in it will be my turf too."

Kelly glanced at the CAD—computer aided dispatch—screen in her car, noting that a call in her beat just popped up. Given that Chris was lead dispatcher tonight who knew how long the call had sat before she got around to dispatching it.

"It will be my turf too, right?" Natalie repeated herself.

"What? Oh, sorry, Nat, a call just came in for me."

"My name is Natalie. Not Nat. I'm not a bug."

"Sorry." She was starting to feel like she was sounding redundant. "So how about it? Tomorrow about 6:30 at Java Jam?"

"I get off work at six."

"Yes, I remember. Could your ride drop you off at Java Jam?"

"I guess. But how will I get home?"

Kelly glanced at the CAD screen and saw the call had elevated from a wrongly parked car to a suspicious circumstance. Either the call had originally come in as suspicious and

Chris didn't think it sounded suspicious, or the reporting party called back realizing that a parked car could take hours, but a suspicious circumstance would produce an officer in about a half-hour. Knowing Chris, if it was a woman on the phone, the caller could have reported hearing noises outside the house and Chris just chalked it up to a hysterical female trying to compete with her for male attention. And that was based on fact and past experience, not speculation.

"I thought you said you walk everywhere."

"I do. In daylight."

"Fine. I'll give you a ride to your home on my way into work."

"If you had called me Friday or yesterday we could have met today."

"Uh-huh. Listen, Natalie, I gotta go, my beat partner is en route to a call and I need to go. I'll see you a Java Jam at 6:30 tomorrow."

Kelly disconnected the call before the other woman could respond. "D-18, en route," she reported and shook her head. Natalie was starting to feel like too much work . . . did she need a roommate that badly?

Then again, Kelly thought, it couldn't be easy trying to find a place to live and dealing with a total stranger like Natalie was trying to do. She pulled up to the residence at the same moment Coburn pulled in.

"Hey, McKenna."

"Jack."

The redheaded officer looked at the house they'd been called to and shook his head.

"What's up?"

"These two . . . you ever been called to this address?"

"No. But then I'm the rookie. You know them?"

He checked his weapon and patted his cuffs. "Not person-ally — we get called out here at least once a week, twice during a full moon. You'd think after all this time the two of them would either go their separate way or find a way to get along better."

"Regulars, huh?"

"Sometimes I think the pair of them wrote the manual on how to do domestic violence."

"DV?" Kelly stopped in her tracks. "The original call came in as a wrongly parked car."

"Ah, yeah . . . that would be Chris. She's not too fond of these two and tends to minimize whatever is going on with them. She'll promise them a unit is rolling and then make a comment that if it takes long enough one of them will kill the other and this nonsense can stop."

"Seriously?"

"Yup. Did it on the air one night so we all heard it."

"And she's still on the radio?"

Jack nodded. "Still employed is the more surprising issue."

"So it probably wasn't anything suspicious?"

"Nope. With Chris she doesn't elevate a call to these two until they call back for the third time or a neighbor calls and complains."

"Wow."

They arrived at the door and Jack knocked. "Warren? Tanya?"

Silence.

Jack knocked again. "Tanya? Warren? Officers McKenna and Coburn. Open up the door."

They heard the click of a deadbolt slide into place in response.

Jack dipped his head and shook it from side to side before speaking again. "Come on now, you two. You know the drill. You open the door. I talk to one of you. Officer McKenna talks to the other and we figure out just what's going on."

"Go away. We don't need you," a teary sounding woman

called from behind the door.

"Can't do that, Tanya. Neighbors reported hearing yelling and other assorted loud sounds."

"They need to start minding their own business and stay out of mine."

"Yeah, well, in this case they didn't, so open the door."

"Come back tomorrow."

"Warren? Warren, do you hear me? Open the door."

"He . . . he's not here."

"Well, if he's not there there's no reason for you not to open the door."

"Wait a second," Kelly whispered to Jack.

He turned with a brow raised in question.

"I heard something . . . something metallic."

"Like what metallic?"

"Like . . . like this may sound weird, but you know the sound of clearing the chamber in an automatic?"

Jack studied her a moment. "Ye-ah. You sure?"

"Well, I'm not one hundred percent sure because I haven't heard that many from behind a locked door, but . . ."

"Jack, Jack," a man called out just about a whisper from a window a few feet from the door.

"Warren?" he softly called back. "Open the door."

"Can't. She's . . . Jack, she's got a gun."

"Aw shit. D-22, Red Oak." He motioned Kelly back way from the door.

"Go to Red Oak."

Kelly noted her partner looked relieved to hear Maria on the radio instead of Chris.

"Need a sergeant, another couple of officers and have an ambulance stage up the street."

"Copy, requesting S-3, additional units and rolling medical."

"S-3, D-22, go to secure channel."

Keeping his eyes on the house, Jack adjusted his radio. "Sarge?"

"What's going on?"

"Not entirely sure, but Tanya Helson won't open the door, Warren seems to be holed up in the living room or den and says he can't open the door. McKenna thinks she may have heard someone clearing the chamber on a gun, but she's not entirely sure."

"You thinking Tanya may have gone off the deep end this time?"

"I'm not sure."

"Red Oak, S-3 is 10-7," the sergeant announced as he pulled up in front of the house.

Kelly saw two other units pull in a bit up the street as she and Jack started for the sergeant's car.

"Heard a weapon, McKenna?" Sgt. Jennings asked her as he got out of the car.

"I'm not entirely sure, sir. I thought I heard something, but . . ." she trailed off.

"Warren didn't sound so good," Jack told him.

"Let's see if we can get him to open the window a bit more and talk to us." Jennings headed toward the house while keeping his focus on the front door. Kelly and Jack followed at a slight distance, also keeping the house in view.

They each took a position on either side of the window before Jack called out low, "Warren? You still in there?"

"Yeah, Jack. I'm here."

"What's going on?"

"I . . . well, you might not believe this but Tanya, she . . . she shot me."

"Where?" Jack asked.

"Here in the house."

"Warren, did she hit you?"

"Well, yeah, she did that before she shot me."

"I mean with the gun."

"No. She hit me with her fist."

"Warren." Jack sighed. "Are you shot?"

"Yeah. And I'm hurting."

"Where did she shoot you?"

"She was aiming for my heart but missed, got me in the shoulder, but I'll tell you, man, I'm hurting."

"I imagine you are," Jack muttered. Then louder, "Warren, can you open the window?"

"I think so. But you know if I do and you come in here she's gonna be mad, really mad."

"Warren, we don't care if she's happy, sad or mad. Right now we want to get your butt out of there. Now as quickly and quietly as you can, open the window."

"You won't hurt her now, will you? Because she can be quite . . . well, she can get pretty angry, you know?"

Coburn sighed. "Open the window, Warren."

Slowly the window opened. Before the man inside could react, Jack reached in, grabbed him, and none too gently pulled him out the window. Against the white of the man's t-shirt, there was a large dark stain, and the metal scent unique to blood filled the air.

"Typical Chris fiasco," Jack groused to Kelly after they returned from booking Tanya at the jail and stopping by the hospital to check on Warren. Not surprisingly, like with most domestic violence matters, Warren was declining to press charges.

"So what happens next since Warren isn't pressing charges?" Kelly asked him.

"We still complaint request to the district attorney's office. Given how many times we've been called out there over the past few years it won't be hard to charge her."

"So there's a good chance of a conviction?"

Jack shrugged. "Never know. She could plead in exchange for a deal, judge might believe him . . . anything could happen. So any decisions on the roommate thing?"

"Maybe. That one woman, Natalie, didn't sound really all that bad. I'm all for neat and clean."

"You got a point."

"I think part of the problem, my hesitation, is Susan and I roomed together for a lot of years. Like back through college. It's not that anyone else wouldn't be a good match—it's getting used to someone else, you know?"

"Yup. I had some winners in my time. Makes me glad I'm married with three kids. Now *that* is stability!" Jack chuckled.

"Sounds like."

"So, you and Michaels? Looking at tying the knot yourselves before long?"

Kelly shrugged. "I think we both know that's where we'll ultimately end up but for now . . . well, we're good where we're at. For myself I need to, or want to, be settled in my job for a while, you know?"

Jack nodded. "Yeah, I do. I don't think Marcy . . . that's my wife . . . and I would be as good as we are if we'd gotten married at the same time I started as a cop."

"If you don't mind my asking, which did come first? The wedding or the badge?"

"The badge, but that was after dating through college and for a year or so after. Like you guys we knew that's where we'd ultimately be but I wanted to get through the academy and have that steady income before we got married. Not everyone makes it through field training, you know?"

"Yeah. Not first hand, but it was something they covered at the academy—how being a cop can change your relationships and how, if you don't make it, it can change things as well. Some guys, I guess, don't handle the failure well."

"No, some don't. We had this one guy who was hired

because his dad was a friend of one of the captains. Kind of a weird one, the captain, Lyles, was active in his church and this kid was one of the deacons or some such's son. Alan, that was the kid's name, almost didn't make it through POST but since he was guaranteed a job here and Lyles said he'd be fine, they passed him. Reluctantly, but passed him. Word is he had to redo several of his exams three times and ultimately graduated with two classes after his own, but he finally made it through."

"Well, not everyone does well in class work, right? Like just because you can't get the book learning doesn't mean you can't do the job?"

"Yeah, that's true."

"So what happened?"

"They tried him with pretty much every FTO, every shift, did a bunch of remedial work with him and he just didn't get it. Mixed it up with all of the dispatchers because he'd do what he wanted and then one day he mixed it up with the wrong one."

"Let me guess . . . blonde and never met a man in uniform she didn't like."

"You got it in one. Specifically we had a call about a drunk and disorderly one morning. Carson, you know, the school resource officer, was pulling an extra shift on the beat the D&D was at and headed out. Alan was sent as back up. They got the guy to the hospital and instead of securing him Alan just kinda stood there not paying attention. Next thing the guy grabbed Alan's gun and Carson got nicked. It was damn lucky the guy was a lousy shot and too drunk to know what the hell he was doing. Captain Harris went out to the scene . . . fortunately Lyles wasn't on duty that day . . . and picked Alan up. In the car Alan started pounding on the dashboard and started to cry about how he had to pass or his dad would be upset. Apparently it was pretty dramatic. He was released from duty that afternoon and Lyles tried to save the guy's career but no one was going to stand by and get shot because Alan got sloppy again."

"Gees. So both Alan and this Captain Lyles are gone?"

"Yup. And so are the rest of the guys that Lyles brought in as favors to his pals."

"That's kind of scary — that people got jobs as cops as favors . . . if that's what you're telling me."

"It is. We've got a good team now and seriously, McKenna, it's good to have you on board."

"Thanks. And for what it's worth, Ryan is supportive of my job."

"That goes a long way. And if you don't make it? Not that I'm thinking you won't . . ."

"Then I'll go back to reporting or find something else interesting."

Jack nodded. "Well, we all think you're doing great and personally I hope the roommate thing works out for you."

"I do too. I do too."

CHAPTER ELEVEN

"Hello, Natalie?"

"Yes?"

"It's Kelly, Kelly McKenna. How are you doing?"

"Well, except for an allergy attack and a little stiffness in my mid-back today for having to sit at the reception desk at the car dealership all day yesterday I'm good. How about you?"

"Fine. Two more days on shift and then my weekend, you know?"

"Uh-huh."

Kelly waited a moment to see if the other woman had anything else to say before continuing, "So I've thought about it and I think we'd be a good match as roommates."

"Really?" Natalie squealed. "That's wonderful! I'm so excited. How soon can I move in?"

"Anytime now."

"Okay, great. I'll give notice with the current landlord and get my stuff packed. I don't have that much, but you know how when you move you have to do some packing and cleaning."

"Yeah, I remember. It's been a couple of years, but I do remember."

"Can I call you in a day or so to let you know when?"

"Sure. Just give me a couple days' notice so I can be sure I've got the keys made and everything. By the way, did I tell you that your room has its own phone line and cable hook up? Susan, my former roomie, thought that worked better for us."

"You did, but thanks for the reminder. I prefer having my own phone and even though it sounds like we'll be working different sides of the day and week it's still good to have my own TV set up. Oh! And I'll bring a security deposit over tomorrow if that's okay."

"Sure. That would be great."

"I like to get the business side of things settled as soon as I can."

"Me too. So, let me know and I'll talk to you later."

Kelly hung up and looked at Ryan. With a shrug, she told him, "So that's it. I've got a new roommate."

"She's not going to be another Susan." Ryan quietly reminded her.

"I know. To be another Susan she'd need to have been my friend for most of my life and gone through all of the things Susan went through with me. She'd have to be . . . Susan."

"She's only a phone call away."

"I know."

"Or a flight."

"I know. I'm okay, really. It was way past time when she should be on her own, living her own life."

"That's karma, babe. You did what you had to to resolve whatever was hanging over you. She made an agreement a long time ago to be there for you."

Kelly shook her head, momentarily puzzled. "You'd think that when I remembered how I caused Adrian to . . . to . . . stalk me, that once I released him, released all of us . . . I guess that's why she was finally able to make a job decision for herself instead of thinking of me."

"You aren't feeling guilty that she stuck by you all these years, are you? You aren't thinking that you somehow held Susan back against her will?"

Kelly looked at him and blinked back a tear.

"Because she'd tell you no, absolutely not. Susan never did anything she didn't want to do. Even without that karmic, past life oath, she's the kind of friend everyone wants and needs and you were lucky, *are* lucky, to have."

"I know. And now there's room for a new friend. Maybe."

"Natalie will be fine. Just don't expect to have instant camaraderie, right?"

"I don't. In fact, with our schedules most likely I'll never see her."

"Good point. So now what?"

"Hmmm, I want to give the room and bathroom a quick go round and check to be sure everything is set for when Natalie moves in."

"How long?"

"She's going to let me know — "

The phone ringing interrupted her thought. "Hey, Natalie!"

"How did you know it was me?"

"Caller ID?"

"Oh, yeah. Right."

"What's up?"

"I wanted to let you know my current landlord said it was cool with him if I moved out this weekend. Is that too soon to move in?"

"No, not at all. I go back on shift Friday afternoon, but if we can't meet up over keys and such before then Ryan can be here to take care of that."

"Ryan . . . you said he's not always there, that's true, right?"

"Uh, yes, I mean it's true he's not always over. It would be a favor to me . . . and you . . . for him to hand over the keys. Otherwise we'll have to find a mutual time for both of us, you know?"

"Oh. Yeah. Good point. I have off on Friday so I'll come by

sometime during the day before you go to work, okay?"

"Sure. No problem. I'll let him know just in case we miss each other."

"Natalie?" Ryan asked her when she hung up.

"Yeah. She seemed surprised you'd be around to hand over the key. I think she thought maybe something had changed about you living here and I just didn't mention it."

"I take it the fact that I have a key didn't come up?"

"No. And since it's my house she doesn't need to know that. Or anything else about my personal life."

"Susan knew," he told her with a smile.

"Yeah, but like we said not so long ago, there wasn't much about my life Susan didn't know or that I didn't know about hers."

"True. Natalie will notice."

Kelly shrugged. "I'll cross that bridge when I come to it. Right now, tell me I didn't talk out of turn when I said you would be here to give her the keys Friday if I've left for work."

"Not at all. I look forward to having a little time to get to know her."

If there was one thing Kelly knew about her boyfriend, it was that he'd be doing a little more checking on Natalie than the reference check Kelly'd done. His protective instincts never seemed to turn off where she was concerned. Even now, when she'd graduated from the police academy and was in field training with the Red Oak department, he still had a need to protect her.

Friday afternoon Kelly had just finished French braiding her hair for work when the doorbell rang. A quick glance in the mirror and she headed down the hall. Ryan was already at the door greeting Natalie.

"Natalie! Hi." Kelly greeted her. "Glad you made it before I had to leave."

"Me too." The other woman looked her up and down. "You look pretty good in your uniform."

"Thanks. I gotta get going, but . . ." She turned to the sideboard. "Here are the keys. This is to the button lock, the deadbolt and garage. And here's the clicker. I park on the right and there's room for your car or storage for you."

"I thought I told you, I don't drive," Natalie told her while stringing the keys onto her key ring.

"Oh, well then, you've got plenty of room for storage out there."

"Great." The group turned as footsteps sounded on the front steps. "Good, you're here." Natalie had turned to the person who'd just arrived.

"Right on time," the dark-haired man answered her while peering into the house.

Ryan had stood by watching the scene unfold and now extended his hand to the newcomer. "Ryan Michaels."

"Gus Boatman. I'm here to clean the carpet."

"Clean the . . ." Kelly looked over at Natalie.

"I have allergies and need to make sure the hallway to the room and my room is clean as possible. Don't worry, I'm paying for it. The maids will be here shortly to clean the bathroom and kitchen. Since I'll be able to store things in the garage I'll have them clean out there too. Will you be taking your car to work? Cause I'd like to get the whole thing cleaned."

"Bath and . . . um listen, even though Ginny, my cat, is relatively young and well behaved, I'm not keen on chemicals around . . ."

"Not to worry," Gus told her. "I use empowered water. No chemicals."

"Thanks, but, well, Ryan, can you check with the . . . house cleaners to make sure . . ."

"I'll take care of it," Natalie told her. "Ryan can go ahead and do whatever he was going to do."

He arched a brow at Kelly. "Well then, I'll be in the library working on my report."

"Wait. What?" Natalie looked from Kelly to Ryan. "What do you mean you'll be working in the library?"

Ryan studied her for a moment. "Just that. I'll be in the library working on a report." With that, he turned and headed down the hall.

"I thought just you and I lived here." Natalie turned to Kelly, clearly not happy to hear that Ryan would be there without Kelly or that he made himself at home.

"Yes, just us. But I told you, Ryan does spend time here with me and he was gracious enough to work here today to make sure if you needed something he would be able to help out."

"Oh. Well, that's okay I guess. I'm a pretty private person and if I have to live with someone I only want it to be that person. When we met you said there wasn't a lot of in and out with people."

"There's not. With my work schedule I don't have a lot of downtime so I . . ."

Natalie had wandered away toward the kitchen. Figuring she was going to check on what the house cleaners might need to do, Kelly headed off to the library and Ryan.

Entering, she closed the door and whispered, "Well?"

"Well, what?" Ryan turned in his chair and smiled.

"It's going to be okay, isn't it?"

He stood and pulled Kelly into his arms. "I'm sure it will be . . . especially with the maids. She did say maids were coming, right? She's just nervous about moving and you're not exactly the best person when it comes to change."

"Excuse me? If you'll remember I spent a lot of years living out of not just a suitcase but a backpack and bouncing from airport to airport and hotel to tents in the jungle doing investigative reports. And yes, she did say maids."

"Yes, you did. But when it came to your home life it's been pretty stable, right? At least in terms of not a lot of disruption once you moved here, yes?"

She stuck out of her lower lip in a pout. "You're right. And since she is paying for the cleaners, and the . . . *maids* . . . well, that's a nice touch don't you think?"

"It is. I wouldn't mind if she paid for mine."

"Well, maybe you should invite her over for dinner and she'll bring em along."

"Only one coming to dinner is you—and that's because I'll be looking for dessert—before we eat."

CHAPTER TWELVE

After a relatively uneventful shift, Kelly was home by 3:30 a.m. While the shift was called graveyard, it started at 5:00 p.m. with briefing and ended at 3 in the morning. Usually, she'd grab a quick shower at the station before heading home to avoid waking Susan in the middle of the night. She'd include Ryan in that except, if he was staying over, he'd usually be up waiting for her or would wake the moment she entered the house. Not that he was a light sleeper—he just seemed to have a knack of waking up at just the right time. Kelly figured it was a throwback to his days as a Marine even though he flew jets and didn't spend a lot of time on the ground.

Tonight though, knowing Natalie was moved in, she hadn't bothered changing out of her uniform before heading home. That, and the desire to avoid another conversation with Jess. Her disappointment that Kelly hadn't seriously considered her offer to move in with her was a bit odd, especially given how moments after expressing how bummed she was Jess had gone on to talk about her plans to move in with Don.

Now, even with Ryan in the house, she felt a little antsy about what she'd find when she got home. The whole issue of the carpet cleaner and cleaning people . . . make that the maids . . . coming in unnerved her a bit. "Probably an artifact of the old Adrian stalking days," she muttered to herself. During those terrifying years, Kelly closely guarded her every move. Always looking behind her, never walking out the door without her keys between her fingers in case the stalker

76

attacked. She never let her guard down.

The sad thing was Susan was also impacted by it. She, too, had to develop a sixth sense of people around her . . . the pair were always looking to see if someone seemed too interested in them . . . too interested in Kelly.

The frightening thing was the stalker turned out to be a man she trusted and almost married. Despite her awareness that Adrian James stalked her because of a spell she cast on him in ancient Atlantis centuries before, she also knew he had some level of free will. He had to know what he was doing was wrong and that it terrified her. Every time he did something — sending her a Barbie with a knife in it and tainted chocolates, trying to run her down in the street . . . he had to know what he was doing and that one day he'd be caught.

She pulled into the garage, knowing Natalie might have stored some of her moving boxes and other unused items in there.

What she didn't expect, though, was the sparkling clean garage. Not a cobweb in sight. Boxes were neatly stacked . . . both Natalie's and hers. It looked like even the garage floor had been scrubbed. Not that it was dirty or had oil stains and such on it. It just looked . . . scrubbed. With a shrug, Kelly turned off the engine, got out of the car, grabbed her duty bag, locked the door, and headed through the doorway into the house. Looking forward to a hot yet quick shower, followed by a quick cuddle with her guy, she did not anticipate what she found in the kitchen.

She and Susan weren't slobs by any means but Kelly sure felt like it when she saw the kitchen. It looked like something out of a home and garden type magazine or at least like a model home that was up for sale. The microwave had been moved from an L shaped portion of the kitchen counter near the sink to a counter space near the stove. It had been thoroughly cleaned.

The electric can opener had the cord wrapped neatly around it, as did the espresso maker and coffee pot. The rice cooker she usually left out because of almost daily use was nowhere to be seen. She noticed the toaster oven had been put on the other side of the stove.

"Okay, well, if that makes her feel more comfortable . . ." Kelly mumbled as she reached into a cabinet for a glass to pour some water from the refrigerator spigot. She couldn't help but utter a small gasp when she opened the cabinet where the glasses were kept . . . they'd been arranged by size and color with labels at the edge of the shelf, indicating which size was to go where. Peeking into the dish cabinet, she cracked the door just a little bit just in case . . . in case of what? Natalie jumping out?

Just as she suspected after seeing the glasses, the dishes had all been arranged as well. Not that they hadn't been in size order before. Now they were arranged by size and color.

"Well . . . I wonder if she discussed this with Ryan?"

Glass and duty bag in hand Kelly started down the hall but stopped short at the kitchen door when she saw Ginny sitting on the floor, glaring at her. She put the bag and glass down before reaching for her cat. "What's going on, baby girl? Huh?"

Ginny growled. She truly growled, which was so unlike her not so little gray cat.

With that, Kelly gave the room another look. Ginny's food and water dishes were nowhere in sight. Normally they sat next to the pantry closet door. This morning they were nowhere to be seen.

"I see, baby. Well, let's get you something to eat, huh? It looks like Natalie did the floors or had the cleaning service to it and trying to keep out of her way, Ryan forgot to feed you."

She swore Ginny grumbled before she set the cat down on the floor. Grabbing a can of food and one of Ginny's dishes,

Kelly scooped out her food and set it down before pouring a bowl of water. In between bites of food, Ginny meowed in her not so happy meow. Clearly, her cat wasn't keen on Natalie's housekeeping style.

"We'll explain it to her, Gin," Kelly assured the cat before heading down the hall to her bedroom.

Even knowing Ryan would wake the moment she entered the room or more likely was already awake, Kelly gently turned the doorknob and tiptoed into the room.

"You come in through the kitchen or front door?" a sleepy sounding Ryan asked.

"Kitchen."

"Nice job in there, huh?"

"Hmm. Do I need to see the rest of the house or can that wait till morning . . . my morning?"

"It can wait. I stopped her from going into the den and library explaining that those are your domains. She wasn't too happy about that, but the . . . maids . . . didn't want to mess with me too much. I think when they saw my credentials they were afraid I was something other than an ATF agent."

"Thought you were ICE, huh?"

"Could have been. Natalie though really pushed to have them go in and clean and I was quite surprised when my best federal agent glare didn't stop her in her tracks."

"So did she clean in there?"

"Nope. Doesn't mean she won't try. The housecleaners let her know they were on a schedule and she'd have to choose between the kitchen and arguing with me over the library and den . . . she picked the kitchen."

"It did look clean. Guess she forgot to put Ginny's food back down."

"Actually she didn't. She said that cats and dogs shouldn't be in houses and should eat and do their business outside. I stopped her before she put Ginny out."

"Wait. What?"

"I stopped her before she put Ginny out."

"What do you mean put her out?" Kelly stopped undressing and sat on the edge of the bed. "Did she pick Ginny up to put her . . . where? The backyard?"

"No, she didn't pick Ginny up. Not that Ginny would have let her. She opened the door and asked me to put her out."

"And you said?"

"Absolutely not. Ginny is an indoor cat, has never been outside and she's not going to start now. Natalie then informed me that with her allergies you were going to have to either put her outside or get rid of her."

Kelly shook her head and started to toe-off her socks. "She knew when she came to look at the room and we agreed to give rooming together a try I have a cat, an indoor cat. She didn't say anything about it then."

"Well, she did mention something about allergies."

"Yeah, but come on, she's an adult. She sees a cat she has to know the cat lives here. If she can't be around the cat fur or has a dander issue she needed not to move in."

"Well, I'll let you take that up with her. Meanwhile I grabbed bowls for food and water and fed Ginny in your bathroom. Then she and I hung out watching Animal Planet until Natalie went to bed."

"And then what?"

"Me?"

"Yes, you."

"I checked out the house, checked over all the rooms she'd been in . . . and the garage . . . to see just what she'd done."

"I take it you felt things were okay."

"Yeah. You're gonna have to set some rules with her but she strikes me as the type who if she has rules, lives by them."

"I sure hope so. I sure as shit hope so."

CHAPTER THIRTEEN

The sound of pots and pans rattling, rather loudly, in the kitchen not long after Kelly had gone to sleep startled the couple awake.

"What the heck . . ." Kelly twisted from the warm cocoon of Ryan's embrace to look at the clock. "It's barely 8:00 a.m."

"I'd wager it's your new roommate," Ryan sleepily told her.

"Mmm. I'd say you're right." Kelly raised her head and let it bounce back down on her pillow. "What kind of normal person gets up before eight on a Saturday morning?"

"Maybe she runs or meets with a group of whatever."

Kelly closed her eyes just as one pot crashed against another. At least she hoped they were pots crashing against each other. "If that's so, why the sounds of a major cooking event in the kitchen?"

"Maybe she's unpacking her kitchen stuff."

"She didn't do that yesterday? When I got home this morning it looked like there was some serious rearranging in the kitchen."

"Don't know." He turned his head enough to look at the clock. "I should be getting up and out of here anyway."

Kelly snuggled back up against him. "Sorry, but why?"

He shrugged. "It's the nature of the business. We got a lead on D-1 yesterday and I need to get into the office and check it out."

"Mmm. I don't like this I think."

"Yeah, well, your first few years you'll be among the last

to pick a shift and probably get all the ones no one else wants so if this is what you want . . ."

"Yeah, I know, get used to it. And it is what I want, Ryan. Seriously what I want." Kelly scooched up to lean on her elbow and rest her head in her hand. "I'll tell you this—I do like working nights and weekends. Unfortunately that one dispatcher, Chris? She likes working them too."

"If I had a choice of shifts those'd be the ones I'd want too—not a whole lot of admin around."

"You don't deal with admin that much, do you?"

"No. But that's because I've got enough seniority they figure I'm working my cases."

"And you are."

"That I am." After a quick kiss, Ryan rolled to his side of the bed and sat up. His mussed, collar-length blond hair looked sexy in its disarray. "So why does the badge bunny like that shift?"

Kelly shook her head. "From what one of the other women said Chris slept her way through day and swing shifts and all that was left was graves. Apparently there's also an officer, a sergeant actually, who went to graves because she was pursuing him and he did it to get away from her. As you can see, that worked out well for him."

"Yeah, the more serious badge bunnies don't care if someone is married or not when they're on the trail of a victim."

"Ry?" Kelly snuggled closer and rubbed her tummy against his back.

"Mmm?"

"We haven't talked about this before but . . ."

"As long as you don't have any male dispatchers I'm not worried about a badge bunny coming after you."

She play slapped his upper arm. "That wasn't my question!"

He chuckled. "Oh no?"

"No. You. Badge bunnies . . . any women at your office ever get their sights on you?"

Ryan shrugged. "It happens."

"And?"

"And . . . I learned early on mixing bread and honey is not very smart at all. And . . ." He turned serious, very serious.

"What?"

When he didn't answer, Kelly asked him again, "Ryan?"

"I always knew that there was someone I was going to fall in love with. That there was someone I was meant to be with and that I'd know her as soon as I saw her."

Kelly leaned over and kissed him lightly on the lips.

"And I did," he told her.

"Me too."

"I—"

They were interrupted by a frantic knocking on Kelly's door.

"Kelly? Kelly, are you awake? Kelly, I need you."

"Natalie," she whispered to Ryan.

"Sounds serious," he whispered back.

Kelly got up from bed and grabbed her robe. She cracked open the door. "Natalie, morning, what's . . ."

"We've got an *infestation*! A major infestation."

"Infestation? Of what?"

"Ants, there are *hordes* of ants all over the kitchen."

"Ants? Give me a sec."

She closed the door and glanced over at Ryan, who merely shrugged and raised a brow as he grabbed the top sheet to cover himself before heading to the bathroom to shower.

"Ryan," she whispered, "there shouldn't be any ants—there was no food left out, not even Ginny's food, and it isn't even ant season. And the kitchen was pretty darn clean when I got home this morning."

"Well, you'd better deal with that infestation."

"It's not funny so stop laughing."

"I'm not laughing," he whispered.

"You're trying not to . . . but you're about to."

"So are you."

"Yeah, well, a horde of ants isn't funny."

Pulling her robe on, she opened the door and followed a rather frantic Natalie to the kitchen expecting to find the floor covered with ants. Anticipating a moving black floor, Kelly was moderately surprised to find the floor was spotless. Not a bug in sight. She glanced around before turning to Natalie. "Where did you see them?"

"All over." Natalie gestured about the room.

Kelly peered into the corners and opened a few cabinets before telling Natalie, "It looks like you scared them off."

"I don't know . . ."

"Where exactly did you see them?"

"On the floor."

"Hmm, well . . ." Kelly walked over to the laundry room, opened the door, and peered inside. "Nothing in here. Maybe you have a hidden talent you didn't know about before and you can make ants disappear."

Natalie looked doubtful. "Maybe."

"Well, crisis averted." Kelly turned to go back to her room.

"Um, Kelly, is Ryan here?"

Kelly stopped and slowly turned. "Yes."

"He's not going to be staying all the time, right?"

"No. Sometimes I go to his house."

"Okay. Could you let me know ahead of time?"

"When I'm going to Ryan's?"

"When he'll be here."

"Uh, sure. If I remember."

"Please try." She seemed to direct instead of ask. "I like to be prepared."

"Right. Well, I work tonight so I'm going to try to catch a

few more winks before I have to get ready to go."

Kelly walked back into her room and shut the door to find Ryan scratching Ginny behind the ears. "Thought you were heading to the shower."

"I was and then little cutie face here let me know she needed some ear scratch time. So, the mighty ant horde vanquished?" he asked her.

"For now," Kelly wryly answered him.

"I thought you woulda been mopping them up for hours."

"Yeah. If there were any." She sat beside him on the bed and reached over to pet her cat.

"None?"

"Not a one and she looked kind of confused when I didn't see any."

"Maybe you need glasses?"

Kelly snorted. "Trust me. There were no ants."

A moment later they heard water running down the hall in Natalie's bathroom.

"Think that will keep her occupied for a few," Ryan whispered.

"Could be . . . whatcha got in mind, cutie?"

"This . . ." He pulled her to him and they met in a kiss that was at first gentle and welcoming and then with a hunger for each other. Amid quiet giggles they whispered about being quiet because of the woman down the hall. Till Kelly knew her better, there were some things they didn't want to share.

"Love you," Ryan told her. "I love you so much."

"Love you too," Kelly told him.

"And as much as I'd like to spend the day between the sheets with you I need to . . ."

Chapter Fourteen

"Gosh, you really aren't ever here." Natalie greeted Kelly on her way out to work late Monday afternoon.

"Oh, I'm here. Just not when you're awake I think."

"I didn't hear you yesterday," Natalie told her.

"Yesterday . . . Sunday. I went over to Ryan's right after work and left from there."

"Do you usually spend Sunday's over there?"

"Mmm, we don't really have a set pattern or routine. It depends on whatever is happening. He wanted to see a movie yesterday that was playing near his house."

"Must be weird doing your dating during the day."

"It has its moments. I sleep a little when I get off shift and then take a nap before leaving in the afternoon."

Natalie took in Kelly's utility belt. "Is that a Taser?"

Kelly glanced down. "Yes."

"Are those real handcuffs?"

"Yup."

"Do you use them on Ryan?"

"On Ryan? Uh, no. If I have to use them at all I make sure they are totally sanitized and ready for the next person I have to take in custody."

"Germs?"

"Could be."

"Is your gun loaded?"

Kelly studied Natalie for a moment before answering, "Yes. It doesn't do you much good not to be loaded. But nothing to worry about — I keep it locked in a gun case when I'm not using it."

Natalie nodded. "Good to know."

"Well, if that's it I gotta go."

"Sure. I guess I'll take a bath and turn in."

"Okay, well, have a good evening."

As she headed toward her car Kelly shook her head — that was one of the strangest conversations she'd ever had.

Tired after her shift all Kelly wanted was a hot bath when she ran into Natalie heading into her own bathroom when she arrived home Tuesday morning.

"Running late," Natalie told her as she hurried by.

Kelly nodded and bent down to pick Ginny up and give her a snuggle before heading into the kitchen to feed her. Absentmindedly she heard Natalie turn on the water in her bathroom.

Ginny fed, Kelly started down the hall to her room, unbuckling her utility belt as she went. She'd just put her gun in the lockbox when her phone rang. "Ryan, hey."

"How's my favorite cop?"

"Good. Tired. I'm about ready to crash and sleep for the next twelve hours."

"Well then, sleep well."

"That's all? Sleep well?"

"I was going to tell you I'm all hot, hard and bothered just thinking about you, but I don't want to keep you up."

"Ah, I see. But it wouldn't be me who was kept . . . up . . . that would be you."

"Yes, it would."

"I could take care of that when you get off work tonight."

"Could you?"

"I think I'd enjoy that."

"Your place or mine?"

"I've got an interview up your way later today . . . how

about we go to Mama's and then . . ."

"I like the way you think, agent."

"Do you now?"

"I do."

"Then shall I tell you what else I think?"

"Please do."

"I think when I get you alone tonight I'm going to slowly . . . but not too slowly, peel off your top and then I'm gonna nibble on those luscious breasts of yours for a few and while I'm doing that I'm going to slowly, so very, very slowly, pull down the zipper on your pants and after I peel them off I'm going to go to work on your thong."

Kelly sat down, her breath hitching at the images Ryan was creating for her. "And what about my thong?"

"I'm gonna peel it off with my teeth."

"Mmm. I'm thinking I hope that interview goes mighty fast and that maybe we should skip dinner out and go right to dessert."

"Is that so?"

"That is so."

"Well, I'll think on that. Maybe I'll have some very sweet dreams about that."

"I look forward to hearing about those dreams."

"I look forward to having a very hot and naked Ryan between my sheets with me."

"And so you shall."

After they hung up Kelly stood, stretched, and padded into her en suite bathroom thinking a hot shower before turning in was just the ticket. Arms raised and twisting side to side she was peripherally aware of what sounded like the water in Natalie's tub running out. Kelly stepped into her shower, turned on the hot water, and let it start to pound down on her. That lasted all of about two minutes before suddenly the water started to run cold.

"What the . . ." Just as quickly the water turned hot before turning cold again. "Oh man, I need to tell Natalie about the water heater . . ." She and Susan knew the tank ran out after two showers and that it needed at least a half-hour to warm up again. Knowing that, they timed their showers, and when Ryan was over they conserved water by showering together. With Natalie and her working different hours of the day it seemed like they'd never be crossing wires or showering time.

She turned off the water in her bath to hear it still running down the hall in Natalie's. Kelly stepped out of the tub and started to dry off, shrugging at whatever was going on down the hall. She pulled on one of Ryan's t-shirts and snuggled down into the bed. Just as sleep was about to take her, a knock sounded on the door.

"Kelly? Are you in there? Kelly? It's Natalie."

"Natalie?"

"Yes, we have a problem."

Kelly looked at the clock and thought that yes, indeed, she did have a problem. She hadn't even been in bed ten minutes and was bone tired. "Is it something that can wait till tonight?"

"I suppose so, but you may want to get up and get the water fixed so you can shower tonight."

"The water?" Kelly slid up in bed and shook her head. "The door's unlocked, come on in."

"Are you alone?"

"Except for Ginny, yes."

Natalie cracked open the door and took a step into the room.

"What's wrong with the water?"

"There's not enough hot water."

Kelly furrowed her brow in thought. "Not enough hot water?"

"No. I took my bath and when I went to take my shower

first it was really cold and then it got really hot and I was finally able to get it comfortable. I should be able to have a nice
hot shower after my bath."

"You took a bath and then a shower?" Kelly was confused.
It was way too early in the morning or late in her night to be
having this conversation.

"Yes. I do every morning and night."

"O-kay. Well, aside from us being in the middle of a
drought, there's nothing wrong with the water. It's an older
tank and if two of us are in the shower at the same time one
of us ends up with cold water."

"Oh. Well then, you'll need to wait for me to finish before
you take yours." Natalie turned to leave.

"Um, if we each take one shower . . ."

Natalie turned back to her "Well, how many would we be
taking in the morning? You take one and I take one after my
bath. Because I work during the day, and you don't do anything but sleep all day, I should be able to take mine first."

Kelly was too tired to have this conversation and figured
she'd table it for another time when her pillow wasn't calling
out to her. "Right. Fine. See you tonight, Natalie."

"Okay." The other woman walked out of the room and
thankfully pulled the door shut behind her.

Kelly listened to Natalie walk down the hall and was nodding off just as she heard a horn honk outside. A moment later
she heard the front door slam shut and the car's engine roar
as it took off. With a quick look at her clock it made sense to
her that Natalie's ride had just picked her up for work, and
for the next nine hours Kelly was alone to sleep.

CHAPTER FIFTEEN

"She really told you you'd have to wait for her to have her shower first?" Ryan chuckled as he confirmed what Kelly told him.

"She most certainly did. And for whatever reason she took a bath and then a shower not only this morning, but when she got home tonight. Apparently she does that every morning and every night—even with the drought."

Ryan picked up a fry and chewed on it and shook his head. "Well, depending on the bath . . . we sometimes shower after we've taken a bath."

"Yeah, but that's when we . . . you know . . . do a little something special in the tub with massage oil and . . ."

"Probably TMI, but she could be as well only by herself. She's probably sore and achy from all the moving."

"Yeah, you're right. And probably a little nervous about moving in and rooming with someone new. I know I'm having some adjustment issues and it's my house or hope for it to be my house . . . I've been here longer and it's my name on the mortgage. Anyway, whatever, I'm sure it will all work out. At least she's clean and seems to be neat."

"That is a plus. Not that I was a neat-nick in my college days but I was better than some of my roommates."

"Me too. Well, Susan and I always roomed together, but from what I saw in my classmates' rooms, yeah, I could have ended up with someone less tidy."

*

"Kel, Kelly?" Ryan whispered to her late the next morning. "You awake?"

"Mmm." She reached over and slid her hand over his abdomen and lower along his happy trail. "Appears you are."

"I am . . . because someone is at your door, knocking."

Jolted awake by his statement, Kelly shot up. "What?"

Again the sound of someone tapping on the door and calling her name was heard.

"Shit," Kelly whispered. "It's Natalie."

Ryan cocked a brow at her. "Who else would it be?"

Louder, Kelly called, "What is it, Natalie?"

The door cracked open just a bit.

Kelly whispered to Ryan, "She's gonna get an eyeful she might not want."

With that he slid far under the covers and curved around her as if that would hide him from sight.

"Kelly?" Natalie peered around the door.

"Yes?"

"Oh, you're not alone. I'll come back or maybe you can step out?"

"Sure. Sure, I'll be there in a minute."

The door closed and Ryan chuckled.

"It's not funny."

"It might be. Do you know what she wants?"

"Could be a horde of ants or hot water or who knows."

Kelly got up, grabbed her robe, and headed toward the kitchen where she heard sounds that could only be Natalie. She walked into the kitchen to see Natalie bent over with her head inside the refrigerator. "Natalie? What's up?"

The redheaded woman stood and looked over at her. "The light is out in the refrigerator."

"What?"

"The light in the refrigerator. It's out."

"Okay."

"Well, it's not okay. I can't see what's in there."

"Oh. I see. Well, is there some reason you can't put another one in?"

"A few. I don't know where you have the spares and I didn't want to do it without telling you first."

"Don't worry about things like that. If it's in a common area there's no reason why either one of us can't change a bulb or whatever."

"Okay. So where do you have the spares?"

"I don't think I have any. Whoever of us going shopping first this week will need to pick one up."

"We didn't talk about things like this when we met to interview."

"About?" Clearly Kelly thought she needed more sleep because the conversation was making no sense at all.

"About replacement bulbs. You didn't tell me I'd have to pay for things like that, it's not in our agreement. It should be included in the rent."

"Fine. I'll pick one up when I go shopping this week." Kelly turned to go back to bed.

"When will you be going?"

"I . . . don't know. Maybe Thursday. Why?"

"I'd like to know when I can see the refrigerator and that's two days from now. And if I know when you're going I can give you a list of other things that you need to pick up for the house, right?"

"Sure. Sure." Kelly felt a quick moment of relief at the sound of a horn honking outside. "That sounds like your ride is here."

"Oh yeah. He'll wait for me. Is that Ryan in bed with you?"

"What?"

"Ryan. Your boyfriend. Did he spend the night? *Again?*"

"Yes. Ryan spent the night. He usually does when we go out up here."

"I thought we talked about that."

The horn sounded again.

"It sounds like your ride is getting anxious." Mentally Kelly shook her head, what the hell had she gotten herself into?

"Right. Well, we need to come up with some sort of schedule when he'll be here. I think if it's more than one night a week my rent should be lowered to account for that."

"Natalie, it's not going to happen now. I had a late night after a heavy shift and right now I just want to get back to sleep. We'll talk later this week."

"And what about the things we need?"

"Just make a list and we'll talk about it."

Natalie beamed at her. "Thanks! I'll see you tonight. We can talk then."

The woman breezed by Kelly and headed out the front door. Shaking her head for real Kelly started back toward bed but stopped and looked at the spot where Ginny's food dishes sat . . . or where they were supposed to be. "What the . . ."

She looked around the kitchen and found the dishes had been stuck in a far corner next to the garbage, which was no longer in a container, but a plastic bag hung it its place. Ginny, who had followed her into the kitchen, looked up at Kelly with a mournful look on her face. "Sorry, baby. Let's put your dishes back where they belong, huh?"

Ginny meowed and followed Kelly and her dishes back to where they'd always been.

"Ants, hot water, light bulbs and lists . . . what next?"

Ginny apparently had no answer for that and turned her head into her breakfast.

"What was the emergency?" Ryan asked when she returned to her room.

Kelly shook her head. "The refrigerator needs a new light bulb."

Ryan stretched and folded his hands behind his head. "New light bulb, huh? For her brain or the refrigerator?"

Kelly tossed off her robe. "Yup, for the frig. And she's not sure if she can wait till I go grocery shopping on Thursday to get a new one and she thinks expenses like that should be part of her rent and not extra things for whomever to pick up."

"Hmm."

"And . . . she was concerned because you were here even though it's my weekend and we were, in reality, pretty quiet last night."

"And you say that because . . ."

"Because she didn't know you were here till she came into my room this morning."

He peered under the covers. "Did she see something we don't want her to see?"

"It's not funny, Ryan. She thinks her rent should be low-ered if you're going to be here on a regular basis."

"Like I'm a roommate too?"

"I told you, it's not funny." She slid back into bed beside him.

"She's just settling in."

"Yeah . . . well, we're supposed to talk about all this later tonight."

"Stick to your guns, sweetheart. Remember, it's your home. You were here first."

CHAPTER SIXTEEN

"So how goes it with the roommate?" Jack Coburn asked Kelly a few weeks later while they were writing reports at the end of a shift.

"S-okay," Kelly told him around a yawn.

"Just okay? She cute?"

"Mmm, not my type. She's about thirty-five, red haired, but don't call it red in front of her. She says it's a warm auburn."

"Nice figure?"

"Curvy, not quite full. I'd say she's about one hundred and sixty, hazel eyes that tend more toward brown than green."

"Good observations."

"Thanks. It's not so hard when I see her pretty much every day."

"And she's in car sales you said?"

"Receptionist at the Jaguar dealership."

"Mmm. Discounts?"

Kelly looked up from her computer screen and turned slightly to face her partner. "Jack, are you interested because you want a car or a date?"

Jack shrugged. "Either or both. You gonna invite her to the shift party?"

"That's coming up isn't it?" Kelly commented in regards to the end of the bi-annual shift party. The officers on each shift had their own barbeque or pot luck—a chance to say goodbye before some of them moved to other shifts. It wasn't really goodbye because the shifts overlapped, they just wouldn't be working as closely as they had the past six months.

"Yup, week from Saturday. You gonna bring her?"

"I hadn't thought about it. Ryan's in town and of course I'd rather be with him."

"Bring 'em both. That way I can check . . . what's her name? T

"Natalie. Maybe."

"That's a flat sounding maybe. Give. What's going on?"

"Nothing really. I had a roommate for years—like a decade or more. You know, Susan. You met her at a few of the earlier shift parties."

"And?"

"And you get used to how one person is, especially after so long. Then you meet someone new and it's an adjustment."

"Uh-huh. Is this a kind of adjustment I wouldn't want to date?"

"Depends. I'm weighing whether I want to run the risk of having you as my back up and you not showing up because things with Nat didn't work out."

"I wouldn't . . ."

"I know." Kelly blew out a breath. "She's . . . needy."

"Needy?"

"Yeah. Like the morning after she moved in she woke me up all upset because of a horde . . . her word mind you . . . of ants. I didn't find a one. Who knows what she saw or thought she saw. Then, she takes a bath *and* a shower *every* morning and night."

"In this drought? Every day?"

"Yup, twice a day. We've had some chats about it and she says she needs to take the baths . . . in full tubs from what she says . . . as a preventative against having her back hurt from sitting all day. I told her she could ask for a standing desk. She said she couldn't because it would make her look less feminine. Then she needs a shower to get the soap from the bath off—which I can see."

"And twice a day?"

"Cause her job is so stressful."

"Sitting at a reception desk is stressful?"

"Apparently so. They took away her internet and she's not supposed to chat with her co-workers when she's on duty or whatever it is they call it at the dealership. I have a feeling it's for her neediness. They don't want to hear it. So yeah, apparently it's stressful. And then there's the laundry."

"Lot of it?"

"No . . . just every day."

"She taking in someone's?"

"No." Kelly started to laugh. "This is wrong. This is so wrong."

"What?" Maria ambled into report writing to sit for a few with the officers.

"My roommate. She does her laundry as soon as she gets in every night—takes off her clothes outside her bathroom, puts them in a laundry bag, slips on a robe and puts whatever she was wearing that day in the wash."

"Wait." Maria stopped her. "She's a receptionist?"

"Yup."

"Not a mechanic?"

"Nope."

"So how do her clothes get so dirty that . . ."

"Germs."

"Germs," Maria repeated.

"Maria, why do I feel like you've heard this before?" Jack asked her.

"Because I have. She called here not long after she moved in because of something going on with the washer. She explained it all to me."

"That's our Natalie," Kelly told him. "The other day I found out about the electricity usage. Not that I found out first hand, but when I got the bill I was kind of shocked. Susan and I used to get bills about $75 a month. The first month's bill with Natalie there it was $250."

"Someone tapping your meter?"

"Nope. Natalie. She leaves her TV, radio, computer, bathroom and bedroom light on all day every day."

"What? Why?"

"Because she has the sound levels set at a certain level and if she turns off the TV or radio then she has to figure out the sound level again. She mutes whatever one she isn't using, but they're on. Same with the lights—they're on dimmers and she doesn't want to have to reset them when she turns them on so she leaves everything on all day every day. When I told her how much the bill went up she said that wasn't possible because we don't pay for electricity."

"How do you manage that?"

"We don't. We *do* pay for it. She actually argued with me about it. Even with the bill right there she argued with me about it."

"Sounds like it's time to get a new roommate," Jack told her, laughing.

"Yeah, I know. Ryan and I talked about it and it's only been about two months. We're just settling in, getting to know each other. I'll see what happens the next month or so. She might even decide to go on her own because she's told me she isn't comfortable with a gun in the house, let alone two because of Ryan's and she doesn't think it's fair for Ryan to be there more than one day a week."

"And how does that set with you?" Maria asked her.

"Not real well. I stay at his place on Tuesday and Wednesday—weekends he's up here and sometimes on Mondays if he's working up this way then. She says he's the reason the water and electric bills are up there. But, like I said, it's an adjustment period."

Deciding to be . . . generous . . . if not friendly when Kelly caught Natalie coming in from her weekly grocery shopping and Kelly was on her way to work on Sunday afternoon she thought she'd catch up with her roomie a bit. "Hey, Natalie."

"Kelly, I'm glad I ran into you."

"Oh? What's up?"

"The light's still out in the refrigerator."

"Oh. I haven't been in there so . . ."

"I bought a bulb. It was $4.99 so you can just take it off my rent for next month."

"Right. Say, listen, next weekend, actually Saturday, is our end of shift party. Would you like to come?"

"I don't know. Can I bring a date?"

"Um, well, it's not like a party for just anyone — it's our squad and pretty much immediate family. One of the senior members of the department suggested I invite you because you're my roommate. Beyond that . . ."

"So it's just cops?"

"And their families."

"Can I let you know?"

"Sure. It's not a formal party — just the squad and their families."

"I'll let you know."

CHAPTER SEVENTEEN

K elly listened as a call went out. "All units with special attention to S-1, D-18, 24, 32, 44, standby for emergency traffic on channel two. Go secured." Maria calmly went out over the air and waited a moment. Once the air was cleared, and the units responded they had switched channels, she continued, "Report of suspicious package found at 444 Grand, corner of Grand and 2nd. RP advises the package is approximately eight inches by eleven inches and has red digital numbers counting down. Approximately . . . two minutes ago numbers shows what appears to be two hours and twenty-four minutes."

"Copy. En route," each unit responded.

"RP advises his name is Ken Lewis and he is standing at the end of the block and wearing a white button-down, dark brown Dockers and will flag down the approaching units."

Once again, the responding units acknowledged Maria's transmission.

"D-18 on scene," Kelly called over the air. "Approaching RP."

"Sir? Mr. Lewis?"

"Yes, that's me."

"You reported a suspicious package?"

"Yeah . . . actually I reported a bomb. I didn't threaten one . . . I think that box, that one over there, might be one."

"Understood."

Two other units and the sergeant pulled in.

The sergeant advised the units to maintain radio silence

and stay off their phones until they knew what they had before heading over to where the package was sitting on the pavement. Kelly glanced over her shoulder as he bent over the package and shook his head before quickly moving away from it. The others stood by as he walked a little further up the street and over the air called for dispatch to roll the bomb squad.

"So it is a bomb," Lewis stated.

"We don't know that for sure, yet," Kelly told him. "It could just be a suspicious package or a really bad practical joke. Can I get your address and phone number?"

"Sure, sure. I live at 7520 Promenade in San Rafael. My number's 415-555-3365."

"How long have you lived there?"

"Um, maybe four years."

"Wife? Family?"

"No, my girlfriend and I live there. We moved there when we decided to live together. Kind of a long engagement, you know?"

"Uh-huh, I can understand that," Kelly told him. "Did you handle the box?"

"No, no. I came out of my shop . . . I work in the classic record and tape store over there, and saw the box. Soon as I saw the numbers, those red digital numbers, I went back inside and called you guys. Then I came back out here because, well, would you want to be in a building near where a bomb might go off?"

"No," Kelly answered him. "Talk to anyone?"

"Not talked. I did tell a few people who were walking by to stay away from it. A couple of them looked at me like I was crazy, but everyone moved on and away. Was that the right thing to do?"

"Yes, it was."

Sergeant Jennings came over at that point with the other

units moving closer. "Bomb squad should be here in about thirty minutes. Let's get the area cleared out, at least a two-block radius. McKenna, you get this gentleman's information?"

"Yes, sir. This is Mr. Lewis, the person who found the package."

"Thanks for calling it in Mr. Lewis. You work around here?"

"Yeah, at Retro Records."

"Any customers still in your store?"

"No. We were . . . I was getting ready to close when I saw the box. I went ahead and locked the door after I called about it."

"Good thinking." Memories of Adrian James leaving a bomb on her car just a couple of years ago flooded to the surface. She and Susan had been out to dinner at one of their favorite restaurants, and when they came out there was a pipe bomb on the windshield of her car. Devastated when the car blew up, there was one ray of sunshine — it was the night she met Ryan. Actually she'd met him before at the police station after reporting another of Adrian's attempts to scare her into marrying him . . . for her protection. But that night she was too shook up after receiving a Barbie doll with a knife stuck in her and a note with something about Kelly being next. When Ryan showed up when Adrian blew up her car there was a connection she couldn't ignore, one that was more than just a past life memory of him. The flesh and blood Ryan in this lifetime was all she ever wanted in a relationship. She considered for a moment that if she didn't have the happier memory of Ryan entering her life that night she'd be more shaken up by Lewis's find.

"So is it a bomb?"

"We don't know yet. Bomb squad will have to determine that. You can head on out if you want."

"Um, I'd kinda like to see what happens, you know? I've never had something like this happen to be me before, you know?"

"Sure. Just keep a safe distance."

Lewis moved on down the street and then crossed over to the other side.

"You think he's behind it?" Kelly asked Jen Donally moments after she arrived.

"Mmm, not really. It's probably big news for him and will be even bigger if it's the real deal. Why don't you run him just to be on the safe side?"

"Right."

Kelly headed back to her car to run Lewis through warrants, AFS, and several other systems to be sure he was on the up and up and not on any watch list. When he came back clear she came back to where Jen was standing. "He's clear."

"Good. Never know."

"Now what?"

"Now we wait for . . . and here they come."

A large, heavily armored truck pulled up alongside where the patrol cars blocked off the street. Jen and Kelly headed over to meet the officer getting out of the truck. After shaking hands and some brief introductions Jen turned the scene over to the bomb tech.

"Package is over there. The last time I glanced at the red LED it was showing about an hour and a half left."

"Not that that means anything. Bomb makers can make mistakes setting their clocks or do it on purpose so we rely on their numbers but it ends up blowing. Well, let me get Mighty Mike out here."

"Mighty Mike?" Kelly whispered to the other officer.

"The robot."

A moment later a little remote car looking device rolled down the truck's ramp and with the bomb tech at the controls, headed over to the package. For a few minutes the device circled the box.

"Mike's taking pictures," the tech told Kelly.

"Ah. Guess looking for fingerprints is out of the question."

"Since there was no threat and Red Oak's not a hot bed of crime and terror the likelihood of there being fingerprints or catching the guy . . . not so good. And it's safer to just grab the thing and blow it."

"I thought you could check for explosives."

"Yup, we do that inside the truck. Watch . . ."

Over the next half hour *Mike* slowly rolled around the package another couple of times before a little platform rolled out and two prongs moved under the box. Very carefully, the little robot rolled around and headed toward the large canister that had been taken out behind the truck.

"Looks like an oversized R2-D2, doesn't it?"

"Yup. But R2-D2 wouldn't have been able to withstand the kinds of explosions that device does."

Once it was inside the officers made one last sweep of the area to make sure no one was in the immediate area, and then they themselves pulled back. Inch by inch Mike rolled back toward the truck. Once the little robot was clear the bomb tech touched a button on his remote and the canister shook with two percussions.

"Definitely an explosive device," the bomb tech told them.

"How do you know?"

"Two concussions and the meter here on the remote detects some of the bomb-making materials."

"Wow. Amazing."

"A lot safer than the old days when we'd try to disarm a device. Not that we don't. Just if there's a choice we go with Mighty Mike."

"Now," the sergeant told her, "we try to figure out who and why the device was left."

"I guess the detectives will handle that side of it."

"Don't look so bummed, Kelly. Sad to say your time will come. But, you can always take a look at their reports and I'll let them know if they need some help with interviews I'll task you to me."

"Thanks. I shouldn't be pleased that it happened but what a great learning experience, huh?" She wasn't about to go into her own up close and personal with a bomb. Some things were just best left in the past.

"It can be." He turned to the tech. "Well, I'll leave you to your clean up. You know where to reach me when you're ready to take off."

While most of the officers went back to their beats, Kelly, along with several other officers, canvassed the area looking for possible witnesses and motives. When she got back to the station a few hours later it was to hear a shrill shriek. "Shit, why do all the good calls happen to *that* woman and when I'm not on duty!"

CHAPTER EIGHTEEN

"So Chris missed out on another one?" Ryan asked Kelly when she called him the next morning.

"Yeah. It was pretty funny how she went on about how I was conspiring against her to miss out on what she considers the best calls. I don't know about you, but I'd rather not have those kinds of calls here, you know?"

"They can be nasty. At least the guy at the record store knew enough to call and take the steps he did."

"So will you be handling this one?"

"I don't know about me, but someone from ATF will be involved."

"Why not you? Is it because I work here?"

"No. I'm working on the D-1 gang initial hearings coming up in a few weeks. Depending on how much of a threat your incident is perceived to be will be the deciding factor on how involved we'll be and if I'll be needed."

"I probably shouldn't admit it, but I'd kinda put the D-1 gang issue to the back of my mind. That and I have to admit it brought back memories of Adrian bombing my car. But then if he hadn't, I wouldn't have you, would I?"

"We would have found each other, babe, I promise. I'll always be there for you. But why would you feel bad about D-1?"

"I wouldn't want you to think I don't care about your cases."

Ryan chuckled. "I know you're interested. This one has been percolating in the background — we're hoping some of them will turn in the big guy. By the way, not that I want to stay on unpleasant people from your past, I heard that your former boss is coming up for trial soon as well."

"Clarissa . . . yeah. The D.A.'s office called with some questions and I need to go for an interview in a few weeks. She . . . Clarissa . . . has managed to postpone her trial a few times which doesn't make sense to me because she's just sitting there in jail. It's not like she's sitting home planning her next corporate takeover."

"No, she's sitting in jail doing it—free room and board, internet, books. That woman is probably planning world domination from her cell."

"No doubt. If it were me though, I'd rather be doing it from the comfort of my home. It just doesn't make sense to me if she's innocent why she wouldn't want to get to trial and prove it."

"It does make you wonder what she's up to."

"Speaking of up, you coming up this way tonight?"

"Not tonight. I'll be there for the shift party tomorrow though. They have someone covering your shift tomorrow, right?"

"Yeah. Tomorrow and Sunday . . . I'm back on Monday night."

*

Just before Kelly was leaving for work the next day, Natalie came in and saw Kelly had stopped in the living room for a few minutes to watch the news. The redhead came in and sat down instead of rushing to her room and doing whatever it was she did at night. When the news switched to the story of the explosive device Kelly worked the night before she quietly told Natalie, "That was one of my calls last night."

"The robot?"

"Yeah. We had a call on a suspicious package and then it

was pretty clear it was a bomb so we rolled the bomb squad. That little robot is called Mighty Mike and it actually goes and picks up the device and puts it into an explosion canister. The thing blew and the bomb tech said it was most definitely a bomb."

"Oh." Natalie paused a moment before continuing, "Well, you know what happened to me today?"

Kelly shifted to look at her roommate. "No. What?"

"Well, I was sitting there at my desk, the reception desk at work, and this guy came in. He was dirty, really dirty and smelly and he had this old backpack and he put it on my desk. It was a bomb."

"A bomb?"

"Yes. This dirty and smelly, really dirty and smelly guy put his backpack right next to me and I knew it was a bomb."

Kelly watched Natalie's eyes shift back and forth as if she were looking for the right answer. "How did you know that?"

"I knew. I just knew."

In the short time they'd roomed together Kelly'd noticed that Natalie exaggerated at times, but given what had happened the night before, what was to say there hadn't been another scare. Thinking Natalie might have seen the suspect, she asked, "How?"

"I *knew*."

"But, Natalie, *how*? Did he say something? Did you see a timer or something in the backpack that led you to think that?"

"No. He didn't say a word. He just left it on my desk and walked out."

"So this guy walked in, left a backpack on your desk and just left?"

"Yes!"

"What did he look like?"

"I told you, he was dirty, dirty and smelly."

"Aside from that, did you notice what color hair he had? Eyes?"

Natalie looked up at the ceiling, thinking before finally answering, "I think . . . I think his hair might have been blond. But it was dirty. Dirty and smelly."

"Blond. And his eyes?"

"His eyes . . ." She glanced up to the right for a moment before her eyes rapidly shifted back and forth several times as if she were looking at something moving on her lap. "Um, he was wearing glasses."

"Glasses? What kind? Wire rims, horn rims?"

Again Natalie's eyes shifted back and forth at a rapid rate. "Oh, he had on sunglasses. I couldn't see the color."

"I see. And did you call the police?"

"No. Why would I do that?"

"Because if it was a bomb, wouldn't you want them to do something about it?"

"I suppose."

Something didn't sound right . . . or rather it sounded like one of Natalie's stories. "Natalie, you're telling me someone walked in with a suspicious package and for some reason you thought it was a bomb and you didn't do anything about it?"

"I was too scared."

"So tell me this." Kelly was finding it hard to keep the incredulity out of her voice. "Why would someone want to bomb a Jaguar dealership reception area?"

Natalie thought about it for a moment. "Because we didn't repair his car the way he wanted."

That was over the top, even for — horde of ants — Natalie. "Nat, a dirty and disheveled, smelly as you say, homeless guy comes into your business, leaves a backpack with what you think is a bomb because he wasn't happy with a car repair? If a guy was that bad off, why would he be driving a Jag instead of selling it? Where would he get the money to repair it? It doesn't make sense."

"Yes, it does. You just don't want to believe it because it didn't happen to you. And my name is Natalie, not Nat."

"Okay, right. Natalie. Natalie, I want to believe you. Do you see that if there was a bomb at your dealership that the two incidents might be connected?"

"Oh."

"So if we know why the guy walked into your dealership and if we can figure out if there were any disgruntled customers at any of the businesses where the bomb we found is maybe we can see if there is a connection. Can you tell me more about what the guy looked like?"

"Hmm." She looked up, and once again her eyes flickered side by side as if she were thinking. "He was really dirty and smelly."

"Was he white, black, Hispanic?"

"I'm not sure."

"No?"

"Well, he was dirty."

"All of him?"

"I was really too busy to look at him much."

"What was he wearing?"

"I don't remember."

"Did he say anything?"

"No. He just put it on my counter and left. I was so scared. It's not every day someone puts a bomb on your desk."

Kelly considered that. Something wasn't adding up, and as much as she didn't want to think it was another of Natalie's stories, it was beginning to sound like it. "Did anyone else at your work see him?"

"I don't know. Remember I'm not supposed to chit chat with anyone." Natalie had told her a week or so after she'd moved in that her boss had not only cut her internet connection but told her she had to stop socializing and engaging in minor chit chat with anyone who happened by. Natalie had told her cutting off the internet didn't make sense because people would ask for directions, and now she couldn't run any mapping or direction programs for customers because of no service. When Kelly asked her if she used the computer and internet for anything other than helping customers her roommate stammered for a few minutes and then admitted that she'd been looking up something like Southway products from the site. It didn't make a whole lot of sense, but given the clientele that probably frequented the dealership customers probably didn't want to know anything beyond high-end products.

As to speaking with people . . . the woman was a receptionist! How could her boss tell her not to talk to customers? Wasn't part of customer relations and service having a bit of friendly conversation?

Kelly mentally shrugged to herself before continuing, "But, Natalie, if the guy left a suspicious package on your desk, telling your boss or someone else wouldn't be chit chatting."

"It was a bomb!"

"Uh-huh." It was becoming more and more clear the whole incident was one of Natalie's fantasies. "Who confirmed that?"

"Confirmed it?"

"Yes, who confirmed it was a bomb?"

"I *knew* it was."

Kelly blew out a breath. "Natalie, you must have told someone and they must have called the bomb squad or at least the police out. Did you tell your boss and have the video of him coming in pulled?"

"No. The guy came right back to my desk and took it. I figured since we were safe there was no reason to tell anyone."

Kelly did a mental head shake. "Let me get this straight— a guy walks in, puts his backpack on your desk, you decide it's a bomb, he comes back in and takes it and does what?"

"Went home."

"Got ya. Okay, well, I need to go so I'll see you later."

"Yeah. Fine. Ryan won't be around after the party tomorrow, will he?"

"We haven't talked about it."

"He's here an awful lot. I think he uses all that extra water."

"Mmm, I need to go." Not wanting to get into it, again, about Ryan or hear more of Natalie's stories, Kelly took off.

"I'm serious," she told Maria a short time later before taking off on her shift. "I told her about the bomb here at work and the next thing *she* has one at her work."

"Did she?" Jess had joined them in the break room.

"No. At least I don't think so. She didn't report it. She didn't call the police. No one alerted the bomb squad and suddenly the bomber turns around, grabs the package and just leaves? Really?"

"It does sound kind of out there."

"Like most of what she says." Jess put in. "Maybe having me move in would have been a better idea."

"Is it really worth having her there?" Maria ignored Jess's comment.

"I'm starting to wonder about it. It's only been a couple of months. I thought it was going to be an easy situation because we work different hours and days ... she works Monday through Thursday, I work Friday through Monday — we should almost never see each other. When we do though, she always has some weird or incredible story. It's like whatever you tell her she has to tell something that sounds bigger and better. The thing is, who cares? Who really cares? It's not a competition for who has the, I don't know, crazier things happen at work."

"She does sound a little unstable," Maria told her.

"I don't know. I think she's just really insecure and doesn't have a lot of self-esteem and feels like she has to make herself bigger than life to be important."

"Yeah, but faking a bomb?"

"It's not like she faked it—I mean she might have made it up, but . . . it was basically a harmless story, right?"

"Harmless until someone calls the cops about one of her stories and it turns out to be a total lie, a false police report and she gets someone in trouble."

"That's true. I do need to talk to her about the tall tales."

"Just don't tell her you think she's telling tales."

"Boy, you got that right."

CHAPTER NINETEEN

"I'm rethinking the party," Ryan told Kelly as they got ready to go.

Kelly spun around. "You are? Why?"

"Cause you look good enough to eat and I don't much want to share you with anyone."

"You don't, huh?" A thrill of anticipation and pure pleasure ran through Kelly and centered in her girl parts. She sidled up to him and reached up to run her hands across his shoulders and behind his neck. More than happy to oblige the intent he read in her eyes, Ryan lowered his head so their lips met. Softly gentle he nibbled along her lower lip till she sighed. Savoring the moment Kelly leaned closer into her guy and rubbed her chest against his. The matching teal blue t-shirts between them did little to keep either one from feeling the delicious friction of their rubbing against each other.

Kelly hummed softly against Ryan's lips and cupped his balls while she enjoyed the moment. No past lives or memories flooded in—no worries about the future. Just there in that very moment, feeling all the love Ryan had for her and hoping he felt hers ebbing back to him.

She slid her hand up over his hip to caress his butt so she could rub her groin against his. She smiled when she felt the hardness of his cock. Taking matters into her hands, as it were, she started to back him toward her bed. When he groaned in acknowledgment of her intent, she smiled into the kiss.

Ryan lifted his head just enough to whisper, "You giving

up on the shift party?"

"Ohhh." Kelly shook her head. "I wish. I really wish . . . but it's probably not a good idea for the new girl to blow it off, huh?"

"Much as I'd like to myself, no. You're still new enough you need to make it, at least for a little while. Besides, didn't you say a few of the guys were interested in meeting Natalie?"

"Yeah. She was pretty happy to hear that there was going to be a few single guys there. This might explain some of her issues — her ex-boyfriend wasn't really an ex."

They'd sat side by side on her bed and Ryan took Kelly's hand in his and traced little heart patterns on the top. "No?"

"No. Apparently he committed suicide."

"Seriously?"

"That's what she said."

"Uh-huh. Natalie of the dirty smelly guy with the bomb said the guy she was dating committed suicide?"

Kelly shrugged. "He might have."

"Excuse me for sounding disbelieving and cold, but we're talking Natalie here."

Kelly chuckled and then caught herself. "Okay, that was a wrong thought."

"What?"

"It crossed my mind . . . Oh, Ryan."

He chuckled in return. "Consider it dark cop humor — for a moment you were thinking if it was the only way he could get away from her . . ."

"Yeah. I don't know if it's true or not, but even if it's not, that she'd make up a story like that shows she's gotta be pretty sad and lonely, right?"

"Right."

"And if we didn't go, she'd be pretty disappointed, right?"

"Maybe."

Kelly turned and looked at him. "You think she'd mind blowing off the party?"

"She might not mind, but we're back to you're new in the department and even though women have been on patrol for a few decades, you really do need to go."

Kelly blew out a breath. "You're right. But . . ." She rested a hand on his thigh a moment. "We're going to finish . . ." She slid her hand up to his groin. "When we get home, right?"

"You'd better believe it, babe. You'd better believe it."

"Natalie? Ready?" Kelly called from her doorway a short time later.

"Yes, I think so. Do I look all right?"

Kelly gave her roommate a quick once over. As usual, the woman was dressed pretty much to the nines. Well, maybe not the nines, but a solid seven and a half. Kelly'd quickly found out that Natalie didn't set foot outside the house without full makeup, even just to run a quick errand to the store. In some ways the other woman was like a throwback to maybe the fifties . . . as in the 1950s. Not that there was anything wrong with being well-groomed, clean, and neat. But it was the way Natalie carried it off — like she'd read about how to dress and act and was playing at doing it. Well, whatever made her happy. It wasn't for Kelly or anyone else to judge. For the party Natalie was wearing a pressed, plaid skort with a royal blue golf-type shirt. Knee-high white socks and penny loafers. Okay, she looked like a catholic school girl on her way to class. On Natalie it worked.

"Yeah, you look fine."

"You sure? You're in jeans . . . should I change and put on jeans?" The way Natalie said jeans it sounded like it was a dirty word. Kelly thought for a moment, not so much about Natalie's question but whether or not the other woman even had a pair of jeans. She'd told Kelly once that classy women didn't wear jeans—if that was so, did Natalie even own a pair?

"Um, would you feel comfortable in jeans? It's just a casual party, nothing special or demanding. Whatever you're most comfortable in."

"Okay. I'll stay dressed in my skort. If you're sure I won't stand out . . . at least in a bad way."

"No, no, it's cute." Ryan had walked up and Kelly turned to him. "Isn't Natalie's outfit cute?"

Ryan gave the redhead a quick look over. "Cute. Yup, cute."

"Okay then, I'm ready. How are we getting there?"

"Ryan's driving."

"Okay. You guys ready?" Ryan asked.

"Yup. Let's do it." Kelly headed off into the kitchen, poured some crunchies into Ginny's dish, and grabbed some deviled eggs out of the refrigerator.

Walking out to Ryan's car, Natalie glanced over at the dish Kelly carried. "I don't have anything to bring."

"No worries. You're my guest. I have plenty for everyone."

"Well, if you're sure. I mean we could stop at the store if I needed to bring something."

"Nope. We're good," Kelly assured her.

Ryan steered the car out of Red Oak city limits towards the freeway.

"Does he know where he's going?" Natalie asked Kelly from the back seat.

"Sort of. Jen lives in Petaluma and I've got directions once we're up there."

"I'd hate to get lost," Natalie told them.

"I've got GPS," Ryan assured her.

"Oh. Yeah. I guess you'd need it being a spy and all. You need to know how to follow people and spy on them and stuff, right?"

Ryan glanced over at Kelly and caught a brief eye roll.

"Um, well, ATF doesn't spy on people."

"Really?" Natalie sounded like she didn't believe him. Not for a second. "Then how do you catch people before they blow up houses and cars and stuff? You know, like when Kelly's car was blown up?"

"My car?" Kelly asked Natalie.

"That was your red Ford Mustang that was blown up a few years ago at Max's, wasn't it?"

How had Natalie learned about that? And right after the bomb scare at work? Not that it was any big secret. After all, the media wasn't going to sit home and pretend a fairly expensive car wasn't demolished in a busy restaurant parking lot in the middle of the dinner hour. As a professional courtesy they'd kept Kelly's name out of the paper when it happened. Months later when Adrian James was arrested for not only that incident but several others, his name wasn't publically linked to the car bomb. In a way, his actions that night, setting the bomb on Kelly's car when she and Susan had gone to dinner, was the catalyst that brought her and Ryan together. The couple had met briefly at the Red Oak police station earlier — because of Adrian sending a doll with a knife in its chest to another restaurant Kelly and Susan had been eating at. It was after Kelly had been interviewed by one of the Red Oak officers, Misha Campbell, about the doll, and as Kelly was leaving, she'd run, literally, into Ryan. They'd only had a brief exchange that night. Then a few weeks later when Kelly found a pipe bomb on the windshield of her car, after it exploded, Ryan became involved in the investigation . . . and Kelly's life. With Ryan, it was coming home after a long, long time away.

"If we know something is up we try to find the suspects," Ryan told her.

"Did Ryan have anything to do with blowing up your car?"

Natalie leaned forward in the back seat to ask.

"No, not Ryan. It was my car. Someone else blew it up and that's how Ryan and I met. He was sent to investigate it because at the time they didn't know if it was a terrorist or a personal attack. Much as I liked that car, if that was the only way I could have met Ryan . . ." Kelly trailed off while she reached over and squeezed his thigh.

"Did you catch the guy who did it?"

"Ultimately."

"What did you do to him?"

What indeed, Kelly thought.

Ryan put a stop to the conversation, at least momentarily, when he announced they were nearing the exit they'd be pulling off on to. "Which way?" he asked.

The next few minutes Kelly gave Ryan directions to Jen's house. Street parking was pretty minimal by the time they pulled up and headed to the house.

Still surprised at her own actions Kelly turned to Natalie. "Do us a favor, okay, Natalie?"

"What?"

"Don't mention anything about my car or Ryan's involvement at the party, okay?"

"Ryan was involved?"

"No. He had nothing to do with it."

"I'm glad because you know someone tried to blow up one of our cars. It was a red Jag."

"Right, the dirty and smelly guy, right?"

"No, that was another guy. That dirty and smelly guy took his bomb away. The other one was a few years ago and he put a bomb on one of our cars — a red Jag."

"Sorry to hear that," Kelly told her. She was sorry because given Natalie's propensity to tell stories that she truly seemed to believe, it didn't lend itself to great party talk.

"Yeah. I was really scared."

"Well, Natalie." Ryan stopped them on the walkway. "It's a good thing it's over. We certainly don't want that memory to ruin our time tonight, do we?"

With a cunning glint in her eyes Natalie looked up at him and chewed her lower lip.

CHAPTER TWENTY

"McKenna! You made it!" Misha Campbell saluted Kelly, Ryan, and Natalie with a beer as they walked in the door. "Come on in."

"Are we late? Last ones here?" Kelly looked around, nodded to a few of her shift-mates, and handed the large tray of deviled eggs to Misha.

"Mmm, love deviled eggs. These are what you made for the in house shift pot luck a couple of weeks ago, aren't they?" Before Kelly could respond Misha continued, "Not the last ones at all. A couple of the guys pulled some OT on day shift today and will be up in a while. Don't think you've met all the spouses and partners, though, huh?"

"No. You know Ryan, but I don't think you've met my new roommate, Natalie."

"Nat, good to meet you. Welcome to the outgoing B shift party!"

"My name is Natalie. Not gnat. I'm not a bug."

Misha turned to Kelly with a brow raised before answering Natalie, "Sorry. We're a pretty friendly bunch. Hang around with us for a while and Nat will sound like a plenty mild nickname."

Kelly'd seen the mulish tilt to Natalie's lips a time or two before. It was not going to go well if the discussion continued. At least for Natalie. While she could dish it out and state her personal rules of life, her fellow officers could definitely give back in kind. They'd tease her mercilessly about her name if Misha continued the subject. Not that it would stop them from sharing a chuckle about the very prim and proper car dealership receptionist later on. If there was one thing Kelly learned on patrol was everything the public saw was professional and on the up and up, when it came time to blow off steam politically correct didn't factor in all that well.

"That beer looks mighty tempting, where can we grab one?" Kelly asked Misha.

Misha winked and pointed off through the wide-open living room out to a patio and a large cooler sitting near several barbeque grills.

"Thanks. I'll catch you in a bit," Kelly told her.

As she, Ryan, and Natalie headed outside Natalie told her, "I don't drink beer. It's uncouth."

"Um, well, I'm sure there's soda, wine or iced tea."

"I hope so."

"I'm thinking something stronger, way stronger," Ryan muttered in her ear.

Kelly leaned back and whispered to him, "Be nice. This has got to be a strange situation for her."

"I'm thinking it's not the situation that's strange."

"What are you two talking about?" Natalie had turned to glare at them.

"Um." Kelly thought for a moment. She didn't like to lie but . . ."Whether I'm going to want chicken or steak."

"I like a nice medium cooked steak," Natalie told them. "On my budget I can't afford much in the way of steak or even white meat chicken. You know, with rent and all it gets pretty expensive."

Ignoring Natalie's latest bid for a rent reduction, the threesome headed over to the coolers. On the way Kelly stopped to introduce Natalie to a couple of the single male officers. "Derek Goodrem, Matt Lasky, this is my new roommate, Natalie. Natalie, Derek and Matt."

"Nat, we heard you moved in. Good to meet you."

"My name is Natalie. I'm not a—" Natalie started to tell them before Matt cut her off.

"Sure."

Kelly had to smile to herself. Matt acted like a player, but word was he was very much a one-woman man and had been looking for someone as low key as himself to date. It was Derek who initially appeared quiet and introspective who was the playboy of the department.

"So, Na-at-a-leee, what would you like to drink?" Derek asked her.

"Well." She moistened her lips and looked around. "I'd enjoy a nice white wine."

"You got it." Derek reached past Matt and took Natalie's hand.

"And the game is on," Kelly murmured to Ryan.

"He does like the redheads," Matt told them.

"Do they need to be natural?" Ryan asked.

"Michaels, be nice!" Kelly tried to bite back the smile at Ryan's assessment of Natalie.

"I am."

"So tell me, Goodrem, you were all over asking me about bringing Natalie. We walk in and you just hand her over to Lasky?"

"Sure. He'll do his charming routine for oh, fifteen, twenty minutes and then I'll meander in when he gets going on his spiel and sweep her off her feet. She seems kinda shy, nice."

"Yeah. At least around new people I think. This is the first time I've gone to a party with her."

"Don't hang with the roommie much?"

Kelly took a swallow of her beer and enjoyed the hoppy taste going down before answering, "Our work schedules aren't really conducive to doing much together."

"Good point. What shift are you going to?"

"Actually as the low person, I'm staying on graves. You?"

"Days. My best bet to avoid . . ." Matt glanced around the room. " . . . you know who."

"Is she here?"

"First to arrive. She's holding court somewhere over by the pool or Jacuzzi."

"Wait. Hold on. Jacuzzi and you didn't tell me?" Ryan tugged a strand of Kelly's hair.

"Musta slipped my mind."

"Either that or she's not into sharing even the sight of your bod, Michaels." Jen Dunlap joined them.

"You got that right. Your spouse here?" Kelly asked her

"Yup, kitchen last I saw."

"Ry, you know Jen?"

"We've met. How's it going?"

"Well. Really well. You?"

"Can't complain."

"Heard through the grapevine you've got a major one in the works."

Ryan glanced around the room before answering, "Give me a hint."

"San Rafael . . . human trafficking."

Ryan nodded. "Something like that."

"If it's any consolation or assurance, I was appointed to that task force last week."

Kelly nodded again. "Thought I heard something about that. It's ugly stuff."

"It is. It definitely is, especially when it's kids and kids who don't speak English or speak it well."

"Um," Kelly interrupted them. "Are you two going off into territory I shouldn't be hearing about?"

This time it was Jen who looked around. "I'm guessing practically living with Michaels here you've heard a bit about it here and there."

"Well, that said, I'm thinking it's time to let the

conversation go till we meet up next week, huh?" Ryan asked the Red Oak sergeant.

"Totally agree. So have you guys had the tour?"

"Not much. We heard something about a Jacuzzi?" Kelly glanced over Jen's shoulder toward the backyard. From the kitchen window she could see the yard was large with a combination deck and patio area just outside the back door. A short yard area, now more dirt and stone than grass due to the ongoing drought lay beyond that. It looked like an old fashioned croquet set was up and ready for use. Over to the side of the patio was a basketball hoop, but no one was playing right then. Several of her co-workers were in shorts or bathing suits over to the other side which led Kelly to believe the hot tub had to be just beyond them.

"Yeah, nice one. Sits ten to twelve people. You two bring suits?"

"No. Being it's my first shift party and all . . ." Kelly's answer trailed off but it was clear Jen got her meaning.

"Not to worry. Chris will be out there before long showing off her less than admirable assets sans clothing."

"You serious?"

Jen nodded. "Happens every party. Even the ones she isn't invited to. She never ceases to amaze."

"Well, hope no one minds if I pass on that sight," Kelly told her, trying her best to keep from chuckling.

"Oh, trust me, it's a sight almost all of us would like to miss."

"What's that?" Lasky meandered into the kitchen, a long neck beer in his hand.

"Chris."

Sgt. White glanced out the window over the sink. "She starting already?"

Jen turned to look as well. "Nah, everyone out there seems pretty calm so I'm guessing the show hasn't started."

Natalie walked into the kitchen. "What show?"

"Oh, just some of the officers acting very un-policelike," Kelly told her. "What happened to Derek?"

"Nothing."

"Everything okay?"

"Of course. He just went to take a quick phone call. Then he's going to show me his motorcycle."

"Ah."

Before Kelly could say anything further Derek joined them. "Nat, ready?"

"My name's Natalie . . . I'm not . . ."

"Right, I forgot. Natalie. Ready?"

"Yes. I've never ridden on one before."

"Ah, sounds like fun."

"I hope so."

Kelly shook her head as the twosome headed out the door.

"Reservations about big D and your roommate?" Jen asked her.

"No, not really. Should make for a good story when we get home later. Meanwhile, Ryan appears to have wandered off."

"Nah, he's in the play room shooting pool with a few of the guys."

Kelly nodded and headed off to find Ryan. They'd missed Chris's show of practically stripping after she'd had a few beers. None of the women present were too thrilled about her rather awkward strip tease—although there were quite a few chuckles when Napolitano's wife commented that Chris appeared to have left her breasts at home. A few other comments were made about the resident badge bunny—none of which were very flattering. Given how she could carry on and retaliate none of the comments were said loud enough for her to hear. When she passed out, rather drunk, one of the guys carried her into the den, tossed a blanket over her, and shut the door as he walked out. The party could now continue without her blatant displays of poorly done seduction.

Derek returned with Natalie in tow a short time later. With her face pinkened from the wind and her usually well-styled hair slightly fluffed, Kelly thought her roommate looked fairly relaxed, happy, and even a little pretty.

"That was fun!" Natalie chirped.

"Glad to hear it." Kelly smiled at her.

"And I had to hold on to Derek's waist. That was nice."

"I imagine it was. Listen, Ryan's got an early call tomorrow so we need to be taking off soon. Did you want to get a little something more to eat or are you ready?"

"Oh . . . I'm ready I guess."

"We can wait a bit if you're hungry or want to grab something to drink."

"No, that's okay. I'm ready."

"You can't leave!" Jess burst into the kitchen. "I just got here. After me taking an overtime shift so everyone else could party you need to at least party with me for a bit."

"Hey, Jess." Kelly greeted the recently arrived dispatcher.

In response to Kelly's greeting Jess threw her arms around her and planted a kiss on her cheek.

Surprised Kelly tried to step back, but Jess held on tight. "Um, Jess, we're kinda blocking the way here."

"Food's on the patio, Jess. Go help yourself." Jen tugged Jess away from Kelly and sent her out the door. As soon as the dark-haired woman was on the patio, Jen turned to Kelly. "Any idea what that was about?"

"Not a one. Kinda weird."

"I'll say." Natalie put in. "I'd never do something so uncouth."

"Well, we'd better get going while Jess is distracted, huh?" Kelly made the rounds saying goodnight and a thank you to Jen for hosting the party. With a few more comments about who she'd see on shift the coming week, Kelly, Ryan, and

Natalie were on their way home.

They'd barely hit the freeway before Natalie piped up, "You know, I have a Southway convention next weekend."

"Uh-huh." Kelly nodded with a glance at Ryan, who was doing his best to keep from smiling.

"I was thinking, do you think Derek would like to come with me?"

"To a Southway convention?"

CHAPTER TWENTY-ONE

L ater, at home, Ryan asked, "She's not really going to ask Derek to go to a *Southway* convention, is she?"

Kelly shrugged. "With Natalie you never know."

"Southway?" Ryan could barely keep the laughter out of his voice.

"He did take her for a ride on his bike and she did seem to have a good time. She's usually pretty meticulous about her hair and makeup, but didn't seem to mind how she looked when they got back."

"Uh-huh."

Kelly settled down next to Ryan on her bed and toyed with a button on his shirt. "Seriously. I think she's lonely and just needs something or someone to get her off the dime and out there having fun. Whatever happened to her before probably set her on the path of being . . . well, depressed or kinda shy. It could have made her, you know, kind of OCD."

"*Kind* of OCD?" Again Ryan seemed on the verge of laughing.

"Well, she is kind of OCD."

"Kind of? Kelly, she's a control freak of epic proportions! The whole cleaning routine is . . ."

"Something wrong with a clean house?"

"You didn't — you and Susan never seemed to do a bad job of it and you weren't as compulsive as she is. Seriously . . . she sets an alarm to get up on Fridays even though she's off work so she can clean. On top of that you have to admit last week when you didn't leave for work when she expected you to she got all wonky because it meant she was going to have to wait what? Ten minutes to start cleaning the kitchen which, might I say, wasn't in bad shape at all."

Kelly shrugged.

"Kel, you've commented on the whole cleaning thing."

"Well, yeah. But mostly I've noticed the whole bath and shower twice a day thing and . . . I hadn't mentioned this to you before, but she leaves her TV, radio and computer on all day, has the ceiling fan going in her room twenty-four-seven and never opens the window. It's like she is afraid to step out of those parameters, like something awful will happen to her if she does."

"Hadn't seen that, but I did see the shoes lined up outside her door. Mind you she gave me the brow action when I left *my* shoes inside the front door with a comment about tracking dirt in the house. Apparently hers are okay to a point, but they have to be outside her door."

Kelly started to laugh and then put a finger to her lips before getting up and tiptoeing over to the bedroom door. She opened it, peered out, and seeing the hallway dark quietly shut the door and tiptoed back to Ryan.

He pulled her into his arms when she sat back down. "Some deep dark secret you're about to share?"

Kelly smiled and nodded. "You know Ginny isn't all that fond of her?"

"I've noticed she avoids Nat."

"That's Nat-a-lie! She's not a bug you know." Kelly mimicked her roommate's voice and lightly pushed him while she giggled. "So yeah, Ginny isn't too fond of Natalie for whatever reason. I came down the hall the other day and Gin was squatting over Natalie's shoes."

"Seriously?"

"Uh-huh. So I asked her, *Gin, you aren't peeing in Natalie's shoes, are you?* Ginny looked me in the eye and I swear she smiled. I could hear her purring from the other side of the hall."

"Did you tell Natalie?"

"Are you kidding me? At a minimum she'd insist I buy her new shoes, but with how she can get I'm pretty sure she would have demanded I get rid of Ginny."

"No way."

"Meow!" Ginny jumped from the window sill she'd been sitting on and pounced on the bed.

CHAPTER TWENTY-TWO

"So are you ready for your new shiftmates?" Ryan asked her the following Friday.

"Yeah. It's not like it'll be different, being low woman on the totem pole and all."

"You say that now."

"One good thing, apparently Chris is going to swings so I won't have to see or hear her for at least part of the shift. From what I hear, Jess is going as well."

"Good ole Chris. She left you alone the past few weeks, didn't she?"

"Mmm, for the most part. She was pissed about the bomb call because she wasn't on the radio when it happened. It was kind of funny — she was complaining about me getting the call and how she's sure I'm making sure she's never there when what she considers the good calls come in."

"Drama queen."

"Yeah. Anyway, we're on different shifts so it's not like I'll be running into her as much and having to deal with her back-stabbing or sneak attack calls."

"And the other drama queen?"

"Ah, you mean DQV?"

"DQV?"

Even though they were in her room Kelly looked around before answering, "Drama queen victim."

"Cute."

"I thought so."

"And has Natalie's mad bomber returned?"

"Apparently not. I'm sure something else will have happened. I just haven't seen her to hear about it."

"No doubt you will as soon as she thinks it up."

"Yeah, well, rent is due today and as long as she pays it we should be good. At least she hasn't complained about you being here this week."

"I think complimenting her on her outfit at the shift party might have gone a long way to bridging that gap."

"That was quite the outfit she had on."

Kelly giggled. "I know it's mean, but the guys sure enjoyed it. I don't know, sometimes she seems made up. Like you know those movies where a guy falls in love with a character or a cartoon in a book and the character doesn't really know what to do and imitates what she thinks she's seeing on TV or whatever?"

"Yeah."

"Doesn't Natalie remind you of that kind of character sometimes?"

"Now that you mention it . . ." Ryan rolled to his side, put his arm around Kelly, and pulled her to him. "Not to change the subject . . ."

"But?"

"But, have I told you recently I love you?"

"Hmm, I'm not sure."

"Well then." He kissed her forehead. "I think." A kiss was dropped on the tip of her nose. "I need to remedy." His lips hovered above hers. "That."

"You do," she whispered before sliding up against him and wriggling just enough to get her man to growl low.

Kelly ran her hand up his arm, pausing at his bicep to squeeze it ever so slightly. While she enjoyed the feel and texture of his arm muscle she slid her leg over his thigh so her mons rubbed against his groin causing him to rumble low in response.

"Hey, Michaels," she whispered.

"Yeah, McKenna?"

"I want you."

He gently thrust his hips against her lower belly. "You got me."

"I'm ready for you."

"Are you now?"

"Slid on in and . . . feel for yourself."

He told her, "I love you," as he slid into her and began to thrust his hips to match her breathing. As her breaths came closer and closer together, the faster he thrust until the twosome climaxed.

When Ryan went to shift off her, Kelly wrapped her legs more tightly around him. "No, stay. You know I like it when I get to hold you close, with you still part of me."

"Mmm."

Chapter Twenty-Three

Tuesday morning, after her shift, Kelly walked into a quiet house and paused for a moment. With paperwork she'd gotten off a little later than usual, and apparently, Natalie had already left for work. It was the first time in weeks . . . months maybe . . . she had the house to herself, even for a few minutes. As close as she and Susan were, there were times when she just wanted to roam the rooms without anyone else around. Fortunately Susan had jobs often enough that necessitated her staying overnight in a different city.

When Kelly and Ryan first got together, whenever Susan was going to be out of town, Kelly would have him come up — in the early days of a relationship even a minute apart felt like a week too long. For the most part Ryan's assignments were local, and on the rare occasion he went out of town, they'd still talk for hours on the phone . . . and Susan was usually around if she wanted company.

Natalie . . . with Natalie it was like she was always *there*. That wasn't entirely true — she did get up and go to work every day, and the woman didn't seem to be late, and in the time she'd lived here with Kelly she never called in sick. Every Sunday she went and did her grocery shopping leaving precisely at 1:30 and turning pretty close to 3:30, and it didn't take long for Kelly to live for those two hours of peace and quiet, at least the part where she was awake.

Not that it was entirely peace and quiet . . . despite several conversations about it Natalie still left the TV and radio playing 24/7 . . . but right now, at this moment, it was peaceful and quiet. Kelly drew in a deep breath and wondered if she could swing the house on her own.

Before she could do the math Natalie burst in the front door.

"Kelly! Hi!"

"Hey, Natalie, how goes it?" While mentally she cursed that apparently she hadn't returned all that late at all.

"Good. Are you alone?"

"Yeah. I just got in a few minutes ago."

"Great. It's nice not having Ryan around all the time."

Kelly ignored the comment about Ryan and started down the hall but was stopped when Natalie announced, "I have some great news."

She turned. "Oh yeah?"

"Yes. Wait till I tell you." The redheaded woman motioned for Kelly to follow her into the library and gestured for her to sit on the couch. "Wait till you hear."

Tired as she was she followed Natalie into the library. They both sat down and Kelly looked expectantly to Natalie who sat there grinning ear to ear. Finally, when nothing was being said, Kelly asked, "Well?"

"You will never guess."

"Apparently not. What's going on?"

"Well, two things."

Again Natalie sat there grinning.

"Two things?" Kelly prompted.

"Yes, first, I got a raise!"

"Awesome. That's great."

"Well, not that great. It's only $300 a month."

"$300 a month isn't bad."

"I would rather have $500 or more. I've worked there four years and should get a better raise."

"Is this your first raise?"

"No. I get one every year. Last year was $200 and I got a

bonus."

"So why is $300 not enough?" After she asked Kelly realized that probably wasn't the smartest thing to do because given how convoluted Natalie could be, this could take a while and ultimately not make any sense at all.

"Because I deserve better."

"I see. Did you tell your boss that?"

"No. He should know better."

"Right."

"I'm glad you agree."

Kelly nodded. When Natalie continued to sit there smiling Kelly debated telling Natalie she needed to get some sleep, getting up and leaving. It really seemed like the conversation was over. But years as a reporter kicked in and Kelly prompted, "You had other news?"

"Yes! Remember I told you about the mailman?"

"Mailman?" Something tickled at the back of her mind . . . something about the mailman and donuts . . . or was that someone else?

"He always chats with me for a minute or two when he brings the mail."

"Uh-huh."

"So you know how I sell Southway?"

"Uh-huh."

"This coming Saturday is the big Southway team-building meeting. It's huge. Everyone from California goes and it's great for networking."

"I see." Not that she really did, but it seemed like the right thing to say, especially since originally Natalie had talked about inviting Derek. This might, however, be a good thing since she really didn't think having Natalie dating one of her co-workers was such a good idea. Sure, she'd invited Natalie to the party to introduce her to some of the other officers, but in retrospect . . . with the Southway thing . . .

"It's in Sacramento."

"Sacramento."

"Right. So I asked Louis, the mailman to go with me and he said yes!"

Sacramento? Saturday? A day home alone? Kelly wondered. "Good news."

"Yes, we're leaving Friday night from work so we can get up there and be ready for the first lecture Saturday morning. Isn't that exciting?"

Friday night *and* Saturday! "Oh, yeah, very. So Louis, the postal carrier, is going to drive you both up there?"

"Yes. It's all day Saturday and Sunday morning there's a brunch and closing ceremony type thing and we're going to be there."

Friday night, Saturday, *and* Sunday morning! Kelly could hardly contain herself. "Sounds like fun," Kelly told her while thinking it sounded like one of the dullest things imaginable until images of Jones Town back in the late 70s and Rajneesh and a host of other cults gone south came to mind. Southway had been around for decades and Kelly'd never heard a breath of scandal around it. Not that she would have been on the front lines about it, and as an investigative journalist she was certain she would have heard something. But if Natalie was involved . . . Kelly mentally shook her head. That didn't mean anything, and at the same time it was mean.

"Yes. These team-building events are part of what makes Southway such a great company.

"You've been to a few of them?"

"No, I've never been to one because I never had anyone to give me a ride before."

"Well, that's nice that Louis is interested and wants to go."

Natalie furrowed her brow. "I'm not sure he's interested, but when I told him about going up to Sacramento he mentioned some things he thinks are fun up there so we might go up Friday since I have off and do some of them."

Now that, Kelly thought, was a great idea . . . three whole days without Natalie underfoot. It would give Kelly some downtime to think about things and whether this roommate deal was really for her. Deciding maybe she needed to get to know Natalie a little bit better—after all they *were* living in Kelly's house, she asked, "So you and Louis, you're moving things along? Like maybe I'll be meeting him soon?"

"Moving things along?" Natalie sounded a little perplexed by that.

"Yes . . . like you're moving into having a relationship? Romance?"

Natalie gave her a small smile . . . one that looked like the idea of romance with Louis hadn't occurred to her, but now that it was on the table it was an appealing one. "Maybe. I hadn't thought about it."

"No? But you asked him to stay at the hotel with you, didn't you?"

"Sure. It's where the convention is."

"Natalie . . . not that it's my business, but he's staying with you, isn't he?"

"No. He'll have his own hotel room."

"Oh. I see." So much for Natalie getting into a romance where she might be at the guy's house a night or two a week. "Well, I misunderstood. For some reason I got the idea you and Louis had more going than just the conference this weekend."

"Well, we might." Natalie bit her lower lip. "We didn't talk about it."

She couldn't help herself and asked, "Does he know he's going to be in his own hotel room?"

Natalie blinked. "Sure."

The conversation was winding down for Kelly, and right now she wanted to get out of her uniform and into bed. "Well,

I hope you guys have fun."

Just as she got to the door Natalie stopped her, "Kelly, do you think he thinks we're staying in the same room?"

Kelly turned at looked at the forty-something woman standing in front of her. For a mature adult sometimes she sure had a naïve way of looking at things. "I don't know what Louis thinks. I don't know him — haven't even met him."

"But you know what men think." She sounded petulant — as if Kelly was holding something back from her.

"Some men. Like I'd know what Ryan would think and expect. I couldn't begin to speak for a man I've never met."

"Do you think I should tell him about the room?"

Kelly turned, walked to the door and back, and sat back down. She blew out a breath before speaking. "Natalie, I can't give you relationship advice. You need to do what you think is best."

"What would you do?"

"Well, we're two different people. Our experiences are different." There now, those old psychology classes of hers were kicking in. Who would have thought it would be useful in her own home life?

"Please?"

"If it were me, I'd lay it out beforehand. I'd . . . well, I'd probably ask him what his expectations were and tell him mine and that since we're not at a point where we're intimate yet it was my thought we'd need our own rooms. Then I'd tell him what the rooms cost so he could decide. I'm pretty sure he's thinking he's going to be getting some so to soften the blow of no nookie I'd offer to pay for the gas going up there."

"Pay for the gas?" She really sounded shocked by that.

"Yes. He's taking his time to drive up there and going to have to pay for a hotel room, probably some meals, at least for himself — the least you can do is pay for gas."

"That makes it sound like I'm . . . I'm a hooker or

something. Like I'm paying for favors." She really sounded offended by Kelly's suggestion.

"Just sayin what I'd do. You have to do what you think is best for you."

"What's best for me is if he drives me up there and stays in his own room."

"Natalie, like I said, you need to decide what's best for you. We're two different people coming from different places."

"Yeah, well, if I were you I'd pull my gun and demand he drive me up there and pay for both his room and mine."

Kelly made a note to hide her gun because knowing Natalie . . .

CHAPTER TWENTY-FOUR

"Sometimes your roommate just amazes me," Maria told her as they took their meal break together.

"I know. Ryan said pretty much the same thing, only with a few expletives to go with it and more definitely from a guy's perspective."

"What's from a guy's perspective?" Chris entered the break room causing Kelly to groan inwardly.

When the blonde badge bunny wasn't looking Maria rolled her eyes and winked at Kelly and mouthed that Chris would certainly know a guy's perspective.

"Oh, my roommate is going away with a guy for the weekend."

Much to Maria and Kelly's chagrin, Chris sat down at the table with them. "At least someone is getting some. I haven't been laid in two weeks. How about you, Kelly, getting any?"

Kelly shot a look at Maria before shrugging. "I don't kiss and tell."

"Uh-huh." Chris shot her a nasty look. "That's what all the women who aren't getting any say."

"So what are you doing here at this hour, Chris? Work late on swings?"

The blonde huffed out a breath. "This sucks. It really sucks. Lifeman's wife found out he and I had a thing going and got all pushed out of shape about it."

Maria coughed. "Jeannette Lifeman is out of shape because you were sleeping with her husband?"

"Can you believe that?"

"Chris, most wives would have torn the hair out of your head after they cut off their husband's dick."

"I don't see why. I provide something they obviously can't."

"So do hookers," Maria mumbled.

"What did you say?"

"Nothing."

"You called me a hooker."

"No, she said they need to be lookers." Kelly took a last swallow of her coffee. "I need to get back out there."

"Like the street is gonna get you any," Chris snidely told her.

Kelly shrugged.

"But what are you doing here now?" Maria pushed, causing Kelly to stop at the doorway.

Chris let out another loud breath. "Because we're short in dispatch I can't get any admin time off pending an internal affairs investigation so I've been moved back to graves until they hold the *Skelly*. Sucks."

"Yeah," Maria agreed. "It does."

Completely missing the double meaning of Maria's response Chris mused, "The good news is I can get some alone time with either Lt. Lemeroni or even Chief Berger and see if I can get them to see things my way . . . if you get my drift."

"I see. So you'll bribe them into letting you off?" Unable to help herself Maria spat.

Kelly figured it was time to step in. "Maria, it's probably a good idea for you and I to stay out of it. We don't want to end up being called as witnesses or anything, right?"

Maria blinked and recalled where she was. "Right. Well, I need to get back to dispatch."

Kelly started her routine car check when she got out to the parking lot. The first thing she noticed was something rather odd sitting on the seat. A closer look revealed someone had put a snake in the car. Swallowing a scream, she started to key her radio to report it. A prickle down her spine had her turning around only to see the back door to the station closing. Someone had been there. She knew without a doubt there had been. And her sixth sense told her it was Chris. Not that the blonde had put the snake in the car—she never seemed to do the dirty work herself—but she would have definitely instigated it.

Kelly looked around the parking lot and spotting one of the other officers waved him over.

Larry Gates headed over in response to Kelly's motion. "McKenna, how goes it?"

"Not so good." She gestured to the car.

"What the he—" Gates took a step back and instinctively reached for his gun.

"I'm not sure it's a shooting matter." Kelly couldn't help the slight, nervous laugh, she made.

"Yeah, right. How the hell did that get in your car?"

"Not a clue how . . . but I can take a guess at who."

"Tanner?"

"Possibly. Not that she herself would handle it. Do you know what kind it is?"

"Not a clue. Any ideas?"

"I'm thinking of calling animal control and having them come out."

"Sounds like a plan." He went to key his mic and Kelly stopped him. "I'm thinking we should keep this quiet. Maybe let the sergeant know and call animal control ourselves?"

"Dispatch can handle it."

"I'm sure they can." Kelly glanced around the parking lot. If Chris was behind it she didn't want to give the malicious woman any enjoyment out of the situation. Even if she weren't behind it, she would certainly use it to her advantage.

145

"I'm thinking the news media listens on the scanner. It probably wouldn't be a good idea to have them hearing about something like this — even if this guy got in my car on his own."

Gates stroked his chin. "Yeah, you're right. You want to run in and get the sergeant and I'll keep an eye on things?"

"Either you or me."

"Go for it. I'm good."

Kelly headed for the building and into the sergeant's office. "Sarg?"

"McKenna, heard you go 10-7 about fifteen minutes ago. What's up?"

"Somehow a snake got into my car."

"A — are you sure?"

"It's coiled up in the driver's seat. Black. Looks maybe three feet long, but I can't really tell the way it's in there."

"Can't get it out?"

"Without knowing what kind it is I'm not sure that's a good idea. I thought we should call animal control."

He reached for the phone. "Good point."

Kelly sat in the desk chair next to him, glad he didn't raise any issues about having dispatch make the call.

When he hung up he told Kelly, "They'll be out in about ten minutes. You seriously have no idea how it got in there?"

"Not a one."

"We don't have problems like this on day shift."

Kelly shrugged. "There's a first time for everything."

"I hope it's not trouble following or starting with you."

"I hope so too. Then again, I'm not the only carry over to this shift."

"You suggesting something, McKenna?"

"No, sir. Not at all. Not at all."

CHAPTER TWENTY-FIVE

"So it was just your average Indigo snake?" Ryan asked her after taking a swallow of coffee.

"Apparently so." Kelly placed her half-eaten slice of toast on her plate and picked up her own cup. Normally she would have just gone to bed when she got in, especially with how tired she felt after the night's shift. Ryan had arrived minutes before her, and when she asked he admitted he was hungry. She made a quick breakfast for him and brewed up a pot of decaf so she could sleep after they ate.

"And no idea how the snake got into your patrol car?"

Kelly took a swallow of her coffee before answering, "Oh I have an idea. Trust me, I've got an idea."

"She's working swings now though, isn't she?"

"Now how did you know who I thought it was? And no, she's not on swings. She was sleeping with one of the married officers, his wife found out and flipped so to make peace, command moved her back on graves."

"Just a wild guess. That was pretty quick."

"Yeah. She doesn't see that having sexual congress with a married man as being a problem because she believes she provides a service to the men in blue."

Ryan coughed at that. "Is that what they call it at Red Oak?"

"You don't have them at ATF?"

"Not so much. Different mindset plus our SAC's give us our assignments, not dispatchers. So what happened?"

"From what I can gather — based on what the other officers

said in addition to Chris herself, she was having quite the fling with John Liveman and his wife found out. Since Chris usually conducts her business in a trailer in the big storage yard or in the station itself, I don't think the wife actually caught them. More like someone had enough of her and turned her in."

"From what friends of mine at local PDs have said, there can be a lot of backbiting between the women, at least the dispatchers. I'd be willing to bet one of the other women was carrying on with the officer and Chris lured him away from her so she turned around and turned Chris in."

"Well, whatever it was, since she's so . . . popular . . . with the male brass she wasn't put on admin leave pending an investigation. Instead they just moved her to another shift. Well, she said it was because we're short staffed but . . . Anyway, what surprised me more than that was how brazen Chris was about it. She actually told Maria and me that she planned to seduce either the investigating lieutenant or the chief into making things right for her."

"Now that is one dangerous woman."

"Who's a dangerous woman?" Natalie walked into the kitchen.

Startled at her roommate's appearance after all her talk of going away for the weekend, Kelly turned toward Natalie with her mouth open.

It was Ryan, however, who spoke up. "Getting a late start on your weekend in Sacramento, Natalie?"

"No, I'm not going." With a pout, the redhead plopped down in a chair at the table.

Kelly found her voice. "Not going? What happened? You were so excited about leaving yesterday." And she'd been so looking forward to having at least one night without the other woman being there.

Shaking her head Natalie told them, "You were right,

Kelly. He thought I was planning a romantic weekend getaway. He didn't understand that we couldn't sleep in the same room in front of all those Southway people. We haven't even been to dinner or kissed — how could he think I'd sleep with him?"

"Well, Natalie, men can be hound dogs," Ryan told her.

Natalie nodded. "They sure can. I really wanted to go and I even offered to split the gas with him but he said no. So . . . here I am."

"Did you have to pay for the conference?" Kelly asked.

"No. Southway doesn't charge — you just have to pay for the hotel room and except for the big breakfast I heard they have in the morning, your meals. I was able to cancel ahead of time so I didn't lose a deposit or anything."

"Well, that's good," Kelly told her.

"Yeah. With how expensive my rent is, I can't afford to lose money like that."

Ignoring what was becoming a never-ending bid for reduced rent Kelly told her, "I'm sorry things didn't work out with you and Louis. At least this time with going away. You think you'd like to do things with him locally?"

"Sure. Why not? Are you guys going to be here all weekend?"

Ryan and Kelly exchanged a look. Kelly answered, "I'm on duty tonight."

"Does that mean Ryan will be leaving?"

Again they looked at each other. Ryan answered, "Probably in the morning, but if you need some girl time with Kelly I've got some things I can take care of."

"No. I just like it when it's just Kelly and me."

Ryan chuckled. "Yeah, me too."

"Yes," Natalie told him, "but you don't live here. *I* do."

CHAPTER TWENTY-SIX

"Well." Kelly giggled as she lay down beside Ryan after they'd finished their breakfast. "She sure told you."

"She most certainly did. That woman . . . Kel, she is an odd duck."

Kelly studied him for a moment. It'd been a long shift and she was tired but felt like she needed to clear the air with Ryan. "Odd doesn't quite cover it."

He rolled toward her. "Look, I know this is your deal. Your house, your decision . . ."

"I'm hearing a but." Wanting to let him know she was good with whatever he had to say she reached out and stroked his arm.

"This is not me being overprotective, okay?"

Kelly nodded.

"This is just me being your boyfriend, the man who loves you and wants a future with you."

She nodded again.

"That woman . . ."

"Ry, are you trying to tell me that beyond odd she's annoying the shit out of you?"

"That's putting it mildly. Look, I know you feel you need a roommate right now . . ."

"Would it help if I told you that she's starting to bother me too? A lot?"

"Is she?"

Kelly sat up. "Oh, man, like you wouldn't believe. You see a little of it when you're here, but Ryan . . . it's never ending. She needs this, she needs that . . . not wants, but needs. The constant reminder that she feels the rent is too high . . . which it is not, the never-ending litany of what she wants fixed, or done to the house . . . *my* house. I'm glad there isn't a lease and I can just give her thirty days to send her on her way."

He lay back down but turned his head to look at her. "You've definitely put up with more than most people would at this point."

"So you don't find her antics all that humorous either?"

"No. No, I don't. Are you thinking of asking her to go?"

Kelly thought about it for a moment before answering, "No. Well, maybe. I keep thinking maybe it's me because Susan and I roomed together for so long and knew each other so well, that this is all new for Natalie and that maybe I'm bunching her in with a new job and dealing with Chris.

"Trust me, it's not you. Yeah, you have a lot on your plate, but Kelly, it's not you. She's definitely got a screw loose somewhere."

"I've been wondering if there's a past life connection."

He shifted back up on to his elbow to be better able to see her. "Do you sense anything?"

Ryan and Kelly both remembered past lives together, starting with long ago Atlantis. Then and there she, as Khorla, was promised to Ryan but coveted another man. To have him, Kelly cast a spell and did indeed win the man who became Adrian James in his lifetime, but not his heart. It was an empty relationship, based on want and desire, not true love. The die was cast, and only she could undo the spell that bound them together. One simple spell set lifetimes of Adrian pursuing and catching her, but neither ever finding happiness. In lifetime after lifetime, Ryan would come into Kelly's life, try to save her from whatever disaster was about to befall them only for one or the other of them to die.

Then, in this lifetime, Kelly was stalked from an early age. Adrian tried to possess Kelly. The two entered into a relationship, but from the beginning Kelly felt reservations. Despite several attempts on her life, Kelly never realized it was Adrian causing all her problems—after all, he had told her he loved her. But unable to possess her completely, Adrian made several attempts on her life. It was when he blew up her car that Kelly met Ryan. Her falling in love, almost instantly with Ryan, enraged Adrian, and in an act of desperation, he kidnapped her.

Engaging in the dark arts himself he began a ritual to sacrifice Kelly. As he began the ceremony, Kelly remembered that long ago lifetime in Atlantis and the spell that had set the disaster her life had become, in motion. Quickly, almost before it was too late, she recited the words to the spell that righted the original wrong. In the moment before Adrian cast the death blow, all four present—Kelly, Ryan, Susan and Adrian—remembered that first life time. They were all, finally free.

"No. I don't think Natalie was part of any of the past lives. Maybe . . . but not an integral part. I think she's just one of those people in this life that . . ." Kelly shrugged.

Ryan stroked her upper arm. "That what?"

"That just happen in your life, you know? Someone just passing through. I don't feel like there is a karmic or past life link."

"And what about Chris?"

Kelly chuckled. "No. I wondered about that too. If that's so, she's part of someone else's karmic payback. I just happen to be on the receiving end now and again."

"Well, that business with the snake wasn't some minor issue."

"I know. I just can't prove she was behind it. All I have is a feeling she got someone to do it. At least the snake decided it wanted to sleep on the seat and didn't crawl underneath and climb out when I was on my way to a call. From here on I'll be checking inside the car and under the seats and every nook and cranny before I get in and take off."

"Definitely watch your back with that one. You still don't know why she dislikes you so much?"

"I'm a woman. Apparently that's all she needs. From what Maria told me, she's gone after every female in the department, even the gay ones. Chris would like to live on a planet where she's the only woman."

"Well, if we were back in the early days of Australia that could have easily been arranged and I'm sure they would have loved her."

"Hmm . . . past lives . . . I wonder if we could find a way to time travel her back there?"

"On another note, Natalie makes no bones about not liking me," Ryan told her with a half-smile forming on his lips.

"Oh, I don't think it's that she doesn't like you. I think she's one of those people who does better on their own, but for whatever reason needs to live with someone right now. She doesn't bother me . . . much."

"Only when you see her?"

Kelly laughed. "Almost. Seriously, our schedules are different enough that we aren't running into each other much. And I think she's lonely and doesn't know how to connect with people. Like her and Louis. It never occurred to her he'd think she was offering him some hot nights between the sheets on an all-expense-paid weekend. I also suspect when he found out it was a Southway conference he'd heard the stories about how it's like a cult and decided that it wasn't his thing."

"Could be. So next question — do I take her up on her hints and go home tomorrow or . . ."

"No! Absolutely not. As long as I'm paying the mortgage here I'll have anyone I want staying over."

*

Ryan left with Kelly when she took off for her shift that evening. Standing by her car giving her a kiss, he happened to look up to see the living room curtains flick closed. Apparently Natalie found her entertainment watching them say goodbye to each other. No matter what Kelly thought, the redheaded woman was trouble. There was something unsettling about her. Nothing he could put his finger on, but he'd never been wrong about someone he thought was off.

He thought back on Natalie's interview to room with Kelly—she was pretty definite about what she was looking for—as was Kelly. They seemed pretty much on a par with each other—they both wanted the same things—someone who was reliable, paid their bills on time, neat, clean, quiet, professional. Natalie did get a little demanding and had a hard time deciding things on her own. Could be though, as Kelly said, the redheaded woman was nervous and just very aware of moving into someone else's home.

Then why did she make him nervous? Was it simply because Natalie had issues with Ryan being over a few nights a week? Would introducing her to someone of her own to date change that? Not that he was going to get into matchmaking. *That* never turned out well.

There was just something off about the woman.

Then there was Chris. He'd heard all kinds of nasty stories about dispatchers over the years, but the ones who engaged in really bad behavior were few and far between. Kelly'd never done anything to the slutty blonde . . . so why was his lady on Chris's shit list? They'd talked about it, and like with Natalie, Kelly had no inclination that there was a past life connection.

Clearly he was spending way too much time thinking about Kelly's situations than focusing on his job, mainly the D-1 gang. Kelly had things under control with both Natalie and Chris. She was probably spot on about what was going on with Natalie being nervous and her sergeant and up through her chain knew there were issues with Chris. There was nothing to worry about.

He, on the other hand, needed to focus on making sure the witnesses against the gang leaders were still on board. Turning to his computer he brought up the witness list, making note of their locations and who to have contact those in witness protection.

Twenty-two witnesses had come forward and they'd named at least forty more . . . forty more who might or might not speak up. Forty more who might have already gone underground rather than deal with D-1. He pulled up a mapping program and started noting the last location for each witness. Most were clustered in the Mission district in San Francisco and El Monte in Los Angeles, and then there were a series of anomalous locations — right in Marin. He'd known about the San Rafael connection from Diego, but looking at the secondary witnesses, it appeared there were more. Diego had been their inside guy, but after he'd turned state's evidence there was little chance he'd go back out there and even less that they'd let him back in. What he needed was a link to the big wig . . . they needed to find the top people.

Ryan picked up his pen and absently tapped it on the desk. How to find the top person . . . how to get someone, anyone, to expose them.

He was pulled from his reverie by a knock on the doorframe from his partner, Keith.

"Hey."

"How's it going, Michaels?"

"Going."

Keith walked into the office and parked his butt on the edge of the desk. "Personal or case?"

"Case. D-1."

"Ah. And?"

Ryan looked over at the monitor to organize a few stray thoughts before answering, "I'm trying to see if there's a pattern to where the witnesses live, work and what they may have seen. I've got twenty or so who were directly involved in some way . . . twenty that came forward."

"Are they solid?"

"They were when we first interviewed them. Now?" Ryan shrugged. "Even though we've got them relatively secured outside the immediate area, it doesn't mean that D-1 hasn't gotten to them in some way, threatened them or their family. You know how it goes."

"Yeah. I do."

"And from what we know, none of them ever came in contact with the head members — that's who we want, that's who we need to bring down."

"No clues at all?"

Ryan looked back at his monitor. "None that we know of. Even Diego, the guy who came to us to get his girlfriend out, never had any contact with them, not that he knew of and he was pretty well connected."

"So now what?"

"Now? I'm going to do an org chart of sorts — maybe looking at the connections will give me some ideas."

"Sounds like a plan. Can I help?"

"Maybe. What say I start plugging in the names and you read off any data we have on them. You see commonalities let's mark it."

With that Ryan brought up a blank Visio document and started to notate the names and locations of the witnesses they had so far. Keith read off the crimes committed against them as well as what each of the witnesses had done to protect themselves. As each connection fleshed itself out, tie after tie, led them back to San Rafael. And wasn't that odd?

Chapter Twenty-seven

"Ry?" Kelly turned from the oven where she was pulling out a casserole she'd thrown together before turning in after her shift Tuesday morning.

"Ryan?" she called again.

"Huh?" Clearly startled, he looked up from the notepad he's been doodling on while sitting at the kitchen table.

"I asked if you could grab whatever you want to drink from the frig and grab me a glass of buttermilk."

"Oh. Sure." He turned back to the notepad and drew another box.

Kelly put down the pan she'd pulled from the oven and sat down beside him. "Wanna tell me what has you so pre-occupied?"

"D-1."

"Ah. A break in the case?"

"No." He put down his pen, closed his eyes, and stretched backward. "I wish. I spent most of yesterday and today working out a spreadsheet and organizational type chart of the witnesses and their locations and who saw or said what."

"And connections?"

"Oddly enough a lot of them relate back to San Rafael."

"That's odd?"

"I thought so . . . why? don't you?"

"Well, given their primary businesses are drugs and human trafficking, I'd expect it to be happening more in the port or border areas or a larger city. We have a Latino community in San Rafael, a close-knit one, but if we're talking crime, mostly drugs and some prostitution, right?"

"Right. No different from a lot of areas that draw certain, shall we say, populations."

"But San Rafael . . . okay, canal area?"

"Once again, oddly, no. There are some there, but a lot in the Gerstal Park area. A lot of them seem to relate back that way."

"Hmmm, I wonder . . ."

"Hello?" Natalie called from the front door interrupting Kelly and Ryan.

"In the kitchen, Natalie."

The redhead started into the kitchen and stopped short when she saw Ryan. Her tone conveyed that it was more like they, or specifically Ryan, was interrupting her when she asked, "Oh. Am I interrupting something?"

Kelly looked at Ryan and raised a brow. It wouldn't do to tell her roommate she had, in fact, interrupted them, especially with Natalie's tone.

"No. Actually we were getting ready to put dinner on the table. Would you like to join us?"

"Maybe, what do you have?"

"Simple chicken noodle casserole. Nothing special, but I like it."

Natalie shrugged. "Sure. Let me put my purse down." With that, she turned and left the kitchen. When Kelly heard Natalie's bedroom door shut she looked at Ryan who was trying not to laugh.

"You know, Ry, she's trying to sort out changing her routine without changing it . . . watch . . . she's going to walk back in here and ask if we can wait till she has her evening bath and . . ."

They heard the door down the hall open, followed by Natalie's footsteps heading toward the kitchen. At the doorway she stopped and appeared to be checking out whether or not anything had changed in the room before asking, "I was wondering . . ."

"Yes?" Kelly smiled at her.

"Would you mind waiting about fifteen minutes so I can take my bath and shower and change? It's been a long day and I really need a bath."

"Sure. Why not?" Ryan answered for them.

"Kelly?" Natalie asked without looking at Ryan.

"Of course. That'll give me time to set the table."

They shared a look when the sound of water filling the tub sounded down the hall. A short time later, without trying to listen, they heard the water running down the drain, followed by the shower turning on.

"Told, ya." Kelly smirked.

"She still hasn't gotten the memo about the drought, has she?" Ryan asked.

"She got it. That's one of her arguments for you not staying here more than one night a week—after you shower, bathe or whatever at home."

Ryan shook his head.

"And check this out. When I told her she needed to start turning off the radio, TV, computer, ceiling fan, etc. in her room when she left for work she told me, once again, that would mean she'd have to re-set them every night when she came home. I told her that with spare the air days and our being in that special savings plan the electric company has for the summer months we needed to cut our electric use she told me that didn't make sense because we don't pay for electricity."

"Seriously?"

"Uh-huh. So I showed her the bill along with one of the bills from Susan and I and her response was that if *you* were here less the bill would go way down. Apparently your electric shaver eats up quite a bit of power."

"My . . . Kelly, I don't use an electric shaver."

Kelly smiled. "I know. And now Natalie does too. But you still use a lot of electricity and she thinks you should be paying for some of it."

"Uh, sure. No problem. I'm ha . . ."

Kelly sat and reached for his hand. "No way! I'm down at your place as much as you are here and seriously? You were here as often before as you are now—and almost all of our bills—water, electric, gas—have doubled with Natalie here."

"Cable?"

"No. She has her own and she uses her cell phone rather than activating that extra phone line Susan had put in for her business. But seriously, the utility bills have just about doubled."

"What are you going to do about it?"

Kelly glanced up at the door and listened for a moment to be sure Natalie wasn't on her way back to the kitchen before answering, "Raise the rent in three months."

"Three . . . why three?"

"She'll have been here a half a year then."

"You know she's going to insist on a year."

"Yeah, well, she'll try to negotiate it either time but I'm hoping she gets the 411 on the drought and power savings before then."

They heard Natalie padding down the hall as Ryan said, "Good luck with that."

"Smells good," Natalie announced a few minutes later as she walked over to the refrigerator and grabbed one of her sodas.

"Like I said, just a simple chicken and noodle casserole," Kelly answered.

"Oh," the redhead primly answered. "I just thought since you're this jet setting federal agent you ate caviar and other expensive stuff with champagne all the time."

Ryan laughed. "No. Trust me. Most of your feds eat your basic deli sandwiches and quick crockpot meals if we cook."

"That doesn't sound very sexy to me. James Bond wouldn't eat that."

"I wouldn't know."

Kelly picked up a breadstick and slid it into her mouth, pulling it out slightly before sliding it in and all the way out before putting in, "Oh, I think any food can be . . ." She looked down at the eight-inch breadstick. "Sexy if you take it the right way."

Ryan all but choked on the swallow of water he'd just taken.

Chapter Twenty-eight

"Kelly." Ryan slid his arms around her as she joined him in bed. "She seriously has a screw loose."

"Just one?" Kelly chuckled.

"I was being polite."

"I know. Ry, you don't think she's unstable do you?"

"Kelly, I *know* she's unstable."

"Well, there is that. But not like Adrian or Clarissa were, right? With Natalie it's just her own idiosyncrasy, right? She's not a danger to anyone . . . like me. I mean, I'm not picking anything up, but I didn't with Adrian . . . not really, either."

Ryan shrugged before pulling her closer. "I don't think so. I'm not getting any prickly feelings like I do around a perp, but there's something not right there."

"That's the thing. I don't feel anything about her. I mean, I feel she's annoying at times, but it's all internal for or with her. I get it that she's OCD and can't help herself with some things and I try to be patient . . ."

"You've been more than patient with some things. If you didn't keep such a firm hand on things she'd be running all over you."

"You don't like her." Kelly scooted up in bed, intent on an in-depth discussion about Natalie.

"I don't like or dislike her. She's someone who lives in your house. Someone still relatively new. She's either going to make it or not but ultimately it depends on you. If you feel unsafe about her, ask her to leave. If her OCDness starts to drive you nuts, ask her to leave. And if she gives you a problem about it I'll be here with you."

"No, I don't feel unsafe about her . . . she's like a . . . like a gnat! Like a bug. Just buzzing around in the background, but not really there. I know how unsafe feels. After Adrian and Clarissa I have a good bead on that and remember, I said that about Clarissa right after I met her. It was my own stupidity and drive for a story that I disregarded those feelings and almost got myself killed. The feelings I had about Clarissa were exactly the same as I felt about Adrian . . . which yes, I ignored those too except I didn't know what they were about at the time. Trust me, if I ever feel those things again I'll be running, not walking, away. No, with Natalie it's like there's nothing there if you know what I mean. But still, I'm starting not to like her."

Ryan studied her a moment. "Do you mean like she doesn't exist?"

Kelly chuckled. "I don't think she's a ghost."

"So just that she's a little annoying, but not worth asking her to leave?"

"Maybe. If she moved out it would be fine. If she stays, she's going to have to bend a little to live the way I want in my house. I'm not so sure she can do that."

"Seriously?" Maria asked Kelly during a meal break the following Friday.

"For real seriously," Kelly answered her.

"Natalie really asked a guy to go to a Southway conference and pay his own way?"

"Yup. And when I told her he was going to expect to share her room and . . . gracious me . . . her bed and that since she invited him she should expect to pay for it, she was stunned."

"What century is she living in?"

Kelly shook her head and chuckled. "I'm not sure. Maria, sometimes it's like she's playing at living, that she's playing a role. Know what I mean?"

"I do." Jess had walked into the break room. "It's like she watches some old TV shows and then thinks that's still the way life is. That sound about right?"

Kelly had turned and looked over at the other dispatcher. "Yup."

Jess took a seat and looked between Kelly and Maria. "Kind of like Chris, you know?"

Maria looked a little surprised. "I've dealt with Chris's crazy since she's been here, but I can't think of any TV show that she could be pretending to be in."

"Maybe not a mainstream TV show, but doesn't she remind you of someone who could be the star of a really bad reality TV show?"

Maria chuckled. "Oh yeah. I got it now. Badge Bunnies Gone Wild."

One of the officers walked into the break room and joined in the laughter. "I can see it. Chris in a sleazy looking bikini lazing on the hood of a police car, a baton between her legs, moaning, only her moans are like her voice — nails on a blackboard so she sounds like a siren."

"That's mean, you guys," Kelly told them, although she couldn't help but chuckle along with them.

"You say that," Jess told her, "but I can see you smiling. Admit it, she'd make a great reality TV star."

"Yeah, maybe. But what does that say about the rest of us who are professional — not that I'm saying she isn't a professional."

"And of course you wouldn't, would you?" Chris stood in the doorway, an ugly smile on her face.

Nervously, Jess rose. "Who's covering dispatch?"

"It's only Sophie and Misha out there. They're fine," Chris spat at her and strode over to the soda machine.

"Chris?" Jen's voice was soft but commanded authority.

"You have officers on the street, no call takers on and no one in dispatch?"

Chris shrugged. "It's only for a minute. I 1023'd them over the air." She looked pointedly at Kelly. "I bet even the trainee knows that means I told them to stand by for a minute while I took care of some personal business."

"Chris, you have two other dispatchers in the building. If getting a soda was that crucial you could easily have asked one of them to take a moment out of their code to take the radio.

Again Chris shrugged and turned to put her money in the machine. "Take it up with Captain Berger. He's picking me up for a ride along in about fifteen minutes. I'm sure he'd love to hear it. By the way, Jess, good luck with getting a ring from that plumber of yours. With any luck that cubic zirconia he's getting you won't fall in his butt crack before he gives it to you."

"He's a carpenter, Chris."

"Whatever. Hey." She smiled at the women in the group. "Just so you hear it here first, Bruce Edwards, the new sergeant over in San Rafael? It looks like we're going to be getting married. You know what that means?"

The other four shook their heads.

"Silly, girls, my initials will be C-U-T-E — Chris Ursula Tanner Edwards. Nice, huh?" With that she sauntered out of the room.

Once she was out of earshot, Jess spoke low but loud enough for the others to hear. "She's wrong about that . . . it will be Chris Ursula nee Tanner . . . C-U-N . . ."

The others chuckled low.

CHAPTER TWENTY-NINE

When dispatch broke Kelly for her meal break, she headed home. While most nights she brought something to the station both to avoid dealing with Natalie and, at the same time, to have a chance to mingle with the other officers, tonight she hadn't had time to put anything together. She quietly let herself in the house and had just reached the kitchen when Natalie came up behind her.

"Ack!" Kelly spun around with her hand on her gun. "Natalie! Don't sneak up on me like that."

"Like what?"

"Like you were tip-toeing. It startled me."

Natalie shrugged. "Sorry." But her tone said she really wasn't. The glint in her eye told Kelly she had been hoping to startle her.

"You're up late."

"I guess. I was on the phone with Harry."

Kelly reached into the refrigerator and pulled out some sandwich makings. Ginny, always on the lookout for a little something special, wandered into the kitchen with a squinty-eyed look at Natalie.

"You aren't feeding her that good chicken, are you?" Natalie asked from where she'd sat down at the table.

Kelly shrugged. "A little bite won't hurt her." What concerned Kelly more was Natalie settling down at the table— clearly her roommate was planning on having a little chat. Silently admonishing herself, Kelly reminded herself that Natalie did live there and was probably feeling a little lonely.

166

Besides, how many nights . . . days . . . times . . . had she and Susan sat at the table talking long into the night. Maybe it was time to broach at least a little friendship with Natalie.

"So," Kelly began, "who is this Harry?" With luck, he'd be romantically interested in Natalie, and the other woman would start spending a night or two out of the house on a date.

Natalie leaned back in her chair and raised her legs in front of her. Closing her eyes she looked like she was going to swoon before she answered, "Only the handsomest, most wonderful guy in the world."

"Sounds serious." But then with Natalie, everything was serious.

Natalie laughed, not a natural, emotionally free laugh, but one that sounded almost forced. "Well, not yet."

"You haven't mentioned him before."

"We just met." Natalie rose and poured herself a glass of water from the spigot on the refrigerator. "He came into work on Monday to get his car fixed. We talked for a few minutes, but you know my boss — he gets all pissy when I talk to a customer for too long. Harry stuck around though, even with my boss giving me looks. Then he came back on Tuesday and brought me a coffee — one of the fancy ones from Starbucks, not a cheapo from the grocery store. And then he came again on Wednesday and brought me another coffee and asked me if I was free for lunch yesterday. I was, but I didn't want to appear easy so I said I had plans."

"Uh-huh." Kelly crossed her fingers that Natalie hadn't blown off a potential romance and chance to get out of the house for a few hours . . . maybe even a weekend.

" . . . but that I was free for dinner Thursday night."

"You asked him to ask you to dinner last night?"

"No, of course not. A lady doesn't invite herself out to dinner. I just put it out there that I was available if he wanted to take me to dinner. Lunch is cheap, you know? And if someone is going to date me he needs to be able to take me to nice places all the time, you know?"

"I suppose."

"You don't agree? You don't care if you're taken to some cheapo dive?"

"It's the company that matters. After all is said and done, it's the person you're looking at your future with that matters, not the outer things they can give you. On one of our early dates Ryan took me to a pool hall and it was one of the best times I've had."

"Maybe. My mother used to always tell me it's just as easy to fall for a rich man as a poor one and I plan to fall for a rich man. How else can you tell if he's rich if you let him take you to some sandwich place for lunch? It doesn't make sense to get involved with someone and then find out he can't support you in the lifestyle you should be pampered in?"

Kelly thought back to her early dates with Ryan—mainly the first time they'd gone out. He'd taken her to a small beer and burger place with pool tables and they shot pool with some of his ATF buddies. The next time they'd gone out was to a local art and wine festival and they'd had hot dogs and funnel cakes. Money and how much Ryan might or might now have never entered her mind.

Then again, in those early days, Kelly was afraid for her life. Would it have been any different if she'd met Ryan under less stressful and frightening circumstances?

Probably not. But that was Kelly and Ryan . . . they were meant to be together in so many lifetimes. In each one they'd been torn from each other again and again. Now, hopefully, they'd have their happy ever after as well as future lifetimes with each other.

As that thought went through Kelly's mind a chill raced through her . . . No. No. Ryan and I are meant to be together.

We know what tore us apart before, I broke the spell, and now we have our life together, the one we deserve. "I don't know, Natalie. Aren't you concerned you might miss the love of your life, someone who is the perfect guy for you, if all you're doing is looking at how much money he has?"

"Nope!" She leaned back in her chair, thrust her legs out, and stretched her arms in front of her. "Like I said, it's just as easy to fall for a rich man as a poor one."

Kelly glanced at the clock and noted she had maybe seven minutes before she had to be back on patrol. "So did you go to dinner?"

"Not last night—but we're going tomorrow night which is even better."

"It is?"

"Of course." Natalie's tone indicated Kelly was perhaps too stupid to live in the dating game if she didn't know that Saturday night was better than Friday.

"How?"

"Because, silly, if you go on a Thursday, some people have to work on Friday. They can't buy you wine or as much wine as you might like. On a Saturday night you don't have to get up the next day—he can take you some place really nice, maybe even the city and you can have some good drinks and dessert and everything."

"Ah. I see. Well, I need to get back on patrol. Maybe I'll see you in the morning."

"Either that or before we go out tomorrow night. Harry is coming about five to pick me up. That probably means we're going into the city and someplace really expensive where the only reservations available are earlier in the evening. But that's okay as long as it's a really good restaurant."

Mid-way through patrol, Kelly met up with Misha in a favorite report writing stop in the city. They sat driver side to driver side in the nearly deserted parking lot, completing paperwork from the first half of their shift.

"You never told me there was this much paper, Mish," Kelly told her friend.

"If I had, would you have still come on board?"

"Yeah. I think so. Ryan has a lot more paper that he deals with than I have."

"Trust me, there's even more of it in detectives."

"You looking to go back into investigations?"

Misha shrugged. "Maybe in a couple of years. Some of it was interesting, but when you're always the one getting the rape and child abuse cases because you're a woman, well, sometimes you need a break, you know?"

"I can imagine. So tell me . . . Chris?"

"That was pretty funny when Jess offered up Chris's initials if she gets married, wasn't it?"

"Yeah. And you know if she ever gets wind of it she's going to have an internal affairs investigation into that person and will settle for nothing less than their job."

"She's said a lot worse in her time."

"And the brass just keeps giving her a pass?"

"Yup."

"So was the business over Jess maybe getting engaged just a one-time thing with Chris?"

"Oh no, she's been after Jess forever."

"Why?"

"You mean aside from Jess being a woman . . . a single woman in dispatch that a couple of the single male officers showed an interest in?"

"Even Chris's leftovers?"

"*Especially* her leftovers. In Chris's world she left them and they're supposed to spend eternity pining for the queen bee. The issue with Jess goes back to dispatch academy. Chris is one of those women who got where she is in life based on sex . . . not her looks . . . sex. If you ever get the guys to talk they'll tell you they find her personally to be butt ugly. Oh, maybe a few think she's attractive, but on the whole they'll tell you she's ugly. Chris and Jess went to the same high school, but Chris was a year behind. Her grades weren't so good and she got left back one year. She was able to graduate because . . . well, for the same reason she gets where she's at in the department. Chris's plan, from what I hear, was to meet an older man who would quickly leave this earthly existence and her enough money to live in the lifestyle she wanted to be accustomed to for the rest of her life. She hung out at casinos, targeting what she thought were well-to-do guys . . . but apparently they all turned out to be your average Joe's who liked to gamble. No rich guys in sight. At least in her sight.

"Jess, meanwhile, went to dispatch school and did pretty well. We hired her right after she graduated. The mistake Jess made . . . or her first mistake . . . was telling Chris about what she was doing. All Chris heard, apparently, was men and just sitting there taking calls. Just the bare minimum. So she got herself in dispatch school and voilà here she is."

"She got into dispatch school and passed, right?"

"Right."

"So she wouldn't have been hired if she hadn't, right? Even sleeping her way to the top she couldn't, right?"

"Right. But Jess has seniority over her. And for Chris, that's almost as bad as a guy looking at another woman. Jess gets to pick shifts and vacations ahead of her. Then Christ will bid the same shift based, of course, on the most eligible men. Chris constantly tries to sabotage Jess. Then if and when Jess steps away or is on break, Chris will slide over and either send CAD messages in violation of the FCC regs, run people she shouldn't or *accidently* delete messages that Jess needs to do her paperwork."

"And the brass does nothing about it?"

"Not a thing. And you know what's kind of weird? Jess could bid for a different shift than Chris, but she keeps opting for the ones the blonde is on."

"Why?"

"Who knows? Anyway, you saw what Chris did when you were behind that stolen . . . how she acted after. And when you and Coburn went out on that domestic not sending back up? I never feel safe on the streets when she has the radio. Seriously. Even the guys don't."

"Someone needs to do something about her."

"Yup. The question is who?"

"So, McKenna, what's the deal with the roommate?" Chris asked Kelly the next night when she stopped into dispatch to pick up some paperwork before going out on patrol.

"My roommate?" She'd managed to leave the house before Natalie's date showed up—if, in fact, he was real and did show up. There'd been any number of times the past few months when Natalie would tell a story that turned out to be quite different from the real deal.

"Yeah. Nat . . . is that her name?"

"Natalie."

"Derek was talking about her. About her asking him to go to some kind of pyramid scheme type party with her?"

"Oh. Yeah. She sells Southway and they were having some sort of training or other a few weeks ago. Somehow it fizzled and she was going to go with someone else. I don't pay much attention to her business although she apparently had a date tonight so I'm thinking the whole thing with Derek is over and done if that's your worry."

"You live with someone and you don't know about them? And about Derek and me, we dated shortly after I came here, we're so last year." Chris actually sounded surprised about Kelly not knowing much about her roommate.

Kelly leaned against the dispatch computer console and crossed her arms over her chest. "She rents a room in my house. If you remember, I had an ad posted on the general info board, but someone kept taking it down."

"You didn't check her out before you let her move in?"

"What I did or didn't do when I checked out a tenant is on me."

"So you didn't check her out," Chris smugly stated.

Kelly decided to turn the tables, if possible, on the condescending and troublemaking dispatcher. "Sounds like you know a lot about roommate hunting. How do you go about checking references?"

Chris shrugged. "I've never had a female roommate."

"But you do check out the male ones," Kelly probed.

"Oh, I check them out . . . I have them audition if you get my drift."

"Ah." That was more information than Kelly was looking for but knowing Chris . . . what could she have expected.

"And I only live with cops."

"I see." She turned toward the door to leave because clearly this conversation wasn't going to go anywhere practical or even interesting.

"Before that it was firemen . . . emphasis on the men." Chris smirked.

"Sounds like any man in a uniform would do."

The skinny blonde shrugged again. "I suppose I could go for a fed if he was hot enough. The whole gun thing is kind of a turn on, you know?"

It was Kelly's turn to shrug. "Personally I prefer someone with a good personality and a sense of humor helps."

With that, Kelly made her escape. With Chris there was never really anything substantial to see or hear. She made a mental note to herself to remember that before she ventured into dispatch with that woman in there alone again.

Jess ran into her while she made her way out of the building to her car. "You look lost in thought."

"Oh, hey. Jess. How goes it?"

"Good. You okay?"

"Yeah. I just made a mistake is all."

"Ohhh, not good."

"Nothing serious—just got into a conversation with Chris."

"A conversation? You mean you really talked with her and exchanged information and pleasantries?"

Kelly laughed. "Something like that. It was more like Chris trying to prove she is desirable to anything with testosterone and I am a bad judge of character."

"Well, she does have that down." Jess looked up and down the hallway before checking her watch. "I've got a few. What were you guys talking about?"

"Surprisingly she asked about my roommate."

"Neurotic Natalie?"

"That would be the one."

"She do something new?"

Kelly leaned against the wall and put her right foot up against it behind her. "No, just Natalie being Natalie. Chris was curious about her which . . . in itself . . . was odd."

"I'll say. The only reason Chris gets interested in someone else's doins is if she's looking for a way to mock them or cause problems."

"That's what I thought."

"I take it you didn't give anything up?"

"Nothing of consequence."

Jess shook her head. "How is it going with the OCD one?"

Kelly blew out a breath. "If I don't see her or have to talk to her, fine. If I try not to think about some of the things she does like two baths and a shower twice a day, laundry every night because even though she has several weeks' worth of underwear—her assurance, not my having asked—she does laundry every night because there might be icky things in her undies."

"Euuuu."

"Yeah, I know, but you asked."

Jess laughed.

"So if I don't think about the things she does or her wacky rules, she's okay."

"Do you see her being a long term renter?"

Kelly chewed her lower lip a moment before answering, "Not really. She's been there almost six months, but if she decided to move out tomorrow I'd be plenty pleased. It would be tight paying the mortgage, but doable."

"Do you have a lease with her?"

"You know, that's one thing I did do right . . . no lease. Thirty days written notice if she's going to move or I want to send her packing and there are times lately I'm really thinking about it."

"Yeah? That bad?"

"I don't know if it's bad as much as annoying. I'm still on probation and having to deal with her . . . her . . . stuff is a distraction at times. She's needy about attention and is determined to have everything her way even though it's my house. I'm good compromising on some things but others . . . no way."

"Like?"

"Ginny."

"Ginny?" Jess's voice rose when she said Ginny's name.

"Yeah. She knew when she moved in I had a cat—an *indoor* cat—a long-haired indoor cat. She moves in and suddenly she's allergic and the cat shouldn't eat in the kitchen and the litter box smells. Typical non-animal or non-cat person comments."

Jess shook her head again.

"And then there's Ryan. She knew when she moved in I have a boyfriend and that he stays over. Natalie said she was fine with it, but then a day after she moved in she starts in about how Ryan should only be allowed to stay one day every other weekend or if he's going to be around *every day*, which he is not, then her utilities should be reduced. Trust me, he doesn't use half the water or electricity she does . . . and she's not paying half. She does pay one-third."

"Does she know that?"

"Yup. I told her. But with Natalie . . . well, she's one of those people who think everything should be or is a negotiation."

"Sounds nasty. And sounds like you plan to invite her to leave sooner rather than later."

"Yeah. Maybe." Kelly glanced at the door leading outside. "I could just be tired right now, you know? And then the conversation with Chris . . . well, that's always a downer and in this instance I brought it on myself."

"Well, if there's anything I can do, let me know. Remember, I did offer to move in with you when you were looking."

"Thanks. Just having someone to talk to about it helps, you know?"

"I do. Well, I gotta get going before Chrissy has a hissy . . . and who knows, Natalie may decide to go on her own and you won't have to deal with it."

"That would be nice . . . real nice. Good luck with shriek-a-lina tonight."

"Shriek . . . oh, Kelly, that's hysterical."

"Jen came up with it — and don't you repeat it!"

CHAPTER THIRTY

As she headed down to the southern portion of the city to cover her beat for the night Kelly radioed in to dispatch she was available for calls. One of the many things she liked about the city, which was more like a small town than a city of 50,000 residents, was the different enclaves. Parts were rural with cows and rolling farmland. There were homey domestic valleys with cute houses, suburban shopping areas, and a small section of urban office buildings. All in all, about 24 square miles. Red Oak city services covered most of the city with a small portion being covered by the county. While it was convenient to work near home, at the same time, it could feel awkward, and Kelly preferred the southern or northernmost beats—she just didn't want to be called in on a quirky or worse, domestic situation in her own neighborhood.

Since Red Oak had only three bars situated in the downtown area there was little chance of many drunk drivers, even on a Friday or Saturday night unless the races were in town the next county over. Even with overly dramatic Chris on the radio, the night looked like it would be a rather mellow one.

With light chatter on the radio, different units calling in their positions, Kelly slowly cruised the streets of her beat. Everything was looking peaceful and calm. Her mind wandered briefly to Natalie and her latest drama. It was looking more and more like she'd have to make a decision about the OCD tenant—one she didn't really want to make. Other than that, it was peaceful, so peaceful her cell phone ringing startled her.

"Ry! What's up?"

"Are you alone?"

"Why, you want to talk dirty to me?" Kelly giggled.

The memory of the goose walking over her grave the night before tickled at the edge of her mind when she heard him say, "I wish."

"Ryan, is everything okay?"

"Yeah. Yeah. I was just calling to . . . oh hell."

"Ryan?"

"I'm at San Francisco General."

"Ryan?" Panic gripped Kelly's breath. Ryan had to be okay. He was on the phone to her, right? He was talking to her. Right? So he was just . . . just . . ."Ry? Tell me you're okay."

"I'm fine."

"You wouldn't lie to me."

"I absolutely would not. Keith was shot earlier tonight. They're operating on him now . . . we should know soon."

"Ryan. What happened? You weren't even supposed to be at work tonight."

"I wasn't, but this morning we got a tip and couldn't wait on it."

"Can you tell me what happened? What it's about?"

"One of the D-1 snitches called early this morning with a tip that there was a major drug deal going down tonight. We got a team together and apparently this guy was playing both sides against the middle because we walked into a trap."

"Ambush."

"Not quite. A trap. We had a solid team together on it including SFPD, DEA and a few of the other alphabets heard we were going in and asked to come along. If the intel we had was right we didn't want to say no."

"Did the snitch know you'd be bringing in that many agents?"

"No. That probably saved us. If it were just Keith and I we probably wouldn't be having this conversation."

"Ryan. No."

"I'm okay, not even a scratch. I was on the other side of the building from him. But like I said, apparently this guy was playing both sides. He set us up."

"And now?"

"Well, he won't be setting anyone else up."

Ryan called Kelly several times over what she considered her weekend of Tuesday through Thursday, updating her on Keith's status. He said little, if anything, about the investigation or what happened.

To say she was relieved when she felt him slide between the sheets with her late Wednesday morning would have been an understatement. She hadn't slept all that well the past few nights with worry about Ryan. Maybe if she hadn't had that chilling feeling the night Keith got shot, it wouldn't have hit her so hard. She knew that Ryan's job was just as dangerous, if not more so, than hers. But it didn't make it any easier to deal with what happened. At least Keith was going to pull through.

She generally tried to keep her schedule to her shift hours on her off days both so she wouldn't have such a hard time staying up all night. That . . . and to avoid Natalie if she could. Running into the other woman now and again was fine—it was her constant need for companionship and never-ending complaints when Kelly was home that drove her a little nuts. So far she'd avoided any in-depth conversation about Natalie's date with Harry. Aside from hearing he'd taken her to someplace in the Mission—which didn't set all that well with Natalie because, according to the redhead, the Mission was for poor people. She didn't hear much. As it turned out the place he took her too was actually pretty nicely decked out, and after they'd gone dancing at some club where there was a hefty cover charge. To Natalie's mind, a large cover charge and long line equated with a rich person's club.

The past couple of days Natalie's phone rang a bit more than before . . . actually, it rang, which was something Kelly hadn't heard much off. Maybe this thing with this Harry was taking off.

For the first time in a few days Kelly felt completely at peace when she turned in to bed and fell into a deep, dreamless sleep. It was the warmth of Ryan's body, that delicious warmth she felt whenever he held her, that brought her to wakefulness and she realized that she'd slept through the soft sound of Ryan slipping off his clothes and the slight dip in her bed when he climbed in beside her and slid his arm around her.

Eyes still closed, Kelly slid ever so slightly toward Ryan, just close enough to run her lips over his nipple. When he groaned in pleasure, she opened her mouth to suck on that same nipple, at first gently, coaxing his arousal, and then more deeply. His low moans and soft sighs were more rousing than if he had done the same to her. When he reached for her, Kelly stilled his movement when she rested her hand on his bicep, a silent, ageless communication that she wanted . . . needed . . . to be in control.

When she'd had her fill of sucking and nibbling on his nipples, Kelly rubbed her mons against Ryan's swollen penis. With her belly and legs shifting in sensual movement, she showed him what she wanted, what she would want, how they would join. Not a word was needed, only the softly, yet ever more urgently, more rapid breathes letting the other know how strong their desire was growing.

Slowly, ever so slowly, Kelly raised her lips from Ryan's chest and kissed her way to his chin, his lips. Planting little kisses along his jaw, she whispered, "I love you, I love you, I love you."

In response, he groaned and told her the same. "More than life, more than my life, Kelly, I love you."

Their lips met, tongues joined, and a surge of moisture gathered at the juncture between Kelly's legs. "Ryan, I need you. Oh how I need you."

"I'm yours, now and forever, I'm yours."

With that, she eased on to her back and opened her legs, her body, her heart, and soul to the only man she could ever truly love.

Ryan entered her slowly, gently, his breath straining as he seemed to fight his desire to take her hard and join with her quickly. They'd given in to their passion, taking each other hard and fast . . . and they'd joined slowly and seductively. Their joinings always left them suspended in time. Each time was sweeter than the one before. This morning Kelly needed their lovemaking to be slow, steady . . . that moment in time needed to be suspended for a span . . . in her heart, she knew this needed to be a full and complete heartfelt joining. And Ryan's response, his steady, evenly paced thrusts, told her he too felt this need to prolong their coupling.

When they came, together, they lay entwined in each other's arms, murmuring, "I love you" until they fell asleep.

CHAPTER THIRTY-ONE

Tuesday morning, all was quiet when they woke, lips meeting in sweet kisses before they were fully awake. With the sound of Natalie leaving they exchanged pleased smiles and made love with unrestrained abandon for the first time since the redhead moved in.

A few hours later, rested, showered, ready to meet the rest of the day, Kelly and Ryan ambled into the kitchen. While they pulled out makings for omelets and coffee, Kelly asked, "So what happened when Keith was shot?"

Holding an egg, his hand over the bowl, Ryan paused, collecting his thoughts.

"Ry, if you're thinking of a way to . . . I don't know, protect me, from the realities of your job, don't. I don't try to protect you from mine so . . ."

"My job is a little different, Kelly."

She put down the plates she'd been holding and stepped over to him. Taking one of his broad shoulders in her hands Kelly made sure he was looking at her. "It's not all that different. You carry a gun and go after bad guys. I carry a gun and go after bad guys."

"Not the same kind of bad guys I do."

She turned to give him a look at that comment.

He met her gaze, caught the narrowing of her pupils that generally indicated she was getting annoyed. "Kelly, I'm not saying your job isn't dangerous. I'm saying . . ."

"I get it, Ryan. Really I do. You, your job, is at a broader level. We get the essentially small time dealers, things like that, especially in a quiet little town like Red Oak. You deal with the big wigs, the ones sending the major shipments of guns, contraband. But when the day is done we have a similar job — we bring in, hopefully, the bad guys. Someone got shot. That much I know. You're okay, at least physically, but I also know you, you're trying to figure out, wondering why, you couldn't stop it from happening. And maybe you're blaming yourself."

He lowered his head, his gaze on the floor as he blew out a breath. "You're right. You are spot on and I'm not trying to shut you out. Really, I'm not. And I'm not diminishing your job."

"I know you're not."

Ryan blew out a breath. "Let's get breakfast on the table and I'll fill you in, start to finish — even the parts I'm not supposed to share. Okay?"

"It's a deal."

With breakfast on the table a few minutes later Kelly gestured with her fork for Ryan to begin.

"Okay. So we had word — one of the D-1 informants — told us there was a shipment of guns coming in over at the port in Oakland. We called in Coast Guard, DEA and a few others to come along, notified Alameda sheriff and Oakland PD we'd be in the area. They sent some units, as did CHP. If anything we were top heavy in law enforcement, but this was going to be a major shipment, over three thousand automatic weapons if the intel was spot on. CHP even put their chopper in the air at a discrete distance. We got there, got staged and then nothing."

"What? Then how did Keith get shot?"

"Nothing happening at the pier was where the source told it would be at. After the ship got in, after we boarded we did a search, and there was nothing. One of the guys races sailboats, long distance, like Trans Pac, noticed quite the flotilla of boats in the bay, coming into the estuary. He commented it looked like opening day on the bay and it would be a wonder if some of the boats in the estuary didn't collide."

"So that was odd?"

"We weren't sure . . . but we started to give them a look. That was when a few of them opened fire on us. We were like pigeons at a carnival in the shooting gallery—just standing there to be picked off."

"Oh my god, Ryan!"

"Yeah. We were lucky only Keith got hit. If he hadn't been wearing his vest he'd be in a lot worse shape."

"Chopper pulled up over us and was radioing boat numbers he could see until they turned some of those weapons on him. They had an arsenal on those sailboats, we couldn't compete except they weren't all the best of sailors. Fortunately for us some of them had gotten seasick out in the ocean, we were better shots, even with our lower grade weapons than them, and we had sheer numbers."

"Did you get them all?"

Ryan shook his head. "We don't think so. Some of the boats turned and headed out to the bay and Coast Guard picked up the ones they could—but they don't have that many boats available. Several other choppers came in, but short of sinking a boat there's not much you can do with that many. We're talking maybe sixty boats out there."

"So they what? Met the ship out in the ocean and offloaded the weapons?"

Ryan nodded. "Their only mistake, at first, was for all the sailboats to enter the bay and head into Alameda. If they'd sailed some to Monterey, Santa Cruz, Pacifica, even sat outside the Gate for a day or so we'd never have gotten them or at least not as many as we did."

"And your source?"

"Funny thing that . . . he disappeared."

"Then, do you think you were set up?"

"No doubt about it. And that gets me to you, Ms. McKenna."

"Me?"

Ryan reached for her hand. "This is not me being overprotective or thinking you can't take care of yourself."

"Uh-huh." Kelly couldn't help but think of all the times Ryan tried to stand between her and trouble. And how many times they'd argued about his protective streak. It was never going to stop—that need to protect her went beyond their time together in this lifetime. It was a blood oath he'd taken many centuries and lifetimes before. He couldn't help it, and she knew that, but still, sometimes . . ."Yes?"

"I don't know for sure, okay? But the informant, he made contact with me. He may have been watching me and by extension, you so, Kelly, please, please, please be extra careful. Make sure you're aware of your surroundings, of anyone strange around you. Just be extra vigilant. Please."

CHAPTER THIRTY-TWO

Natalie was starting to make her dinner when Kelly and Ryan walked into the kitchen a few hours later. With a glance at the couple, the redhead conveyed exactly how she felt about Ryan's presence. *That* was never going to change. And neither was Kelly going to ask Ryan to make his visits a bit fewer and far between. Chances were after Kelly gave Natalie the heads up to be a bit more cognizant of who was around her, Natalie would feel she had a little more ammunition to have Ryan around less.

"So, Natalie. How goes it?" Kelly tried to ask nonchalantly.

After turning, she looked the couple up and down, and she answered, "Fine."

"Whatcha making?" Ryan asked as he pulled out a kitchen chair and sat down.

"Baked potato."

"And?"

Natalie looked over at him with a decided stink-eye look. "Just the potato."

With a look at Ryan that spoke volumes about what she really thought, Kelly cut into the conversation. "Natalie likes authentic baked potatoes and cooking them in the microwave ruins the flavor, right, Natalie?"

"Right."

Taking a breath, Kelly sat in another chair facing Natalie. "So, Natalie, there's something we wanted to mention to you."

Fork held upright, Natalie spun to look at them. "Look, if

you're going to tell me you are getting married and I have to move out I hope you know I expect a certain amount of notice. And since I've only been here a short time I expect—"

"It's nothing like that, Natalie." Ryan cut her off.

Kelly knew that while her tenant was pretty darn good at scamming things out of people, being called on something, cut off mid-rant, was not something she was used to. If there was one thing Kelly had learned over the past few months, it was how to out Natalie, Natalie . . . always be prepared for the most outlandish response, demand or solution to a problem. Always be ready for Natalie to expect some sort of special accommodation because she saw herself as a delicate flower. And maybe she was. But what they needed to tell her tonight needed to be done in a way that wouldn't send the other woman off the deep end.

They'd decided to raise the issue in general terms rather than a potential incident due to Ryan's job. While not outright lying, they opted for a version of the truth that would work for a woman, like Natalie, with an otherwise very active imagination.

"Natalie," Kelly began. "I'm not sure if you've heard the news reports . . ."

"I don't listen to the news. It's too depressing."

"Generally I'd agree with you. However, what we're . . . what's happened . . . well, there have been some incidents here in Marin that you probably should be aware of."

Hand on hip, fork sticking out to the side, Natalie asked, "What kind of things?"

"There's been some drug-related incidents."

"Oh, that." The hand holding the fork flashed up in front of Natalie like she was flipping a baton. "There's drug issues in San Rafael all the time."

"This time, though," Ryan put in, "it's more than just some sales."

"Of course it's more than sales. Anyone who knows anything knows that."

"Really?" Kelly was surprised to hear her roommate say that given how flighty she could be.

"Sure. I'd think being a cop and a big-time spy the two of you would know that."

"What do you hear, Natalie?" Kelly asked.

"They sometimes steal cars or license plates. And they get girls high and take advantage of them. That's why I don't drink when I go to parties."

Kelly found she couldn't help herself and asked, "Is that why you don't go to any at all?"

"I go to parties. If you remember, I went to yours and that police officer took me for a ride on his motorcycle."

"That's true," Kelly conceded. "But is that all you hear about with drugs . . . in San Rafael?"

"Isn't that enough? I'm surprised you two don't know about that."

"We do know about these things, Natalie," Ryan dryly told her. "Lately though there's a bit more going on. There have been some instances of women being attacked and sometimes being injected with one of the more popular street drugs."

With that, Natalie walked over to the table, fork held upright, and a bright light in her eyes. "You mean like sex trafficking?"

"There could be an element of that, yes."

"Wow."

"So," Kelly looked at Ryan for support, and when he nodded, she continued, "we want you to just be aware of your surroundings. If you hear or see anyone or anything strange, make note of it and then move on. If it feels just really uncomfortable, tell someone. Okay?"

"Should I call the police?" she whispered.

With another look at Ryan, because they both knew of

Natalie's penchant for telling stories, Kelly carefully chose her words. "If you really and truly feel that there is danger and no one else is around you, then yes, call the police. But nothing should happen. After all, we're in Red Oak and the problems are in San Rafael, right?"

"Right. But we *are* the next town over and the criminal element can find their way here too, right?"

"That's possible," Ryan told her. "But based on what we've heard nothing should happen. We just want you to be aware of what's going on around you."

Natalie winked. "Got it. Well, my potato is done so I'm going to go eat."

With that, she got up, turned off the oven, took out the potato, and began to prepare it to eat. With a shrug, Kelly looked at Ryan and nodded to the doorway.

Ryan rose and offered her his hand. As they walked through the door, he moved his hand to her waist and pulled her close.

"Do you think we got through to her?"

"Short of outright telling her someone might take a shot at her? Yup."

"Ry, you don't believe that, do you?"

"No. It will most likely be nothing. I just feel better knowing the two of you are on guard about anything or anyone strange being around you."

"And with Natalie, you better believe she'll be very aware and by tomorrow night there will be three stories about how she escaped with her life at least six times."

Chapter Thirty-three

"So how goes it in Boringville?" Chris asked Jess, her voice as snotty as ever.

In an attempt to ignore the blonde, even though it would be reviewed during briefing, Jess looked over the hot sheet.

"Know why they call it a *hot* sheet, Jess?"

Jess shrugged.

"Because hot cops use it to catch bad guys. Know why you don't need to bother looking at it?"

Even though Chris regularly taunted the other women dispatchers with equally as snide and really ludicrous comments, that last one caught Jess off guard. "You got me curious, Chris."

"Because you'll never get near someone hot."

Jess shrugged again and started to put her duty bag away and set up for her upcoming shift.

"I'm serious, Jess. You can't really think that your plumber with his butt crack hanging out is remotely sexy, can you? Admit it, you want a cop, but you just don't have what it takes."

Jess turned and watched Chris thrust what existed of her chest out. It took all her will power not to call Chris the other women's pet name for her — zipper. "Don's got substance, Chris. He's smart, he's a great conversationalist and he's a carpenter, not a plumber."

"He's got substance," Chris mimicked. "But I bet he's a wet noodle in the sack."

"You'll never know."

"You're right—because I only do cops."

"Yeah . . . and they do you because you're handy . . . and then they go home to their girlfriends and wives. They take you out in their cars, they take you to back alleys on patrol, but I don't see any of them setting up house with you let alone asking you to marry them."

With that, Jess turned and walked out of dispatch into briefing. Jess may not have a lot to say, but when she said it, it zinged and hit its mark.

Briefing was the usual round of summation of the last three shifts, updates on reports the officers were writing, and a review of the hot sheet. Jess had already pretty much memorized the cars they were fairly certain would likely turn up in Red Oak. At least the colors and makes along with the first letters of the license plates. That was just routine with her.

"And fire has asked us to keep an eye on this one." Sgt. White brought her attention back to the table. "Apparently there's been a few suspicious fires popping up inside buildings. What makes it especially odd is that they're inside the ductwork areas. Could be bad wiring setting off old insulation, because the buildings are in the older part of town, but there's a pattern forming. They seem to be moving down Grand."

Jess made notes and studied the map of where the fires had occurred. They wouldn't respond outright, but if a fire grew or if there were more than usual dangerous materials, the department'd be called on for traffic control.

Back in dispatch, she brought up a Google map of the area and highlighted where the fires had been set.

Chris meandered over to Jess's console and hip bumped her chair. "Doing your homework?"

Before Jess could answer, the shift units started out on the street, calling their 10-7s, in service, as they pulled away from the station. Jess confirmed each on-duty call and marked them in service in the CAD.

"You're soooo detail oriented," Chris nastily purred from the other side of the room. If there wasn't some decent traffic or a larger incident, it was going to be a long, long night with Chris in the same room as her. It occurred to Jess that she had enough vacation on the books to take three or four months' time off. That was one way to avoid Chris's spiteful attacks. Someone should have done something about the woman years ago.

It was quiet for a few minutes both from the radio and from Chris's side of the room. For a moment or two Jess thought that maybe tonight wouldn't be all that bad . . . maybe it would be so quiet Chris would take off early . . . or maybe even go on a suck-along with one of the guys . . . yeah, that would be the ticket . . . they all knew Chris gave blow jobs to the officers she rode along with . . . maybe . . .

"So is she a wimp or up to something?" Chris broke into Jess's thoughts about finding some peace in the station.

"Huh?"

"Weren't you listening?"

"Not really."

Chris sighed. "I asked you if you thought McKenna was a major wimp or was she getting something out of that crazy roommate of hers."

"You'd have to ask Kelly."

"Oh like she'd tell me."

Once again, Jess shrugged.

"What! Is that gonna be your main answer tonight? A shrug for everything?" Chris all but shrieked.

Jess turned and looked at her. "Chris, I don't know what your problem is, but yelling here in dispatch, particularly about something that is neither your or mine's concern is not how I plan to spend the night. And why do you care about Kelly's living situation?"

"Whatever. The roommate is crazy. She's nuts."

"And you know this how?"

"I hear things. In the hallway. Before briefing, in the gym. She calls here almost every shift with some weird-assed story. Everyone knows that woman is driving McKenna crazy. Maybe crazy enough that she's going to have to quit or even kill that Nat person."

"Oh, Chris, come off it." What Jess wouldn't give for a rolling traffic stop . . . or even a car that had been parked for more than three days so she could run something and have some kind of radio traffic.

"Would you put up with the crap that McKenna is with that nutball roommate?"

"What you would or wouldn't do is immaterial, Chris."

"Yeah, well, I think she's putting up with that Nat person to get that fed she dates to ask her to marry him. Either that or she's hoping one of our guys will want to step in and rescue her from the crazy lady."

"Chris. Natalie isn't crazy. She just has some issues, she's just . . . just . . ."

"Crazy, Jess. She's just crazy and you know what happens to crazy people. Well, I'm taking my dinner break," Chris announced as she stood up and headed out of the dispatch office.

Jess had already turned to her monitor to catch up on where her units were and the calls they were on. It was a bit out of character for Chris to be so interested in someone else's situation, particularly Kelly's with her roommate. Yeah, Natalie was a bit over the top, but as she'd told Chris, it was Kelly's problem. She'd do whatever she needed to. And Chris was wrong—there was no way Kelly was using Natalie to get Ryan to move in with her. If anything, it was more likely Ryan, with his protective streak regarding Kelly, that would be the one to suggest they move in together than the other way around.

Once again, she shrugged. It wasn't her problem.

Chris, on the other hand, was a problem . . . every female in the department's problem, and it was going to be a long quarter if they had to work together for most of it. It was a blissful half-hour while Chris was on her dinner break. While there was some radio traffic, it wasn't a very heavy night. Mainly it was officers calling in license plates on different vehicles that had either committed a traffic violation or on the brink of one. No arrests, no drunk drivers . . . for the most part, it was a pretty easy evening. Jess had a passing thought . . . hope . . . that Chris would go on one of her famous ride-alongs.

The pace of the evening was interrupted by a frantic 911 call . . . from Natalie.

CHAPTER THIRTY-FOUR

Without calling Chris to come back to dispatch from her lunch break both because it probably wasn't that high a level of a call and out of protectiveness for Kelly and just not wanting to deal with Chris, Jess handled the dispatch as discretely as possible. If Sergeant White said to go out over the air with it, she would. Absent his order to do so, she was going to handle it on the QT.

While she quickly dispatched officers via private CAD messages, she called her sergeant. "We just got a rather panicked 911 call from McKenna's roommate. Until I get further I've sent them CAD messages and plan to call McKenna on her cell. That sound right?"

"Good plan. Send me the 20 and I'll head over there myself," he told her, asking for Kelly's address when he asked for the 20.

Disconnecting from White, she called Kelly.

"McKenna."

"Kelly, it's Jess."

"Hey, what's up?

Jess swallowed and quickly organized her thoughts. "We just got a 911 from Natalie."

"Natalie? My Natalie?"

"Yeah, we have units rolling but I wanted to give you a heads up in case you want to roll that way."

"Roll what way? Jess, spit it out. What's going on?"

"We got a 911 from your house and I could hear a woman whispering, asking for help. She said that there was someone trying to break in the house before the line disconnected."

"Oh crap. I'm on my way. Can you let Sgt. White know and . . ."

"He's already on it. They know you'll be coming. And since Chris is in the station I've sent all messages over CAD. So far she's not on it."

"Thanks, Jess."

A flood of thoughts ran through Kelly's mind. Had Adrian gotten out of jail and somehow slipped back into his stalking persona? She shook her head on that thought—she was supposed to be notified if and when he was released. Was it someone from the D-1 gang trying to get to Ryan directly or through her? Given that had happened earlier today with Ryan, that was definitely a possibility. Then again, could it be someone she had arrested who had had a short jail term and now wanted revenge? Or was it some sort of past life connection breaking through into the present? It didn't much matter which—what mattered was something was happening at her house.

"Jess, you've tried to call her back, right?"

"Of course. We've been trying, no answer."

"Oh, okay. Please, keep trying."

"Where are you?"

"I'm heading from the southern end of town, I should be there in maybe seven minutes max."

"Take it slow and safe. White and two units are pulling up to your house now."

"Keep me posted. I know you're on the radio, but keep me posted."

"You got it."

Kelly and two more units pulled up outside the house. She saw the sergeant and two of the Red Oak PD officers had exited their vehicles and were approaching the house. The sergeant signaled to the other two to approach from either side and they started to surround the house.

She quickly sent a private CAD to Jess that she was on scene and exited her vehicle. White signaled to her to approach him.

"What's going on? Have you been able to reach Natalie?"

"So far it's quiet — we're setting up around the house and will start assessing."

"Jess said Natalie told her someone was trying to break in."

"Uh-huh."

"I need to call Ryan."

"Do you think it was him?"

Kelly looked over White's shoulder and shook her head. "No. He's in the city tonight. But I need to let him know that something . . . well, he's working this case and in case one of those suspects is out and about I need to give him a heads up, but I want to be sure Natalie and Ginny, my cat, are okay. I guess I should have told you as well but it didn't seem that critical."

"Step on over to the street and call your guy and let us handle the approach to the house, okay?"

Before Kelly could answer, Natalie came running out of the house. "Help! Help!" The redhead sounded hysterical.

"Natalie!" Kelly called her. "Over here."

"Kelly! Oh my god, Kelly. I was so scared."

Kelly tried to draw Natalie over to her car and protection on the side away from the house. "Natalie, come on, we have to get you away from the house."

"Why?"

Kelly stopped in her tracks. "Why? In case the intruder is in the bushes or somehow got in the house."

"Oh. Well, I don't think there's anyone there."

"Did you see them leave? Did you hear anything?"

"No. But I'm not so sure."

"Sure that they left or are still around?" White asked from behind them.

"Well, that I really heard an intruder." Natalie coyly looked up at the sergeant. "You see I'm so used to Kelly's boyfriend hanging around—he's *always* over—that when I had some time by myself in the house by myself for a change I *think* I heard noises I never heard before."

"Natalie. You called 911 and reported someone was trying to break in."

"Yes, well, I heard a noise, but it could have been a tree branch hitting the house. Like I said, Ryan is always here and I think I just never heard that noise before and then when I did I jumped to conclusions."

Kelly looked to her sergeant, wondering if he would hold her accountable for her roommate's actions if it turned out to be nothing.

"Natalie, did you actually *hear* a noise?"

"Well, it could have been the TV."

"Ms . . . Natalie." White drew her attention. "What did you hear?"

"Wellll, actually, I think it was the TV."

The sergeant blew out a frustrated breath before keying his radio. "All units clear."

"Copy?" Jess couldn't keep the question out of her voice.

"Will call you in a few," he told her.

Kelly rounded on her roommate. "Natalie, are you sure?"

"Yeah. I put on this old movie and the woman in it was alone in a house and she heard something and it scared me. Maybe if Ryan wasn't here all the time or your cat didn't sneak around I wouldn't have been afraid."

"McKenna, you want me to check the house anyway?"

Kelly considered her options—and her private concerns. Natalie might have read some things about Kelly in the paper, but she didn't know the whole story. She didn't know about Adrian and his attempts on her life. He was supposed to be in jail and she was supposed to have notice when he was up for parole, but the system had been known to fail in that task now and again. And she only knew a small bit about Ryan's investigation, only what they'd told her earlier that night. It could have been Natalie's movie, or it could have been either one of those situations.

"It might be a good idea."

White nodded. He was aware of both of Kelly's concerns. "Better to be safe than sorry."

As her sergeant finished up his check, Natalie came to stand beside Kelly. "I'm glad it was nothing."

"Me too."

"And you agree, don't you, that it would be a good idea to tell Ryan he shouldn't stay here anymore. If he hadn't been around so much . . ."

"No. It's not a good idea."

"Well, then the cat has to go."

"No, Natalie, Ginny doesn't have to go—and I'm telling you right now, I won't be very happy if anything . . . *anything* at all . . . happens to Ginny. You knew I had a cat and a boyfriend when you moved in. You knew it was a packaged deal. I suggest you resign yourself to those conditions or maybe renting from me isn't your best situation."

"But . . ."

Kelly had enough. "It's my house, Natalie. My name is on the mortgage, not yours. I pay most of the mortgage, you only pay a very small portion which includes utilities. You rent a room and a bathroom and have access to a few common areas, end of story. And while I don't mind coming out on a legitimate 911 call, in the future make sure it's not your TV that has you freaked out."

"Someone could have been breaking in."

"Yes, they could. It's just embarrassing when it's a call from my house that turns out to be a television show that freaked someone out."

"Maybe this isn't the best situation for me." She didn't sound resigned — rather, she sounded like she'd thrown out a challenge to Kelly, a troublesome challenge. A shiver raced down Kelly's spine, not unlike the ones she'd gotten just before Adrian would engage in one of his stalking actions. For a moment, a brief sliver of time, Kelly could have sworn she saw Clarissa, her former boss at the accounting firm, the woman who killed two of her co-workers there, standing in Natalie's place. Kelly blinked, and once again, it was Natalie standing quite clearly in front of her.

"You need to decide what's right for you, Natalie. Right now I need to get back on patrol."

With that, Kelly turned and headed toward her patrol car. With her hand on the door, she stopped and looked back to the house. She lowered her head a moment before turning and heading back inside. "Ginny? Gin-Gin?"

Inside the house, Ginny came running and wound her way around Kelly's ankles with a soft meow.

"Hey, pretty girl." Kelly reached down and picked her cat up, feeling along her fur to be sure she was okay. Ginny immediately started purring and head butting Kelly, letting her know all was well in her world.

Kelly turned Ginny in her arms. "Would you like a treat?"

Ginny's purr became a shade louder.

Setting the cat down, Kelly reached for the bag of treats and gave the cat a few. "When you're done why don't you head into my room and catch some zzzs, huh?"

Intent on her treats, Ginny didn't look up but twitched her tail at Kelly. Kelly stood there a moment longer before heading out of the house without speaking to Natalie again. She didn't know if she should be pissed or concerned that maybe Natalie had heard something and whoever it was left before anyone arrived.

"D-18, 10-7." She called into dispatch to let them know she was back in service. Cruising down the street, back to her assigned beat, Kelly thought about Natalie's words. Maybe it was time to ask the redheaded woman to leave. She'd only been there several months, but she had been a disruptive energy from day one. As Kelly thought about it, it seemed from the moment Natalie answered the ad she'd been disruptive. While her incessant need for attention and dramatics made for some chuckles at work, the bottom line was Kelly was on probation, and she couldn't afford the never-ending distractions caused by Natalie. Tonight was one of the most blatant. Yes, it could have been an intruder, but after checking the house and Natalie's admission, it was pretty clear it was just another of the other woman's plays for attention.

Tomorrow Kelly'd walk the perimeter of the house just to be sure there were no strange footprints or signs of an intruder around. And then . . . then she'd have to decide what to do about Natalie unless, of course, Natalie decided she would be moving on by herself.

Back at the station, just before the end of her shift, Kelly wandered toward dispatch. Seeing Chris had already left, she entered and sat across from Jess.

"High drama at chez McKenna tonight, huh?" Jess asked her with a smile.

Kelly shook her head. "She's got issues."

"Natalie?"

"Yeah. You heard, right?"

"It was her TV or something like that."

"Yeah. She tried to say that if Ryan wasn't around so much it wouldn't be so noticeable when he's not there."

"Oh come on."

"I know, right? And then she tried to say that both Ryan and Ginny had to go."

"No way!"

"Yeah. She never stops. Sometimes she, I don't know. I've never met anyone like her before. She can seem perfectly normal and then she comes up with these pronouncements and expectations."

"You think she's an escapee from a lunatic asylum?"

Kelly chuckled. "You could be on to something there. Anyway, tonight when we were leaving she started to insist that Ryan not come over anymore and I give Ginny away. I told her it was my house and she knew about Ryan and Ginny when she moved in and if she didn't like it she could move."

"If you don't mind my saying so, it's about time."

"Yeah, well, we'll see what she does. With Natalie I've found it will be whatever eeks out the most drama for her."

During a lull in radio traffic and calls, Kelly called Ryan and updated him on what had happened.

"So there was no sign of any intruder?"

"None that I could see tonight. Sgt. White detailed the outside with me and the two of us checked the inside of the house. I'll give it a closer look in daylight tomorrow — when Natalie is out — and see if there's any sign of attempted entry."

"Good idea. Let me ask you though . . ."

"Could Natalie have faked it and had enough smarts to go out and mess with the windows?"

"Got it in one. Could she? Would she?"

"With Natalie you never know. But that doesn't mean a check of the outside isn't a bad idea."

"If you wait till I get up there I'll help you lay some tracking devices — some wires and whatever to put on the windows just in case it was someone and they come back . . . or if down the line someone does decide that's something they want to do."

"Thanks, Ry. I hadn't thought about that. That's a good plan. And I figure installing an alarm system is a good idea as well."

"I can't believe I'm back to Adrian 101."

Natalie was waiting for Kelly when she came home the next morning. Normally Kelly had a few minutes peace to unwind before being accosted by Natalie and her latest round of needs. Today, not so much.

"Hi." Natalie greeted her.

"Hey. You're up and about early."

"Actually I didn't sleep last night."

"Oh? Well, you wear sleepless really well."

"What do you mean?"

"No bags under your eyes — you're lucky it doesn't show on you."

"Oh . . . well, I did get a little sleep. But it was with one eye open."

"Mmm." Kelly moved to head down the hall to her room.

"I was thinking."

Kelly turned. "Yes?"

"I need a gun. I was thinking a Magnum Forty-four like Dirty Harry has."

"A Mag . . . Natalie, do you know how big and heavy that kind of gun is?"

"Isn't that the name of the game? She with the biggest gun wins?"

"Uh. Can we talk about this later?"

"I'm going to buy it today."

Well then, guess we'll talk about it now. She gestured to the kitchen. "Let's talk about this."

Knowing this probably wasn't going to be a quick conversation, Kelly pulled out some milk to heat up some hot chocolate. "Natalie, guns are nothing to be taken lightly."

"You have one."

"Yes, for work."

"And Ryan has one."

"Yes, for his work."

"Well, I need one."

"Natalie, your job doesn't require you . . ."

"But if I'm going to be safe around here I need one."

The kettle whistled, giving Kelly the chance to stand up and gather her thoughts. While she stirred her hot chocolate, she waited to see if Natalie would say anything further. When she didn't, Kelly took her cup and sat down. "Natalie, guns are nothing to take lightly. If you have one you need to be ready to use it."

"I will."

"No. Natalie—really use it. If you are picking it up in self-defense you need to be ready to use it to kill."

"Oh, I'd just wound whoever."

"It doesn't work that way. Natalie, you need to be ready to shoot to kill because the other guy will be ready to kill you. And you need to be ready to fire and make it count because bad guys, if they see you with a gun, if they have their own they're going to shoot to kill you or they're going to try to get yours. Guns aren't toys and people who aren't ready, really ready to use them, are walking targets."

"I know that."

"Do you?"

"Yes. You may think I only watch game and reality shows, but I watch some police shows too."

"Uh-huh." To keep from commenting on the police shows, Kelly took a long swallow of her hot chocolate.

"I do. I even know some of the code talk you guys do."

Kelly almost spit out her drink. "Oh?"

"Sure. One Mary 7, proceed to Sepulveda and some other street."

"One Mary . . . 7 . . ." Oh no . . . Kelly thought. "Natalie, you're watching reruns of CHiPs?"

With a proud smile, the other woman answered, "Yes. You don't think I'd waste my time on some unrealistic show like CIS, do you?"

"CIS? You mean CSI?"

"Whichever. Everyone knows Erik Estrada was really a highway patrol officer who played an actor."

This was Natalie at her finest. And Kelly was too tired to continue with her nonsense. "Look, I don't think you having a gun is a great idea . . ."

"You just want to think you're special because you have one. You think you're so special because you have a boyfriend who's a spy and you have a gun, but you aren't. You're jealous of me because I can wear perfume and pretty dresses to work and you have to wear that ugly uniform."

Kelly pondered the change in Natalie. Clearly her world view was even more distorted than Kelly previously thought.

"Natalie, for what it's worth, when I worked as a reporter and then in the accounting firm I wore dresses and if I thought perfume was attractive I would have worn it then too. I don't think you should have a gun because, as far as I know, you don't know how to handle one."

"Well, I'm going to learn."

"Sure." Now she really was too tired to continue the conversation. "Look, let's table this discussion till the weekend and then if you still think you want to get a gun I'll take you out to the range. We'll have them outfit you with one that both the range master and I think would be a good one for you and I'll teach you how to shoot it."

"Fine. I'll look at my calendar and see when I have time to fit it in."

"When you . . . sure. Fine. Right now I need to get some sleep."

CHAPTER THIRTY-FIVE

Any hope that Natalie would forget about her plan to get a gun was quickly dashed when she joined Kelly and Ryan in the kitchen early Saturday afternoon. Dressed in black camo pants, a faux camouflage sweater with sales tag intact, and knee-high black boots, Natalie strode into the kitchen. After giving Ryan a derisive look, she busied herself with her coffeemaker—not the *Nespresso* Ryan had bought Kelly for Christmas the last year, but your basic, every day, *Mr. Coffee*. When Ryan lifted a brow in question at Natalie's outfit, it was all Kelly could do not to laugh. Clearly Natalie thought clothing made the woman when it came to going out to the range.

After starting her coffee, Natalie turned. "So, Kelly, what time are we leaving to go out on the range?"

"Um, well . . ."

"You aren't dressed for it. We should get going soon, right?"

"Um, well . . ."

"We are going to buy me a gun today, aren't we?"

"Um, well . . ."

Sounding like a petulant eight-year-old, Natalie whined, "You promised."

"I didn't promise it would be today—just that at some point, when it seemed right, we'd do."

"Well, I'm ready to go today."

"And we'll go. Just give us a few minutes and we'll head out, right, Ryan? Be sure you've got your license for ID, okay?"

"I don't have a license. And why does *he* have to come?"

"But you do have California ID, don't you?" Ryan ignored her question about his participation.

"Of course I do. Do you?"

If she meant to intimidate Ryan, it so was not going to work.

If she meant to entertain him by providing some comedic relief, she was going a great job, but the laughter would have to come later.

"Of course I do. And I also have a concealed weapon permit. Do you?"

"I'll be buying one on the range today."

"Well. Good. Ryan, finish your coffee so we can head out."

"He's not coming, is he?" Since Ryan hadn't addressed it, Natalie turned to Kelly.

"You got a problem with that?" Ryan answered before Kelly could, his tone clearly intimated that she'd better not. Fortunately for Natalie, she got the message, at least for the moment.

"Well, great. I'll go get my ID." Natalie stopped at the door. "Say, do I need one of those leather things to put it in?"

"Holster? No. No. We're just going to show you how to load and a little about firing, that's all."

"And I'm buying a gun. There is no way I'm going to be caught here in the house unprotected again." Kelly watched as Ryan bit his lip clearly in an effort to keep from laughing as Natalie flounced out of the room.

Ryan leaned back in his chair and looked down the hall. When Natalie was safely out of hearing, Ryan leaned back in and toward Kelly. "I take it you didn't tell her about the background check and waiting period? And just so I'm clear, you didn't really promise to buy her a gun?"

"No. No how, no way. It's a good bet she can't afford one

even if the sound doesn't have her ears ringing for a few days. And the smell of the used powder will definitely put her off. What did you think of the outfit?"

"Nice. Really nice. I'm thinking you'd look pretty good in a similar one."

Kelly slid over to him and, with her hand on his crotch, answered, "Yeah?"

"Uh-huh, and even better having it peeled off of you."

"Michaels, you say the nicest things."

"I don't know why *he* had to come," Natalie groused a short time later at the shooting range.

Kelly sighed and shook her head rather than answer until Natalie persisted. "Kelly, why?"

"We routinely come out here to practice. And since he's also a firearms instructor for his agency it makes sense you'd want to learn from the best, wouldn't you? And you did agree it was a good idea before we left."

"I suppose. It's just . . . well, you're the only friend I have and we never do anything together."

Kelly looked over at Ryan and then back to Natalie, narrowing her eyes at Natalie. "You've got friends, Natalie. What about Martha? And now you're dating what's his name."

Natalie shrugged. "Martha and I aren't speaking right now. She's jealous because I've got such a good situation with you, even with Ryan always there."

It didn't make sense. There was no way the redheaded woman was making sense. And worse, it gave Kelly a chill of foreboding. She shook off the feeling as Ryan came back over to them.

"I thought a twenty-two was a good one to start Natalie off with."

"A twenty-two?" Natalie wrinkled her nose. "Is that what you have, Kelly?"

"Me? No, I have a Sig Sauer."

"Then that's what I want."

"Um, mine's police issue."

"Then what do you have?" she asked Ryan.

"Me? I carry a Glock."

"And is yours police issued?"

"Uh, no. It's my preference . . . based on using guns for years. Once you've handled one for a while and know just what they can do . . ."

"I know what they can do!" Natalie snapped. "They can kill so I can protect myself. I want a Sig sober."

"Sauer," Kelly muttered.

"Natalie." Ryan tried to say as patiently as possible. "The range master isn't going to allow a total novice out there with any kind of major firepower. You either use the twenty-two or we leave."

She got a mulish expression on her face, one Kelly'd seen before right before Natalie started in with her drama. Once again, a chill raced through her. She closed her eyes a moment to see if she picked up anything relating to a past life, but nothing registered. This shooting lesson wasn't going to lead to anything good, so why where they here doing this? With a mental shrug, Kelly reminded herself that if she and Ryan weren't here with Natalie, the woman would go out and find a way herself to do this. It was much better to control the situation as far as they could.

The threesome started down the short walkway into the shooting area.

"It's ugly in here," Natalie flatly stated as she took in the heavy cinder-blocked hallway. A moment later the sounds of gunfire began to penetrate the thick walls and the smell of burnt powder evident. "And it stinks. I thought it was supposed to be nice and clean and appealing."

"That's gunfire for you," Ryan dryly commented.

"I don't like it."

"Um, do you want to leave?" Kelly couldn't keep the hopefulness out of her voice.

"No. We're here and I want to feel safe."

"I'll take it," Ryan told the women.

"*You're* going to teach me?"

"You want the best, don't you?" Kelly was feeling more and more exasperated.

"I suppose."

"Good. Kelly go on and get a few rounds in. I'll explain gun safety to Natalie."

Fighting the urge to watch Ryan and Natalie's interaction, Kelly took a position at the counter, put on her ear protectors, checked her weapon, and began to fire. Even over the sound of rapid fire, she could hear an occasional squawk from her roommate. Whether it was the repeated concussion of the weapons firing which were bothering Natalie or her disagreement with whatever instructions Ryan was giving her, she figured she'd hear all about it . . . with a little extra drama thrown in . . . later.

As Kelly reeled her target in Natalie and Ryan walked up.

"You only hit it once?" Natalie sounded incredulous.

"No," Ryan explained, "if you notice the hole is a pretty good size. Kelly hit the target in the same place each time."

"Well, what good is that?"

Kelly looked at Ryan. "It means the shot is dead on."

"Yeah, but don't you have to hit people a bunch of times to kill them?"

"Uh, one good shot in a significant organ is enough," Ryan dryly told her. "So, do you want to fire a few times?"

Natalie shrugged. "Does it always smell this bad?"

It was Kelly's turn to shrug. "I never really noticed."

"Okay, Nat, let's get these ear protectors on." Ryan plopped the headpiece over her ears and turned her toward the firing line before she could protest that she wasn't a bug.

After firing wild a good six or seven dozen times, Natalie put the gun down. "It's getting too heavy for me."

"Yeah, it can get heavy," Kelly commiserated.

"Let me see how many holes I got in it."

Ryan obliged by reeling the target in. Not surprisingly, there wasn't one mark on the silhouette.

Nonplussed by it, Natalie told them, "See this is why I need a bigger gun, like Kelly's Sig syrup."

"Sauer."

"Whatever."

CHAPTER THIRTY-SIX

Kelly joined Ryan on the couch in the den and sat with a sigh.

"Kelly, my love?" Ryan said as he put his arm around her.

"Yes, dear."

"Kelly, promise me the next time Natalie decides she wants to learn to fire a gun, you wait till I'm out of town before you agree to go?"

"She didn't want to learn to fire a gun, Ry, she wanted to buy one for protection."

"Uh-huh, and the difference is?"

"You seriously don't know?"

"For a normal person, no. Any sane person would make sure they knew proper gun safety before even considering firing one the first time."

"Ah, see there's that sane part. And seriously, would you want Natalie out there on her own looking for a gun?"

Ryan started to laugh.

"What?"

"I can see it now . . . dark alley, Natalie appropriately dressed in black turtleneck, black jeans, knee-high black boots and a black scarf covering her too red hair."

"It's not red, Ryan. It's auburn."

"Yeah . . . not any color that occurs in nature."

"And she wouldn't be caught dead in jeans . . . they'd be nicely pressed linen slacks."

"But definitely black."

"Definitely black."

"So there she be, in a dark alley, money gripped tightly in her fist, making an exchange."

It was Kelly's turn to laugh. "Uh-huh, and she'd wrinkle her nose and tell the guy that the next time they did business they'd need to do it in a cleaner, better smelling place."

"Seriously, you don't think she'll go out and buy a gun on her own, do you?"

Kelly shivered. "I hope not. The whole registration process would probably put her off. With her luck I can see her hitting someone or something really, really bad. The good news on that score is that she probably doesn't make enough money to buy one . . . at least she's always going on about how broke she is."

"Let's hope so."

"Anyway, I need to get going . . . you staying up here?"

Ryan quirked a brow. "After today?"

"She may not notice you're here."

"Natalie doesn't miss much, including things that aren't there like hordes of ants."

"Well, there is that."

"Actually I need to head into the city. We have an early meeting on the shooting earlier this week first thing in the morning."

"Mm?"

"Debrief, who saw what, next move."

"Got ya."

"And you?"

"Hopefully Natalie will have forgotten her whole need to buy a gun. With any luck yesterday and time at the range put her off that subject."

"One can only hope." Ryan paused a moment, clearly thinking over his next words. "Kelly . . ."

"Mm?"

"I'm not telling you what to do. And I'm not going all

protective mode on you, okay?"

"Uh-huh . . . but?"

"No but. Just a thought."

"Uh-huh."

"Natalie."

"Yes."

He swallowed, clearly nervous, clearly aware of his history of trying to protect her from anything and everything life tried to throw at her.

Kelly turned and put a hand on his cheek. "What?"

"She's disruptive."

"Yes, she is."

"She's a drama queen."

"DQV."

"DQ . . ."

"Drama queen victim. She loves her drama and always sees herself as the victim."

"Yes, she does. Kelly, she's not Susan."

"Not even close."

"She's . . ."

"Ry, are you trying to work up the nerve to tell me that maybe I need to be thinking it's time to ask her to leave?"

"Yeah."

"We're on the same page . . . as much as I hate to admit it I've been thinking about it since the day she moved in."

"I've been hoping you'd have that talk since she moved in."

"Thing is, I kept thinking it was me . . . that I wasn't being patient or understanding or that I have a problem relating to people . . . but I feel myself tensing up, my stomach starting to churn every time she's around. Sometimes just the thought of her sends me over the top. Ryan, I don't think it's me. She's too needy, too demanding, too . . . too . . ."

"Crazy."

"Don't say that to her!" Kelly laughed. "One time I said something about crazy people and the kind of calls they make to the police and she got all twisted about how she wasn't crazy . . . like she thought I was talking about her."

"Were you?"

"No! That's the thing, it had nothing to do about her, but she made it about her. Like she makes everything about her."

"So?"

"So I think I'm going to talk to her tonight and tell her she either needs to stop the weirdness or she's going to have to move. She and her rules and OCD needs are too disruptive for me . . . she forgets it's my house . . . that I own it and her demands on my time and making changes here have to stop."

"I think you're on the right track."

"Thanks. So if you aren't going to be around tonight I'm thinking it would be a good time to do it."

"Call me when you're done . . . or if she goes sideways on you, call me and I'll come up."

"I will."

CHAPTER THIRTY-SEVEN

It wasn't a conversation she wanted to have and then to potentially be home alone with Natalie. There would be tears. There would be recriminations. In short, there would be drama. Natalie would be the victim of the piece and she'd *need* all kinds of soothing. By the time the redheaded woman came home from work, Kelly's stomach was in knots. She'd called Susan four times during the day and Susan listened, offered her condolences, and had a few bits of advice like offering to pay Natalie a refund on her rent if she'd leave early.

Like that would happen.

Ginny clearly, too, sensed her angst because she kept climbing up on Kelly's lap and purring as she did so. Whimsically during one chat with Ginny she told her pet feline how she'd read an article that a cat's purr was soothing and lowered blood pressure. Not that hers was high because of Natalie. Nope, not at all.

Okay . . . it probably was.

It seemed pretty clear to Kelly that Ginny understood a lot of what she said and that the cat had little liking for Natalie. When she narrowed those big green eyes of hers into tiny slits at the mention of Natalie's name, it was pretty clear how Ginny felt. Well, there was that and the fact that Ginny had peed in Natalie's shoes twice more in the past month without Kelly saying a word to either cat or human.

And she'd rehearsed what she was going to say — practicing on Susan in two of those four phone calls. Susan cheerfully agreed that she'd want to do the right thing and leave if

Kelly said those things to her.

And then it was showtime.

As usual, Natalie hurried into the house in a flurry — purse and book bag she carried flapping around her. Not that there were books in the book bag — Natalie was not a reader but whatever she carried in there sure did seem heavy.

"Natalie, hi!" Kelly came out of the den where she'd been watching out the window for Natalie's arrival. How Adrian could have spent years looking out or in windows to watch her seemed incredibly boring. She'd positioned herself behind the curtains maybe a half-hour before Natalie was due home and felt like a total nut peering out from the parted drapes to see when her roommate was heading up the walk. Despite telling herself at least a dozen times she'd hear the car door slam she maintained her post.

"Hi." Natalie sounded rather subdued as she walked through the door and hurried to her room.

"So, hey." Kelly followed Natalie a few steps down the hallway. "You got a few minutes?"

"No, not really."

"Um, well, I meant after you put your things down."

"No. I watch Jeopardy at seven and have to start my dinner and take my shower before it comes on."

"Oh, I see. Well, how about after Jeopardy?"

"Then it's Let's Make a Deal. I have my programs to watch."

"Hmm."

"Maybe before you leave for work on Saturday."

"It's kind of important."

"I need to relax after a day at work. Maybe you don't because you have a gun so you don't have to worry, but I have to relax."

Kelly had no idea what a gun had to do with relaxing except . . . well, maybe Natalie thought it meant she'd feel safe.

"We all do after work and that's part of what I want to talk to you about."

Natalie dropped her purse. "Well, I can tell you what will help me relax. Tell Ryan he can't stay here anymore and find a new home for your *cat*." With that, she picked up her purse, turned, and walked toward her room.

And now Kelly was pissed. Royally pissed. And it was going to go a long way toward evicting Natalie.

She took a long, slow, deep breath and then started down the hall after Natalie. "Natalie. We need to talk and we need to do it now. Let's go into the kitchen."

Natalie sighed. "I'm tired. I've had a long day. You have no idea what it's like to have to sit there for hours and look attractive and not even be able to google or do any kind of internet searches. To just sit there."

"No. I don't. But I do know what it's like to work a full day and just want to come home and unwind . . . and not be able to because of things going on in your home."

"Exactly. And I told you what would make it better for me."

Now she had it. She really had it.

"Natalie. Natalie, at this point your never-ending needs and demands are making my life difficult."

"Well, if you'd meet my needs for a change, things would be a lot better."

"I'm sure you think so, but, Natalie, I've told you before, this is my house . . . my mortgage, my house. You rent a room and a bathroom from me. You have kitchen privileges and can use the living room but this is my house and it's time for you to stop making demands for me to change my life to accommodate you."

Kelly watched as the redhead chewed the inside of her cheek for a moment just before she narrowed her eyes and squared her shoulders. "I'll have you know I had plenty of choices of where to live. Lots where they were more than happy to get rid of any animals and just be the two of us, but I decided to move in with you."

Kelly crossed her arms over her chest. "Really? Because you were falling over yourself to move in here. You were more than ready to give me a deposit before you even saw the room. And you knew when you moved in I have a cat and that I have a boyfriend who sometimes stays over. You made your choice and, Natalie, now you have to live with it . . . or not."

"Are you telling me to move out?"

This was her chance. One word . . . maybe two or three . . . and Natalie would be out of her house and life.

But this was Natalie. There would be drama and it wasn't drama Kelly wanted. Weighing her words carefully—not all that different from how she'd approach a guy with a gun at someone's head—Kelly took a breath. "It sounds more to me like you want to leave and don't know how to tell me that's what you want."

"Are you telling me to move out?" Natalie repeated.

"I'm telling you that you sound really unhappy and you need to make a decision of either staying here and not hassling me about Ginny or Ryan or moving on. If you can't do that then you need to find someplace where you'll be happy."

"Then you are telling me to move out."

"No, I'm telling you that you have to make a choice."

"I choose to stay here and to have you get rid of that cat and tell your boyfriend he can't stay here anymore."

"That's not going to happen, Natalie. You either live with me in my house the way I told you things were when you moved in or yes, you have to move out."

"Fine. You're throwing me out. I expect to have my thirty days' notice . . . in writing."

"No problem."

With that, the redhead huffed, turned, and headed down the hall and rather firmly shut the door to her room. In minutes Kelly heard the water turn on . . . it was going to be a night of a long bath followed by an extra-long shower. She knew it. She totally knew it. Even with a drought, Natalie was never going to put aside what she felt was her due and her creature comforts.

Kelly sat down to type up an iron-clad notice letter telling Natalie to get her ass out of her house.

CHAPTER THIRTY-EIGHT

Despite being way tired and needing to get some shut-eye herself, Kelly stayed up until she was relatively certain that Natalie had gone to sleep. Not that she was chicken . . . after all, she'd knocked on Natalie's door and handed her the move out letter as soon as it was done and Natalie was out of her bath and shower. The other woman hadn't said a word. Merely glared at her and took the letter. No, she didn't want Natalie to hear her on the phone to Ryan and Susan telling them what happened.

Maybe Susan would want to move back up to the Bay Area. That would certainly solve a multitude of problems . . .

Feeling like a teenager sneaking around the house after her mom and dad went to bed, Kelly tiptoed to her bedroom door and peered out. Not for the first time, she was glad her room was on the other side of the house from Natalie's. From the bed, Ginny watched her movements. There was no doubt in Kelly's mind the cat thought she was a total nut job. "Yeah, well, Ginny, if you had to deal with her as much as I do, you'd be tip-toeing around, too."

Ginny yawned. Clearly she felt no sympathy for her human's plight.

Curled up under her down comforter, Kelly dialed Susan's number.

"Lo."

"Suze! Oh, Suze, I have to talk to you! Are you awake? Can you talk?"

"Mmm, hmm. Let me turn off the TV." A moment later,

Susan was on the phone again. "What's up?"

"Natalie."

"What'd she do now?"

"She's moving out."

"Really?" Kelly could picture her best friend settling into her chair, crossing her leg underneath her butt, and getting ready for a good story.

"Really."

"So what? She walked in and said she's moving and you need to turn your life upside down this weekend when she's moving out after she uncleans everything she had cleaned?"

"No. Not quite. I told her to move out."

"You kicked her out?"

"I didn't kick her out in the cold or anything like that. I just told her I was tired of her constant demands and it didn't seem like she was ever going to be happy here and she was going to have to stop making unreasonable demands."

"Now really, Ms. McKenna. Since when is demanding someone tell their boyfriend to stop coming by and that they have to give up their cat unreasonable?" Susan quipped.

"For all the people I've met and situations I've been in she's definitely a one of a kind."

"I'm surprised it took you this long."

"Seriously?"

"Yes. Kelly, you may have been in some sticky situations . . . Adrian may have been your worst nightmare, but you didn't put up with his antics. You constantly held your ground and stood up to him. Yeah, you got scared at times, but you always held firm. This Natalie . . . she's really been something. So when is she moving out?"

"Well, by law I have to give her thirty days."

"Even though she's renting a room in your house? Doesn't the thirty days thing apply to like apartment rentals?"

"I don't know. I suppose I need to check it out, but just to be on the safe side I gave her a note and a definitive move out date. Knowing Natalie there will be ongoing drama and she'll probably try to pull something. She's never failed to see herself as the victim in anything and everything happening around her."

Kelly tentative asked, "Suz?"

"Mmm?"

"I'm not being too hard on her, am I? Unreasonable?"

"Kelly McKenna! Absolutely not! That is your house. She had a lot of nerve from the git-go demanding how you clean and then bringing her own . . . what did she call them? The *maids*? Then all her rules and that business about the two baths and two showers a day . . . and you have no idea what she was doing when you were at work either."

"That's true."

"Trust me, you did the right thing. That woman has to go and I seriously can't believe it took you that long. Now, my question for you . . . do you feel okay about her being there while you wait for her to move out?"

"You mean do I think she'll sabotage the house or cause some other kinds of problems?"

"Yeah."

Kelly considered that a moment. "No. No. She's a pain in the ass to deal with and she may have some outrageous stories — like the dirty and smelly guy with the supposed bomb — but she does have a strong sense of ethics. Like she gives me her rental check the night before it's due, she gets up and goes to work every day. She's never late. I don't know, sometimes I get the idea she's playing at being an adult, so I don't think she'd ever destroy anything. She doesn't get mad . . . she just tries to manipulate things to her way and if she doesn't get it right away, she just tries again. So no, I don't think she'd do anything destructive."

"Okay, cause I could come up and stay till she moves out."

"Suz . . . you don't need an excuse to come up. I'd love to have you here even for a few days. I miss you, girlfriend. Talking on the phone and email and texting just aren't the same as curling up in the den having hot chocolate and shooting the shit."

"Yeah."

"But . . . if telling you I'm worried about her will get you up here . . ."

"Uh-huh . . . if you were in any kind of danger Ryan would be all over it. Hey! What did he say when you told him?"

"Actually I haven't yet. You're the first to know."

"So I still rate number one in some things?" Susan giggled her trademark giggle at the other end of the phone.

"Of course. And just in case you were thinking of moving back I wanted to be able to tell Ryan both pieces of good news."

"Ah. Well, no, I'm not in a position to move back yet. Maybe after a year or so if you're in the market for a roommate, but the job just isn't there yet."

"Believe me, I'd be down there in a heartbeat if I had enough time on the job to go down."

Susan sighed. "Sucks to have a great job but not be at it long enough to travel off somewhere and hang with your friends."

"Yeah."

"Well, whatever you decide, good luck."

Kelly clicked off the phone and sat looking into space for a few minutes. It was a genuine relief to know that before long, Natalie and her never-ending demands would be out of her life.

CHAPTER THIRTY-NINE

After two weeks of barely seeing Natalie, which, in and of itself, was just fine because there was no attendant drama, Kelly frowned. Natalie should have said something about leaving by now. At least left a message about not finding the right room or could she have her deposit back early so she could use it for the new place or some built-up story about what Natalie thought or wanted to happen but didn't happen. Not that she wanted to hear it . . . it would just be an indication that Natalie was actually looking for a new place.

Nor were there any calls about references. Not that that was an indication of anything. Not everyone checked references on roommates, and people lied about bad employees and tenants just to get rid of them, so why not a roommate? Kelly was certainly going to focus on Natalie's good points if someone called about a reference.

Of course, there were indications that she was still in the house — Ginny's dishes were still routinely moved into the pantry and there was still the sound of bathwater being run whenever Kelly was home at the same time as Natalie. Natalie just managed not to be around or available when Kelly was home. Not that Kelly sought her out . . .

Maybe she had found a place and would go quietly into that new residence.

Then again . . .

"Kelly! Are you home? Kelly?" The screech of Natalie's rang out.

Well, not really a screech . . . Chris, now she screeched like an owl in heavy labor. This was more of nails on a blackboard. Kelly wondered, not for the first time, how she thought Natalie was soft spoken.

She sighed. "Yeah, in the den."

A moment later, Natalie appeared in the doorway. "I found your cat's dishes next to the refrigerator again."

"That's where Ginny eats."

"No, that's where she used to eat. Remember? One of the things I need to feel comfortable is to have her dishes, if she has to eat in the house, in the pantry. If you let her out, she could hunt for her own food."

"Natalie, don't even think about it. You're leaving in two weeks and ..."

"Actually I wanted to talk to you about that."

Here it came ... not that Kelly doubted it would happen. Just that she was expecting it maybe a day or two before Natalie was due to move out.

"Yes?"

"I need more time."

She knew she was going to regret this, but Kelly asked anyway, "How much more time?"

"Maybe two or three months."

"Two or thr ... no."

"I'm sorry, but that's what I need."

"Well, Natalie, that's not what I need. You were given thirty days' notice, in writing and in reliance on that I've re-rented the room. My new tenant is moving in the day after you move out."

"Then there's no problem. You tell her that she can move in when I've found a new place."

Kelly blew out a breath. That was the problem with lying ... thinking of the next lie or backing that lie up. "Well, that is the problem because I told her you'd be out on the twenty-seventh so you need to be out on that day."

"But where will I stay?"

"Natalie, you're an adult. I'm sure you can figure it out."

"Fine." She turned and walked out. Kelly had a moment's concern Natalie would do something destructive, but that wasn't her normal *modus operandi*. But she was talking about Natalie . . . things could turn on a dime with her if there was a chance for drama.

Kelly stood and followed Natalie down the hall. She knew she was going to regret this . . .

"Natalie, how many places have you looked at?"

"I haven't had time to start looking."

"Well, I can understand that, but you might want to start looking. I'm sure you can negotiate a deposit to hold it."

"Maybe. I don't have any extra money available . . ."

"Well, you find a place and I'll see if maybe . . . and the operative word is *maybe* . . . I can release some of your deposit to me back."

"Thanks. I guess. You got your deposit from the new person, don't you?"

"Well, actually, Susan's moving back." She was so going to hell for lying . . . totally going to hell.

No . . . wait . . . she *was* already in a kind of hell with Natalie, wasn't she?

"Oh. So she can't take some extra time to get here?"

It was time to put an end to the negotiations. Not that they were negotiating, but with Natalie . . .

"Natalie . . . you have thirty days' notice to move out. I cannot and will not extend it. But like I said, maybe we can work out releasing some of your deposit early."

"Well . . . thanks. I'll try to make some time during commercials tonight to see what's on the apartment hunting list."

"Thanks." Mentally Kelly shook her head . . . in between commercials. Watching TV was more important than a place to live?

At work a few hours later Kelly sat with Maria for a few minutes before briefing and filled her in on the latest.

"She seriously said she'd try to make time during *commercials*?" Maria asked.

"Yup."

"What is that about?"

"Oh, she has these TV shows she watches and she can't miss a minute . . . kind of like my great-grandmother when my mom was growing up."

"Huh?"

"My mom used to tell me about how when she was a kid her grandmother, my great grandmother used to have, and I quote, her, unquote, programs like Perry Mason and the Lawrence Welk shows. She would not miss them and no one else got to pick any shows that her grandmother didn't like. And back then they had like three channels and, this used to crack me up, it wasn't the Perry Mason or Lawrence Welk shows, but it was *Perry* and *Welk* like they were old friends."

"Oh yeah, I remember my mom talking about that."

"Yeah. And even though she has, I think, TIVO or a DVD or some such, she has to sit and watch from beginning to end."

"She seriously needs to get a life." Maria shook her head.

"Yeah, well, she's not the only one," Jess burst in and threw her go-bag under her desk. "I'm going to kill her. I swear I'm going to kill her."

Kelly looked at Maria. This didn't bode well for their shift tonight. If Jess couldn't get her temper under control and the duty sergeant picked up on it, things were going to get pretty ugly for her. That and the issue of officer safety if Jess's emotions were out of control.

"Let me guess," Maria calmly said to Jess. "Chris."

"Who else would do something sleazy and slutty and so,

so, I just want to kill her."

Kelly stood and stepped toward the door to prevent anyone else coming into dispatch before they got Jess calmed down. "What did she do, Jess?"

"Don, my boyfriend . . . she . . . in the parking lot she . . ."

Maria looked at Kelly and shook her head. Knowing Chris, this would probably be really ugly.

"What did she do?" Maria asked.

Jess paced back and forth in the small, eight-foot by eleven-foot dispatch center, her fists clenching and unclenching and her breath coming in short gasps. "I'm going to kill her."

"Jess," Kelly calmly but matter-of-factly said her name after glancing down the hall to be sure no one else was coming. "You either need to sit down and talk to us or you and I need to take a walk outside the building. Which will it be?"

Looking exhausted, like she'd battled demons through the night and had just stumbled home Jess sat at the other console. "I saw her and Don in the parking lot in his truck and after her comments a few weeks ago about how he was a plumber and not a cop and he had a butt crack when he bent over I thought . . . I never thought . . . he's not a cop . . . why would she go after him? He's *my* boyfriend! He's not her type! And she's not his . . . why . . ." She bent at the waist, hugging herself, and started to cry.

Kelly looked at Maria and shook her head. They needed to get Jess out of there. There was no way she could get her head on straight and work the radio tonight. She'd be a danger to the officers and if Chris showed up who knew what would happen.

If Chris showed up? Jess just said she was out in the parking lot.

"Is Chris on duty tonight?" Kelly asked Maria.

Maria shook her head. "No, she switched day shift with Annmarie today because Annmarie had something or other going on tonight."

"The badge bunnies keep together," Jess spat.

"Well, that's a good thing . . . that Chris won't be here tonight," Kelly told her.

"Yeah, and if I know Annmarie she'll be on a ride-along for at least the first part of the shift or something will happen so I won't get off on time so we're good . . . kind of good . . . here."

"Okay, so Jess, what happened?"

She took in a shaky breath and swallowed. "I saw his truck and he was sitting in the front seat with his eyes closed and his mouth open and his face looked kind of pink. I started to walk up to the truck to say hello and see what he was doing down here and then I saw blonde hair come up above the bottom of the window and go back down and go back up again and I realized it was Chris giving him . . . she was . . ." Jess broke into tears again.

Maria finished for her. "She was giving him a blow job?"

Jess wiped her nose. "It's what she's known for, isn't it? But why? He's not a cop. She only goes after cops."

Kelly stood and adjusted her gun belt. "Apparently she also goes after men who are with someone else."

"Anything she can do to be mean," Maria put in.

Kelly shook her head. "Jess, I think it would be a good idea for you to tell the sergeant you don't feel well and go home for the night. You're too upset to be here and you need to give yourself some TLC."

"I can't."

"Why?"

"Don and I live together. We moved in together two weeks ago and he's been talking about getting married."

Well, that explained why Chris suddenly went after him. She couldn't stand to see anyone else happy or anyone having a good relationship. That she hadn't made a move toward

Ryan when he stopped by the station was a surprise given he was a cop and quite the hunky one at that. But Ryan was on to Chris or would be if she got near him. More than once, Kelly'd seen him give her the cold shoulder for no particular reason when he'd been in the station.

"Okay. Well, you want to go hang out at my house for a while? Natalie will be there but she usually stays in her room." Then again, Natalie would probably enjoy Jess's drama and feed off it herself. Who knew what kind of stories Natalie would tell Jess—whatever they were though would definitely take Jess's mind off her problems.

"Are you sure?"

"Yes, definitely. You know where I live, right?"

Jess nodded.

"Good. I'll call Natalie and tell her to expect you and let her know you're just going to hang out for a while and that she doesn't need to entertain you, okay?"

"Thanks." She sniffed.

While Jess went to tell the duty sergeant she needed to go home, Kelly pulled out her personal cell rather than call on the department's landline, which would be recorded.

"Natalie, hi."

"Hi."

"Listen, one of my co-workers needs to hang out for a while tonight. Jess. You met her at the barbeque so she's going to be over in a bit."

"Here? She's coming here?"

"Yes. She can't be at work right now and she can't go home just yet so she's going to hang out. You don't need to do any-thing but let her in. She'll just maybe make a cup of coffee or tea and go into the living room and watch some TV. You don't even have to talk to her."

"But what if she comes in the middle of my program?"

Kelly put her hand to the bridge of her nose and took a

deep breath. "Good point. I'll give her my key."

"That's not a good idea."

"Why?"

"How do we know she won't make copies and give them out to everyone and that they'll make copies for their friends? We could be invaded by hordes of people we don't know. And I don't have my gun yet. No. No, don't give her your key."

She had to ask.

"Natalie, Jess isn't going to do anything like that. Trust me. She works for the police department. She had an extensive background and psychological tests and she's my friend. If you won't be able to let her in, I'll give her the key."

Silence reigned on the other end of the phone. So much so Kelly finally had to ask, "Natalie?"

"I'm not happy about this. First you throw me out on the street and now, before my room is even cold, you have someone taking my place."

This was so not going well. Going totally to Nataland but not going well. Kelly sighed. With Natalie no amount of cajoling would get her to change her mind unless she thought she was going to get something out of it. Kelly racked her brain for a few moments trying to come up with something Jess would have or be that Natalie would want. While Jess might have some good stories to tell, once Natalie went into victim mode . . . or deeper into it . . . there'd be no pulling her out. Natalie loved her pity parties and the whole thing with her being kicked out was a pity party of major proportions. Actually it'd been pretty nice the past two weeks or so with Natalie avoiding her as much as possible.

Well, avoiding physically. There were the deep sighs and additional baths and showers to help her relax or destress or whatever the hell she did when something didn't go her way.

Natalie interrupted her thoughts. "Since I'm not expecting

someone don't be surprised if they end up dead when I shoot them coming in the door."

That did it . . . and where did she get a gun? "Natalie, did you just threaten my co-worker and friend? Or was that a threat to me that I'd better be on *my* guard walking into *my* house tonight? Because if that's the case, threatening or attacking a police officer is a felony — that means you go to jail. No plea bargains."

The other woman huffed out a breath. "Fine. I'll let her in. But she'd better not bother me because I'm busy."

"No worries. Jess has enough on her mind that she doesn't really need to speak to anyone."

Just the same, Kelly handed Jess her key. "I'll call you when I'm leaving work so you can open the door for me when I get home . . . just in case she forgets that she's going to let you in."

"Thanks, Kelly. I just can't deal with the chance Chris will show up tonight and I really don't want to deal with Don either. I can't believe he'd give in to her like that. Not just her. I thought . . . I thought we had the real deal but apparently a blow job knocks that out of the equation."

At a loss for words, at least any words that would comfort Jess and not completely degrade the blonde badge bunny, Kelly just shook her head. "I'll see you in a few hours. Make yourself at home and ignore Natalie as best you can."

CHAPTER FORTY

"911, what are you reporting?" Maria answered the emergency line shortly after the shift had begun.

"There's someone outside my house. I think they're trying to break in," the woman frantically whispered into the phone.

Maria looked at the call screen and shook her head. The call was coming, again, from Kelly's house. It didn't mean there couldn't or wouldn't be an emergency at the house, but Natalie's calls came in pretty regularly when Kelly was at work. Muting the call before releasing a breath, Maria closed her eyes and opened them before continuing, "Confirm your address is 676 Rosemont?"

"Yes, yes. Hurry. They're trying to open the door. Hurry."

"Please try to stay calm. I have officers rolling. Can you see the person?"

"What? No. I'm not going to open the door! You have to hurry. They could come in here and *kill* me!" Natalie wailed.

Someone should. Overhead she heard the call go out, noting that Kelly was not included in the round of officers being dispatched out. Chris's mentor in all things sleazy, Annamarie most likely sent the other officers just to rile Kelly. The badge bunny probably thought Kelly'd leave her beat to respond to the call . . . but Chris didn't know that it was probably Jess entering the house with the key Kelly had given her. Kelly was probably on the phone with Jess this very minute telling her what was going on over the radio.

"Are you there?" Natalie stage whispered. If the woman spoke any louder, undoubtedly, the neighbors would have heard.

"Yes. Keep your line open."

"Are you sure they're coming? I don't hear any sirens."

Maria blew out another breath. "There's no reason for them to roll code 3 with lights and sirens."

"I'm not?"

Maria shook her head and wondered how Kelly could put up with her as long as she had. "You don't want to give the intruder a heads up do you? Because if we do then he'll get away and he can come back and get you later, right?"

"Uh. Yeah. Yeah . . . and you know, I have people, bad people, after me all the time. I have a very dangerous job."

"This is Natalie, right?"

There was a pause on the other end. A fairly long pause before Natalie ignored Maria's question but instead asked, "Are you sure they're coming? I don't hear anything, not even the intruder."

"Yes, they should be pulling up." Maria couldn't help herself. "And I've sent them a CAD message that it's Officer McKenna's roommate who's called."

"Uh. Good. That's good, right?"

"I'm going to disconnect now, Natalie. Go on to the door and let the officers and who, I believe, is Jess from here at the department in. I guess you didn't get the message that Kelly gave Jess her key."

A moment later Maria received a call on her cell from Kelly. "I saw the call . . . seriously? Someone outside my house trying to break in?"

Maria laughed. "That's what Natalie said. Of course there's always the chance something is, or was, going on."

"I doubt it. You were there when I gave Jess the keys to my house and told Natalie she was coming over. What is wrong with that woman?"

"You're asking me? You're the one who checked her

references before she moved in."

"And more and more I'm sure they said nice things about her just to get her the hell out of where she was. You know that's what I'll be saying on any reference calls—she's neat, clean, pays her bills on time . . . and the bonus point . . . I hardly ever see her soooo."

"I just hope it's over soon . . . and not just for your sake. I'm getting tired of her phone calls."

"And you think they're going to stop just because she moves out?"

"She might find a place in another city . . . like in Oklahoma or something."

"One can only hope. So any updates? All I see on the CAD is that units arrived."

"Nope. No chatter on this end. I imagine they walked up to the house, said hello to Jess and she told them you gave her the key. And then I figure in ohhhh, three minutes there'll be another call from Natalie that we clearly don't care about public safety because there were no sirens and they let Jess in anyway."

"Probably. Two more weeks . . . two more weeks.

"Yeah. I think most of dispatch is getting tired of Natalie drama too."

"I doubt that's what it is. You've known her longer than me, but Chris never does anything without an ulterior motive. You gotta worry what she's up to."

"Hmmm."

"Kelly?"

"Hmm?"

"What are you going to do if she hasn't found a place by then?"

"I hope you're just messing with me because I can't take a minute more of her than I have to."

"Yeah, well, neither can we. Neither can we."

CHAPTER FORTY-ONE

K elly called her friend at the end of her shift. "Jess, I'm out-side the house."

Jess flipped on the outside light and opened the front door.

"Is she around?" Kelly whispered as she came in the door.

"No. Well, she was in her room watching TV for a couple of hours. Then it got quiet and I have to admit I crept into the hall and saw the light go out. Either she's asleep or she's standing at the door listening to us."

Kelly shook her head. "I can't wait till this is over. I need to kick back a bit. You up to chat or you ready to turn in your-self?"

"I'm all over talking about what happened. Kelly . . . that woman is certifiable."

"Yeah, that's what Maria and I talked about after everyone went code 4 and left."

"It looked like they cleared the scene pretty quickly."

"Uh-huh. Right after they saw I was here and Doug said he'd seen you give me the keys when I left the station to-night."

Together they walked into the kitchen and Kelly pulled a container of coconut milk out of the refrigerator.

"You drink that stuff for real?" Jess asked her.

"Yup. I like the pumpkin and egg nog flavors best, but you can only get them at certain times of the year."

"Whatever you say."

"That mean you don't want any?" Kelly paused as she reached for some glasses.

"You know . . . you only live once so yeah, why not?"

Ginny ambled into the kitchen and, after checking her food bowl, meowed at Kelly before looking at Jess. Kelly chuckled. "That's her *I could starve around here if I wasn't careful* look. As you can see, she has a full dish of dry food."

"But?"

"After all the drama and upset tonight she clearly needs some wet food to help her through to the morning."

After a quick chuckle at the gray cat's antics the two women sat at the table, a plate of cheese and crackers in front of them along with their drinks, Kelly gestured with her glass for Jess to tell her what happened.

"I've got to tell you, I've only met her those few times but based on those times and things you've said . . . typical Natalie. I rang the bell several times, knocked on the door and finally used your key. She's something, isn't she?"

"That's an understatement."

"So I tried to be courteous. I peeked in one of the windows by the door saw her behind it and told her it was me, that we'd met before and she never said a word. Nothing. I waited a minute . . . seriously I counted to sixty and then said you'd given me your key and I was coming in. She didn't say a word but as I came in the door she was on the phone dialing 911 and telling them someone was breaking into the house."

Kelly shook her head.

"Did you listen to the dispatch tape?"

"No . . . I didn't go 1010 to the station at all during my shift. It was busy, but with simple things like a car lock out at the mall, some tow trucks, a couple of wobbly drivers. Nothing special, just busy."

"That must have ticked Annamarie off."

"You know, if she wants twenty-four-seven drama she needs to get a job in San Francisco or Oakland or with the CHP. It's not going to happen at Red Oak."

"Uh-huh . . . unless it's from you stumbling on to something."

"There is that. Anyway, no, I didn't listen to the tape."

"Well, you'll enjoy it when you do . . . she said I had a gun and I was threatening her."

"Gees. How stupid . . ."

"Seriously. The woman is a menace. So Doug and Misha rolled out and I could hear her asking Maria why they didn't have their sirens on and didn't they care she could die if they didn't hurry. I guess Maria made some comment about you giving me the key at the end of the call because she got all blustery when the officers arrived and she hung up. Misha told her how much trouble she could get in for filing a false police report and she was all *It's not false. This woman was breaking into my house.* Doug asked if she knew you and she said of course. And he asked if you'd told her I was coming over and at first she said no. So he asked her if she was sure because it didn't sound like you to give someone a key and not give her a heads up. In the end she finally admitted that yeah, she knew I was coming and she was so absorbed in her TV program she forgot so it startled her."

Kelly groaned and shook her head. "Tell me it's going to be over soon. Sometimes I'm sure the only reason she's still alive is I know orange is not my color."

"It will be over soon. One way or the other it will be over soon. Ginny was great company though."

"Was she?" Kelly reached down to scratch the gray cat's head. In turn, Ginny's purr revved up loud enough to be heard across the room.

"Yeah. Once I got in the house I came in here, made some hot chocolate for myself and she came right up and climbed up into my arms and lay there purring for a long time. She's a sweetheart."

"Yes, she is. I can't imagine life without her. So, did Natalie make an appearance after that?"

Jess chuckled. "No. I heard the TV get really loud and a few times I heard her laughing about something."

"Yeah, she watches some reality TV show or something. We're into different programs, you know?"

"I can only imagine. Doesn't she have any friends?"

"Nope. Well, the one who she sometimes calls . . . but only between her programs if there's time and that's not that often. There *is* the schedule . . . come home, start her bath, put one potato in the oven to bake, take her bath followed by her shower, get her potato and go watch her TV shows. If for some reason she has a few minutes she'll stop and tell me her latest drama which often matches whatever police calls we had that made it into the paper."

"I guess I got lucky and her TV shows kept her busy. Oh, well, there was one thing." Jess started to chuckle. "She did make a comment that I had interrupted her TV show and now she wouldn't know what was going on and she'd have to make time to watch the rerun on the internet or something."

"Yup. That would be my soon to be no longer roommate."

"Man. So I guess looking out the window happened during a commercial and then she had to rush back for her show?" By this time Jess was laughing a good solid belly laugh.

"I'm glad you can laugh at my situation."

"It's going to be over soon though, right? She's supposed to be out in two more weeks?"

"Something like that. Like I've said too many times before, knowing Natalie, there will be drama. Like tonight when she was trying to tell me that she wasn't able to find a place. Not that she looked or has been looking. She's busy, you know. She has work and her TV shows and cleaning to do and her baths to take."

"You've put up with more than anyone else I know would have done. See, if you'd of had me move in you wouldn't be going through this now."

"Jess, honestly, I've had it with her from day one. I can't believe she was the best of the ones who interviewed and that I thought for even a minute she'd be easy to live with. And if you'd have moved in here you wouldn't be living with Don now, would you?"

"Yeah, well, hindsight is great for kicking yourself in the ass. At least your headache is moving on—Chris won't be leaving the PD anytime soon and with all the problems she's caused for the rest of the dispatchers none of us can get out any time soon either."

CHAPTER FORTY-TWO

K elly shook her head when she walked into the kitchen the next day to find a note from Natalie admonishing her for letting Jess in the night before. "Fourteen days," she muttered to herself. "Fourteen days and this will all be over."

At least, as Jess said the night before, Natalie would be moving on. They were all going to be dealing with Chris for a long, long time.

Just as she was leaving for her shift, Natalie came bursting in the door. "Kelly, thank goodness!"

"Uh-huh."

"I left something at work—someone just called me and told me they left some info on a possible apartment for me. Can you give me a ride over there when you leave for your job?"

Kelly shrugged. "Sure, why not. I'm leaving now, you ready?" Inside she gave herself a little fist bump—at least Natalie had a lead for an apartment which was more than she had the day before.

"Yes." The redhead dropped her carry-all bag, kept the purse in hand, and followed Kelly out to her car.

Neither spoke on the ride over to the dealership, but when they arrived, Natalie turned and told her thank you.

Kelly took in the dimly lit building and darker alleyway leading to the garage area. It probably didn't matter since Natalie wasn't a back door kind of person and, after all, she did work in the front reception area. Besides, it wasn't Kelly's problem. "No problem. It's not too dark yet so you should be fine getting home, right?"

"Yeah. I'm sure one of the guys that's still there will give me a ride. I can't believe I left the list there."

Kelly looked past Natalie, and while she didn't see anyone else in the showroom, it didn't mean there wasn't anyone in the service or office area. She doubted the owner or a manager had given Natalie a key to the building, but if she thought she'd get a ride home, that wasn't Kelly's problem.

Based on past experience, Kelly was pretty sure she was supposed to ask Natalie something or other, but she needed to get to work and really was ready to be done with Natalie's drama. Natalie, however, had other things in mind.

"Like I said, it's about for a new place to live."

No matter what she said, it would be wrong. If she said it was good, Natalie would be offended that Kelly wanted her out. If she said something to the effect that there was no rush or she was sorry for her leaving the ads, Natalie would take it as a sign she didn't really have to leave. If she asked about the places Natalie was looking at, not only would Natalie tell her, but she'd take it as a sign that Kelly wanted to be kept up to date on her search for a new home. At this point in time, Kelly just wanted it to be over.

Natalie finally hopped out of the car and started walking toward the back of the dealership leading Kelly to believe that her soon to be ex-roommate knew someone would be in the office or service area. While Natalie was an adult and knew the dealership area and Red Oak was a fairly safe community, Kelly still watched as the redhead made her way to the back of the main building. That sixth sense she had when something was off niggled at Kelly. When another person, wearing a hoodie with the top up, came up behind Natalie and started to follow her, Kelly almost got out of her car to make sure there wasn't a problem. When Natalie turned to the person and stopped to talk, it looked like they knew each other. In fact, Natalie looked downright happy to see whoever it was, so Kelly took off and headed on to work.

*

Jess burst into briefing just as the sergeant was calling the session to order. "Nice of you to join us," he told her with a sour-looking glance at the clock.

"Sorry — but I just saw something . . . weird. I'm not sure, but I think I saw a body when I drove by the Jaguar dealership."

"Say that again, Jess."

"I think I saw a body lying on the ground outside the Jaguar dealership."

"You mean like a homeless person passed out or sleeping?"

Kelly noticed Jess looked not only harried but appeared to be shaking. Clearly whatever she'd seen had upset her.

"I . . . I don't know. It looked like . . . well, I saw a, a . . . blonde haired woman rushing away from where the body was or what looked like a body. At least I thought it was a woman. It could have been a man because of how he . . . she looked and moved."

"You thought you saw a body and didn't call it in?" White demanded.

"Well, um, I wasn't sure. It's a dealership and there was a lot of other debris and they have rags and stuff like that . . ."

White shook his head and keyed down on his mic, "Dispatch, White here in briefing. Jess just came into briefing, late, to advise she saw something suspicious outside the Jag dealership. Can you send a unit over there to check it out?"

"Copy that." Maria was on the radio. "D-44, D-58, roll code 2 to 4458 Redwood, Jaguar dealership regarding suspicious circumstances. Check your CADs for further." She quickly entered the data that Jess had seen what appeared to be a body lying outside the dealership.

"Okay," White told a still visibly shaking Jess, "units are

on their way. Can we now get on with briefing?"

"Yes, sorry. I would have been on time except I saw that, well, I'm sure it was a body and then I watched that other person walking away really quickly. It . . . it almost looked like they'd been . . . well, never mind." Her voice trickled off.

Moments later, the officers in briefing heard dispatch go out over the air requesting medical and fire to respond to 4458 Redwood. Misha dialed into dispatch and confirmed additional units were needed on the scene. Dispatch cleared Kelly and several other units to respond. Hurrying to her car, Kelly mentally ran over her checklist for responding to a fire. Given it was reported at the dealership, chances were there would be chemicals, at least gasoline and oil, involved. She stopped mid-way, checking her vehicle, and shook her head. Coburn glanced over from his car. "Something wrong, McKenna?"

"I hope not."

"Uh-huh."

"It's just that I left my soon-to-be ex-roommate off at the dealership just before I went on duty."

"Uh, right. The drama queen victim."

"Exactly. It wouldn't surprise me if she wasn't pulling some weird-assed act to not have to move out. After calling 911 the other night when Jess went over to hang out, who knows what she'll do as a follow up. Knowing Natalie she probably waited till someone was walking or driving by where they could see her and lay down."

"That woman's nuts. Seriously nuts."

A moment later, both units rolled out onto the street. Kelly hit the lights to roll code 3 to the call. Depending on where the fire was, it could be something as simple as a coffee pot left on to something much more serious if it was in the auto shop. Between the oil, gas, and other automotive appliances, it could be a serious, toxic-laced fire.

Of secondary concern was the drama that would

accompany Natalie hearing about the fire if she'd already left, although, as she'd told Coburn, it wouldn't surprise her to hear Natalie was the supposed victim. Whatever it was, where ever it was, Natalie would blow it up ten times further out of proportion.

She rolled up behind D-15 with D-16 a moment later. Following the fire incident commander's directions, they took up positions blocking off the street and redirecting traffic away. Fire came over the radio requesting the officers to cordon off a three-block radius. Clearly, the fire was a big one, and most likely there were toxic elements involved. Additional units were called for to section off the area. Despite the warm afternoon, Kelly felt a chill the moment she heard one of the firemen radio to roll the coroner because he'd found a body inside the dealership.

Additional alarms went out for fire apparatus. Within minutes a fire captain arrived and set up a command center. Together police and fire set up a perimeter to keep anyone from getting too close to what could be toxic fumes and a potential explosion from the materials in the dealership.

From her vantage point directing traffic a short time later Kelly saw a firefighter-paramedic wheel a gurney with a black body bag on it into the building. A chill raced down her spine. Someone had died in that fire and she had a sinking feeling Natalie was somehow involved. Kelly had a momentary flash that in her never-ending bid for attention Natalie had set fire to the building or worse, to herself, and then quickly dismissed the thought. Natalie might be a drama queen, but she wasn't likely to do anything to disturb her livelihood. No, if anything, Natalie would somehow position herself to be in the center of everything, a victim who was also the one who saved everyone.

Kelly chided herself for her unkind thoughts just as the paramedics wheeled the body out a few minutes later. While the body bag was zipped up, a lock of hair dangled off the side. There was no mistaking the ginger color, not all that different from Natalie's.

It couldn't be. It just couldn't be.

Kelly debated a moment before signaling to one of the other officers. When Coburn jogged over, she quickly told him, "I have a bad feeling I know the victim. I want to check with the paramedics."

He nodded. "Go."

Kelly hustled over to the coroner's van. "Please, just a moment."

In the process of loading the body, the coroner's assistant looked over at her and raised a brow in question.

"I have a feeling I might know the victim." She gestured to the lock of hair that had escaped the bag.

"You sure you want to look now?"

That gave her pause. She'd seen dead bodies before. First as a reporter and then more recently at her own job at the accounting firm when she'd arrived one day to find a co-worker stabbed to death by her former boss. Somehow this felt different, terribly different. "It's a woman, yes?"

"Yeah."

"Is she, was she . . . burned?"

The paramedic shook his head. "Looks like smoke inhalation."

So it wasn't a charred and burnt up Natalie . . . if it really was Natalie. At least not from what he was telling her.

"Then yes, I want to be sure it's not . . . that . . ." Kelly huffed out a breath. "My roommate works for that dealership. She has red hair . . ."

The paramedic nodded and reached for the bag's zipper.

Even though the victim . . . the woman . . . wasn't burned, she still had that lifeless stare, the pale, almost gray skin, of a dead body. It was, clearly, Natalie.

CHAPTER FORTY-THREE

Frozen where she stood, Kelly watched the progress of the paramedics rolling the gurney toward the ambulance. She swallowed and blinked her eyes as if to clear away what she was seeing. It couldn't be. It absolutely couldn't be Natalie. With all of her drama, Natalie just couldn't be dead. Nope, no how, no way could Natalie be dead because if she were, then there would be no more drama and tall tales for her.

"McKenna?" White gently put a hand on her shoulder.

"Huh?" She shook herself and tore her eyes away from the body on the gurney.

"You okay? Do you need to sit down? Any chance you breathed in something toxic and need the EMTs to take a look at you?"

Kelly chanced another look at the body before answering her sergeant, "No. No. I'm fine. The victim . . . It's my roommate."

"What?"

"My roommate. I'm sure it's Natalie."

"You haven't seen the body. Why would you think it's her?"

"I did . . . I saw her hair. When they brought out the body some of her hair was sticking out of the body bag." She raised her hand and pointed. "See, it's red. Like Natalie's."

"Lotta women have red hair."

"Yeah, but how many work in a Jaguar dealership? This is where Natalie works."

"Could be another employee."

"Maybe . . . maybe they only hire women with red hair but Sergeant, I'm sure it's her. I-I-I asked to look and saw her face."

"What was she doing here this late?"

She turned again to watch the EMTs stop to talk with the coroner when the finished loading the body into the ambulance. "She uh . . . she came back because she had a message about a possible place to rent. Someone left it here for her. I gave her a thirty-day notice to move out and she had me drop her back off to get the information."

"Uh-huh."

"Maybe . . . maybe it isn't her. I should look again." Kelly turned to start to the ambulance.

"Hang on a second, McKenna. Let's check with the doc and see if . . ."

Kelly was already moving to the ambulance. "Guys? Just a sec if you don't mind."

White followed her over to the ambulance and stood behind her as if guarding her against anyone else looking on.

"I think I know the victim. I just need to look again."

"Climb on in," the coroner told her. To the others, he advised, "Let's keep this quiet — we don't need any lookie-loos who just want to see a dead body."

Not that there was any question that the woman was dead. After all, you didn't put a body in a body bag if the person was still alive. Kelly climbed in the ambulance and swallowed as one of the EMTs unzipped the bad to show the victim's head.

White stood behind her. "That her?"

Kelly nodded. "Yeah, that's Natalie. I can't . . . how . . . it makes no sense."

"Let's get out of here and we'll talk." Her sergeant spoke a few words into his radio and then guided Kelly out of the ambulance.

Misha met them on their way back to their patrol cars. "What's up?"

"It appears the victim is McKenna's roommate. I want to do a bit of a debrief, find out a little more about the victim before the press gets ahold of this story. Can you get her car back to the station?"

"Sure. No worries. McKenna, can I get you anything?"

"No, Misha, thanks. No. I'm kinda . . . stunned. It's not every day someone you know dies like that."

"That's for sure."

It wasn't until she sat in Misha's car that it occurred to her she should call Ryan. Not that he was going to be all that upset that Natalie was dead. In retrospect, aside from the shock . . . no, not shock . . . surprise . . . that the other woman was dead, Kelly didn't really feel much of anything. Recognizing that there was a level of shock, however, going on, she knew it would hit her later. That would be when she'd need . . . want . . . Ryan's comforting presence. At the moment, whether or not a crime had been committed was still up in the air. It didn't look like Natalie had been burned, but died of smoke inhalation. Only an autopsy would tell them that for sure. The Coroner would likely do a cursory check tonight and then a more in-depth study in the morning. Unless there was something in Natalie's health history, they could find, or someone at her job knew about, they'd be looking at any number of causes of death.

"I hope she didn't suffer," Kelly softly commented.

"Huh?"

"Natalie. The victim. I hope she didn't suffer. She was a pain in the ass, but no one deserves to die like that. She shouldn't have even been there except she got a call about a possible place to move to and she was going to call them tonight . . . or at least I thought that was what she was going to do. Why else would she have wanted to go back to her work if she wasn't going to look for a place to live?" She was rambling and she knew it, but Kelly couldn't stop. She just couldn't stop and make sense that just an hour or so ago, her roommate was alive and well and her annoying self. And now she was dead. She felt like she was going to vomit when it hit her that if she hadn't told Natalie to move out, the woman would still be alive because she wouldn't have gone back tonight.

"If it was smoke inhalation, no, she wouldn't."

"You think that's what it was?"

White shrugged. "We could speculate all night on that and then the coroner will come up with something entirely different. Let's table that for the time being."

"They why are we going off to . . . where are we going?"

"I thought maybe a cup of coffee and a little chat about what happened might be a good thing for you right now."

"I'm fine."

"I'm sure you are. But it's not every day a friend, co-worker or roommate dies under those kinds of circumstances."

"Yeah . . . those kind of circumstances. Do you think it was an accidental fire?"

"Won't know till the arson investigator gets out there and looks around. I did smell fuel, but given it's a car dealership with a body shop and repair bay attached, it's hard to say if it was intentional or accidental."

"I know. I know." Kelly blew out a breath. "Natalie. Dead."

White pulled up to a local coffee shop. As they got out, Kelly looked up at the sky. "I can't believe it. Do you know, did you hear, that I asked her to move out the other day?"

"No. I'm not surprised."

"Why?"

"You were pretty quiet about things going on at your place, but I saw her at the shift party and have heard a few things around the station. She was kinda nutty, wasn't she?"

"That's an understatement. It's not right to speak ill of the dead, but in her case, she was kind of nutty. Well . . . that may be wrong. She was OCD about some things and it made living with her kind of difficult at times. I just had enough and told her it was time for her to move on."

"Looks like she did just that."

CHAPTER FORTY-FOUR

"Ry." Kelly was a tad surprised at the wobble in her voice. Even when Adrian was stalking her, she'd managed to keep fairly solid control over her emotions, especially when it came to Ryan. For some reason she always felt the need to show him she could stand on her own two feet—which was odd in its own way because the man clearly, always, wanted to take care of her.

"Babe? You okay?"

She looked around the sergeants' office, seeing but not seeing the pictures and commendations that lined the walls, the reports on the various desks—only the image of Natalie when she'd gotten out of Kelly's car that night. Talking with Mike White over a cup of coffee steadied her nerves somewhat. Now it was time to start dealing with the situation on her own. There was, however, no going back on the shaky way she'd said his name. "Yeah. I'm fine."

"Not that I'm not glad to hear your voice, but you usually don't call in the middle of your shift. What's up?"

"Natalie."

Ryan blew out a sigh. "What'd the drama queen do now?"

"Died."

"Great. Was it in a southern swoon or Western yi-hah?"

"I'm thinking a gravely gasp."

"Wait. You're serious?" Kelly heard the squeak of Ryan's chair as he shifted, probably sitting up straight in it. "Natalie, the pesky redhead died? Was it her usual drama where she played at suicide and it went south on her?"

"That was kinda mean there, Michaels." Her defensiveness

over the annoying redhead surprised her.

Immediately he picked up that she was feeling unstable and emotional. "Kelly? What's going on?"

"She's *dead*, Ryan. Stone cold dead. She went back to work tonight and somehow got hit on the head or fell and then the dealership caught on fire and they found her body in the fire. She's dead, Ryan." Kelly swiped at a tear that was tracking down her cheek. Surprised at her reaction, she looked at her fingers still damp with the tear. "Ryan?"

"I'm here, babe. What do you need?"

"I . . . can you come up? Now? My sergeant thinks it's a good idea for me to take the rest of the shift off because of the situation, you know?"

"Is someone with you now?"

"I'm in the station and there's other officers and dispatch around. Maria is here in records so I can sit with her till you get here."

"Good. I'm on my way."

Kelly disconnected the call and drew in a breath. She'd wanted Natalie to move out—not die. Was this yet another past life issue to be resolved and she just hadn't picked up on it? Or was it just one of life's stupid little curves? She shivered as she remembered the dream she had of Natalie calling to her . . . it wasn't fog though. It was smoke. It was Natalie trying to find her way out of the smoke.

She rose to head into dispatch, stopped when Mike White walked back into the office. "Sir?"

"McKenna. How are you doing?"

"Fine. I mean . . . I'm okay. Like not going to fall apart but it probably hasn't hit me yet, you know?"

White nodded. "Michaels coming to get you?"

"Yeah. He's on his way. So the notifications . . . do you want me to go with the chaplain to tell her mom? And her job?"

"Chaplain Hayes is on her way. You okay to give me her family's info?"

"Her mom lives local. Down in Corte Madera. Do you want me to go with?"

"No. You've got enough on your plate right now."

"She might wonder why I'm not making the notification."

"That may be so, but you need to take care of you right now. Wait for Michaels and have him bring you home. You can call the family and her job tomorrow."

She knew he was right. The old adage of not being able to take care of someone else if you weren't okay yourself definitely made sense in this situation.

"You know the family?"

This was going to take a few, so Kelly walked further into the office and sat down. If her sergeant didn't want her there, he'd ask her to leave.

"Not really. As far as I know it was just her and her mother. Natalie's dad died when she was a teenager. At least that's what she said. So it was just her and her mother as far as I know. I don't know how close they were. I . . . I never asked. She just . . . she was so annoying that I never asked."

Kelly took in a shaky breath and continued, "Natalie didn't drive so her mother'd come pick her up on Sunday afternoons to take her grocery shopping. With our different work schedules I don't know if they talked or got together during the week. And with Natalie you never really knew if what she was saying was the truth or not. She tended to . . . embellish . . . a lot. And this . . . her death . . ." Kelly shook her head. "I can't believe it. Do you think maybe I made a mistake on the ID? That I saw the hair and . . ."

White shook his head. "Her ID confirmed her as Natalie Valle and the picture on the California ID card looked exactly like the victim."

"But is there a chance she was just unconscious?"

Again he shook his head. "Not from what the EMT and coroner said. And from what I saw of the body she was gone a bit before we got out there."

Kelly blew out a breath and looked down at the floor. "What a sad way to go."

"Could have been worse. She could have been burned instead of smoke inhalation. The way I understand it, that's a peaceful way to go. If you got to go in a bad way, that's one of the least bad ways."

"I guess."

They both turned at the sound of a footstep behind them.

"Remind me not to piss you off." Chris stood there with her arms folded over what passed for her chest.

"Excuse me?" Kelly turned in her chair, a confused look on her face.

"We all knew she was pissing you off. You should have grown a pair and kicked her out before you got desperate enough to kill her."

"You are out of line, Tanner." White started to rise from behind his desk.

Chris shrugged. "It's a fact *Officer* McKenna had an issue with her roommate. Makes sense she'd get rid of her any way she could."

Kelly was too tired and emotionally drained to deal with Chris right then. Fortunately, the on-call chaplain, Vicki Hayes, arrived at that moment and with a smile and a gentle shove pushed Chris out of the way.

"How is everyone doing?" Chaplain Hayes asked.

"Been better," White responded. "Chris was just leaving."

The blonde tossed her hair and flounced out of the room. Kelly had no doubt he'd have to deal with the bitchy dispatcher later, but that wasn't Kelly's problem.

"Maria filled me in a little on the phone. I'm sorry to hear this was someone you know, Kelly," the chaplain told her.

"She was my roommate."

"Were you close?"

"No. Not really. We'd only roomed together a few months and our work schedules were different enough that we seldom saw each other. She had . . . needs that were a bit overwhelming so I'd recently asked her to move out."

"I see."

Whatever that meant. Kelly wasn't even sure right now. The impact of the night and Natalie's death drained her. She's never been a slacker, but taking tomorrow off was looking like an option. Not that anyone would say anything about it. Well, anyone but Chris. She'd cross that bridge when she came to it in the morning.

"Well," Hayes said. "I guess we'd better get going. The family lives in Corte Madera?"

"Her mother. Her dad passed some years ago."

"Okay. The mother is going to ask — cause of death?"

"Preliminary is smoke inhalation. The coroner will confirm it after autopsy."

"In the event the mother doesn't want one . . ."

"Until we know the cause of the fire it's a suspicious death and you know those come with autopsies."

"Got it. Well, then we'll be . . ."

White looked surprised when his phone rang at that moment. "Right. Right. You sure? Well, that changes things, doesn't it?"

He hung up and looked at his desk for a moment before looking back up at Kelly and Chaplain.

Seeing his troubled look, Kelly asked, "Sir?"

"That was the coroner."

Neither woman said a word while he gathered his thoughts.

"It appears your roommate was killed by a blunt instrument to the back of her head."

CHAPTER FORTY-FIVE

"Blunt . . ." At a loss for words, Kelly looked from her sergeant to the chaplain.

" . . . force trauma," White finished for her.

"Accidental?" Chaplain Hayes asked. Kelly didn't miss the hopeful tone of the woman's question.

"Hard to say, but given the position of the body and where she was found it's not looking very accidental."

"Man." Kelly shook her head. "I knew she was annoying, obviously, but for someone to kill her? Really?"

Her sergeant looked at her steadily for a moment before asking, "You ever want to kill her, Kelly?"

That he called her Kelly rather than McKenna was telling. White never called anyone by their first name unless he was reaching out in some way. She supposed, ordinarily, it was too personal for him to be on a first-name basis. In this case, was he letting her know he was on her side? That he was asking the question because he had to, and if someone asked, later on, he could say he did question her?"

"No. At times her . . . neediness . . . was almost entertaining. No matter what you said or did she had some crazy story to tell you that was kind of like what happened to you. You know the type—been there, done that, got the t-shirt and it's better than yours?"

"Yeah. Yeah. I do. So for all her antics you never wished she was dead?"

"No. I hardly ever saw her. Yeah, I know people around here knew some of what she was like because she was always calling 911 about something or other or I'd share her latest tall tale, but she was just . . . there I guess. With our schedules I hardly ever saw her and I asked her to move out the other day because she was clearly unhappy living with me. My house was never going to be clean enough or things the way she wanted in her version of an ideal world . . . and I wasn't going to give up Ginny or break up with Ryan. So I asked her to move out."

"Any problem with her about that?"

"No. She got it. So that was that for us. This though . . . who would want to kill her?"

"That is the question . . . that is the question. So, here's the deal. Because it's someone you know — in your household and it's a suspicious death, I need to put you out on admin leave for a few days."

Kelly leaned forward in her chair. With her hand on the desk, she shook her head. "No. No, I need to work."

White leaned back in his chair and folded his hands over his abdomen. Shaking his head, he told her, "No. You need to be off on leave, but it's not punitive. This is paid leave, Kelly, so you can deal with whatever you need to over your room-mate . . . Natalie?"

Kelly nodded.

"Natalie's death."

"Sergeant, there's nothing to deal with. She rented a room and a bathroom from me, but we weren't friends. We didn't socialize. I hardly knew the woman."

"Be that as it may, you need to take a few days off."

"Sir, I want to help find her killer."

Again he shook his head. "That would be a conflict of interest. You need to take a few days off. That's the procedure."

"What about desk work . . ."

"Can't do it. You take a few off and we'll talk about the investigation when you get back and . . . we need to have some techs go out and go through her things."

Seeing it was going to be a losing battle to keep asking, Kelly finally nodded. "Fine. Do I turn in my gun? Badge? Anything like that?"

"No. Like I said this isn't punitive. This is for you to be sure your head's on straight and going through her things to see if there are any clues why someone would want to kill her. It's most likely a random attack, but we have to follow procedure."

"It is punitive!"

He put his hand up. "I'm sure it feels like it . . . but I can't break policy."

Kelly released a breath. "Okay. I'll grab my gear and head out. Is there any problem with my chatting with Maria and Jess for a bit before going?"

"No problem. In fact they'd probably feel better about what happened if they had a few with you."

"Thanks. So when do I come back?"

He looked at the calendar. "A week. I'll have a memo drawn up tomorrow. Remember, this is for you. I'll have Misha go out with the techs tonight so you can go back home in a day or so. You have somewhere to stay?"

"Yeah, I can stay with Ryan. He'll be here in awhile and we'll go to his place."

"Good. If you need the department shrink or to talk with a debriefer, call me. Okay?"

"I will. And, sir. Thanks. I know this is the right thing to do. I just . . ." She didn't finish the thought, just released another breath, and stood. Without looking back, she headed out of the office. She needed to talk to Ryan . . . and Susan, but not from the station.

Actually, what she needed was to curl up in Ryan's arms and have him make sense of what happened. Natalie had her issues . . . she was annoying . . . but who would kill her?

Kelly peered into dispatch before entering to be sure Chris wasn't in there. She wasn't afraid of the blonde badge bunny — she just didn't want to deal with her after what she'd been through tonight. If anything, if she ran into the snarky bitch tonight, Kelly'd likely say or do something to Chris to extend her time on the beach, only it would be one that would be unpaid. And, since Kelly was still on probation, she'd likely lose her job.

Not that she was worried about finding a job — she could easily find another job doing any number of things. It was finding another job like this one. Being a cop, this was her dream job. This was the one she felt the strongest about. The one that defined her and what she wanted out of life. This was the career she was meant for. Kelly had no doubt about that. And the best way to do that now was to avoid Chris.

Seeing the coast was clear, Kelly pushed open the door and listened a moment to be sure there was no radio traffic. Hearing the silence, she slid into the chair next to Jess. Jess glanced at her monitor before turning and embracing Kelly. After a moment, she asked, "How are you?"

"I'm fine. Really fine." And she was. At least at the moment, she was fine. Just fine.

"Good. We heard . . . well . . . Natalie. Wow. I never thought when I came in and reported I'd seen something weird it would turn out to be your roommate's body."

"Yeah. Wow. She's the last person I expected or would have expected who'd die like that."

"Maria said you ID'd the body."

Kelly nodded.

"So . . . now don't take this wrong, okay?"

"Not at all. Go for it."

"Was she burned . . . bad?"

"Actually — wait — you didn't hear?"

"Hear what?"

"She didn't die in the fire."

She glanced back at the monitor. Kelly figured to see if any of the units still on duty had sent her a message or entered any calls on their own. When Jess turned back to Kelly, she looked serious. "So if she wasn't a crispy critter, how did she die?"

"Okay, that's an eeeuuu moment, Jess. Thanks. Really. Eeeuuu. From what the sergeant told me when I met with him a few ago the initial from the coroner is blunt force trauma to the back of the head."

Jess nodded. "So she probably died from falling and hitting her head trying to get out of the building." She paused for a moment before sliding a look Kelly's way. "I wonder if that blonde I saw hurrying away from the scene had anything to do with it."

"Possible. I didn't see where she was found or how. And that blonde you saw — unless there's camera footage there's no way of knowing if she was even there or saw anything."

Jess glanced back at the monitor again before asking Kelly, "So how did you end up IDing her?"

Maria walked in at that moment. "Hey. How are you?"

Kelly stood and the two women hugged. "Like I told Jess, I'm fine."

"Yeah, well, keep in mind, you could be numb or in shock right now and it will hit you later."

"Maybe. Like I told White, we weren't like friends or close in any way."

Maria walked over to the other console and looked over the pending calls. Not seeing anything, she turned back to Kelly and Jess. "When I first started . . . and we're talking twenty-five years ago . . . I thought I could handle anything. I figured because I sit in the station, in a room away from all the action, I would be immune to feeling anything. And for the most part I was. Yeah, I saw the photos of crime scenes, of victims. I heard the officers talking and talked to people in crisis on the phone. We're just the messengers. All dispatchers really do, bottom line, is accurately convey information from one source to the other. Yes, we lend an ear to people in crisis—but we hand it off to the officers or medical or whoever."

"I'm hearing a *but* here."

Maria nodded. "I'd been here maybe ten years before it happened. Oddly some of the worse calls I took were *before* I joined HNT, the hostage negotiation team. I don't know, maybe the training made me more sensitive or something . . . which it shouldn't have. And it's been only one call that kinda messed me up. We had this dispatcher, Deanna, working here and she was on the radio and I was answering phones and a call came in. This guy said he'd been sick, had had surgery, and they were having a problem paying the doctor and hospital bills. At first I thought he was looking for information on financial help so I started to bring up our EAP, you know, the employee assistance program, information. It wasn't an employee, but there's financial assistance as part of the program and I felt kind of bad for the guy because he was talking about over $50,000 in medical bills they owed. And then his voice got a little wobbly and he said, and I remember it like it just happened, *I took the dogs to the Humane Society today and left a good-sized donation. I know that sounds weird when I owe so much money, but here it is. I just shot and killed my wife and now I'm going to kill myself.* Before I could say another word I heard the shot. I heard him fire the gun and kill himself. I was already putting the call in but I froze. Kelly, I froze for a moment. It felt like I sat there for hours, but Deanna said it was only about three seconds and that I turned to her and told her the guy had just killed himself.

"Our officers were close by and got on scene pretty quickly. They had to evacuate the other houses . . . the neighbors . . . and then they went to make entry. They said it was pretty bad. He'd shot his wife and himself . . . one bullet each but . . .

well . . . they said it was bad. They had to take photos and it was stupid on my part, but I looked at them. Until then I'd thought I was Teflon when it came to feelings. But I was wrong. Way wrong. The first few days I was fine . . . showed up for work, laughed at some really bad jokes . . . just business as usual. Only it wasn't."

Jess had stopped watching her monitor and leaned her elbows on her knees and leaned toward Maria. "What happened?"

"We had a debrief session — a critical incident stress debriefing. You ever done one?"

Kelly shook her head.

"Well, they start by having each person say a few words on what their role was and what they remembered feeling at the time they were brought into the call. While I was talking about my role I started to shake. And then I started to cry . . . not about the people, but about the dogs and how they went from their home to Humane and weren't going to understand what was happening to them. I babbled about the dogs for what felt like an hour. And I cried . . . we're talking a full box of tissues cried."

"So are you saying," Jess began, "that doing the debriefing thing isn't a good idea?"

"No. Not at all. See, I wasn't dealing with the call and what happened. I was going about my life with what I thought was business as usual. But it wasn't. I'd shut down. I wasn't talking to co-workers, I wasn't sleeping at night and if I did I was having nightmares. I'd go a day without eating and then binge on junk food . . . serious junk food. And I showed up for work drunk the day after. No one knew. I kept it pretty low key and managed to do my job without getting anyone killed. And those are just the highlights. I avoided thinking about the call at all and was doing everything I could to bury what happened. To pretend it didn't happen and if we hadn't had the debrief, frankly, I think I would have lost it. There was nothing that was going to stop me from going down the destructive path I was on after. The debrief saved my career and I'm pretty sure my sanity."

"Wow." Kelly shook her head. "I had no idea."

"So what I'm saying is if they offer a debrief, take it. And even if they don't, don't be surprised if it hits you in a few days that someone you knew died under suspicious circumstances. Even if it's not suspicious, someone you know died in a bad way. A young life in a way, cut short."

CHAPTER FORTY-SIX

A short time later, driving separately, Kelly left with Ryan for his place.

She didn't share a bond with Natalie. The woman rented a room and was, for the most part, an annoyance. What she wanted to do was to be able to talk about how relieved she was her issues with Natalie were finally over. Maybe being relieved was wrong, but the fact was Kelly was not going to miss the redhead. Natalie was a demanding nuisance from day one day of moving in now that Kelly thought about it. From the first phone call when Natalie demanded to come on a certain day and time. All the signs were there and Kelly just ignored them. She needed to sort out if she'd ignored those signs because she was in denial that Susan was moving out or was she doubting herself, her ability to make a decision? At least Ryan would help her sort things out.

Now, for the first time since she moved to California, she was going to walk into an empty house. Sure, Susan had taken trips with her various consulting jobs and she lived alone for a few days after Susan moved, but Ryan was there. Until Natalie moved in, Ryan stayed almost every night. And much to Natalie's annoyance and chagrin, Ryan had stayed over several nights a week after Natalie moved in.

Kelly drew in a deep breath and focused on releasing it as slowly as possible. She stared at the house—it seemed darker than ever. Not just because Natalie wasn't there with her lights on—there was an emptiness to it.

"Now why would that be?" She asked herself. Natalie was

an energy suck, so her absence should make the house feel calm, not empty, right?

Right.

Still, there was that feeling of relief that she wasn't going to have to deal with Natalie in the house. And did that make her a bad person? That she was glad not to have to deal with Natalie and her demands anymore?

Nor was she going to have to deal with her death at work. There was no way White or any of the department admin would let her participate in the investigation if it turned out something more than a slip and fall getting out of the building killed Natalie. But she'd hear about it. Someone would tell her things and, of course, there was always the police report. Fortunately that wasn't, Kelly guessed, the same as if say Susan had died.

Kelly drew in another breath and turned the car into the driveway and pulled up to the garage. As she watched the door roll up, it occurred to her that Ginny wasn't going to miss their roommate either. Ginny'd be able to have her food where she liked it, and her litter box could go back in the guest bathroom, and she'd be able to have her toys around the house . . . yes the little cat would undoubtedly be happy to have her little world her version of normal.

Inside the house Kelly called Ginny, and as if she knew something had changed, the gray cat came running with her tail up in the air. Of course, Ginny could have picked up something in Kelly's voice, or . . . there were times and stories of cats knowing the news before humans did. Kelly dropped her go-bag and picked Ginny up. Cuddling the cat to her shoulder, she whispered, "Gin-gin, Natalie is dead. She died tonight. She won't be coming home anymore and for a couple of days we're going to stay at Ryan's."

The cat started to purr . . . whether it was because she understood their roommate was dead or she felt Kelly's relief

Kelly didn't know. Either way, the sound of her purrs was soothing.

Kelly padded into the kitchen, flicked on the light, and settled Ginny on a chair—the chair Ginny always liked to sit on, but Natalie would balk at.

"First things first, Gin." Kelly pulled Ginny's dishes out of the pantry and put them near the refrigerator where they'd sat before Natalie came along. Then she put out some extra fishy-smelling cat food, the kind Natalie hated, and refreshed Ginny's water so the cat could eat before they headed to the city.

Ryan and Misha arrived about the same time a few minutes later. The techs followed Misha in and started going over Natalie's things. As Misha watched the techs start going through Natalie's things, she told Kelly it didn't look like it would take very long, but Kelly didn't want to stay in the house—at least not tonight. Leaving Misha to it, Kelly turned to Ryan and led him into the living room. The moment he pulled her into his arms, she started to relax. The feelings she'd been holding at bay bubbled to the surface. Not just the ones about seeing Natalie's body on the stretcher and her death, but the ones she'd kept down, buried, from the moment Kelly'd met her.

"Oh, Ry."

"It's okay, babe. It's okay. Cry if you need to."

"I don't want to cry. Ry . . ." she looked out the door, down the hall before whispering, "I'm glad she's gone. Ry, I'm sorry she's dead, but I'm glad she's gone. I'm relieved I don't have to deal with her anymore. Is that wrong?"

He rested his chin on her head, held her close. "No, not at all. Truth be told, I got to admit I'm glad she's gone myself. Sad she's dead and the investigation into her death won't be pleasant, but that's not going to be our problem."

Kelly drew in a breath. "Wow . . . I . . . I'm not processing all this . . . I hadn't thought about how the investigation into her death would affect me, but it will in some way, won't it?"

"No, it won't. Let's pack you a bag and go."

Driving to Ryan's a short time later, she wondered about Maria's words, and in reality, they made sense. From her own experience, as a stalking victim, Kelly knew how a day or so after an incident she'd start to shake and have flashbacks — not to events in this life, but of what she now knew were past life events — events where she, Ryan, Adrian and, at times, Susan came in contact with each other and had relationships. More than in touch, her romantic relationships with Ryan and Adrian played themselves out over and over again, each time with Ryan dying in some tragic way. A few days later, Kelly would have a series of nightmares or start shaking for no reason, or seemingly no reason. It made sense that even though she wasn't close to Natalie — that Natalie, in fact, annoyed the shit out of her, that the woman's death would disturb her in some way.

At least the body . . . Natalie . . . wasn't burned or disfigured in any way. She was just . . . dead. Sure. Natalie's mother would have to come get her things and she'd probably cry or carry on, but not the way Natalie would have. And then it would be over.

Ryan broke into her thoughts when he asked if she was really doing okay.

"I'm fine. But Ry . . . Natalie."

"Not the way you expected her to move out, was it?"

"Absolutely not. Ryan, how can you joke about that?"

"I'm not joking. I'm being perfectly serious. You wanted her to go, but never in your wildest imagination did you think she'd end up dead."

"No. No, I didn't."

Once at Ryan's, they quickly settled Ginny in one of the bedrooms and then left her to roam around exploring her new digs. Kelly sat down on the couch and cuddled up against her guy. Myriad emotions bubbled to the surface, happy, sad, scared, confusion chased each other through her mind. "Ryan, do you think it's my fault?"

He toyed with a strand of her hair, his brow furrowed. "How? How could it be your fault, honey?"

"Because I asked her to leave."

He was matter of fact in his response. Rather than cater to her guilt, he let her know in a clear and rational tone. "Tell me how that is your fault. Kelly, she was disruptive. She was set in her ways and even though she was told over and over it is your house she refused to compromise. I'm surprised you put up with her as long as you did."

"You're not the first person to say that. What I'd like to know is why did everyone wait to tell me what they thought? Why didn't you tell me . . ."

"I did."

"Not very forcefully. No, wait, I don't mean it that way. I mean . . ."

"You wanted permission to kick her out and no one was giving it to you."

"Yes . . . that's exactly it. I didn't want to be the grown-up. I wanted someone, anyone, everyone, to tell me it was okay to tell her to leave. I guess that makes me pretty imma-ture . . ."

"No. There are times we want the validation or someone to validate that what we want to do is the right thing."

"Exactly. I wanted someone to suggest to me that Natalie leave so I could act on it and boot her ass out. But I didn't want it to be my idea because if it was, then I would be mean and thoughtless and unkind."

"And there's nothing wrong with that."

"Thanks. Still . . . Ry, the lieutenant said that the initial re-port showed she may have died from blunt force trauma—

murder."

They sat in silence for a few minutes. Ginny ambled into the room and jumped up on the couch to join them, purring loudly. It seemed Ginny was happy in her own way, about the change in living situation.

"So, now what?" Ryan asked her.

Kelly played with a button on Ryan's shirt. "That is the question. There's the *what* of my private and my professional life."

"Well, work life side should be fairly straight forward — they'll do an investigation, find a definitive cause of death and rule one way or the other on it."

"Yeah. I won't be part of it, but I'm sure I'll hear about it."

Ryan nodded. "You may be called to testify at a coroner's inquest if it pans out to be murder."

Kelly drew in a long, slow breath. "There was some joking about that . . . you know, black cop humor, at the station. She was annoying, but who would kill someone for being annoying?"

"That's a question for the killer, if there was a killer. It remains for the coroner and the investigator to determine if she died because she had a slip and fall or if it was murder. You won't be involved in much of that except as a witness about what she did or was doing right before it happened."

"Well, that's easy — she came home and asked me for a ride back to her work. She was alive and well when she walked toward the building. In fact." Kelly snapped her fingers. "Someone approached her as she got to the building. It looked like it was someone she knew and I figured it was a co-worker. She looked just fine walking toward the shop area."

"Shop area?"

"The showroom looked closed when we pulled up . . . I guess the dealership closes early on Friday nights." Kelly shrugged. "Like you say, that's for the investigating officer to look into. All I know is she looked fine walking toward the shop area when I left her off."

Ryan nodded, "You sound like you're fine not doing the investigation."

"In this case, I am. To be honest, except for curiosity about what happened I'm not interested in what happened. I can manage without the rent for a few months . . . it's just having her things there . . . just . . ."

"Creepy?"

"In a way. I'm not sure how I'd feeling moving into a house where someone died . . . well, not died there, but . . . well, once her mother comes to get her things . . . I'm rambling, aren't I?"

"You're allowed, and if you need help making your mortgage payment, I'll help you."

"No, no, I'm fine on money. It's my need for a security blanket on the money thing, you know?"

"I do. I do. So . . . I know you're rattled about her death. What do you need from me?"

"Hold me. Just hold me."

"Happy to."

Ryan pulled her a little closer. "I'm here for you, no matter what, I'm here for you for as long as you need me."

"Would that include a lifetime?"

He kissed the top of her head. "You know it, babe. You know it."

*

Ryan woke the next morning and smiled when he felt Kelly's head resting on his chest. Mornings waking up next to her were always the best. They'd had a long road finding each other—not just in this life, but through centuries. For the first time in his life, he felt complete and secure. Not that he'd felt insecure about himself. It was just that a piece of himself always felt like it was missing until he met Kelly. While he didn't have the complete past-life recall she did of their many lifetimes together, he had glimpses of them. When Kelly recited the spell breaking the bonds of the one that had bound Adrian to her, he knew the words before she said them. They were nothing he'd read or seen—they were parts of his psyche. He knew, without a doubt, he and Kelly had finally and forever found their way to each other.

He also knew that the next few weeks would be hard for her. Not the hardest she'd ever faced—breaking free from Adrian, from the spell she'd cast to have him, that was the hardest. But dealing with Natalie's death was going to be hard for her to get through.

He didn't fear Natalie's ghost would appear or anything like that. And even if she did, her ghost couldn't haunt any worse than her in person. No, it would be the investigation into the death and finding the killer. It was going to be hard for Kelly to stay out of the investigation if it turned out the annoying redhead had been murdered.

Kelly stirred beside him. He smiled to himself as her hand slid ever so slowly toward his crotch. Even in sleep, she knew how to rouse him, make him want her as he never wanted another woman.

She snuggled closer, and as he pulled her closer in his embrace, she placed a light kiss on his pec and another after another, working her way to his neck, his chin, and whispered, "I love you" before lowering her lips to his.

Slowly, sensually their lips met, a slight rubbing across each other's, little nibbles on the rims as Kelly gently undulated her pelvis against Ryan's hip, her hand finding its way to his cock where she began leisurely stroking him up and down.

"You keep that up you never know what may come up," Ryan whispered against her lips.

"I think something has already come up." She smiled against his just before she slid her tongue into his mouth.

"I think you're right," Ryan told her, rolling Kelly on to her back and beginning his own kissing trail along her jaw bone, to her shoulder and then down her chest to her breast. He flicked his tongue back and forth against the nipple until he heard the change in her breathing. At the very moment she drew in a shuddering breath, he pulled her nipple into his mouth and sucked like it was the most decadent sweet ever made. Over and over, he alternated between sucking and licking her nipple while his fingers stroked the other until Kelly moaned in sheer pleasure.

"Ryan." Her voice, laced with passion, lanced through him, surging to his groin, making him even harder.

Without a word, Kelly lay more deeply on her back and spread her legs. Ryan obliged her need by moving between her thighs, spread for his pleasure, and in a stroke, entered her. Both uttered, "I love you," at the same moment.

In a combination of desire and a need to feel alive, they climaxed quickly, completely, and after a moment to catch his breath, Ryan rolled off her and pulled Kelly into his arms. "Are you tired of hearing I love you?"

"Never."

"Good. Because I love you more every day."

"Ryan Michaels, I'm so glad to hear that because I love *you* more every day."

"Seems we've got ourselves a match."

"We do indeed."

They lay in silence for a few minutes, Ryan stroking Kelly's arm. Not hearing a change in her breathing, indicating that she was falling asleep, he softly murmured, "Now that's how I wouldn't mind waking up every day."

"Me too."

"Maybe . . ."

" . . . someday. You have plans for today?"

"Nothing that can't wait. What's on your mind?"

"Nothing special. I just . . . I just don't want to be alone to-day."

"Then you won't be. I'm here for you, Kelly, for as long as you need and want me, I'm here for you."

"Today's a good start . . . on forever. We are forever, aren't we, Ryan?" Before he could answer, she shook her head. "I sound pathetic . . . beyond needy."

"No, hon, you sound like a woman in love and that's a good thing because I feel the same way. Trust me, we are for-ever."

"I'm glad. So today . . ."

"Whatever you want."

"Good. How about some breakfast and then . . . then I don't know."

"Sounds perfect. Shall we do our part for drought relief and shower together?"

Kelly nodded. "And who knows what will come up while we're in there."

The ringing of Kelly's cell woke the couple up after a short nap a bit later. Kelly reached over Ryan for her cell while Ryan fumbled for his landline. Ginny meowed in protest as being jostled from her place on the bed. Kelly answered a second before the call went to voicemail.

"Kelly? Is this Kelly?"

"Uh, yes." She fought to wake up enough to focus on the caller. Hoping it was work calling her back in or even better telling here there'd been a mistake and that Natalie had only been unconscious ran through her mind.

"It's Lorraine, Natalie's mother."

"Oh . . ." She lay back down in the bed, close to Ryan so he could hear the call without her putting it on speaker. "Mrs. Valle, I'm so sorry. I'm so sorry. How are you doing?"

"I'm . . . how could this happen? Why did this happen?"

"We don't know. The police are investigating . . ."

"Why aren't you looking into it?"

"Department policy says I can't because we were room-mates . . . they feel I would be too emotionally involved."

"How could you be emotionally involved when you were throwing her out on the streets?"

Okay, that was enough. The woman was upset. Her daughter had died, possibly murdered. But surely she knew how neurotic her daughter was. "Mrs. Valle, I'm not sure what Natalie told you, but she had plenty of notice that I felt I needed to live alone right now."

Ryan shook his head and mouthed to her not to talk about her relationship with Natalie.

Kelly sat quietly for a few moments, letting the redhead's mother gather her thoughts . . . to collect herself. Finally, looking for safe ground, a way to move the call along, she spoke. "Is someone with you?"

"No, not right now."

"Do you have someone who can come be with you?"

"Yes. Yes. My neighbor came by while the police were here and stayed with me last night. She went home for a bit this morning, but is coming back to stay with me tonight."

"That's good. That's good. It's not good to be home alone right now."

"No. It's not. I've lived alone for several years, but . . . with Natalie. Kelly, they said . . . the body . . . the ID . . . they said I didn't need to."

Kelly debated how much to say. "Mrs. Valle, we can talk about this in a couple of days, okay? Right now all I can say is I'm sorry for your loss and to suggest you keep from being alone."

"Do you think my life is in danger?"

Kelly blinked. It hadn't occurred to her that Natalie's death was about more than Natalie. Could there be an issue with her entire family . . . what little there was of it? She looked at Ryan, who again shook his head. "That's something you need to talk to the police about."

"But what do you think? And what about you? Are you in danger?"

The woman was all over the place with her questions . . . but that was to be expected on the heels of finding out her daughter was murdered.

"Mrs. Valle, I can't discuss the case with you. The police are investigating and they're the ones you need to speak with."

"But why can't you?"

Kelly drew in a breath and sorted out her words. Finally, she thought she had a viable answer, one Natalie's mother could and would understand. "It's best if people who knew her directly don't speculate on what may or may not have happened or why because that way, when the police ask their questions, do their investigation, our answers will be factually accurate and not colored by what we may or may not think happened. Does that make sense?"

There was a moment or two of silence before she answered, "Yes. Well, I guess you're going to want to rent Natalie's room out quickly. When can I come pick up her things?"

The last thing Kelly wanted to deal with right now was a distraught mother coming into the house going through Natalie's things, probably crying, possibly having a meltdown.

"Let me check with the department about that and have one of the investigating officers get back to you."

"Why? Why can't I come get her things?" The woman started sobbing heavily again.

A moment later, another woman was on the phone. "Listen

277

to me, young woman. My friend is *grieving*, her daughter was murdered because you kicked her out of your house and into the streets. If she wasn't living on the streets she'd still be alive."

Kelly blew out a breath and threaded her fingers through her hair. Apparently, Mrs. Valle's neighbor had shown up . . . if she hadn't already been there listening. At least now she knew where the business about Kelly possibly being involved was coming from.

"I will call the station and ask them when Natalie's mother can come and pick her things up. Alternatively I can pack her things and have them delivered."

"And why is that? You don't want to look in the eyes of a grieving mother?"

"I've told you what I will do. I'm going to hang up now."

Kelly disconnected the call and looked at Ryan in disbelief.

"Grieving families . . . one reason why I like federal law enforcement. We don't have to do too many of those notifications."

"I didn't do the notification! The chaplain and officer who went out would have explained it all to her!"

"She's grieving and has a friend who's probably seen one too many cop shows and has you confused with a perpetrator or Natalie's lover."

"Ryan!" She turned away from him and looked across the room. "Natalie would be all over this, wouldn't she?"

"Major drama. Right up her alley."

Ryan took the phone from Kelly. "You okay, babe?"

She looked at him, opened her mouth, closed it, and shook her head. "I'm fine. But that call. I get grief, Ry. I really do. And I get it she wants answers and to get her daughter's stuff. But seriously? Does her friend really think I had something to do with Natalie's death? And that business about her living out on the streets? Natalie was *not* living on the streets! She was paid up till the end of the month and Ryan . . . I gave her a month's notice to get out. Exactly what the law requires. And she *was* looking for a new place."

Ryan pulled Kelly to him and held her close.

"It's not funny! Ryan Michaels, it is not funny."

"I'm not laughing."

"Yes, you are. I can feel your chest moving up and down like it does when you laugh. It isn't funny."

He broke into full-scale laughter. "Sorry, but it is. Not the part about her blaming you for Natalie's death, but you . . . your reaction."

"Oh, so now I'm a joke." She half-heartedly pushed away from him.

"No, babe. Not. But if you could have heard yourself . . . and I get it, you're frustrated with the whole thing. Unfortunately it will probably get worse in some ways till it's all said and done so I'd suggest you have a few laughs about it while you can."

A hand on either side of his torso, she gave him a light shake. "You're right. I know you're right . . . but, Ryan! The woman is nuts! Like I said, I get it that she's in shock and grieving but really? Living on the streets?"

"Kel, consider the source. When you gave Natalie her thirty-days' notice to leave she probably called her mother and in true Natalie fashion she added some extra drama to it. You gave her thirty days . . . she probably told her mother two weeks. And it probably went on from there."

She dropped her hands and let out a breath. "You're right. You're right." She blew out another breath. "What would I do without you to put things in perspective for me?"

"You'd figure it out. And . . . you'd call Susan and the two of you would go to town on it. Speaking of which, we got a little busy last night . . . are you going to tell her?"

She shot him a duh look.

Hands up in surrender, he started to laugh again. "I just know how you guys are."

"I don't tell her *everything*, Michaels."

"No?"

"No . . . there's that thing you do between the sheets . . . ."

He pulled her back into his arms. "I'll be here for you through this and you know Susan will too."

"I know. Have I told you lately how much I love you?"

"Love you too, babe. Love you more than anything too, babe."

"Well . . . how about some brunch while I try to figure out the rest of my day?"

"Sounds good."

Together they walked into the kitchen. While Ryan pulled out brunch makings, Kelly fed Ginny. The gray cat purred loudly, almost as if she knew the dreaded Natalie wasn't going to balk at her eating in Ryan's kitchen.

They worked companionably, cooking their meal, and didn't speak until they sat down to eat.

"So . . . here I am with a week off with pay . . . what do I do? I probably should call the station to tell them Natalie's mother wants to come get her stuff and see if it's all right."

"I would. But it's early yet."

"It's a murder! At least we think it is. How else could she gotten her head hit if someone didn't hit her?"

"She could have been pushed, slipped and fallen . . ."

"It's Natalie . . . she couldn't . . . wouldn't . . ."

"I doubt she'd throw herself down or take something and hit herself in the head with it."

"Isn't that sad? We're so used to her gratuitous drama we even joke about her hitting herself in the head."

Ryan finished chewing the bite of toast he'd taken. "It is. But that's not your problem. By the way, who notified her work?"

"I don't know that they even were. I'd guess the department or her mother. I do need to call in and talk with my sergeant about my call with her mother and see about her going to get Natalie's things. You know, I hate this. I really do. She's gone and I'm still having to deal with her shit. And don't tell me that's the anger part of grief coming out. I'd be pissed at her even if she moved out without incident."

While they finished up their meal, Kelly reached for the kitchen phone, called into the station, and asked for White. "Hey, sir. I know I'm on admin leave but I had a couple of questions and wanted to let you know Natalie's mother called me."

"No problem, McKenna. I was going to call you to come in to talk later today."

"Oh. Well. We can talk then. When do you want to see me?"

"Can you make it in an hour?"

"Make it two—I'm in the city at Ryan's. Is there a problem if he comes?"

White paused for a moment before answering, "Sure, it would be okay. He might have some insight on the case."

"Great. See you in a bit." Kelly hung up and turned to Ryan. "Hope it's okay I asked if you could come . . . you don't have to if you don't want to . . ."

"I wouldn't have it any other way."

Several of the officers came up to Kelly when she entered the station through the front door a short time later. Each one took a moment to assure Kelly they were sorry for what happened and that they were all on board looking for the killer. Any feelings she had about being ostracized or blamed were quickly put aside. It helped that Ryan was by her side. And it was nice that she didn't feel like he was there rescuing her or trying to rescue her. He might have been, but this time she soaked up his support. Maybe she was finally putting her past behind her and ready to truly move on with the man she'd been promised to so many lifetimes ago.

They picked up cups of coffee as White led them into one of the conference rooms.

"Thanks for coming in, Kelly. Michaels, good to see you."

"Thanks. This is weird. I got to tell you it's really weird."

"I can imagine." Her sergeant gestured to Kelly and Ryan to have a seat.

Once everyone was settled in their seats, White sat for a few moments looking down at the blank pad of paper on the table in front of him. Kelly looked out past his shoulder to the garden area one of the volunteers had planted with native trees and bushes behind the police station. A few boulders, large enough to sit one along with some park benches were scattered around the area. Kelly'd sat out there a few times herself, enjoying the peace and quiet when on a break in her shift or to eat a meal.

White reached for his pen and absentmindedly tapped it on the table a few times, seeming to gather his thoughts. Finally, he cleared his throat. "We've gotten preliminary reports from the coroner and the arson investigator regarding the deceased."

Despite sitting quietly, Kelly's stomach was in a jumble, cramping up as if she'd eaten something rotten. She swallowed in anticipation of what she knew was going to be bad news.

When neither she nor Ryan said anything, White cleared his throat again and spoke. "It appears the initial coroner report was accurate—Natalie Valle died from blunt force trauma to the back of her skull."

"So not from smoke inhalation?" Kelly's voice was tinged with sadness at the thought that at least with smoke inhalation Natalie would have more or less gone to sleep and not woken up rather than the stunning pain of being hit in the head.

"No. She was, as the coroner said, probably dead before she hit the ground."

"Is there a chance the building had caught on fire and she was running to get out when she might have fallen and hit her head?"

White shook his head. "Not from how the coroner has described the head wound. One of the officers found a wrench lying near where the firefighters found the body with hair and blood on it."

Feeling distraught, Kelly looked over at Ryan. "Who would do something like that?"

"That's what the investigators need to find out, hon," Ryan told her.

Still not believing what she was hearing, Kelly pressed. "You're sure that it wasn't an accident — that maybe when she walked in the building was on fire and she was running out?"

"Absolutely. Again, the preliminary report indicates that there was an accelerant used."

"So it was arson." Ryan nodded in Kelly's direction.

"It appears so," White told them.

"That's just . . . wow . . . I'm having trouble wrapping my mind around that," Kelly told him.

"Fortunately we don't see a lot of murders like that in Red Oak, but it happens. Sadly this time it's someone we . . . or at least you . . . know."

Kelly drew in a breath. "Well, thank you for letting me know. Um . . . have you . . . has anyone . . . told her mother?"

Her sergeant shook his head. "No. And for now I prefer to keep that information under wraps. At some point we'll give her the full details, but for now we need to keep it close to the vest."

"Understood. Well. Am I still on leave?"

"Unfortunately, for a few days, yes."

"I see."

White cleared his throat. "Kelly, if you're up to it, I'd like to ask you a few questions about what happened last night."

"Sure. Sure. No problem."

"Why don't you start from the beginning."

With a look at Ryan, she began by telling her sergeant how she'd been on her way to work and how Natalie came in just as she was leaving and asked for a ride back to her job.

"Did you see anything strange when you pulled up?"

"No . . ." Her brow furrowed, she thought back to the night before. "It was still a little light out. Natalie hadn't said much in the car—or if she did, I tuned her out. Sometimes she tends . . . tended . . . to ramble and there was usually a bit of drama attached to it. She'd embellish things, you know? If she'd called two phone numbers she'd say she called six. If she looked at one apartment or house she'd say it was five. I tended to take whatever she said with a grain of salt."

Ryan nodded in agreement.

"So we pulled up, Natalie said one of the guys from her job would give her a ride home and she got out of the car."

"How'd the building look?"

"Fine. I don't remember any signs of smoke or anything that would indicate a fire. If I had I would have stopped Natalie and called it in."

"Then she just walked up to the door and went in?"

"No. No. The front was dark, like they were closed for the day and she headed back toward the shop area."

"Did you watch to see if she made it back there?"

"You're asking if I saw her slip and fall?"

White lifted a shoulder in response.

Kelly closed her eyes while she continued speaking. "All I saw was her heading to the back door and then . . . wait . . . yeah, someone came up to her."

"Male? Female?"

"I don't know. I was in the car and maybe twenty, thirty feet away. The person was . . . hmmm . . . about medium build. I think white . . . they were wearing a hoodie, a grayish hoodie." Eyes still closed, Kelly slowly recounted what she remembered seeing. "The person walked up to Natalie. Not fast. Just an everyday relaxed kind of walk. Natalie turned and seemed to be talking to the person, like she knew them. I figured it was someone from her work and I took off. If I'd thought for a moment that the person was a danger to Natalie or they didn't know each other I would have stayed and checked it out. But she seemed fine. Like I said, it was as if she knew the person."

"And you didn't recognize them?"

"No. I didn't get much of a look. Just someone in a hoodie. I can't even really say I saw what kind of pants they were wearing."

"Did you see Jess out there?"

"Jess? Hmmm. No . . . why . . ." Kelly snapped her fingers. "That's right. She did say she saw something weird happening at the dealership on her way in, didn't she? She came in a few minutes after I did."

"Something like that." White tapped his pen on the table again, a gesture Kelly was quickly coming to see indicated when he was thinking something through . . . coming to his own conclusions.

"Jess said something about a blonde . . . a woman who looked like . . ." Kelly trailed off in part because she didn't want to jump to any conclusions and, in part, because she didn't know if White was one of Chris's conquests. It wouldn't do to point her finger at someone without facts to back it up. After all, wasn't that what so many people complained about with the police — that they didn't do a full investigation or just went after the easiest suspect. Kelly had no doubt the majority of her co-workers wouldn't mind if Chris was somehow involved but really . . . that was incredibly far-fetched.

So what *did* Jess see?

CHAPTER FORTY-SEVEN

"We'll be interviewing Jess and Chris," White told them.

"Chris?" Ryan asked.

"She was coming on duty about that time as well and may have seen something coming to the station."

"You've got video as well, don't you? From the dealership?" Ryan asked.

White nodded. "And we'll be interviewing Natalie's co-workers. I know she irritated a number of the staff here so it won't come as a surprise to me, or anyone I imagine, if she also irritated people at her job."

"I'm pretty sure there were issues there. I learned pretty quickly not to ask her too much because she'd tell me and in the telling the story would grow. What she ended up with was very different from the story she'd started with. I doubt her tall tales were reserved just for me. She did tell me when she first moved in that her boss had taken away her internet so she couldn't look up directions for customers anymore. I didn't know her that well at that point so I asked her why and she launched into this story about how she was also forbidden to talk to her co-workers or customers. After seeing her in action both at home and some of her calls here at the station it wouldn't surprise me if she did the same thing at work and rather than fire her, the boss just shut her down."

"Well, we'll find out when we interview her co-workers." White drew a breath. "Kelly, can you think of anything she said, anything credible, about someone being angry with her or threatening her?"

Kelly let her gaze wander out to the community garden and thought for a few moments. Had Natalie ever said anything about someone threatening her? Viable or not . . . was there ever a comment?

She finally brought her focus back into the room. Brow furrowed, she answered, "No. No, I can't think of anything she ever said about anyone saying anything to her, not even that she saw someone following her."

"Well, hang on a second," Ryan broke into the conversation. When he had Kelly and White's attention, he continued, "Didn't she call in a few times that someone was outside the house?"

"You mean besides the other night when Jess came over? Hmm." Kelly chewed a fingernail while she thought. "Okay, yeah, a few times she said she heard something outside the house. And we'd go out and it would be nothing—she'd either have been watching something on TV or Ginny, my cat, was playing with something, but there was never anything real. She was pretty fond of calling 911 when I was on duty to report a lot of nonsense."

"Doesn't mean there wasn't something there though." White looked to Ryan for agreement. "No boyfriend, ex or anything like that?"

"No." Kelly shook her head.

When Ryan nodded in response, the sergeant continued, "We'll pull the calls from your place the past . . . how many months was she there?"

"Almost six."

"Seems longer." White chuckled. "We'll pull those and any from her place of work. I'm guessing we might get a few leads from her job. She may have mentioned something to them about being followed or something."

Kelly blew out a breath. "Man . . . talk about a cluster. I just . . . for as annoying as she could be, I still can't believe someone would kill her for her antics. It just doesn't make sense."

"Murder doesn't make sense, Kelly. It never makes sense," her boss told her. "Well, thanks for coming in. If I have any more questions before you come back on duty next week I'll give you a call. If you need to talk or need help, give me a call. We're done at your house so you can head on home and any time you want to let her mother in to pick up her things they're good to go. Otherwise we'll see you next week."

"Thanks. I'll be fine." Kelly and Ryan rose. "By the way, her mother was pretty distraught and made some comments about how I'd thrown Natalie out on the street and she wouldn't be dead if I hadn't done that. Sarge, I didn't just throw her out. I gave her thirty days' notice to move."

"I know. No one's going to give statements like that any credence."

"Right."

As they walked out, they heard Chris going out over the radio and by tacit agreement walked out through a back door, not taking the time to visit with anyone else on the way out. The last thing Kelly needed right then was to get into a conversation with Chris.

Outside Ryan reached for her hand and together they started down the street.

"You want to get a coffee or something to eat, hon?"

Kelly stopped and looked up at Ryan. "Yeah. You know a coffee sounds good. You have time?"

"I've got all the time you need for me to be here."

"Jamba Jam?"

He let go of her hand to put his arm around her. "Sounds good." Kelly relaxed into his embrace. He never failed her. Whenever she needed his strength, his support, Ryan was there for her. Despite how his protectiveness sometimes irritated her, he never let her down. With Ryan, it wasn't that he was possessive, but that he loved her and would do anything and everything for her.

A short while later, coffees in their hands, they sat down.

"Ry, what if was someone who wasn't necessarily looking for Natalie . . ."

"What do you mean?"

"What if it was just a random act . . . that someone was looking to break into the dealership or something?"

He shrugged. "That's for the investigators to find out. Let them do their job and you, for the next week, just relax. Think of it as a paid vacation."

Kelly took a sip of her coffee and thought about it for a moment. "You're right . . . I haven't really taken time or any kind of break in so long. I need to figure out whether I really need a roommate and seeing if I can live alone for really the first time."

CHAPTER FORTY-EIGHT

A s Ryan turned from locking the door, Kelly wrapped her arms around his waist, reached up, and kissed the back of his neck. "Have I told you recently about how much I love you, Ryan Michaels?"

"I believe you may have mentioned something like that not so long ago, but feel free to remind me."

"Mmm." Kelly released him from her embrace and lit several of the candles set about her room. It had been a long day, and even with the coffee, she was tired. All she wanted to do was curl up with her man. One of these days, she'd be the strong one, just not today.

Seeing what she was about, Ryan turned on a light rock station and dimmed the lights. Kelly pulled back the sheets on the bed, then reached to unbutton her blouse. Mirroring her movements, Ryan removed his ever-present shoulder holster, pulled his shirt out of his jeans, and started to unbutton it. Kelly sidled over to him and reached for the button on his jeans, undid it, and slowly pulled the zipper down. While she worked the zipper, he finished shedding his shirt, and she leaned in to lick his nipple. At his sharply indrawn breath, she took his penis in her hands and began to stroke him.

Step by slow step, he backed her to the bed. When the backs of her knees were flush to the mattress, Kelly slid down on the bed, her hands on Ryan's arms pulled him with her. Sensuously she shifted back on the bed until they were lying side by side, knee to knee, hip to hip, nipple to nipple. With an unspoken word, they wrapped their arms around each other, and their lips met in a torrid kiss. Kelly moaned and rubbed her hips against Ryan's. In turn, his cock hardened even further against her belly. Together they whispered words of want, of need, of love.

When Kelly's soft moans became more needy, Ryan rolled her on to her back. With her legs parted in welcome, he moved between them and slid into her welcoming warmth. She climaxed the instant he was inside her, drawing her legs up to hold him close while she murmured words of desire, telling him what she wanted, what she needed. In answer, he thrust faster and harder. She climaxed again and again with each thrust. She lightly scored his back with her nails, making him move even harder and faster into her. Their mutual need spiraling until they both found their release amid a kiss, sealing them together forever.

Curling up under the covers, Kelly chuckled.

"Am I missing something?" Ryan shifted to look down at her.

"I was just thinking how nice it is not to have to worry about disturbing Natalie. I know it's wrong to speak ill of the dead or to find something good in someone's passing, especially the way she died, but seriously, Ryan, the past few months having to be quiet and act like monks around her . . ."

He smiled, warm and sexy. "I can't say I'll miss her antics when it comes to our sex life."

"I'm thinking we need to start making up for lost time."

"And what we just had was?"

"Pure unadulterated passion. Plain and simple I have the major hots for you and I couldn't stand to go another minute without doing the deed with you."

"I'm all for passion . . . unadulterated and any other kind."

From under the covers, Kelly fondled him again. "I see."

"You see or feel?"

"Hmmm, I feel, oh do I feel."

This time she pushed him to his back and climbed on top of him. "Have I ever told you why I like to be on top?"

With his hands on her hips, guiding her movements, Ryan quirked a brow in question.

"Because, Agent Michaels, I like it when you play with my girl parts. All of my girl parts, but when you . . . ohhh, ahhh, that, that, ohhhh . . ."

She leaned over till her breasts hovered above his mouth. With a slight upward movement, he captured a nipple in his mouth and sucked just hard enough to cause her quick intake of breath. In response, she clenched her vaginal walls around his cock while she moved up and down over him. "Ryan . . . oh . . . Ryan."

When he shifted his lips to her other nipple, Kelly climaxed in response. She began to move more quickly above him, murmuring her desire, telling him how he made her want, need, couldn't live without him buried deep inside her.

This time when they came together, Kelly collapsed on top of him.

Kelly and Ryan called Susan the next morning to fill her in on what had happened. "You've been here for all the big things that have happened in my life so I figured you'd want in on this too."

"Dang," Susan murmured. "That's awful. Are you picking up any kind of strange vibes in the house? You know, like Natalie's ghost or anything like that?"

"Bite your tongue! Having her here in the flesh was bad, I can't imagine an OCD ghost floating around here."

"Yeah, that would be bad. Have you spoken to her mom or any of her friends?"

"Her mom, who, justifiably, isn't doing well with this. I don't think they were all that close, but still, murder, no matter how close you may or may not be, is always hard on family."

"So no clue what happened to her?"

"No. The only clue we have, if you can call it that, is I saw someone in what looked like a gray hooded sweatshirt approach her outside her job when I dropped her off that night and then a short time later Jess said she saw someone meeting that description leaving the area. Oh, and she also said she thought the person was skinny and blonde . . . and I quote *looked a lot like Chris.*

"Jess, your BFF who loved you forever for standing up to Chris, that Jess? Jess, the woman who tells you all her dating problems because Chris picks on her, that Jess?"

"The one and the same," Ryan dryly replied.

"She's not that bad, Ryan. I mean think about it . . . she's not Natalie."

"Trust me. No one could ever be Natalie."

"She was something else. But anyway, that's all we've got. The investigators are looking into anyone she may have pissed off or just had issues with. She was honest . . . at least in terms of paying her bills on time. Her stories, not so much, but in business things she was fine."

"Have you picked up any psychic impressions about her at all? I mean, if there was something there before you would have said something . . . or not let her move in in the first place."

"Right." Kelly considered Susan's question for a few moments. "I wonder though if all her chatter . . . how she was always carrying on . . . could have blocked me picking something up."

"I don't know enough about what you do to know for sure but it would make sense. What about since she's dead?"

"Hmm. I'm not a medium. At least I've never had any kind of mediumship skills and I don't think it would be starting now. Mostly it's picking up intuitive impressions about my own past lives. That sounds pretty self-centered, doesn't it?"

"It is what it is." Susan told her, "Maybe your past life issues are also other people's so if you tune into yours, you'll be able to solve theirs."

"Maybe. But it would be nice if I could do it before someone dies, you know?"

"Don't know. So Natalie?"

"Nothing. All I knew was that every time she came near me she just drained me. Psychic vampire stuff. I just never knew what was going to come out of her mouth and most of the time there was an embellishment to whatever she was saying."

"Sounds like you did pick up things from her."

"Picked up or got sucked dry."

"Okay. Now . . . what about Jess?"

"Jess?"

"Yes. Jess."

"What do you mean . . . Jess?"

"You know her better than I do, but . . ." Susan hesitated.

"But what? I'm not the only intuitive person in this conversation. Tell me."

"I'm not talking stalker country here. Not like Adrian. And maybe I'm totally off base and some of the things you told me about Jess were colored by Natalie's antics. You know, how Natalie would do something weird and she'd call the station and it was Jess getting the calls. They annoyed her as much as they annoyed you and Jess wanted to be close to you so she'd maybe stir things up too? Encourage Natalie in her own way? And didn't you say she and Chris go at it?"

"Almost all the women go at it with Chris. Even some of the guys do when she's done with them . . . like when they find they have the gift that keeps on giving and that they got it from her."

"Gift that . . . she's giving them herpes?"

"Uh-huh. You can tell who Chris has been with based on when they go looking for penicillin or another antibiotic. Apparently she doesn't do a thing to curb her activities when it's active. Rumor has it she's passed it on to some of the women via them having relationships with some of the guys after they've slept with Chris."

"Whoa, whoa. Let me get this straight. Not that it doesn't happen elsewhere—like even in my company, but Chris sleeps with the male officers, right?"

"Yup."

"And she's got an active herpes infection when she does?"

"Yup."

"And then when she breaks up with them they go and sleep with some of the other women in the department?"

"Yup."

"And rumor has it that Jess slept with someone who had it and now she has it?"

"Maybe. She never said. But if it were me, I'd be pissed. The issue with Jess and Chris though is that Jess is involved with this guy, Don who is a plumber or carpenter or something and Chris constantly antagonizes her about it. She makes all kinds of rude comments about him and Jess. I lent her an ear a few times about it and in turn she listened to some of my issues with Natalie. And yes, she took a number of those phone calls Natalie made. The woman annoyed everyone, not just me and not just Jess."

"So when Jess saw whatever she saw the night Natalie died and she said the person looked like Chris, she might have just been projecting or wanted to point the finger at Chris out of revenge or to get even?"

Kelly nodded. "Could be."

"And since Jess would like to, I don't know, somehow be a heroine to you, to show you how she's on your side she's embellished on her own to somehow tie Chris and Natalie together?"

"Plausible. It makes me look like the prize and kind of egotistical, but definitely plausible." Kelly drew in a breath. "But whatever it is, it's up to the department to figure it out. As long as I can go back to work next week and start looking for a new tenant-roommate I'm good."

"So you aren't going to try to solve this?"

"As much as I might want to be involved, it's not my problem."

"Glad to hear it."

"I know what you're about, Susan. I am so on to you. You know I have a hard time not getting involved in something. In this case, however, I can't get involved cause I'll major lose my job if I do."

"Well, I'm sorry Natalie died and that her death is so disruptive to your life."

"Thanks."

CHAPTER FORTY-NINE

"Jess, need you to come in to chat for a few. Maria will cover your station," Sgt. White told her from where he stood at the dispatch door.

Jess shot a look at Chris sitting at the primary radio before following White out the door.

"You need a rep?" Maria whispered to her on her way out, referring to the possibility that the other woman would need a union representative about whatever White wanted to discuss.

"I don't think so. I wasn't served a Robinson notice so it's probably just part of the investigation into McKenna's roommate's death."

"That's a mess, isn't it?"

Jess shrugged. "She was a mess."

"She may have been, but she's still dead and if it was a blow to the head that couldn't have been an easy one."

"Well, she's not hurting now. And she deserved it. The way she was always dumping on Kelly and calling here. We're better off without her around. Now Kelly can get a good roommate and hopefully this one won't be a nut job."

"Jess . . . that's cold. Just cold. Yeah, she may have been a little nutty, but she was killed."

Again Jess shrugged and turned to follow the sergeant into the interview room. She smiled as she sat across from her sergeant.

"Jess, this is Detective Daniels from the Sheriff's department. Because the deceased was related, in some fashion, to a member of our department, they will be doing the primary investigation." White referred to the buff, sheriff's deputy. With his close-cropped hair and smile lines around his eyes, he could have been anywhere from his early thirties to late forties. With piercingly clear blue eyes, he appraised Jess a moment before beginning. "Ms. Clarkson, you may be our best witness on Ms. Valle's death."

"Uh-huh."

"Yes. Why don't you start from the beginning and tell me what was going on before you saw what may have been Ms. Valle's attacker. I'm going to turn on the recorder, okay?"

"Sure." She settled back to begin her story.

"This is Sheriff's Deputy Daniels and I am with Jessica Clarkson, known to her peers as Jess. Today's date is October 11, 2020 and we are in Interview One at the Red Oak Police Station. Ms. Clarkson, for the record, please state your name, date of birth and job title."

"My name is Jessica Clarkson and my date of birth is October 27, 1985 and I am a dispatcher at Red Oak Police Department."

"Thank you. This is an interview into the death of one Natalie Valle and you are here as a possible witness and not in the official capacity as a Department employee. As such are you comfortable proceeding without representation?"

"I am."

"Okay, for the record, please start by telling me how you came to be in Red Oak on October 2, 2020 and what you saw as might pertain to the death of Natalie Valle."

"Sure. I left my apartment in Sonoma County about 3:30 p.m. so I could arrive in time to store my gear and be ready for briefing for work that day. I got into Red Oak City limits about 4:15 p.m. because traffic was pretty bad going southbound. I came down Grand and as I was driving by the Jaguar dealership I saw someone in a gray sweatshirt rushing away from the back of the building. When I looked past them I saw what at first looked like a bunch of rags on the ground . . . but it looked strange, like not really a big bunch of rags, so I slowed down for a closer look. At that time I thought I saw smoke or flames coming from the building. So when I saw that I got out of the car and went to get a better look. When I saw a foot sticking out of the rags . . . or clothing I realized it was a person. I smelled smoke so I came to the station to get help."

"You didn't call 911?"

Jess looked confused for a moment and then said, "I forgot. Anyway, the person in the gray sweatshirt had blonde hair and was skinny. I almost thought it was Chris because she has that kind of sweatshirt and uh, I think she comes that way too."

Daniels looked at her as if trying to make sense of the detour in her story. "We'll get back to the person you saw in a minute. Can you tell me why you didn't call 911?"

"Oh. Well, I knew Chris was working the early shift that day—working mids and whenever I've called 911 before and she's either answering the phones or on the radio she has always decided that my calls didn't have merit."

White turned his head as if questioning what Jess was relaying. White remembered that when Jess rushed into briefing that day, she'd said the person walking away from the dealership looked like Chris. Now, however, she was saying she knew Chris was working the early shift that day.

Jess looked at White. "I've told you that before—you and the other sergeants. Chris always disregards anything I call in so I usually wait till I get to the station if I see something and tell one of the officers or dispatch a unit myself."

"Okay. So even though you saw what you thought was smoke and flames and possibly an injured person, you thought coming to the station would get a quicker response?"

"Yes. Although since I thought I saw Chris on the street I guess I should have . . . could have called 911 because she wouldn't have been here to interfere. I was so shook up by what I saw, or thought I saw I didn't do that though. Obviously." She ended on a nervous laugh.

"When you saw the smoke and possible flames, you didn't think about going up to the dealership to alert anyone who might have been inside that they needed to get out of the building?"

"There was no one inside."

"How do you know?"

"Well, it was after five and the lights were out so I was pretty sure they were closed."

"After five? Jess, briefing for your shift starts at five. You should have been station by then."

"Yeah, but . . . because of the traffic and seeing Natalie lying there and the fire . . . well, I was nervous about it all and the building looked dark."

"I see. How did you know it was Natalie?"

"Natalie? Oh, well, I didn't know it was her, not at the time."

"I see, now this person you saw walking away from the building . . ."

"Not walking. She was rushing. That's what caught my attention . . . this person was rushing away from the building like something was wrong. I thought maybe they were going for help too, but I still came station to report it. And I came right into briefing. I didn't put my bag down or stop on the way in. I came right into briefing to report it."

"Okay. Let me make sure I have this straight." He paused to look at his notes for a few moments before continuing. "You got into Red Oak about 4:15 and came down Grand to get to the station. On the way you saw someone hurrying away from the Jaguar dealership so you slowed down to take a look. When you looked into the driveway area?"

Jess nodded. "Yes."

"You saw a bundle of what you first thought was just a pile of clothes. And when you looked past the clothing you thought you saw smoke . . ."

"And flames. I thought I saw flames."

"Right. So instead of calling 911 . . ."

"Because I knew Chris was on the radio and would ignore the call."

" . . . you came right to the station to report what you saw."

"Right. And the person I saw hurrying away was skinny and had blonde hair and was wearing a sweatshirt that looked like one that Chris has."

Daniels nodded. "Got it. Now, have you had any interactions with Ms. Valle?"

"Yeah. Just about all of us did. She was annoying, always calling with made-up problems and dogging Kelly."

"Kelly?"

"Officer McKenna. Kelly McKenna. Natalie was her roommate. Her very annoying roommate."

"I see. So you took emergency calls from her here at the station?"

"They weren't emergencies. She'd call about things like there were ants in the kitchen or there wasn't enough hot water for her bath and her shower."

White released a long, slow breath. "Jess, you should know by now that even mentally ill people and frequent flyers can have emergencies. It's up to the officer on scene to make that decision."

"Exactly. And that's why it's always a problem with Chris . . . she'll decide something doesn't merit an officer without having someone really check it out."

"As long as you know that whether or not something is an emergency can be a matter of perception. So you took calls from Ms. Valle on the emergency line. Any other contact?"

"Yes. She'd call here for Kelly with things going on in the house. Like if she got mad because Kelly left out her cat's food where Natalie didn't like it she'd call."

"She ever come station to report anything?"

"No. But she was at one shift party and was kind of weird there." Jess looked up as if trying to see the scene she was describing. "She and Chris got into it about something, but I don't know what. She just had some choice things to say about Chris."

"Uh-huh. And did something come up recently between you two? Ms. Valle and you?"

"Yes. My boyfriend and I had a little problem so Kelly said rather than go home I could go hang out at her house for awhile. She called Natalie to tell her I was coming over and to let me in. Natalie was kind of weird about it—argued with Kelly about it so Kelly gave me her key to get in. When I got there and was trying to open the door Natalie called the police because she thought . . . she said she thought . . . I was breaking in. That's the kind of thing she was always doing."

"I see. Anything else?"

"No. I think that's enough, don't you?"

The detective nodded.

"Okay. That's all I have for now."

"Sure." Jess rose to leave.

"Oh, one more thing." White stopped her at the door. "Next time you think you might see something happening, call 911."

"Right. And then when there's no help going it'll be on Chris."

"Jess, I know the two of you don't quite see eye to eye and I will chat with her about routing calls. You, however, need to pay attention to your own issues and procedures. You see something, you call it in—you don't drive up the street, pull into the parking lot and report it. That building could have burned to the ground because you drove to the station . . . fortunately in this case someone did call the fire in before you got here."

"Sarge, I was worried, upset. It completely caught me off guard and I panicked, you know?"

"If that's the case you need to consider how that kind of panic can affect your job. If someone called something in that was close to you, you need to consider how you'd handle it. I would hope it would be professionally."

"Yes, sir."

*

Jess stopped in the ladies' room to wash her face and hands before heading back into dispatch. She stood looking at her reflection for a few minutes and then shook her head. Why didn't Misha and Maria and the others see what a problem Chris was? The blonde did, regularly, close out calls without sending an officer. There had been any number of times the caller called back wondering why no officer had arrived and the others had to scurry around trying to get whatever it was taken care of. And they'd report it to their duty sergeant who, in turn, would do nothing.

And Natalie. Her death wasn't a loss to anyone. Sure, her mother would be sad, but anyone who knew her or who had contact with her . . . really? No loss. If she'd just tried to get along with Kelly, Kelly wouldn't have had to make her move out. And if she'd just tried to find a place sooner, she would have been gone instead of going back into her job late at night. Okay, it wasn't late, late at night, but the business was closed. She shouldn't have been there, but it was her tough luck she was, and now she was dead and wouldn't be a problem for anyone anymore.

And really, killing her was the kind of thing Chris would

do.

Jess snapped her fingers. Of course! Natalie might have called 911 that night because she heard or saw something on her way back into the Jag dealership and Chris probably just filed the call away.

But if that was the case, how could Chris have been there and killed Natalie because Jess was sure she'd seen Chris rushing away from the scene. How many skinny blondes were out there? Seriously?

CHAPTER FIFTY

"Right . . . okay. See you tomorrow, Misha." Kelly hung up the phone and turned to Ryan. "Misha said Natalie's funeral is day after tomorrow."

"And you're going?" Ryan's raised brow said more than the calm tone of his voice conveyed.

Kelly shrugged. "I kind of have to. Aside from her being my roommate the department wants some sort of police presence there to see if her killer shows."

"Makes sense." Ryan reached for her and pulled her into an embrace. "I'll be there with you . . . if you want."

He felt so good, so solid when she leaned into him. "I want."

The next day, with Ryan by her side, Kelly entered the church where Natalie's funeral was being held. She hadn't gone to the viewing . . . even though it was a closed coffin, in deference to Natalie's mother's belief that that was what she would have wanted, Kelly still couldn't bring herself to enter the funeral home. Several of the officers, along with Misha, were also at the cemetery. Kelly watched as Misha scanned the other graveside attendees. Natalie's friend Martha stood by her mother. It looked to Kelly as if the entire dealership staff was present, which, given the funeral happening in the middle of the day, was saying a lot — not that a lot of Jags sold in the middle of the day in the middle of the week. Some of Natalie's co-workers looked distraught, others looked bored, while still others were there to be seen.

Kelly turned a surprised look in Ryan and Misha's direction when she spotted Jess enter the cemetery.

Misha shrugged. "You know Jess."

Kelly's brow furrowed in confusion. "Yeah. Sort of. For all of complaining about Natalie and her calls . . ."

"Maybe she feels bad about complaining about someone who turned out to have a real emergency, but didn't have a chance to even call 911 before she died," Ryan whispered.

Jess ambled over to Kelly and Misha. Before she caught up with them, Misha murmured, "I'm going to see what I can get out of them at the reception."

"I'll let you know if anyone talks to me," Kelly answered, and Ryan nodded.

"Hey." Jess greeted them. "How are you doing, Kelly?"

"Fine. You?"

"I'm good, but it's not my roommate who got offed."

Before anyone could say anything, the further mercifully short burial service began. Kelly, Ryan, and Misha didn't speak through the service but scanned the area the entire time, looking at each person in attendance. No one looked like they felt anything but grief or resignation at Natalie's passing. Most of her co-workers looked bored. Clearly, they were there because their boss had told them it would be a good idea or that they owed it to her. People who seemed to be Natalie's friends, few that there were, along with her mother, cried. Surprised at her reaction Kelly wiped a tear from her eye.

At the end of the ceremony, despite the chilly reception she'd gotten from Natalie's mother on the phone, Kelly, with Ryan by her side, approached Mrs. Valle to express her condolences.

It was Ryan who spoke first, telling the older woman how sorry they were at the tragic way Natalie died. The members from the police department in attendance were rather shocked at her response when she spat, "You have a lot of nerve coming here. Come to gloat that you've got her out of your house, that what you're about?"

"No, Mrs. Valle, not at all. I would have hoped Natalie had explained to you that because of our conflicting schedules . . ."

"And whose fault was that? My daughter may have had issues, but you could have been nicer to her. You could have gotten rid of that cat and hired a house cleaner to come in a few times a week . . ."

Ryan tried to interrupt what looked to be turning into a long-running diatribe of the dead woman's needs.

"I see it now. You wanted my daughter out so you could live in sin with this man. Is that it?"

Kelly shook her head, reached for Ryan's hand, and turned to walk away.

"Ignore her. She's upset," Ryan told her.

"That sounds like a plan," Misha softly concurred. "Just don't be alone with her, okay?"

"Not a chance of that," Kelly told her.

"I'll come when she's there if you need me to," Jess told her with a glance back at Natalie's mother.

"Thanks. Well, since we're probably not going to the reception I'm thinking we should adjourn to Cat's Meow for some lunch?"

Misha and Jess nodded in agreement at the suggestion to go to a favorite local cafe. "We'll meet you there."

Together Kelly and Ryan walked toward his car. "You doing okay?"

"Yeah. I'm glad that's over. I did have to go, didn't I?"

At the car, Ryan opened the passenger door for Kelly. "It was the right thing to do. But I'm glad it wasn't me. Seriously though, don't even think about meeting the mother alone. More likely than not she'll try for a lawsuit or at least to try to get some money out of you."

"Well, she is entitled to the security deposit."

"True. But don't be surprised if she turns out to have a shopping list of demands to rival Natalie's. Natalie learned that constantly needing to negotiate for something else from somewhere and I'm betting it was Mom."

"Man, I wish I'd had an inkling of what was coming when she moved in. Ry, I really and truly thought she was just going to be a bit of a neat freak and she'd get over it."

"Mmm."

"And now, just the thought of looking for someone else . . . given what showed up the first time . . . I don't know. Maybe I can swing it on my own for awhile."

"Is it the money?"

"Not just the money. More that living alone is . . . I know Adrian is in prison and it's going to be awhile before he gets out and I know why he did what he did. But knowing and accepting are two different things, you know?"

Ryan nodded.

"So the extra money is nice, but it's really more about fear of living alone because of all the shit Adrian was always pulling except I didn't know it was Adrian. The other thing is, from what Misha said at the service, they've ruled out an accident and still don't have a clue who killed her."

"They'll find him."

"It's my department."

"I get it that it's hard for you to stay out of it . . . just call me or Misha if you find yourself starting to get into it."

"I will. I will."

CHAPTER FIFTY-ONE

"Well, I need to get going," Jess told them at the end of the meal. "Misha, you heading back to the station?"

Misha dabbed her napkin against her lips. "I figured I'd take a swing around the city and see what's up."

"Oh. Okay. I guess I'd better go then."

"You're on duty for graves tonight right?"

Jess nodded. "Yeah, Chris and I. Kelly, when will you be back?"

"Umm, I think White is moving me to days for a few weeks starting Sunday."

Jess sat back down. "You won't be on graves with me from Wednesday to Saturday?"

"Not for a couple of weeks. At least until they close the books on Natalie's death."

"Oh. Well, maybe I can switch with someone to your end of the week."

Kelly glanced at Misha and picked up a silent communication from her friend. "Don't you think that would make it hard on everyone else, Jess? Your officers rely on you to be there for your shift. You know, being part of the team they expect their whole team to show."

"Yeah. Yeah. But you're my team too."

"I appreciate that, Jess. Shifting your whole schedule around for what could just be a few days doesn't make much sense."

"Mmm. Well, we'll see. At least you won't have to deal with Chris." With her purse on her lap, she sat back down and looked around the restaurant as if to be sure no one would hear her. "That reminds me. I've been meaning to ask. Has anyone looked into where Chris was the night that Natalie died? Didn't I see that they found a scarf or something that looked like hers and put it in evidence?"

Misha quickly swallowed the mouthful of coffee she'd just taken. Eyes wide, she looked from Kelly to Ryan. "Where did you hear that, Jess?"

"Oh. Well, I pulled the report. I wanted to see if there was something I could do to help."

Shaking her head, Misha answered, "Jess, Jess. You know better than that. This is a priority investigation because it involves what could be considered family of someone in the department."

"Yeah, but I want to help."

"Well, you can do that by showing up for your shift and letting the detectives do their job. Stay out of the reports that don't concern you, okay?"

"Okay," she muttered as she stood up to leave. "I'll see you at the station, Misha, and you next week, Kelly. Bye, Ryan."

Misha, Ryan, and Kelly bid her goodbye. When they saw her leave the restaurant Ryan turned to Kelly and Misha. "A bit of hero worship going on there?"

Brow furrowed Kelly answered, "I'm not sure. I know most of the non-sworn read the reports on the more interesting cases —"

"Yes, however," Misha interrupted her, "that report is locked in the detectives' office. She would have had to go out of her way to get in there, get the key and pull it out. If any of the detectives or Elaine, the secretary, saw her in there they would have said something. And checking out the evidence . . . that's a little odd. I know it happens, but in this case . . . well, I know she and Chris clash."

"That was odd," Kelly told her, "for her to point out that

the scarf looked just like the one Chris recently lost or misplaced. And she's said that several times, hasn't she?"

Misha nodded. "Or as Chris said, it disappeared from the locker room a day or so before Natalie died."

Ryan spun his spoon in a small circle and then tapped his finger on the table. "Chris lose things often?"

Misha shook her head. "Not that I've ever heard her say."

"Is the scarf they found hers?"

Misha looked around the restaurant and when she was sure no one could hear her. "It appears to be hers. She swears it was in the locker room and had been there for about a week. She says she wore it into work the week before and then kept forgetting to bring it home. Chris swears she didn't pay any attention to it . . . that she knew it was there and figured she'd grab it at some point. When Sterling brought it in to book it into evidence she was a little surprised that they'd found a scarf, that she said, looked like hers. When she went into the locker room to get hers was when it started to look like it was hers."

"So is it Chris's?" Kelly wanted to know.

"We don't know. Not for sure," Misha answered her. "Motive is a big issue with that one. Yeah, your former roommate annoyed her. She annoyed pretty much everyone at the station that came in contact with her. Chris though . . . she might get into petty squabbles with what she feels is the competition at work, but going after Natalie because of what she might have felt were excessive phone calls? That doesn't sound like Chris. I'd believe it more if she caught Natalie in a clinch with one of the male officers Chris considered hers."

Kelly looked at her watch. "You've known her longer . . . aside from having to call for help the past few years first with Adrian and then with Clarissa, my only real contact with her is as an officer. She's a pain to deal with when you need back up or information on a call at times. Most of the time though, she's on top of it. I just can't see her killing someone because they made too many 911 calls, you know?"

Misha nodded. "Well, I need to get going. I'll probably talk to you before you go back on duty Sunday."

"Sure. Come by if you get a break."

"We should get going too, honey," Ryan told her.

They headed to Kelly's house. She stopped at the door and shook her head. "Even though she was only here about six months, it still feels a little strange to walk in the door and know Natalie won't be there."

"And Susan?"

"Only a phone call away."

Ginny came running to the door when they walked in, tail upright, and her purrs could be heard. "Someone is happy to see us . . . and not have Natalie here," Kelly commented. "Want some hot chocolate or something stronger?"

"You have a beer that would be good."

Ryan headed into the living room while Kelly went to get them a couple of brews. When she joined him in the living room, she smiled at the scene before her—Ginny lying across Ryan's lap, her eyes half closed in sheer contentment, purring loudly while Ryan stroked her soft fur.

"Know what strikes me?" Ryan asked as Kelly settled down beside him and shook her head. "How much Jess is bent on putting the blame on Chris."

"I noticed that," Kelly told him. "The night Natalie died, in briefing, almost the first words out of Jess's mouth were that she thought she saw Chris out there."

"And what did Chris say?"

"Interestingly she *was* late for briefing that night. Chris was supposed to be on days but she got someone to switch with her that night so she was on graves. And then she was late because, hmmm, there was something about traffic being bad on the way down . . . and since she and Jess come from up north they were both late. Jess got to the station first and Chris a few minutes later."

"And no famous scarf on either of them?"

Kelly shook her head and scrunched Ginny's ears. "I can't remember what either of them was wearing. Not very observant of me, but who thinks to look at their co-workers as suspects, you know?"

Ryan nodded in agreement. "I wonder what they were able to pull from the camera outside the dealership."

"Oh, Misha mentioned something about that. The suspect seemed to know the one camera was there and kept his or her head down. So far they can't tell if it was a man or a woman. And no one from the dealership or the shop area can remember seeing anyone back there."

"She say anything about the fire?"

Kelly shook her head. "No. Only what I heard that night and the day after that the fire marshal thought there was an accelerant. That seems a minor issue though since the coroner said she died from blunt force trauma to the head."

"All things considered, that was probably an easier way to go. Quicker."

"Had to hurt."

"But not like trying to breathe and not being able to."

CHAPTER FIFTY-TWO

K elly opened the door the next morning to find Natalie's mother standing there. The woman looked lost for a moment before shaking her head.

"Mrs. Valle?" Cautious after the scene at the cemetery, Kelly spoke loud enough to alert Ryan as to who was at the door. "Won't you come in?"

"Thank you."

Kelly studied the woman who walked into the foyer. There was a passing resemblance to Natalie in that the women were the same height and their eyes were the same color. The older woman's hair was threaded with gray — something Natalie would never have tolerated. She might not have made a lot of money, but one thing about Natalie, she put whatever she needed to into her appearance. She'd do without a meal if it meant she needed the money to pay for hair color or makeup or the god-awful perfume she wore. At the first sign of gray, Natalie was using one of those color wands to tide her over until she could color her hair. Fortunately, because the woman was such a neat freak and so OCD about cleaning, there weren't any stains in the sink. Mrs. Valle would be getting Natalie's entire cleaning deposit back, that was for certain.

"How are you doing, Mrs. Valle?"

She shrugged. "How are you supposed to be doing after your daughter is murdered?"

At least she wasn't ranting that the death was Kelly's fault. "I don't know, Mrs. Valle."

"No." She paused as if sorting her thoughts. "I found a few things that I don't think belonged to Natalie. I'll admit," the older woman stated, "I don't know all what Natalie owned, but this doesn't look like something she would have used, does it?"

Kelly reached for the earphones and threaded the wires through her hands. She pondered her next words before speaking. "I'm not sure. I never saw her at her job and for the little she said about it I don't remember her ever telling me if she used a headset or other device for answering phones . . ."

"Oh, they gave her one of those things you put over your ear . . . in your ear . . . a blue . . . blue . . ."

"Bluetooth?"

"Yes. Sorry, I'm not up on all the modern equipment and all."

"No problem. I'll check it out with her boss and if it's theirs I'll return it if you like."

"Thanks. Yes. And this . . ." She held out a garish looking red belt. "I don't think it was Nat's. She was never that thin. It is a belt, right?"

Kelly studied the other woman for a moment. That she'd called Natalie *Nat* was telling in its own way. Did she really not know what a few simple items were? Or was it the shock or puzzlement of finding that some of Natalie's things were a bit . . . different? Than her perception of her daughter was wrong? Still, the belt looked familiar.

Of course she could have seen it in a catalog. But it was more than that.

"And she'd never wear earrings that look like these."

Kelly looked at the long, dangling silver earrings. No, Natalie would never have worn any earrings that looked like that. She wasn't a clubbing kind of girl. At least not in the short time Kelly's known her. Natalie had worn small, gold earrings or pearls. Kelly reached for the earrings . . . she'd seen them before. Not so long ago, she'd seen them . . .

"I don't think they're Natalie's, Mrs. Valle. They might be a friend of hers from work."

"A friend? Natalie never told me about a friend from work."

"Oh. Well, maybe it was someone that started recently. You know, someone new and Natalie may have invited them home for a lunch break or something."

"You don't know?"

"Me? We worked different hours. I hardly ever saw her."

"But you know the belt isn't hers." The woman stated it matter-of-factly.

"Yeah . . . but I'd run into her. I never saw her wear it and . . . like you said, it looks a lot smaller than what she'd wear."

"Oh . . . yes." Natalie's mother looked worn. Just worn and tired. "You're right. Who would kill her? Who would do this?"

"I don't know, Mrs. Valle. I don't know. But the police will find out who did it and why."

"I hope so. I imagine you'll have a cleaning service come in to clean up her room and bath . . ."

"Natalie was very neat and clean. I'm sure it won't take much. In fact, I have a check for you for a full refund on her deposit and for the last week since she wasn't . . . Mrs. Valle, I've never dealt with anything like this before. I know you haven't either. We're both kind of struggling here. But I do have a check for the return on the deposit."

"Thank you. Her company paid for her funeral . . . I suppose because they're afraid I'm going to sue them for not having better security or causing her death."

Kelly bit her tongue rather than ask. If the woman was going to sue the car dealership, was she also going to try to sue Kelly for kicking Natalie out? Not that she did anything wrong. She'd given Natalie a month's notice in writing. Still . . . grieving people did strange things to deal with their grief.

"Well, if I find anything while I clean the room or we're getting it ready to rent again, I'll call you."

"Thank you."

As the woman drove away, Ryan guided Kelly back to the house. "You doing okay?"

"Yeah. Ry, some of the things her mother found were . . . odd."

"How so?"

Inside they headed toward the kitchen, and without speaking, Kelly started to pull out makings for soup. That was one of the things about their relationship that was so comforting for Kelly. They knew what the other one was thinking or going to do without speaking. At least most of the time. Ryan peeled carrots and cut up some already roasted chicken while Kelly sliced broccoli and a clove of garlic.

"Kelly? What was odd?"

She paused mid-slice and softly exhaled. "There was a headset in her room."

"Okay. Natalie listened to music, right?"

"It looked like a dispatch headset — like what we use at the station. There's a volume control and a foot pedal override switch on it."

Brow raised, he asked, "Any chance it's from her work?"

Kelly shook her head. "Her mother said they used a Bluetooth there. No, this definitely looked like a dispatch headset. It will have a serial number on it. I'll have Misha run it tomorrow."

Ryan nodded.

"And she found a belt and earrings. I could be wrong, but both of them look like things I recently saw Chris wearing. She came into the station one night on her way out to a party or some such event and I swear she was wearing that red belt and those earrings."

"Any chance she was hanging out with Natalie?"

"Are you kidding me?"

Ryan chuckled. "Yeah, I can't see those two even sitting in the same restaurant."

"Since I can't participate in the investigation I'm going to run them by Misha."

"Not Chris?"

"No . . . Jess has been saying how she saw Chris at the crime scene . . . I . . . I can't believe it but still . . . Wait . . . are you joking about asking Chris if they're hers? Ryan . . . if they are . . .then maybe Jess isn't going for the drama."

With a shrug, Ryan told her, "You're right to turn whatever you find over to Misha. Keep the evidence trail clear and be cooperative."

Kelly studied the items a moment before looking up at her guy. "Ryan, someone really could think I killed her, couldn't they?"

He nodded. "You kept your distance from her physically and emotionally, but she was still a drain or kept putting herself in a position of draining you if you let her. She was a time and energy suck and that was without even trying. It would be easy to see you just having enough and either shoving her out of the way or even popping her one."

"Ryan! I didn't! I couldn't kill another person. You know that."

"I know you didn't . . . but I wouldn't go down the *I couldn't kill another person road* all that closely. You're a cop. Red Oak may be a small town, but criminals don't care if they're in a little town or big city and if it comes down to you or the suspect I need . . . you need to know if it's you or him he's going to go down."

Kelly looked up into his eyes. It wasn't the first time she'd seen the cold steel in them. It was, however, the first time she'd seen it in relation to actions she might need to take. More than once, she'd seen Ryan in action during a criminal takedown, and before this lifetime, she'd seen him . . . the men he had been . . . defend what was his. There was just something chilling in his look, and while it didn't scare her, it made her aware of just how dangerous Ryan Michaels could be. "I'm pretty sure if it came down to me or some guy out to kill me I could handle it."

"Not handle it, Kelly. Make the decision and end it. Can you do that?"

"I think so . . ."

"Do you know so?"

"Ryan, why are you acting like this? Why are you acting like you *want* me to be a killer?"

"Because if they don't find someone with a solid motive and the evidence to prove it, when the D.A. starts looking at what's there and starts hearing stories, particularly from her mother, they're going to take a long look at you. You need to be able to stand there and say yes, as a cop I can kill; but as a person, dealing with a pesky roommate, no. That she was going to be leaving and you wouldn't be seeing her again."

She swallowed. It hadn't occurred to Kelly that someone . . . her fellow officers . . . could or would think she had killed Natalie. Sure, she knew the woman's mother blamed her. But that was grief. Wasn't it? The need to blame someone and just picking on the easiest person to say did it?

And then it struck Kelly. Was her mother right—that by telling Natalie to leave, did she set things in motion to have her killed? If she hadn't told Natalie to leave, to move, then would she have gone back to work that night? No. Plain and simple. No. Natalie would not have been back at her job that night. She would have been home watching her TV shows.

So was it Kelly's fault? Maybe. But this was Natalie . . . did she really forget the apartment listing? Or was it a play for sympathy by saying she left it at work . . .

"Where'd you go, babe?"

"Ryan?"

He raised a brow in question.

"Ry . . . I was . . . for a moment there was I blaming myself for her death. That if I hadn't told her to leave she would have been home that night except given her penchant for drama, what if she left the apartment listing at work on purpose? Or just said she did in a sympathy play?"

"Are you ruminating or going somewhere?" He sounded compassionate, interesting, caring . . . not like she was off on a tangent she didn't need to be going.

"Thinking I'm going somewhere. I'm not sure if they'd tell me, but what if she went back, timed it so I'd need to take her because of her usual dramatics? If the list she was talking about was here in the house then she was going for another reason. If she had it with her — same thing. But if it was at work then she really did forget it and for some reason didn't want to wait till the next day to get it. Although with Natalie she tended to want to deal with things as soon as they came up. That OCD thing of hers."

"Okay and?"

"I'm just thinking — someone lured her back to work. Someone called her and said they had a room or information on a room. I don't think they ever found a note or anything that was about a room for rent. Not that Misha or the investigating detective from the sheriff's department would tell me."

He shrugged. "Are you looking at it this way for your own peace of mind or are you thinking someone had an in for her rather than a crime of opportunity? I ask because personally I think it was a crime of opportunity. I think someone was either in the middle of something in that alleyway or there was a look out just outside the shop because something was going down inside that they didn't want a witness to."

Kelly blew out a breath. "It's making my head spin. No matter how annoying she could be I can't imagine anyone wanting to kill her. Swat her away like a gnat, sure. But to kill her? That just doesn't make sense. And I'm trying to figure out if I caused her death in some way because I asked her to leave."

"Babe, trust me, you aren't the reason she's dead. Truly, it wasn't your fault. She was in the wrong place at the wrong time."

"Still . . . I'd like to get a look at her cell phone and see who she called and who might have called her. I need to talk to Misha and if they don't have Natalie's phone she needs to ask her mom for it."

"Are you grasping or is your intuition kicking in?"

Eyes closed, Kelly thought over his question. "I think someone set her up. I think she was set up and whoever set her up intended to kill her."

"Then we need to make sure there really was a list of apartments for her to check and get Misha to look at her phone."

Kelly reached for the phone and dialed Misha's cell. Her sergeant and friend answered on the second ring. "Campbell."

"Misha, it's Kelly."

"What's up?"

"I know you can't give me details, but Ryan and I were just talking about Natalie's murder."

"Uh-huh." Her tone was distracted, yet there was a hint of mild interest.

"Can you talk?"

"Give me a few. Are you home?"

"Yes. Shall I put on a pot of coffee?"

"That would be good."

When Misha arrived a short time later, Ryan met her at the door and showed her to the kitchen. Kelly handed her a cup of coffee as she sat. "So what's up?"

"Well." Kelly and Ryan had sat at the table with her. "Like I said we were talking about Natalie and what happened. As part of Natalie's OCDistic behavior she was methodical. *Very* methodical. She left nothing to chance. If she could help it she had every minute of every day planned down to the slightest detail. For instance, when she'd come home at night she'd look at the clock and you could set your watch by her actions. She'd come in, say hello, put her lunch bag in the kitchen in exactly the same spot every time after taking out any dirty dishes. She'd wash them out and put them in the dishwasher. If I left a cup or spoon in the sink I'd hear a sigh . . . a *loud* sigh . . . that it was, according to her, messy. She'd then head down the hall . . . depending on the time she'd either walk at a normal pace and go into her bathroom and start drawing her bath. If she was running late for her TV show she'd move a little faster. She'd get undressed, take her bath and then her shower and then come into the kitchen to start her dinner. While it cooked she'd watch her first program. Then on the long commercial break she'd come get her dinner. If she somehow had her dinner ready a minute or two early she'd stop and chat and then go back and watch her next show. Usually she'd find a few minutes to talk about whatever she did that day, but she was always back in her room at the precise end of the commercials."

"Wow. Seriously?"

"I told you she was OCD."

"Yeah, but I had no idea it was so . . . Kelly, for real?"

"I saw it myself," Ryan told her.

"Wow. Just wow. So what about her murder?"

"Misha, it wasn't like Natalie to forget a list of apartments or potential living situations. And that night she said someone called her with apartment or rental information — she would have been very precise about that. And that night I just wanted to drop her off and get into work so I didn't pay a lot of attention. The day she came to interview with me she had a list and was very precise. So if she forgot it, if it even existed, it had to be calculated. When you guys went through her room, did you see any apartment listings or roommate type ads or something from a potential roommate? And did you go out to her job and look through her desk? Were there any there? It sounded like she never made it into the building the night she was killed but were there papers or notes with the body? I'm betting the ad was in her room and that something or someone got her back to work."

Misha nodded. "You took her back there that night, right?"

"Yup. I was on my way to the station and she asked for a ride. When I started to wonder why she was going back out at night, after her work she got antsy and said she had to meet someone about a room. It struck me a little strange even for Natalie, but I had to get to work and with her you never knew if the story you were getting was the real one or an embellished version and frankly at that point I didn't really care what was motivating her. All I knew was I only had a few more days to deal with her and then we were done, you know?"

Again Misha nodded.

"So what if someone lured her back to work planning to kill her? What if it wasn't a crime of opportunity where she was just in the wrong place at the wrong time and someone wanted to kill her for some reason?"

"Sounds plausible. Can you think of a reason?"

Kelly looked to Ryan and finally answered, "No. Except for being annoying I can't imagine Natalie had anyone in her life who was out to get her. I can't see her doing anything worth killing for."

Misha toyed with her spoon a moment and drew in a breath. "We are looking into the Jag dealership's finances and transactions the past few years."

"Are they in trouble?"

"No more than anyone else coming out of this economy. Just a precaution."

"Do you have her cell? Can you check to see if she was called or made a call right before she came home that night? If someone lured her back there with the intent to killer her they might have called her right before it happened."

"Kelly, you aren't grasping are you? You *do* know she could just have been in the wrong place at the wrong time."

"I know that, Misha, I know that. I just have a feeling that based on her regular behavior and actions that normally she wouldn't have forgotten a rental listing or gone back to work at night unless someone called or drew her back there. And remember I told you that when I drove away someone did come up to her and it looked like she knew them. I think she knew her killer."

CHAPTER FIFTY-THREE

When the doorbell rang the next day, Kelly was fairly speechless to see Chris standing there. She stepped back from the peephole to gather herself before opening the door. What on earth could the blonde badge bunny want with her? And why all of a sudden were people she had no interest in seeing or talking to showing up at her door?

Well, she wasn't going to find out by standing there looking at the closed door. With a deep breath, Kelly gripped the handle and turned.

"Chris?"

The blonde surreptitiously looked up and down the street before whispering low, "Yes." With another glance up the street, the woman whispered, a drastic change from her usual screech, "Can I come in? Please?"

It was hard to miss the edge of panic in the other woman's voice.

And that was something new and different—Chris sounding worried or panicked. What was that about?

Again, Kelly wasn't going to find out unless she invited the other woman in. The question was, did she want to do that? Aside from how generally unpleasant Chris could be, according to Jess, Chris was the person who killed Natalie. And given the level of vitriol Chris could dispense, was Kelly safe with her in the house?

Now she was being silly. *I'm a cop.* And after years of dodging stalker Adrian and the stunts he used to pull, she could certainly hold her own against the skinny badge bunny.

"Uh, sure." Kelly opened the door a little wider and stepped aside so the other woman could enter. With one last look up the street, Chris hurried inside.

"Thanks."

They stood there a moment, looking at each other. Not really sizing each other up, although Kelly did feel that element of being ready to take Chris down if she had to. Deciding she needed to say something, Kelly finally managed, "Well, this is a surprise."

Instead of answering, Chris looked down the hall and then turned to peer into the living room. "Uh-huh."

"Chris?"

Startled, the woman looked at her. In turn, Kelly looked at Chris's hands and then checked as best she could to see if there was any kind of weapon within each reach. There was a haunted look in the blonde's eyes she'd never seen before.

"How about a cup of coffee?"

Chris nodded but continued to stand there with a deer in the headlights look in her eyes.

Kelly slowly put her hand on Chris's arm to guide her into the kitchen. She had a passing thought of that maybe not being the best idea given there were knives and other sharp objects in the room. Given how slowly her guest was moving, Kelly began to wonder if maybe she was on drugs. Not something Chris ever appeared to do, but you never knew what someone did on their off time . . . like killing other people's annoying roommates.

"Here, have a seat." For such a thin woman Chris sat heavily and sighed as if she'd just walked several miles. Kelly pulled out some beans and began filling the coffeemaker. With the coffee perking, she reached for mugs and then, figuring there was no cause to be rude, reached for a package of scones and set them on a plate. She may be skinny as a rail, but Kelly'd seen her co-worker power down some pretty hefty meals at the station. Clearly, Chris had the kind of metabolism most other women would kill for.

And wasn't that the wrong thought to have?

She placed the scones on the table and pulled milk out of the refrigerator. "Hope you don't mind if I don't stand on ceremony and just put the carton out."

"No problem." For the first time since she showed up, Chris sounded somewhat normal . . . normal for Chris anyway.

"Great. Coffee should be up in a minute."

Chris nodded.

Kelly glanced at the clock. Ryan should be calling before long. His D-1 case had heated up again the past few days and he'd been working in the city as well as staying there last night and would be again tonight. With Natalie not only gone, but dead, being alone in the house with basically nothing to do left her feeling a tad unbalanced. At least she had Ryan's calls to look forward to until things settled down. At least he wasn't going all protective on her worrying that the killer was going after her instead of Natalie.

They sat there looking past each other while the coffee brewed. Neither seemed to feel the need to speak. Then again, what did they really have to say to each other? When the coffee stopped dripping, Kelly stood up and poured them each a cup. Sitting down again, she poured milk in her mug before handing it to Chris, who shook her head.

After sitting for another few moments in silence, Kelly finally spoke. "So, you stopping by is a bit of a surprise. What's up?"

"I didn't know who else to go to."

"About?"

Clearly nervous, although if it was from whatever was on Chris's mind or just being in Kelly's house, wasn't clear, she took a deep swallow of her coffee before speaking. "About what's happening."

Kelly sat silent, waiting to see if the blonde would elaborate, but at the same time wondering if she should be calling Ryan or Misha. Finally, she figured it was time to cut to the chase. "What's happening, Chris?"

"I . . . I'm not sure. I . . . I think I'm being followed and I don't know if it's work, you know, if they think I killed your roommate, or if it's someone who is just following me, or if I'm just being paranoid. But I don't think I'm being paranoid."

"And why is that?" Kelly had to fight the urge to snap at the other woman. After all, she'd gone out of her way to make life for Kelly difficult, especially while she was on probation at the police department.

"Because of some things that have happened."

"Like?" She so didn't want to be pulling teeth to get Chris to talk. It just didn't make sense for the woman to be there in her house unless she was up to something. Or did it? Or . . . was she in the house with a killer?

"Well, some of my things have been missing."

"What kind of things? From where?"

Chris looked surprised, like she had no idea why Kelly would ask such a thing. "My things. One of my belts, a scarf, my phone . . . I couldn't find my phone for two days."

It wasn't lost on Kelly that they were the same things Misha had told her Chris had claimed was missing. "Where did you lose them from?"

"I didn't *lose* them, Kelly. Someone took them. And someone's been following me. You know how that is? You know how you know someone is following you? I know you know. Well, now I do too. Kelly, I need help."

"Help to do what, Chris?"

"Help to prove I didn't kill Natalie."

Well, there it was—out there, totally out there. "Well . . ." And wasn't that an intelligent response? How would Ryan handle this? Or Misha? If Chris was the killer, how much danger was Kelly in? If she was and she was denying it, was it because she didn't think she'd done it or that she was trying to cover it up? Whatever it was, one thing was certain. She needed to keep Chris calm.

"Okay. What makes you think someone thinks you did?"

Chris stood and turned around in a circle. "Because of how people are acting. Because of the investigators finding my things . . . some of my things at the crime scene. I didn't do it, Kelly. I didn't do it. Someone is trying to set me up."

"I see." Kelly paused a moment before asking, "Chris, have you talked to anyone at work about this? Have you gone to Misha or any of the investigators? I'm not sure how you think I can help you."

She sat back down. "She was your roommate. And . . . and no one likes me. At work. They don't, I know they don't. They'd love for me to be the killer. But I'm not. I may have done some crappy things . . ."

"You certainly have." As soon as the words were out of Kelly's mouth, she regretted them. If she was sitting with a killer, antagonizing her was not the smartest thing to do. "But our department is professional. We're all professionals. No one is going to jump to a judgment without careful investigation."

"I know that. I know that. But someone is creating evidence against me. Look, your roommate annoyed me. She annoyed all of us. I need help to prove I didn't do it and I'm afraid that whoever killed her is going to come after me. That they're already coming after me."

"You need to report that to Misha, Chris. Whatever you've seen or anything weird you need to report to Misha. I'm on admin leave. I can't do anything . . ."

"Yes, you *can. You* can. You can tell them I didn't do it and have them look in another direction. She probably annoyed a lot of people. Enough to make people want to kill her. But it has to be, it would have to be, someone who dealt with her all the time, like someone from her job or . . . or she had to have driven you crazy. I heard you more than once say she was driving you a little batty. Way batty. And you were the last one to see her alive."

Kelly inadvertently leaned back in her chair. The blonde was starting to lose it. Or maybe that was her plan all along — to lull Kelly into some sort of complacency and then get Kelly to react emotionally so Chris could go back to work and tell them Kelly'd lost it.

But the problem with that was Chris would then have to admit she'd come to see Kelly and no one would believe she just dropped by to say hello. Something just wasn't adding up. But with Chris . . . who knew.

One thing she knew for certain, she had to gain control of the situation and quickly. Kelly stood. "Chris, stop. Stop and take a breath."

She waited while Chris managed to compose herself.

"Good. Now, I can understand why you came to see me. Okay. I can understand why you thought I'd be a good person to talk to because I've had some unpleasant situations in the past."

"Unpleasant? Some guy — your old boyfriend, tried to *kill* you!"

"Yes. Yes he did. But that's over. He's in jail and everything is fine now."

"But it wasn't always. That former boss of yours was a major whack-job. She tried to kill you too."

"Well, yes, she did. But she didn't and . . ."

"What if Natalie wasn't the target, Kelly? What if someone wanted to kill you and thought when they went after her it was you?"

"I suppose that's a possibility. How do you think you

figure in with that scenario?"

"Everyone knows you and I don't get along. What if someone was coming after you and just got Natalie and they're trying to pin it on me."

"Chris, you need to get a grip here. Okay? You need to report all this to Misha and tell her what you think is going on."

"She hates me!"

"Chris, she's a professional. Okay? She's not going to let personal feelings get in the way of doing her job and right now she has a murder to solve. If you tell her what's been going on and what you think you can help her find the person who killed Natalie. Right?"

The blonde looked around the kitchen without seeing anything there. Her mind was clearly in another place. It took a few minutes but she finally nodded. "Can you . . . will you . . . call Misha and ask her to come over?"

That was probably the best idea Chris had had since she showed up on Kelly's doorstep. "I sure will." What she wanted to do was call Ryan.

No, what she wanted was for Ryan to be there and to handle it.

And wasn't that a switch. Since she'd met Ryan, they'd had these little set-tos about him always trying to step in to protect her. And now the one time she should really be standing on her own, she wanted him—yup, definitely a switch. For now, she had to play the card she'd been dealt.

*

"So . . . what's going on?" Misha asked when she arrived a short time later.

Kelly had met her at the door and glanced over her shoulder to be sure, at least as sure as she could, that Chris couldn't or wouldn't hear. "Chris is here."

"Chris as in *Chris*, Chris?"

"That one."

Misha pulled Kelly out the door and pulled it partly closed. "Why?"

"She wants me to help her prove she didn't kill Natalie."

"What?"

"Yeah. Based on what you can tell me, is she a suspect?"

"More than you are."

"What?"

"Just kidding. About you." Misha rolled her eyes upward. "There is some evidence that she may have been involved."

"Wow, really?"

"Seriously. Nothing specific right now . . . you have to totally keep that under wraps. I know you know she reported some of her things were missing and some of them were at the crime scene."

"I know, I know. So with what she was saying I told her she needed to talk to you. Apparently she believes someone has been following her and they had been for some time and that this person was going through her things at work to set her up to take the fall for Natalie's death."

"That would be some serious planning. Whoever it was would need to know Natalie's schedule and that she would leave the list of apartments she was looking at after you told her to move out. They'd have to know exactly what was going to happen that night and the likelihood of that? Not likely. Personally I think Natalie's death was a crime of opportunity — possibly, probably by someone who knew her and who she annoyed."

Kelly nodded. "That's my thinking. She's inside . . . Chris . . . we should go in before her paranoia gets really out of control."

Misha agreed and followed Kelly inside and to the kitchen. "Chris?"

"Misha! Thank you for coming. I need to talk to you and

I . . . at the station . . . I didn't want anyone to know."

"Sure, Chris. I get it." Misha slid into a chair across the table from the blonde.

"Get you a coffee, Misha? Refill, Chris?"

When both women nodded that they wanted the brew, Kelly was relieved — it gave her something to do while everyone gathered their thoughts. After she served them both, Kelly looked from one to the other, "So would you like me to stay or go?"

"Stay," they both told her, so she sat down.

"You know, Chris, we should be talking about this at the station."

"I know, I know." She looked around the room. "You're right. I just . . . look, I'm scared, okay? I'm afraid that whoever killed Kelly's roommate is trying to set me up."

"I understand. Listen, Chris, we were going to talk with you about this anyway."

"You think I did it." She sounded utterly defeated. On Chris it wasn't a good look.

"No, no, we don't. We're gathering evidence. And you know as well as anyone, Natalie's death could have been a crime of opportunity."

"But someone is setting me up!"

"Why and how would someone do that?"

"Someone has been following me and taking my things."

"From the station?"

"Yes!"

"Then we need to take a report on it. You know this, Chris."

"Fine." She slapped her hands on the table and stood. "I thought you could help me, Kelly. And I thought you could too, Misha."

"And we will try to . . . but . . ." Misha blew out a breath. "We need to treat this as an official interview so that down the line no one can say we were biased one way or the other."

Chris shook her head. "You're right. You're right. When do you want to do it?"

"Let's check coverage tonight . . . do you want a union rep or . . . an attorney with you?"

"Why would I need an attorney?"

Kelly watched as Misha gazed at Chris. It was pretty clear why Chris would want an attorney there . . . that she asked could seem to indicate that she really was in the clear.

Before either of the other women could answer, Chris raised her hand. "Nevermind. I know. No, I don't need an attorney there. Jess and Maria are on tonight with me. So yeah, let's do it then."

"Great." Misha nodded at her. "Are you okay to head back to the station?"

"Yeah. I'm okay. Kelly, I'm sorry. I don't know what I was thinking."

"You were thinking you needed help and came to the person you felt you could trust," Kelly told her.

"Yeah." Chris rose and reached for her bag. "I'll see you at work. Thanks, you guys." Despite her words, she looked and sounded defeated.

Kelly stood and started to the door with Chris. Before she left the kitchen, she turned to look at Misha and with raised brows let her friend know she wanted a few minutes with her.

Misha was refilling her coffee cup when Kelly returned a few minutes later. "She gone?"

"Yeah. Misha, that was weird."

"It sure was. After the way she treated you? Seriously?"

"There is that. She's not stupid. She may have gotten where she is in life spreading her legs or opening her mouth, but she's not stupid."

"No, she's not. I probably shouldn't say anything just yet but I know you'll keep it close."

"You had a break in the case?"

"Not a break per se. We ran the numbers in Natalie's cell phone."

"And?"

"She hadn't been calling anyone about room rentals and certainly hadn't gotten any calls about rooms."

"How do you know that?"

"Because the only number in her call list for the past two weeks was Chris's."

CHAPTER FIFTY-FOUR

"Why? Misha, that doesn't make sense. Why would Chris be calling Natalie? Unless . . ." Kelly sat, shaking her head.

"Yes?"

"Well, given Chris's penchant for deciding how calls should be handled, if she got tired of taking Natalie's version of emergency calls, could she . . . would she . . . have called Natalie to tell her to stop calling?"

"That's a possibility. She has done that with a couple of the other frequent flyers before. But always in the past she's called from one of the station lines."

"One of the recorded ones?"

"Yeah. The woman's ego has no bounds."

"So she'd seriously call someone and tell them to stop calling?"

"Yup. And when citizens would complain Berger would always give her a pass. His reasoning, as you know, is she is too valuable to the department to question her judgment . . . or lack thereof."

"And getting Natalie's number wouldn't be that difficult. All she would have to do is just write it down whenever she called with one of her emergencies."

"Exactly."

"So what are you thinking? That Chris got so fed up with Natalie's calls she lured her back to her job one night, I don't know, saying she had a living situation for her and then waited to kill her?"

"Could be. We found a belt Jess swore was Chris's along with a scarf and top, among other things. We fingerprinted the things we found and Chris's are all over them."

"And the murder weapon?"

"Based on some of the debris in Natalie's hair the coroner is pretty sure she was hit with a wrench. We picked up a few of them around there, but not a one had fingerprints. If there was pre-meditation she would have had gloves. Add into it that Jess swears she saw Chris at the scene right before Natalie died . . . along with you seeing someone approach her and that Chris was late for work that night it seems to add up to Chris killing your roommate."

"As much as any of us would like to see Chris gone, it doesn't feel right to me. Chris is about being a bully, about being one of the mean girls. Killing someone takes away her victim."

"How was Natalie her victim?"

"Not a victim like Jess is. But Natalie fed her need to be a bitch. Think about it . . . Natalie was always calling with some sort of drama. Chris likes to take charge and bash people. She certainly had enough derogatory things to say about Natalie whenever she took one of her calls. I'm not entirely sure Chris knew Natalie was looking for a new living situation because I didn't say anything about asking her to leave in front of Chris and I'm pretty certain no one talks to her about anyone else's business. So it doesn't add up . . . she wouldn't want to lose one of her points of drama and she's not likely to waste her time killing someone."

Misha slowly nodded in agreement. "She does like her drama. So do you think someone is following her and taking her things?"

"Yes. I do. And I think it could be the killer."

"I have to agree. I know Investigations is leaning toward a random killing, but nothing was taken either from Natalie nor was there a break-in at the dealership. There haven't been any thefts or similar violence in the area."

"Do you think it was someone Natalie knew?"

"Maybe."

"Both Jess and I saw her respond to someone who walked up to her right before she was killed."

"True. True. Not to change the subject, but to change the subject . . ."

"Yes?"

"How's things going with Ryan?"

Kelly smiled. "Good. Really good. He's . . . he's my soul mate. I know that sounds trite, but he is. It's like he's that piece of me that was missing for most of my life."

"So he's relaxed on that protection business of his?"

"To a point. He's always going to be *that* guy . . . but he is working on toning that need to always guard my virtue down."

Misha laughed. "Good. You know, when you first decided to become an officer I was a little concerned about his reactions."

"I was too. Especially since the decision came right after Clarissa and her bevy of sycophants tried to kill me and the other women from Hamilton & Myers. But he's been supportive of anything I've wanted to do since day one. Well, okay, there was that one incident when I was coming back from the transport to the city and I got behind that stolen vehicle."

"You mean how he heard what was going down over the radio and raced out to intercept you in the middle of the pursuit?"

Chuckling along with her friend, Kelly nodded. "He's been very well behaved since then. Then again, he's been working on that big drug dealing/human trafficking case of his."

"How is that going?"

"From the little he's told me, that he can tell me, okay. Not as great as he'd like, but you know Ryan . . . perfectionist and driven. He won't be satisfied with just getting half of the D-1 gang. He's going to want to bring in, try and convict all of them."

Misha nodded.

"And that's one of the reasons I love him. He doesn't do anything halfway. I miss him when he's not here, but I wouldn't want him to change who he is and what he does."

"He is a one of a kind."

Kelly shook her head. "I disagree. Oh he's got some one of a kind attributes, but in terms of work ethic, professionalism and drive—most of the guys he works with are like that. If there are any that aren't I haven't met them."

"Well, anytime you're ready, introduce me!"

"Happy to. If you're serious, any time. Well, any time after this case concludes."

"Any idea how close they are?"

Again Kelly shook her head. "Two things seem to happen—and I know you've seen it in your own cases. Either you get someone who is reluctant and clams up or you get someone who either wants out or is afraid or wants a deal . . . someone who cooperates . . . and just when you think you've caught them all in your net, they produced someone else. I'm not sure how far it all goes except there are cells in San Rafael, San Francisco, Los Angeles and San Diego. Ryan's made a few comments about New Mexico and Arizona, but he only goes to L.A. At least as far as I know. The nice thing about that is he does meet up with Susan for at least lunch when he's down there."

"And how is she doing?"

"Great. I wondered a few times right after she moved but when we talk she sounds like she's clearly in her element."

"Which reminds me . . . you ready to come back to work?"

"In a heartbeat. When?"

"You ready to report Friday night?"

"You bet. Uh . . . is Chris still on that shift?"

"I don't think she'll ever voluntarily take another shift. They're her best hunting grounds, you know? If she worked days she wouldn't be able to sneak off for quickies for her flavor of the week."

"Mmm. No changes on that shift then?"

"Nope. Chris and Jess on radio, Maria on phones and records. Same officers."

"You'd think Jess would try to get on another shift for the way they clash. That reminds me of something I wanted to ask you. Since Jess keeps pointing the finger at Chris as the killer, and Chris must know she is, why hasn't the brass moved one of them to another shift?"

"Surprisingly they've been pretty cordial to each other. Yeah, Chris has a good idea Jess keeps pointing the finger at her although her showing up here today to ask for your help because she thinks she's being framed . . . that throws a different light on it. I'll have to talk to White about that and see if maybe one of them should be moved."

"Well, I'd vote for Chris. You can always tell her it's for her safety that she be able to travel in daylight just in case someone is after her."

Misha stood. "That's a good idea. So I'll see you tomorrow night?"

"You bet."

Together they walked to the front door, and Misha turned to give Kelly a hug before leaving. "It'll be good to have you back on duty."

"It'll be good to do something besides clean house and read!"

Kelly immediately picked up the phone to call Ryan. She

frowned at the phone when it rolled to his voicemail. Given how his investigation was going, she'd wanted to give him some good news. "Hey, Ry. Misha just came by. Well, interestingly, Chris came by and had an interesting story and because of what she said I called Misha and she came by. Anyway, I'm back on shift Friday. So . . . give me a call. Miss you. Love you."

She drew in a deep breath and called for Ginny. When the gray cat ambled into the kitchen, she meowed. "Didn't like all the traffic today, did you girl?"

Jumping up onto Kelly's lap, the cat settled down and began to purr. "Well, here's the news. Natalie, as you know, isn't coming back and on Friday Mommy is going back to work."

Ginny stretched out a paw and yawned. Clearly the news, neither bit, was very exciting to her. Kelly shook her head. Clearly, Ginny had the best perspective on life. Just purr and stretch.

CHAPTER FIFTY-FIVE

"**K**elly! Welcome back!" Maria greeted her as she walked in the door. After a brief hug, Maria suggested they catch up when Kelly came in for her code break. Kelly promised she'd pick up whatever take out Maria was in the mood for.

On the way to briefing, she stopped at the bulletin board to catch up on any department news. There was nothing much new aside from the usual items about an upcoming shift party and range day. In briefing, everyone greeted her warmly. Even Chris sent a smile her way. Clearly, the woman was concerned about the finger pointing toward her being the main suspect or having something to do with Natalie's death or she was still worried she was being followed. Kelly nodded to her in greeting without giving any indication that the blonde had come by her house the day before.

"McKenna, good to have you back." Sergeant White greeted her.

"Yeah, now we can get back to regular patrols and shit." Doug sent a smile her way.

"That mean you've had my beat?" Kelly asked him while she reached for the daily hot sheet that detailed stolen cars and other high felonies.

"We shared," Misha told her.

"Okay, people, let's get to it," White called the briefing to order. "Jess Clarkson is on leave for a bit so Kate Morrissey will be joining Chris on radio tonight and for the foreseeable future. She usually works day shift so give her a break while she adjusts to our graveyard traffic."

"Oh, you mean call in a lost skateboard or car parked for more than seventy-two hours in between our stolens and armed robberies?" Doug joked.

"Now, now, they do have an occasional armed robbery on day shift. I'll remind you of the bank robbery two months ago. Kate was lead on that one and did a darn good job."

"Sure. All our dispatchers are awesome," Misha put in.

"Is Jess okay? What happened? How long is Jess out for?" Kelly asked.

"We're not sure."

Kelly studied her sergeant. What he wasn't saying was the reason why Jess was out on leave. No one was asking, so either they didn't care, or they did know and were admonished not to talk about it. Kelly was going to go with at least a few knowing the reason why and choosing not to discuss it in public. She looked over at Chris and was somewhat surprised to see the woman wasn't gloating. In fact, she looked as surprised as anyone at the announcement. Interesting twist given what had happened the past few days. She hadn't spoken to Ryan since she got cleared to return to work. This would certainly make for some interesting conversation when they did sit down to talk. That would be after she had her wild and wicked way with him.

Doug stopped Kelly as she headed toward her car. "You know why Jess is suddenly on leave?"

"No, I was going to ask you. Is she sick? Her family okay?"

Doug looked over his shoulder and seeing no one else was around told Kelly, "She kinda wigged out last night."

"How?"

"A few things. She and Chris never got along . . . we all know that . . . and since Jess has seniority she gets to bid shifts first. Thing is, before Chris came along Jess always worked days or swings and never weekends. She only took them when she had to. Chris got off training and you know how it is, with newbies, they always end up with night and weekends. Me, I like em. A lot of us on graves do. But the dispatchers, unless they're like Maria, prefer days or at least want weekends off. Even when she got seniority Chris bid for nights and weekends . . . good hunting for her I guess. Anyway, right after Chris got off training and said she preferred graves Jess suddenly starts bidding graves. For the past three years the two of them have been on the same shift even though they can't stand each other."

"That makes no sense. Well, at least to me that's just stupid. Why would you want a job like this . . . such a high stress one . . . working with someone you don't particularly care for? And why didn't admin or management move one of them to a different shift or end of the week?"

"Union contract."

"Uh, yeah. Right."

"Anyway, the two of them go at it but at least they make sure their personal issues stay out of it although there have been a few screaming matches while they're both on duty."

"Yeah. I've been privy to a few of those. I just can't believe management lets it go on."

"Well, based on Jess being out on admin leave I'd say they've about had it."

"Thing is, why Jess? Why not put Chris out or . . . did she get something through some pillow talk?"

Doug looked over the parking lot again. "Word is Jess has been following Chris around — outside of work."

"Huh? That's kind of creepy, isn't it?"

"That's putting it mildly. Her fascination with Chris is creepy too if you think about it."

Kelly shook her head. "You know, you think that of all people or jobs the police department would have the most stable. I mean look at it — we go through a polygraph and a psych eval . . . the dispatchers do too. So then you get a situation like Jess and Chris . . . or even Chris with how she handles calls and sleeping around. Talk about odd ducks."

"Yeah, and then there's us!"

"True . . . anyway, we'd better get out there."

Kelly headed out toward her beat, thinking over everything that had happened since Natalie's death when her phone rang. She checked her CAD for any traffic in her area before answering.

"Hey, handsome."

"How's my favorite cop?"

"Miss you. How goes your case?"

Ryan released a long sigh. "Slow going, but it's going. We have a few more names that we've plea bargained lighter sentences and new identities for."

"Any word on the leaders?"

"No . . . it's a pretty convoluted network. Clearly works for them but not so great for us. How's it being back at work?"

"Good. It feels really good. Of course it's my first night back and they've got me on a slow beat. Check this out though. Jess is on admin leave."

"Jess? Really?"

"Yeah. I would have thought if they were going to put anyone out it would be Chris except because of her relationship with those in high places."

"Is it because of her and Chris in general or something to do with Jess supposedly seeing the person who might have killed Natalie?"

"Natalie. Ry, I know it's only been a short time, but they still had no idea whether or not it was random or a planned attack . . . although I've been going over this in my mind. Not just Natalie's death, but the whole situation."

"You mean the relationship with Chris and Jess?"

"Or lack thereof. Apparently they've never gotten along. Doug told me tonight that even though Jess is senior to Chris in tenure and could easily get a better shift, she keeps picking shifts that she knows Chris will want. She . . . okay, I know I'm going to sound paranoid here and that I'm seeing stalkers behind every fence post. Before I started with the department Jess was always friendly. If I called in about a problem and Chris just closed the incident Jess would open it up again and send an officer. And when I started FTO she was great about clueing me in on things, explaining things, telling me what dispatch needed. Maria did too, but with Jess . . . I'm thinking back now, it was . . . more intense if that makes sense."

"Uh-huh. It does."

"And while Misha and I were friends before and she sponsored me into the department, during training we tried to keep a professional distance although we did get together. She had nothing to do with my training so we were all above board. Thing is, do you remember a few times when we got together Jess would turn up?"

"Maybe."

"No, seriously, she did. Without an invite. The dispatchers have an encumbered lunch—they get paid for lunch and can take off from the radio, but need to be close by in case of emergency. Usually they bring lunch or order in and eat in the station. In fact I can't remember any time when any of them went out to lunch unless it was something really special and they were sure there was a lot of coverage. In the past eight months I think Maria went out with Misha and I twice. Thing is, we never invited Jess. She'd show up where we were . . ."

"Did someone else invite her?"

"No. It was usually Misha and I and we never planned ahead. We do put out in the CAD where we are in case we need to call something in."

"Right."

"So anyone, an officer or dispatch for sure would know. Just a sec." Kelly watched as several calls popped up on the CAD. After checking through them it appeared they were all non-emergencies in other beats.

"Problem?"

"No, bunch of calls just came in, but none are mine. So anyway, Jess would show up. No matter what time or where we were, she'd show up and act surprised to see us. She's too good at her job not to have paid attention to where we were. She'd stand at the table, acting like she had no idea we were there and would wait for us to invite her to eat with us. And remember when Susan was first moving out Jess had asked about possibly moving in?"

"Vaguely. I remember the drunk guy and the one who didn't show and, of course, Natalie."

"Jess asked me about it but . . . I had one of those flashes and told her I didn't think it would work because we work together. Too much togetherness. She said she got it and she'd been thinking that too but didn't want to hurt my feelings."

"Wait. Did she come to you or did you ask her?"

"She came to me. That's why the whole hurt feelings thing was kind of odd. With everything going on I didn't think much of it. Then when Natalie moved in and started with all the 911 calls she mainly irritated Chris. Jess still kept showing up places I was . . . I sound like I enjoy being stalked, don't I?"

"No. Not at all. I do remember her turning up places at odd times."

They sat quietly for a few moments, each gathering their thoughts.

"The odd thing, or maybe not, is Jess keeps trying to point the finger at Chris for killing Natalie. Even though no one knows whether it was intentional or a crime of opportunity."

"Maybe not. Kelly, if she was following you and she has a history of taking shifts that Chris is on . . ."

"D-18, Red Oak."

"Sec, Ryan." Kelly keyed down on her mic. "Go to 18."

"18 with 34 and 42, 1183 Parker and Hamilton. Two vehicles involved, white Nissan Sentra and green Volkswagen Jetta. 1141 rolling, unknown injuries."

"18 copies, code 3." Kelly started rolling towards the accident and told Ryan, "Gotta go, accident with ambulance rolling. I'll call you back."

Kelly rolled in to the accident scene moments later, arriving about the same time as the paramedics. At first glance, all of the parties were out of their vehicles starting to exchange information. One woman leaned against one of the cars holding her neck. After calling in her arrival, she grabbed her notepad and headed toward the involved individuals. The paramedics approached the woman holding her neck and began to take her vitals. Two other individuals talked to them, but only one person was going to be transported as a precaution. After assessing the incident, Kelly called into dispatch and advised them it was only a minor injury accident and she didn't need the other units to respond.

Just as she was wrapping up the scene, Kelly looked over and, for a moment, thought she saw Jess standing across the street. One of the drivers from the accident called to her, and by time she turned back Jess, or whoever the person was, had left.

Or maybe she hadn't seen her at all. Maybe talking about Jess showing up places had just started to play on her mind. There wasn't a stalker behind every bush.

The rest of her shift ran relatively smoothly, and toward the end, she headed in to do the paper on the accident. It appeared everyone had come in early. While not totally out of the ordinary, two sheriff's department patrol cars were present. As she keyed in the building code to enter, the door opened, and two deputies walked out with Chris between them.

Kelly's first thought was that Chris had moved on to servicing or seducing the Sheriff's department . . . not that she hadn't hunted there before. Then she realized there were tears in the blonde's eyes and her arms were cuffed behind her.

"Wha . . ." Before she could ask, the officers escorted Chris down the stairs to the waiting cars. One of the officers placed his hand on top of Chris's head and guided her into the back of the car.

White appeared at the door as Kelly stepped inside. "Everyone's in briefing," he told her.

Kelly nodded and started down the hall to briefing. Clearly, the accident report could wait. She spotted Misha and Maria and sat down beside them. "What's going on? Whose got the radio?"

"Radio traffic and calls have been transferred down to County." Misha nodded toward several of the officers and day shift dispatchers. "Day shift was called in a little early and any units not already on their way in have been called station."

"I saw two deputies walking Chris out—she was handcuffed. What's going on?"

Chief Berger entered the room with several of the other officers who had just come station. "Ladies, gentlemen."

"Sir," came the unanimous response.

"I'll be brief. As you know a few weeks ago Officer McKenna's roommate was killed just before Officer McKenna came on duty. Based on evidence from the scene and an eye witness it appears Chris Tanner is the most likely suspect. The district attorney proffered charges against her earlier today or rather yesterday and her arrest was effected tonight. Since some of you will be called upon to testify, especially you, Kelly, I can't say much more but the evidence seems to point strongly in her direction. Now, if you have any questions I'll try to answer them."

Like virtually everyone in the room, Kelly was stunned, but not so stunned that she didn't take a moment to look at the faces of those assembled. No one seemed surprised to hear about Chris's arrest.

CHAPTER FIFTY-SIX

As the officers sat processing what they'd been told, Jess walked into the room.

"Jess." The chief nodded to her and ignoring the fact that he had been the one to put her out on admin leave told her. "Thanks for coming in."

Jess nodded and took a seat. Kelly surreptitiously studied her. If nothing else, Jess looked overly confident and smug. Not the look of someone who was surprised or shocked at what had happened.

"So is dispatch for day shift gonna be here or down at County?" one officer asked with a glance in Jess's direction.

Kelly turned her attention from Jess and smiled to herself. Leave it to her co-workers to focus on the logistical aspects rather than what was going on with Chris. Then again, it was self-preservation—while the County dispatchers were good, some of them damn good, they didn't know the roads and officers' quirks like the home station dispatchers did.

"Dispatch will stay up here. We'll ask for volunteers to cover. We've worked short-staffed before and we will again."

Heads around the table nodded in agreement. Someone finally asked, "So Chris—will they set bail?"

The chief shrugged. "That's up to the D.A. right now. She'll probably be arraigned in the morning."

"Can we go down and see her?" another asked.

"I can't tell you what to do on your own time. I would ask you not to wear your uniforms or make it appear official in any way."

Again heads nodded.

Kelly half listened to some of the talk around her, but she mostly watched Jess. The other woman didn't stop grinning, not a full grin, but close enough that you knew she was thrilled at Chris's arrest. With few other questions, the meeting broke off soon after.

Misha, Maria, and Kelly headed out to leave.

"Wanna grab a coffee?" Misha asked.

"Sounds good," Maria answered.

"I'm in," Kelly told them.

"Good. I think Java Jam is open this early."

"It is," Maria laughingly told them. "I learned that when I was on days."

"See you guys over there," Misha told them.

The hairs on the back of Kelly's neck rose and she turned to see Jess standing at the top of the station stairs, the same glint in her eyes she's seen when she'd walked into briefing. It was the same feeling she'd had so many times in the past just before Adrian would strike and, more recently, when Clarissa Siegel would engage in one of her more nefarious plots. Since graduating from the police academy, she'd felt it a few times, but not quite as strong as she had when she herself was the target. Those times it seemed to happen when they'd have a suspect in their sights, or they had stopped someone and that person was lying. Feeling that uncomfortable prickle on the back of her neck, not unlike cold, bony fingers tracing a pattern along the column of her spine, now had her making a mental note to start tracking when those feelings happened.

Jess looked over each of the women standing on the various steps leading out of the building before focusing on Kelly. "Where are you guys going?" she demanded more than asked.

Misha glanced over at Kelly and Maria before answering

for them, "Just heading out. It's been a trying few days."

Jess took a step down toward them. "I'm hungry myself. Do you guys want to go to . . ." She looked them over again, one by one. "Maybe Java Jam and get some coffee and food?"

What could they do? It wasn't like Jess was one of the bad guys. She was one of them and it was her eyewitness report that had led them to Chris.

. . . Her eyewitness report . . . Kelly's vision blurred for a moment and she caught a misty scene playing out. Only instead of skinny Chris approaching Natalie, the figure was larger, and that prickle traced down her neck. She shook her head.

"It's been a long night for me so I'm heading home. Maybe before we go on days off we can all grab something together. Jess, didn't you come in to cover the rest of the shift?" Kelly told them before turning toward the officers' parking lot and her car. If she knew Misha like she thought she did, Misha would shortly follow her to her house. They'd either call Maria or Maria would figure it out on her own.

"No, I'm in for days so I have some time. Not to worry."

"I'm pretty beat myself." Kelly heard Misha tell Maria and Jess. "And since I'm in early later today I need to hit the sack. I'll see you guys tonight."

In the parking lot, Misha caught Kelly's eye over the hood of her car. The message was clear. Misha would meet Kelly at her house.

"Guess that leaves us." They heard Jess tell Maria. "Want to grab some breakfast?"

"Um, I'm surprised you're awake enough to want to go out. After all, it was your detective work that led to Chris, right?"

"Yup. I should go to the academy, huh? But I'm not tired. I'm feeling pretty jacked up. So breakfast?"

"Well . . . it sounds good, but I need to call Gabrielle before

her classes start and since we have that thee hour time difference . . . well, I need to go. But hey, you're on paid admin
leave, right? Enjoy the time off!"

"But I'm in now." Jess pointed out.

"Well, soon. We'll go soon." Maria told her before taking
off herself.

Misha pulled out of the lot while Kelly had busied herself
ostensibly looking for something in her trunk. She didn't
want to leave Maria alone with Jess and unable to get herself
out of a situation Kelly was pretty sure her friend didn't want
to find herself in.

"Sure. Whatever," Jess muttered.

Coming back around to the front of her car, Kelly watched
as Jess headed back up the stairs and opened the door to the
station. Maria hurried down the stairs and practically ran to
her car. As Kelly climbed in her own car, she nodded over at
Maria and started out of the lot. Jess was once again standing
at the top of the stairs, holding the station door open, looking
over at them. This time Kelly felt a chill go through her. Something was not right with her co-worker.

A few minutes later, Kelly pulled into her garage and
headed into the house. She had just gotten to her back door
when Misha hurried around the corner. "Hey."

"Hey, yourself."

Kelly looked over at the driveway. "Where'd you park?"

"Three blocks south."

Kelly nodded, to head up to Sonoma County where she
lived Misha would have had to go north through town. The
neighborhood to the south was heavily residential, with several streets turning off into twisty courts. If there had been a
lot of crime in the neighborhood, those streets would have
been a great stomping ground for suspects to hide.

"I called Maria," Misha told her, "and told her to park a

little east of me. Hopefully Jess won't put it together."

They were no sooner in the house and there was a knock at the back door.

"And," Misha continued, "I told her to come to the back."

Kelly opened the door, and Maria stepped in. "Aren't we like a bunch of high school bitches trying to lose the less than popular girl."

"Something like that. So breakfast?" Kelly asked.

"I'm starving," Misha told her and headed to the coffee pot to start brewing some coffee.

"I could definitely eat," Maria told them.

"Good cause I'm hungry too. I was all ready for some of the Jam's blueberry pancakes with hot blueberry syrup and some bacon," Kelly told them. "Best I can do is some pancakes . . . no bacon in the house right now."

"Sounds good," Misha told her as she started the coffee perking.

"I'm here for the company," Maria told them. "So tell me, I figure I know the reason why, but how come we didn't want to invite Jess?" Maria asked.

Kelly looked over at Misha and shrugged. It was Misha who answered Maria's question with a question of her own. "Did you want to invite her?"

"Honestly? No. I just wondered why you guys didn't want to."

"Well . . ." Kelly began, "sometimes Jess invites herself into things that . . . well, it's kind of hard for me to explain."

"I can," Misha told them. "This stays here, right?"

At Maria's nod, Misha continued, "Sometimes Jess isn't the most stable person, especially when it comes to Chris."

"Well." Maria set the plates down on the table. "We're on the same page where she's concerned on that score. I've wondered more than once how she managed to pass the psych not just once, but twice."

Kelly flipped the pancakes and turned to her friends. "She went through *two* psych evals?"

Maria nodded. Misha answered, "Yeah. Right after she passed probation, when it would have been too difficult to just fire her, we had a call on an armed robbery at one of the banks. Jess was supposed to be lead on that call and she didn't just freeze on the radio. She got up, walked out of dispatch and went into the sergeants' office closet and stood in there, her head in the coats, crying. Berger was a sergeant then, it was right before he was promoted to lieutenant, and while he was never a fan of Jess's she did the things he wanted when he wanted so he just sent her for a psych eval to see if she was fit for duty. She managed to pass the psych and we got her back. We had our chance and Berger blew it for us."

"But she hasn't done anything like that since, right?" Kelly slid the pancakes onto a plate and brought it to the table. Misha meanwhile poured coffee for the three of them.

When everyone was seated, Kelly asked again, "So Jess hasn't done anything else . . . unstable . . . has she?"

"Unstable is a relative term," Misha told her. "She hasn't left the radio in the middle of a call again, but then again she hardly ever gets lead when Chris is on shift with her and, as you know, Chris is always on shift with her."

"Not from Chris's choice though. From what you said, it's Jess who keeps going to the shift she knows Chris is going to want."

Maria nodded. "Exactly. It's so weird to watch those two. They hate each other."

"That's a pretty strong word," Kelly told her.

"Not really." Misha took a sip of coffee. "To be honest, the pair of them have no place in a dispatch center let alone a police department. Jess has . . . since the beginning . . . Maria, correct me if I'm wrong. From the first day she stated with us Jess always seemed to have someone she at least followed if she didn't outright emulate. She'll start to dress like someone, talk like them, show up where they are . . ."

"Stalk them," Kelly quietly stated. "Did she ever stalk Chris?"

Maria answered, "Of course she did . . . and still does. Why do you think she keeps going on the same shift she knows Chris is going to want?"

"And no one does anything about it?"

Misha and Maria shared a look. Finally, Misha nodded and answered, "Nope. And . . . Chris is all about the attention. She'll do anything to stay in the spotlight."

"Even kill someone?"

Misha shrugged. "Maybe. Natalie bothered her. She's skated since her first day because Berger and upper management protect her."

"So I'd say if Chris did do it, because she's gotten away with all kinds of things at the station because of her sexual proclivities, she probably figures she'll walk on killing Natalie as well. What she isn't thinking about, because Chris doesn't think beyond herself, is that chances are the D.A. isn't going to be crawling into bed with her and there may be enough women on the jury who don't much care for her . . . if it gets that far."

"I wonder . . ." Kelly rose and went to look out the kitchen window.

"What?" Misha quietly asked.

"Jess . . . the evidence seems to point to Chris killing Natalie . . . but what you've said about Jess along with some of the things I've experienced with her . . . you don't think . . . is it possible . . ."

"Wait." Maria sat up straighter in her chair. "Are you suggesting that *Jess* killed Natalie?"

Kelly turned back and looked right into Maria's eyes. "Think about it. Chris has given Jess grief since the day she was hired. Even though Jess has had plenty of opportunity to get away from Chris—working different end of the week, different shifts, she keeps going where she knows Chris will go. Chris . . ." making air quotes, Kelly continued, "saves the day from any number of Jess's calls. Jess is the only one who sees Chris or someone who looks like Chris at the crime scene and she's the one who points the finger at Chris."

"And," Maria cut in, "did you see Jess's face when she came into briefing? She wasn't just pleased, she looked . . . okay, this is right out of a romance novel, but triumphant when she heard it. But she didn't look surprised. She looked like she'd won some kind of victory. Like she knew and was waiting for the announcement."

"That sounds well and good," Misha told them. "But what about the physical evidence? Chris's scarf at the scene—and yes, there is DNA confirming it. And the phone calls to and from Chris and Natalie's phones to each other?"

"Chris reported her phone stolen a couple of days before Natalie was killed," Maria told them.

"Where was the proof it had been stolen?" Misha asked. "Anyone can report anything they want stolen. It doesn't mean it actually was stolen."

"I suppose if Chris did call Natalie, Natalie, given *her* quest for drama would have called her back and then kept calling if she was getting attention," Maria said while toying with her spoon.

Kelly had sat back down at the table and nodded. "My gut says that Jess knows more about Natalie's death than just seeing someone who looks like Chris at the scene. I think Jess killed Natalie.

Chapter Fifty-seven

"Seriously?" Maria asked her.

"Seriously. It's just my gut feeling and I don't have any proof but . . . when you look at the personalities . . . it sounds plausible. Doesn't it?"

The three of them sat with their thoughts for a few minutes. Finally, Maria asked, "Why?"

"Why indeed," Misha looked from one to the other.

"Well . . ." Kelly began. "Given what we know about Jess, the things she does, the need for attention . . . I mean, look . . . she tried to come with us again tonight. She's done it before, just invited herself places. She wants to belong and doesn't see that the harder she tries, the more people pull away. And she sees how popular she thinks Chris is. Even though she doesn't see that it's only the men who want to be with her and not for conversation—she feels Chris is popular and she wants that."

"And . . ." Misha picked up the thread. "Jess knows that Kelly bothers Chris simply because she's a woman, a respected woman. So the way Jess wins Kelly's favor as it were, is by eliminating what she perceives as the competition."

"So." Maria again looked from one to the other. "She kills Natalie? Really?"

Misha and Kelly both took and blew out deep breaths. It was Misha who answered, "It's something to think about." She paused a moment before continuing, "Now that I think of it, it's a possibility."

"Then what do we do?" Maria asked.

"That's the question," Misha told her. "We have to look over the evidence again with an eye toward someone else killing her. I'll talk to Lieutenant Napolitano about having a sit down with Chris and see if we can verify some of the information."

"What about Jess?" Maria looked from one to the other.

Kelly blew out another breath. "I'd say we need to talk to her as well — but in a very controlled situation. One where she can't lash out or, if she did kill Natalie, be in a position to fight or attack."

"Then how do we do it?"

"That's a question for Lieutenant Napolitano."

"I'm thinking it'd be best if you raised it, Misha," Kelly told her.

"I agree. In fact, why don't I call him now and get his read in on it?"

Misha picked up her cell and dialed. Whoever answered at the station put her through to the lieutenant quickly. "Sir, can you call me back from a secure, unrecorded line?"

Napolitano hesitated a moment and then told her sure. When the phone rang a minute later, Misha answered and told the lieutenant she was putting him on speaker. "I'm with Kelly and Maria at Kelly's. You're alone, right?"

"Uh-huh. What's up, Campbell?"

The three friends looked at each other and as if one mind nodded. "It's about Chris and Jess and Kelly's roommate's death."

"Go ahead."

With a glance at Kelly and Maria, Misha spelled out their theory. "We think Jess may have killed Natalie."

"Jess?" He couldn't have sounded more surprised than if Misha had told him a space ship landed on the station's roof. "How do you figure that?"

"Her history. Hers and Chris's for starters. They've been

like oil and water from the beginning. Jess was on a solid track at work until Chris started and then Chris started to get everything Jess wanted. Every plumb assignment . . . the officers Jess seemed attracted to. Chris got it all."

"But Jess could have picked any shift or the opposite end of the week that she knew Chris would be getting simply because of her place in seniority."

"Exactly. Jess kept going for the very shifts Chris would end up on. Almost like she was trying to antagonize Chris or . . ."

"Stalk her," Kelly cut in. "Remember, I have a little experience with stalkers and if you take a look at Jess's behavior over the past few years she fits the general pattern . . . always showing up where Chris is, bidding for the shifts she'll know Chris is going to be on, I've done dinner pick up runs for dispatch and any number of times Jess will change her order to whatever Chris is having . . ."

Napolitano blew out a breath. "You can say that about any of us. Haven't you ever been in a restaurant and ordered something and then you hear what someone is having and you change your mind?"

"In isolation, sure," Misha answered. "But Jess has gone out and bought the same outfit, the exact same outfit she's seen Chris wearing."

"So she likes the same clothing."

Misha shook her head and whispered to the other two, "He's not getting it." And then she turned the conversation back to her lieutenant. "It's not just Chris. She's dogged Kelly too. She's shown up places Kelly's been and recently, after Natalie was killed and Kelly went away for a few days Jess had a meltdown because Kelly didn't ask her to house and cat sit."

"So you're telling me Jess has a thing for a number of women in the department."

"*No*. I'm telling you we need to look at Jess for Natalie Valle's murder. Who was it that came into the station saying she'd seen Chris at the murder scene? Jess. Who found Chris's scarf with Natalie's blood on it? Jess. Who had the answers about Natalie's death? All the answers? Jess. And who would benefit most from Chris being found guilty of Natalie's death?"

Napolitano answered, "Jess." He blew out a breath. "And she'd be the hero. The one who solved it and that would give her a lot of cred for a few months. Okay, you have me interested. What do you want me to do?"

"A sit down with Chris. We don't tell her what we suspect, but get her read in on what's been going on with her and Jess. We know Natalie annoyed Chris."

"She certainly complained about Natalie often enough. Yeah, a few weeks ago she asked if we could block her from calling 911 every time she wanted to talk to Kelly."

"So she'd be the hero for Kelly too . . . she would have ended all the problems Natalie gave Kelly."

"She was moving out though, wasn't she?"

Kelly spoke up. "I asked her to leave, but I'm not sure she was actually going. I mean I had every right to evict her, but I don't know if she was really actively looking or just said she was. With Natalie . . . there was always drama."

"The three of them were a perfect storm," Maria mused.

Misha snapped her fingers. "Exactly. Sir, it's like Maria just said—a perfect storm—Jess feels inadequate next to Chris, Chris can't stand Jess because she's so needy and the same about Natalie. Chris was no fan of Kelly's because she felt Kelly would end up on all the hot calls before Chris took the radio or just after when it was too late for her to have lead and Natalie annoyed her. Jess wanted to be close to Kelly . . . and what better way to end all her problems than to pin Natalie's murder on Chris?"

There was silence on the other end of the phone for several moments. Kelly rose and went over to the coffee pot and poured herself another cup before turning and raising the pot to the other two in a silent question if they wanted a refill. Maria held her cup aloft while Misha shook her head no.

He finally spoke. "As much as I hate to say it, what you all say makes sense. In a sick way, it makes sense. Jess wasn't stable before Chris came on board and admittedly since she's been with us Jess has ... deteriorated. So it seems you've given this some thought—how do you suggest we approach Chris?"

"I think," Kelly began, "you and Misha should talk to her first. She's no fan of me and since Maria is non-sworn it would put her in a tough situation."

Maria shrugged but nodded her agreement.

"You and Misha are both senior to all of us," Kelly told him. "And even though she's no fan of Misha's she may be willing to talk to both of you."

"I agree," Napolitano answered. "Okay, I'll set it up. See if we can get in to talk to Chris tomorrow. I'll check with the jail and see if she's gotten a lawyer yet since she may want one present. I'll call down to the jail now and get back to you when I know." He paused for a moment and then said, "I'm sure you thought of this already, but keep it on the downlow where Jess is concerned. She may be completely innocent, but that doesn't mean she wouldn't lose it if she thought you thought she was a killer."

Kelly walked Maria and Misha to the door and hugged each one of them goodbye. Both women walked to the end of the walkway. Misha reached out and briefly put a hand on Maria's shoulder. Maria returned the gesture and then turned and waved to Kelly. Each of them then turned and went their separate ways to their cars. Kelly mused for a moment on how sad it was that her friends couldn't come by, at least not right now, openly—that they had to park on another street and hide their visit. If Jess wasn't the killer, she still had some issues that someone needed to be looking at. Kelly shook her head, thinking about Jess behind the radio and despite how good she'd been . . . was . . . at dispatching . . . was she stable enough not to lose it on the radio. There'd been a few stories about Jess losing it when she was primarily, like the night there was an armed robbery and she simply threw down her headset and went into a closet and cried. Kelly'd never seen it, but Jess liked Kelly. Maybe liked her a little too much.

With a last look down the street, she closed the front door and padded into the kitchen for another cup of coffee and to call Ryan. Before she reached the room, her phone rang.

"How's my favorite police officer?" Ryan's deep baritone sent a pleasant shudder through her body.

"Hope I'm your only police officer."

"You are. How are you?"

"Good. Confused but good. When are you coming home?"

"Soon. I'm working in San Rafael today so soon."

"Not soon enough."

"Because . . . I mean not that I don't want to be there with you, but the confused part?"

Kelly nestled the phone to her ear and poured her coffee. She released a brief sigh before sitting down and filling Ryan in on what she, Misha, and Maria had talked about. She concluded by telling him, "I hate to think of Jess as a killer in the first place, but if we're right about what motivated her to do it . . . if she did it . . ."

"Sounds like hero worship gone wrong."

"At a minimum."

Kelly paused for a moment. "Hmm . . ."

"Babe?"

"It sounded like someone's at the front door . . . that

someone knocked."

Ginny's ears twitched just before she hopped off her chair and led Kelly down the hall to the front door.

"Kel?"

"I'm just checking . . ."

"Where's your gun?"

"I've got . . . Jess?"

Chapter Fifty-eight

Jess pushed past Kelly and into the house. The look in her eyes was a combination of alarm with a hint of madness.

Kelly quickly slid her phone into her back pocket and cast a quick look at Ginny as she slowly backed away and headed down the hall. The cat definitely had a strong sense of self-preservation if Jess was as unstable as she appeared standing there in the hallway.

"Jess, what a surprise," Kelly told her, hoping Ryan was still listening in to the call . . . and then wondering if it wouldn't be better if he hung up and called the police on her apparently crazy visitor.

"Where are they?" The other woman spun on her heel and headed first toward the kitchen and then to the library. "I know they're here. I know you have been plotting."

"Jess . . . Jess, stop. Come into the kitchen and have a cup of coffee and tell me what's going on."

Jess threw up her arms as if trying to embrace the hallway. "What's going on? What's going on? You three dumped me! You are off planning and you dump me. After what I did for you! After I helped you."

"I . . . Jess, let's go . . ." Taking another look at her unwanted guest, Kelly thought better of suggesting the kitchen. After all, there were knives in the kitchen, and if they were right that Jess had killed Natalie and framed Chris, it wouldn't be a stretch for her to pull a knife and come after Kelly. Her gun was in there as well . . . fat lot of good it was doing her in the kitchen. "Come on, let's go into the living room and sit down and talk about what you think is going on."

"*Think? Think?* I know. I *know*! I do everything for you. Everything and this is how you thank me."

Kelly reached out a hand and gently placed it on Jess's arm. "Come on, let's sit down." She tugged on Jess's arm and pulled her toward the living room . . . it seemed the safest place to bring the emotionally distraught woman. Inside the living room, she guided Jess to a chair and urged her to sit down. "I'll be right back. I'm going to get us a coffee, okay?"

Jess glared at her but stayed sitting until Kelly reached the doorway. Jumping up, she yelled, "Don't think you can ditch me again. Don't even consider it. After all I've done for you."

Kelly cleared her throat. "Jess, this is my house . . . where would I ditch you to go to?"

"Fine." She sat down again and crossed her arms over her chest.

Kelly hurried to the kitchen and grabbed two cups before pulling her phone out of her pocket. "Ry?" She whispered.

"I'm here. I heard it."

"What . . ."

"Who are you talking to?" Jess stood in the doorway, a gun in her hand.

"Jess, put the gun down."

"No. You put the phone down." She flailed the hand holding the gun around the room. "Now!"

"Jess. Let's sit and talk about this."

The other woman held her gun hand out and fired off a shot into one of the cabinets. "Next one is for you if you don't put the phone down."

"Okay. Okay. I'm putting the phone down."

No sooner had Kelly laid it on the counter behind her than Jess took a step over and fired a bullet into the phone. With a maniacal grin, she informed Kelly, "Now it doesn't matter who you were talking to. And I don't want any coffee. I want to be with you."

"Well, we're together now, right? So let's go into . . ."

"*No*! We're leaving. Now. Right now. We are leaving."

If there was one thing Kelly learned from her time with Adrian, it was that you did not leave unless you really had no choice. Leaving led to nothing good. She'd placated Adrian over and over again and he'd almost killed her. She thought she'd learned her lesson but once again had allowed herself in harm's way with Clarissa Siegel. Not this time. This time she was going to get the upper hand and keep it.

"I don't think so, Jess. Now you sit down and we're going to talk about this."

"I-I don't think so."

"Unless I'm greatly mistaken, you've already killed once, Jess. You don't want to attempt another murder. Once you might be able to claim self-defense — it's not going to work if you do it twice."

"No. No, they won't catch me. And Chris will be happy. Chris will love me because I will have gotten rid of her two big problems. Don't you see?"

"*Chris* will love you? I thought you said you were helping me, doing everything for me." Kelly stepped around her and sat down in one of the kitchen chairs — the one that sat in front of the butcher block holding the knives. If she needed to, she'd be able to reach for one of them and at least damage Jess while at the same time keeping the other woman from the knives. "How do you figure that, Jess? How would Chris love you?"

"Why . . . why she will."

Kelly swallowed. It wasn't the first time she'd seen a maniacal glow in someone's eyes. Once again, she thought back to Adrian and Clarissa and how they'd looked when they were plotting something nasty. For a moment, she wondered if there were perhaps some evil spirit lurking in the ether who had targeted Kelly and that spirit just kept inhabiting bodies around here. After all, she was a spellcasting priestess in Atlantis, why wouldn't some spirit she conjured centuries ago follow her to the present?

She mentally shook her head at herself. *That* was utterly crazy thinking. Seriously? Spirits following her through time?

Then again, right before Adrian tried to kill her, she remembered the spell she had cast to make him love her in another lifetime. She wouldn't have believed it if she hadn't uttered words to reverse that spell, and the memories of that time come flooding into not only her but Adrian, Susan, and Ryan's minds. If there was a past life . . .

"Jess, if you wanted Chris to . . . love you . . . why did you frame her?"

"I didn't frame her."

"Oh. I thought . . . well, it looked like you tried to blame her for killing Natalie. I apologize if that was wrong."

"Well." Jess wearily sat across from Kelly. "I did say it was her. But there was a reason for it."

"I see. What was that?"

"So I could rescue her."

Kelly heard Ginny moving in the hallway. While Jess had been friendly to the cat when she'd visited and had wanted to cat-sit when she and Ryan had gone out of town, she didn't want to risk Jess turning on the little gray feline. Between the look in her eyes and her actions up to now, there was no telling what she'd do if Ginny wandered into the kitchen.

"Okay, you've lost me. Could you explain?"

Jess smiled. A rather deranged yet self-satisfied smile. The woman had clearly lost it.

Kelly thought back on her psych classes and how you didn't confront someone's delusion but went ahead like everything was normal. They could live in their fantasy world, and you could acknowledge it, but you didn't enter it.

"We love each other, you know?" Jess purred.

"No, I didn't. When did that happen?"

Kelly's head swam. For months it seemed Jess and Chris fought each other. That Chris antagonized and belittled Jess at every turn. Was it an act to cover up their relationship? Where they romantically involved? If so, and Chris was involved with Jess? Did she sleep with every male officer she could wrap her legs around to cover up her relationship with Jess?

And Natalie . . . Jess seemed to get along fine with Natalie. Sure the redheaded woman annoyed everyone at the station, including Jess—but it certainly seemed like Jess dealt with her well-enough. And Chris, Chris seemed to genuinely dislike Kelly's former roommate. Something wasn't making sense, and Kelly had a strong feeling it was Jess's muddled mind. After all, most of the officers had warned her that Jess could lose it during a high-profile call, and for the few felony-in-progress calls Kelly had that Jess was on the radio, there was always this undercurrent that something was not quite up to snuff.

"You know, Jess. We have some time, right? How about I make us some coffee and you start from the beginning."

"Like you care."

"I do. Jess, we're friends, right? We've hung out together and I'm glad you've come to confide in me about what's really going on with you and Chris."

"You are?" She smirked.

Kelly chose to ignore the smirk and answered, "Yes. Of course. So, coffee?"

Jess shrugged. "Sure."

Kelly stood and headed over to the coffeemaker and started to make a pot and then stopped. "You know, I'm thinking I'd rather have some hot chocolate. That sound good or do you want the coffee?"

Jess chewed her lower lip and considered the question as if it were the weightiest thing she'd ever had to consider. She finally answered she wanted hot chocolate.

Kelly smiled to herself when she turned and reached for the cacao powder and sat it on the counter. When she opened the refrigerator, she pulled out the milk and reached for the canister of whipped cream. It might not be the peroxide-like spray Susan had loaded into her little water pistol a few years ago . . . the same substance she'd sprayed into Adrian's eyes when Susan and Ryan burst in on Adrian and Kelly just before the other man killed her, but it just might work to disable Jess long enough for Kelly to take charge of the situation.

She continued preparing the hot chocolate, pulling down some mugs and reaching for spoons. She'd developed a connection of sorts to Jess and now needed to keep the other woman talking.

"Okay, Jess, so tell me about it from the beginning."

Kelly's unwanted guest released a long, suffering sigh. "You really don't know?"

For all the times Ryan had turned up to help her, where was he now? Time and time again, he'd arrived to rescue her, even when she didn't need rescuing. Now that she really did need help, where was he?

Kelly mentally shook her head. That wasn't fair. He'd been there when Adrian had kidnapped and was getting ready to kill her. And there was the time Clarissa Siegal was determined to kill her. But where was he now? Because Kelly had no doubt Jess would tell her story, and unless Kelly could find some way to reach Jess, the other woman would hurt her.

She matched Jess's sigh. "I'm sure I don't know the whole story. And wouldn't you like to tell someone everything?"

Jess sipped her cocoa and, after a moment, nodded as if she'd made a decision.

CHAPTER FIFTY-NINE

"Chris is in love with me."

Kelly swallowed and couldn't decide if she wanted to laugh or reach out and shake the delusional woman sitting at her table. Chris was in love with Chris. End of story. She'd never give someone else's feelings another thought, that much everyone knew . . . or at least anyone who was sane. "I see."

"You don't believe me?"

"It doesn't matter what I think or believe. This is between the two of you, right?"

For a moment, Jess looked confused and then nodded as if deciding something. "Well, she is. She sleeps with all those men to make me jealous. And . . . and to hide the fact that we're in love. She's afraid to let anyone know she's in love with me."

"Why would she be afraid?"

"She's not gay, you know. Neither am I. We're just in love, but we're not gay."

Jess's statement made no sense to Kelly, but then Jess's reality was clearly different from Kelly's and, apparently, everyone else involved. Still, Kelly answered, "I see."

"I was her first trainer at the department, you know."

"I didn't."

"Yes. I was. I taught her how to dispatch. I taught her everything she knows. Before she came a lot of the officers, the guys, were attracted to me. But once she came they all flocked to her. Like she was something special. And she thought . . .

she thinks . . . she's something special. But she isn't, not really. If there's anything special about her it's because of me. Because I taught her everything . . . *everything*. And because of that she fell in love with me. But she isn't sure of my love for her. That I really love her best. That I want a future with her. So she's slept with everyone she can . . . well . . . all of the male officers."

Kelly picked up her cup and considered if she could toss the hot chocolate into Jess's face and disarm her. If she missed or the cocoa wasn't hot enough, Kelly realized she would lose any advantage. Seriously, where was Ryan? This was one time he could show up unannounced and it wouldn't bother her at all. Not for a moment. She finally gestured with her cup for Jess to continue.

"She didn't like you because we're friends . . . or we were. She thought I was leaving her for you."

Kelly thought back to when she'd started with the department. There'd been no indication Jess and Chris even got along. She thought back further, before she became an officer, to see if there was any connection between the two, any indication of whether or not they'd been involved. For as far back as Kelly could remember, Chris always acted like Jess annoyed her and Jess would seem to be one of Chris's victims. Maybe there had been an unrequited attraction on Jess's part, but she never saw it on Chris's.

"I wasn't though. I liked you well enough because you were nice to me. But I wouldn't have left Chris for you. Things were okay when you started, but then you got that Natalie. Natalie caused problems for us. Things were fine. We were working the night shift together. We could be alone and I knew we were going to be okay. That we'd be together. But then you let Natalie move in with you and she was a pest. Always calling, always having problems, always looking for you. She upset Chris. She was always upsetting Chris and

Chris started to pay more attention to you than me. I knew Natalie had to go. And when you said you were telling her to move out I thought maybe she'd just leave. But you said she wasn't moving . . . that she wasn't looking so I decided to help her go."

"So did you ask her to move along?"

Jess shook her head. "I never spoke to her. At first I thought she'd just move away though and that then she'd stop calling. But like I said, you told us you were having problems making her go. So that night I called her . . . I had Chris's phone and I called her and told her I had a lead on a room. All I had to do then was wait for her to come back. At first I was concerned when I saw you dropping her off at her work, but in the end it worked out really well. Really well. I waited till you drove on and I got out of my car, picked up a wrench I saw inside the dealership and let her have it. And you know what? It felt good. It felt good to know Chris would know I did it and love me all the more for it."

Well, that explained why Chris's number came up on Natalie's phone. "I see. But if you killed Natalie, why were Chris's things there? Why was her scarf there?"

Jess laughed. A decidedly maniacal laugh. "Oh Chris was sloppy. When she'd do it with the male officers in the station . . . she did you know? She'd sneak off into the station's gym or they'd go back into one of the offices in investigations and she'd leave items of clothing around. I'd sneak in after her and get them. She'd look for them after . . . but mostly she didn't care. I kept them . . . I kept them because I knew one day she was going to want to be with me and that way I'd already have her things set up for her. I keep them in a drawer in my house you know . . ."

"And her phone? How did you get her phone?"

"Oh . . ." Jess waved her hand in the air. "She's sloppy . . . careless. She'd leave it sitting around and I'd pick it up and make calls. Guess she never checked her bills." Once again, she let loose with a maniacal laugh that was akin to nails on a blackboard.

"Well, you certainly had things figured out."

"Yes. I did. I do. And now you know it." Jess looked around the kitchen. "And I have to make a decision."

"And what's that, Jess?"

"Why how I can pin your death on Chris. With her in jail . . . how can I do that?"

Kelly sat up in her chair. On some level, she knew Jess planned to try to kill her, but having her say it outright . . . well, that made it all too real. She'd been threatened before — had people like Adrian and Clarissa take steps to kill her. But this was different. Then, both Adrian and Clarissa made no bones about planning to kill her. Jess was going to put the blame on someone else.

And wasn't that typical Jess . . . she never took personal responsibility for anything. It was always someone else's fault . . . someone else always carried things out . . . and now that Jess was finally planning to do something she still wasn't going to take responsibility for.

"Well, that's quite a problem you have there, Jess. With Chris in jail . . ."

"I know. I *know!*" she shrieked. "If only those two hadn't interfered."

"What two?"

Jess shot her an *oh please* look. "The M&M twins — Maria and Misha."

"Jess, Chris has been in jail for a couple of days. Listen, I get it that you care for Chris . . ."

"Care for her? Care for her! I *love* her! She's the reason I get up every day . . . and now I'm going to rescue her and she's going to know I'm all that matters to her and she'll give up all those men and be there for me, with me."

"And that sounds like a good plan, Jess. Listen, why don't you and I go on down to the jail and we can visit with her?"

"What? Why?"

"To let her know she isn't being abandoned . . . that you believe in her and want to help her."

"But why would I bring you?"

She had a point . . ."True."

"And I'm not sure she's ready to know about us . . . I have to think. I have to think . . ."

"That sounds like a good plan." Kelly started to stand.

Jess stood as well, waving her gun in front of her. "*Sit down. I didn't say you could get up.*"

Kelly swallowed and shook her head. "Jess, I think going home and thinking things over is a good plan. You need to decide what you want to do and how to do it."

She narrowed her eyes. "But you don't have to be alive for me to do that. I think I figured out how to do this. Stand up."

Making sure the table was between them, Kelly rose.

"Where is your duty weapon?"

"My duty weapon? Why?"

"Because you are so distraught over your roommate's death you're going to kill yourself."

"Jess, no one will believe I killed myself over Natalie. Everyone knows I asked her to move out."

"Yes, but you feel responsible for her death. That's what I'm going to tell everyone. I'm going to tell them you called me to come over . . . that you were crying and upset and you called me to come over. And when I got here . . . get here . . . I found you dead . . . a gunshot to the head. You'll have a great funeral, Kelly. There'll be a police escort and people will line up. It will be very dramatic and then they'll find evidence that you were really the one who killed Natalie and Chris will get out of jail. And then with both you and Natalie out of the way, the two people who caused all kinds of problems and upset for Chris she'll see that we belong together."

"Jess. You don't want to do this. You deserve better than Chris. She hasn't been good to you."

"Because people kept getting in the way."

"Jess . . ."

"Enough! Where is your duty weapon?"

Kelly studied the other woman. Jess had a solid build, but she never moved very fast. She'd stomp down the hall into dispatch like she was speed walking, but she wasn't fast. After a quick mental checklist of what was in the hallway and within reach in her bedroom, she figured she could take Jess before they got to the bedroom.

Once again, she heard a creak in the hallway and looked to see if Jess heard it. It didn't seem she did because all the other woman did was wave her gun at Kelly and then point it to the hallway. Hopefully, Ginny would stay hiding where ever she was and not get caught in any crossfire.

"Fine. It's in my room."

"Good. Good. You can pull the trigger lying on your bed so there's less of a mess for me to find when I discover your body. Let's go."

Kelly rose and headed to the kitchen door. Just outside the jamb, she looked for Ginny, and not seeing the cat, she headed into the hallway. She glanced up and wet her lips . . .

Jess was close behind her, but not so close that Kelly could turn and grab the other woman's gun hand.

Kelly spun just as Ryan slammed Jess's arm against the wall, once, twice, and on the third time, the other woman dropped the gun she'd been holding. Kelly wasn't sure if the howl she let loose with was from the pain of having her arm slammed against the wall or frustration that her murder attempt had been thwarted.

Jess recovered quickly, though, and tried to knee Ryan in the groin. Ryan, however, was faster and quickly spun Jess so her chest was against the wall. None too gently, he grabbed her arm and pulled it back behind her and snapped a handcuff on her. A moment later, he grabbed her second arm and cuffed that as well.

He spared Kelly a glance. "You gonna call for backup or are we going to stand here for awhile and enjoy the view?"

She threw a disgusted look in Jess's direction before going into the kitchen and for once was glad she'd kept her landline phone. While she dialed the station's in-house, private number, she thought about who would be on duty and would take the call. Rachel, one of the dayshift dispatchers she only had a passing acquaintance with answered. Kelly asked for the on-duty sergeant and then quickly explained that she was code four and safe before going on to request a backup unit to respond to her house. Sergeant White acknowledged her request and quickly advised her he had a unit on the way. Fortunately, he trusted Kelly enough to send the unit before asking for more detail.

White blew out a surprised breath. "Jess? Jess admitted to killing your roommate and trying to frame Chris?"

"She did. And the good news is Ryan was here when she made the confession. She might, well . . . will probably lawyer up once she realizes what she did, but yeah, she admitted to it."

"I hate to say it, but gotta tell you, I'm not completely surprised. Jess always was a little unstable."

"A little? Listen, I think the unit is here."

"Go ahead and then come on in and let's get your statement."

"You bet."

Kelly hurried to the front door to let the responding officers in. Looking out past Doug and Chet, she saw Misha pulling up and waited for her friend to get to the door.

"What's going on?" Misha asked her.

"You aren't going to believe this. Jess admitted to killing Natalie and framing Chris!"

"No way!"

"Way."

"What hap . . ."

A shriek from down the hall monetarily silenced both women. Misha stepped through the front door, and together they watched a struggling and screaming Jess Clarkson being led down the hall.

"I'll get you! I swear I'll get you! I'll make you sorry, so sorry. You're next Ryan Michaels, I'm going to get you next! You can't do this to me. You can't do this. I did it for Kelly. Kelly loves me! *Me!*" she shrieked and tried to kick Ryan.

"Hey, Misha." Doug nodded to her. "This is gonna be a bad one so I'm gonna ride shotgun with Chet, but I think we're gonna need a second car at the jail."

"I'm in my car so I'll follow you down."

"I'm coming with," Kelly told her before glancing back to see Ryan shaking his head, not in disagreement, but in acknowledgment that this was nothing less than what he'd expect from Kelly.

"I'll take the back seat."

Both women looked at him, and despite the seriousness of the situation, Kelly giggled. "Of course you will."

Misha looked over her shoulder and saw both Doug and Chet struggling to get Jess in the car. The soon-to-be-former dispatcher broke loose and, with her hands still handcuffed behind her, started to run first up the street and then when she saw a car coming along ran into the street. The car slammed on its brakes and barely missed the hysterical woman by mere inches. Misha, Kelly, Ryan, and the two officers ran toward Jess, who again started running down the street. Two other Red Oak patrol cars had come down the street — it wasn't every day one of their own was arrested and certainly not for murder.

Standing in the middle of the street, Jess turned in a circle, yelling at them, "I did it for you! I did it for Kelly! Kelly, help me. I did it so we can be together. For us! Let me go. Let us go. You can't do this to me!"

Chet started to key down his radio and then catching Misha shaking her head in the negative pulled out his cell. The last thing they wanted was the media descending on them before things with Jess were sorted out.

Kelly stepped toward Jess and reached out a hand. "Jess. Jess, listen to me. We're trying to help you. Okay? Jess?"

"I knew it. You do love me, don't you, Kelly?"

"We're going to help you, Jess. But to do that I need you to come with me now. Okay? Let's get into Doug's car and we'll get you some help."

"*I don't need help!*" she shrieked. "I just need you."

"Well, the only way we can do that is if you get into Doug's car. Okay?" Kelly reached out her hand and grasped Jess's arm. "Come on, Jess. Let's get into the car. Then after we get things sorted out, you and I can talk, right?"

Jess sniffed and then nodded. "You're going to come with us, right?"

"You know Doug doesn't like me in his patrol car. I'll be with Misha and we'll be right behind you."

Jess nodded, unsure. There was a glimmer of sanity in her eyes while she thought about whether or not Doug would want Kelly in his car.

"Ready?"

Jess nodded again, and Kelly led her to Doug's car. Putting her hand on top of Jess's head to guide her into the back seat, Kelly secured the other woman's seatbelt and shut the door.

"Nice job, McKenna," Chet told her.

"Yeah, well, just keep a handle on her at the jail."

"You're coming down too, aren't you?"

Kelly looked over at Misha and Ryan, and the three of them nodded in agreement.

Kelly ran up to the house, made sure Ginny was okay, grabbed her purse, and ran out to meet the other two. A few minutes later, they headed down to the jail. Misha radioed in that she was en route to the jail with two passengers. Kelly called into the station to advise the sergeant what was going on and why and that she and Ryan would be by as soon as Jess was booked to make their statements.

The Red Oak caravan arrived at the jail a few minutes later. Misha radioed in that Jess was behaving erratically and requested the jail nurse be standing by. A subdued Jess let herself be escorted from the car and led into the booking area. A few tears trickled down her cheek as she waited for the officers to complete her booking paperwork.

CHAPTER SIXTY

"I gotta say that's one of the most bizarre stories I've heard. Like something out of a thriller," Lt. Napolitano told the assembled group.

"Stranger than fiction," Misha agreed with a raised brow in Kelly's direction.

Maria, Ryan, and the two arresting officers nodded in agreement.

"So, now what?" Kelly asked.

"Well, for starters, you finish your reports . . ."

Kelly and Misha groaned.

"And then we present the evidence to the district attorney . . . along with Michael's tape-recorded confession . . . and request charges be brought. Jess will be arraigned on Monday and hopefully the judge will deny bail based on how mentally unstable she is. Meanwhile we've already got the paperwork going to have Chris released from the jail. I'm sure whoever Jess gets for an attorney will want to look at an insanity defense, but that's neither here nor there. Either way she won't be coming back to work here."

"Well," Ryan began, "my concern is that whatever charges are brought stick. If she gets out, Kelly could be in danger . . . unrequited love and all that."

With a smile on her lips, Kelly shook her head.

"What?" Ryan asked her.

"You. Always the protective one."

"Nothing wrong with that," Maria told her. "Seriously, what red-blooded female wouldn't want a gorgeous six-foot-three-inch blond-haired, green-eyed hunk being all protective about her?"

"I agree," Misha told them with a smile.

"Oh," Napolitano answered, "and us older, dark-haired . . . with a hint of gray at the temples don't matter?"

"Just sayin . . ." Maria responded as everyone chuckled.

"Well, if we're done, I'm beat. It's been a long day," Kelly told them.

"Agreed. You're not back on duty till Tuesday so get some rest," White told her.

She and Ryan stood and hand in hand headed out the door.

Ginny came running as they walked in the door. Kelly scooped her up and nuzzled the cat's furry belly. "How's my girl."

In response, the cat began to purr loudly.

"I think someone is ready for her dinner. You sure had a scary day, didn't you, girl?"

"I'd say you both did." Ryan reached over Kelly's shoulder to scratch the cat's chin.

They headed into the kitchen, and Kelly put down Ginny's dinner. With a look at Ryan, she asked, "Hungry?"

"I could eat. We probably should have grabbed something on the way home, but . . ."

"I'm with you on that. Eating was the last thing on my mind during that whole ordeal with Jess. How bout we order in?"

Ryan nodded and pulled a menu off the refrigerator and thumbed through the collection, looking for a place that would deliver quickly. "Chinese?"

"Mmm. Sounds good. I'm gonna go grab a shower while you do that, okay?"

Ryan turned to the phone to call in their order.

A short while later, they sat in front of the fireplace, eating their mu shu pork, potstickers, and broccoli beef. Kelly stopped eating for a moment to rest her head on Ryan's shoulder.

"You going to tell me you could have handled it today?" Ryan asked, not aggressively or with hurt in his voice. Rather he was openly curious about her answer.

"Maybe. I'm glad you were there. We make a good team, don't we?"

"We do."

Kelly sat up, put down her plate, and turned to look at Ryan. "Ry, you don't think Jess is another past life whack job and I missed the signs, do you?"

"No. Even if she is, it's not that you did anything."

"Not in this life. I can't help but wonder . . ."

"What?"

"What is it about me that attracts the weirdos? First there was Adrian . . . then Clarissa then Natalie . . . now Jess."

"Well, Adrian was that past life issue you raised. I remembered that spell you did centuries ago the same time you did. And same with Clarissa."

"I don't remember feeling any connection like that with Jess. With Adrian and Clarissa I had, I don't know, flashbacks? Memories? Nothing like that around Jess."

"Kelly, it's entirely possible that she is just a mentally imbalanced person who was attracted to you and tried to win you over. It doesn't matter one way or the other if it's a past life residue or purely something from this life—you cannot murder someone to win someone else's affections and that's exactly what Jess did. Whether or not she is sane has nothing to do with the right or wrong of the situation."

"I agree. The feelings around Jess were entirely different from Adrian or Clarissa. But that doesn't make me feel any better about me being so attractive to people who, I don't know, want me? Think they love me? And then hurt or kill people to win my . . . affection."

"Kelly, if it wasn't you, Jess would have fixated on someone else. Hell, she fixated on Chris! I'm sure as the story unfolds you're going to find there were other people she was always showing up by or being attracted to. She may well have gotten violent in reaction to how abusive Chris was to her—and you've got to admit Chris could be pretty abusive."

"No argument there." She huffed out a breath.

"What?"

"Oh, just thinking. I'm sure I'll get some looks at the station when the story comes out. But more . . . well, Susan isn't going to be moving back, Natalie is dead and I'm roommateless. I'm not sure I'm ready to try to make it alone financially . . . so now I've got to go through looking for another roommate."

Ryan studied her for a moment and then quietly told her "There's another option."

"What's that?"

"Well, I've been thinking . . . it may be time . . . at least I'm ready . . . to take our relationship to the next level. How would you like to not only share your bed, but your house, on a permanent basis, with me?"

"Are you asking me to live in sin with you, Ryan Michaels?"

"I am. That I am."

ACKNOWLEDGEMENTS

While *The Roommate* draws in part on my background as a police dispatcher, it is a work of fiction therefore any errors in what would be current procedure are mine. Some people consider dispatching a stressful job. For me, while there were daily, high pressure moments, the fact that at the end of each day I knew I had done something to make a difference in at least one person's life made it less stressful. Even if all I did was call a tow truck for someone with a flat tire, I did something to help someone. I knew far too many men and women in this profession to acknowledge them individually, but know you are appreciated for the work you do.

Anyone who has had a roommate knows there are good ones and ones you can't wait till they are out the door. I've had both. *Natalie* is a combination of not only the worst of the ones I've had but also from horror stories from other people.

Susan in the book is based on a very dear friend of mine who died too soon and too young and who I miss every day. She was a kind, loving, genuinely good person, one anyone who met was honored to know. For me, she lives on in this book.

In publishing there are rules, policies and procedures. While I may not use a certain phrase, such as *his gaze* publishing requires you use that instead of what is more comfortable and language I would use such as *his eyes*.

In at least local law enforcement we write P.O.S.T. for the Peace Officers Standard Testing, but my publisher does not use periods for such abbreviations so anyone in law enforcement with an objection to the phrasing, I had no choice.

You may also enjoy the following from eXtasy Books Inc:

The Secret
Regan Taylor

Excerpt

Dashing out of work promptly at 5 p.m., Drusilla Montgomery hurried to her car, her very practical gray Honda Civic with a simple AM radio. It was the car her mother, Martha, chose for her and never one to dispute, at least outwardly, what Martha wanted or suggested, Dru complied. Martha would have flipped if she knew where her otherwise obedient daughter was off to tonight.

But Martha could no longer object to or interfere with anything her daughter wanted. This was now Dru's life and only Dru's.

Carefully turning on her turn signal, Dru pulled out of the Midland Savings & Loan parking lot and headed toward the 101 freeway. With glee she pushed down on the gas pedal and let the car hit its cruising speed in seconds. She drew in a deep breath, closed her eyes for a moment and gave into the spark of imagination that it wasn't a dark, hard plastic steering wheel in her hands but the throttle of a spaceship taking her to another world, another life. One where all her dreams would come true.

It would darken soon on this crisp, late fall night, but before then the sky would be painted in the vivid violets and blues she so loved. Tonight the green of the hills of Marin melded with that pallet of color, creating an array of color any artist would envy.

Fog, like a thick, downy, white comforter, greeted her as she approached the Golden Gate Bridge. When she pulled out of the Waldo Tunnel, now known as the Robin Williams Tunnel, Dru laughed to herself, "Well the old saying certainly is true . . . Don't like the weather? Wait five minutes. It'll change. Well I'll take that as an omen. My life is going to change tonight. It is definitely going to change. I just know it."

Racing across the Golden Gate Bridge, she drank in the sight of the fog as it sat like a silent sentinel over the ocean with its fairy-like tendrils reaching into the avenues. Letting that bit of her imagination out, the part she kept hidden from her mother for so long, Dru wondered if somehow, beyond the fog, something wonderful awaited.

Off the coast, beneath the rocky cliffs of San Francisco's Seaside neighborhood, Mile Rocks appeared to hang in the clouds, miles above the earth, rather than being an offshore beacon meant to warn ships of danger as they passed under the Golden Gate on their journey into the Bay. Looking out over the railing of the bridge, she likened the fog to the fabric that is San Francisco. Like magic, its damp grayness cast a spell over all that enter the City by the Bay. By land, sea or air, it greeted each visitor, wrapped them in its damp caress before its tentacles dug in and held on long after you have moved on. Like the detectives of old, the fictional Sam Spade and those of his ilk, anyone who has walked the City's streets when the fog is low to the ground, threading itself around their ankles, it entrances them with its promise. No one can deny its pull.

Then, in the blink of an eye, it dissipates, leaving all in the stark light of day, only to return when it is ready. Then, and only then — when it is ready — does it come again. Like a living thing, the fog becomes one with those who venture into its fold.

San Francisco's fog can be bone-chilling cold. The kind of cold that you never quite warm up from. Not quite the cold sterility of death. No, something else, something more, yet at the same time, indefinable. It is part icy blast that chills to the very marrow of your soul and part safe cocoon.

The fog does that. The fog and the silent toll of the bell at a lighthouse. Sterile, cold, like an ice tomb. Yet at the same time, there is a security to its depths. A feeling of safety in the anonymity its gray embrace can give you.

Her heart beating a tad faster in anticipation of what was to come, Dru headed along Park Presidio toward Golden Gate Park and into the Haight where Gabrielle George's Victorian sat. A full moon rose above the clouds casting a mystical glow to the ground below. It cast the park in a surreal aspect and she half expected to see a vampire or werewolf peek out from the trees flanking the street. The lights from the Asian Art Museum filtered through, giving the area an alien-like landscape. Rather than scare Dru, it mesmerized her. The tendrils of fog surrounding her car were akin to bathing it and marking her for something new and exciting.

"Okay, Drusilla Montgomery, time to reign in that imagination of yours and get your clear-thinking head in place because you really want this job."

A few minutes later she pulled in front of the rather imposing Victorian owned by her most favorite author of all time, Gabrielle George. Wow, plenty of parking out front here. How odd is that? Not wanting to look a gift horse . . . or parking space . . . in the mouth, she parked right in front of Gabrielle George's Painted Lady. Moonlight winked in and out between the trees as Dru exited the car. A chilled breeze came up and traveled up her legs, caressing them. "Definitely the makings of a scary gothic romance," she muttered to herself.

She double-checked the address and walked along the knee-high, black, wrought iron fence to the gate leading into the yard. As she pushed it open, it squeaked as if no one had passed through it for many years. Without warning, the moon disappeared behind a wall of fog creating a scene that only San Franciscans can appreciate—dense fog on one side of the street; blue-gray moonlight on the other.

A dry, dead leaf bounced along the walk momentarily startling her. It scraped on the pavement, unnaturally loud, in the otherwise quiet evening. She glanced up and down the street, surprised that not another soul was out and about. No cars drove by, no birds chirped in nearby trees. It was as if time had stopped the moment she crossed the boundary past the creaking gate.

She paused at the foot of the Victorian's dark wooden steps, painted to a gloss so high you could see each rung despite the darkness, and gazed up at the front door. Dim light filtered out of the entry hallway inside the house. Framing either side were stained glass mosaics of purple and blue flowers nestled among dark green leaves. At the inner corners were the likenesses of fluffy black cats with orange eyes. Potted plants sat on either side of the door, just inside the frame created by the stained glass.

Above the door was another breathtaking piece of stained glass. This one depicted a full moon looming over yet another black cat.

Dru jumped at a scraping sound skittering up the pathway. Relieved to see it was only another leaf traveling on its way, she released the breath she didn't know she'd been holding. Oddly, still no cars traversed the street. Aside from the leaf's scraping and the slight whistle of wind, not a sound was to be heard.

She tilted her head back to take in the entire form of the Victorian with its Gingerbread trim. In the dim light she saw a woman sitting at an upper window, gazing out. Was that Gabrielle George? Gazing out the garret window waiting for her interviewee's arrival?

She stepped back to take a better look and in that instant, the woman in the window disappeared, like a ghost, leaving Dru to doubt if she'd seen her at all. Well, she'd be meeting the famed author soon.

Drawing in a deep breath, she started up the stairs and reached for the bell.

Before she could even touch it, the heavy wooden door creaked partway open and revealed a dark, gaping hallway.

She peered in. "Hello?"

Silence.

"Hello? Is anyone there?"

ABOUT THE AUTHOR

From earliest childhood Regan was an avid reader and upon discovering Alexander Dumas and Charles Dickens she was hooked on books that carried the reader away to a different time and place. Preferring the quiet of her room and a good book to spending time with people she traveled far beyond those four walls.

It was while working as a police dispatcher, first for the California Highway Patrol and then her local police department, she began to write fiction, primarily time travels and romantic suspense. In the spring of 2009 she returned to the day job she always liked best, working as a legal secretary. Although, curled up in her bunny slippers with her furfaced children, Missy, Lulu and Ollie, while writing is one of her most favorite things to do.

www.ingramcontent.com/pod-product-compliance
Lightning Source LLC
Chambersburg PA
CBHW060146260626
47160CB00001B/141